THE
WHITE
TIGRESS

OTHER TITLES BY TODD MERER

The Extraditionist

THE
WHITE
TIGRESS

TODD MERER

THOMAS & MERCER

Published by Thomas & Mercer, Seattle

www.apub.com

Amazon, the Amazon logo, and Thomas & Mercer are trademarks of Amazon.com, Inc., or its affiliates.

ISBN-13: 9781503954298
ISBN-10: 1503954293

Cover design by Jae Song

Printed in the United States of America

FOR ELLA AND JOE

Oh, East is East and West is West, and never the
twain shall meet,
Till Earth and Sky stand presently at God's great
Judgment Seat;
But there is neither East nor West, Border, nor
Breed, nor Birth,
When two strong men stand face to face, tho'
they came from the ends of the earth.

—*Rudyard Kipling, "The Ballad of East and West"*

There was a little girl,
Who had a little curl,
Right in the middle of her forehead.
When she was good,
She was very good indeed,
But when she was bad she was horrid.

—*Henry Wadsworth Longfellow*

A PREDICATE ACT

A felonious act ordered by criminal conspirators rendering
them equally culpable as those who committed said act.

—Title X, Organized Crime Control Act of
1970 (also known as RICO)

The man with the scoped rifle who lay sprawled on the jungled mountainside had not been schooled in distance shooting, although he possessed the same abilities as a trained, battle-hardened sniper. He had an almost preternatural aptitude to will his heartbeat to slow, muscles to relax, mind to clear. He was blessed with perfect vision and uncanny sensory awareness. Instinctively, he could measure distance, angle of descent, effect of wind. He'd honed his skills not with a rifle but with a bow; in a millisecond, he could notch a feathered arrow and launch it into the green canopy, bolting the heart of a monkey a hundred feet above.

He wasn't hunting monkeys now.

His dark clothing rendered him nearly invisible on the densely matted forest floor. Only a portion of his face was visible, where he squinted through the scope. His jet hair was long and straight. His skin was coppery, and in profile he looked to be the twin of the Indian on a Buffalo nickel. His name among his Logui people translated as Older Brother of Those Who Know More.

He'd chosen his position carefully. A few feet ahead of him, the vegetation opened, providing a view from above of a white-sand beach and gentle turquoise sea. Half a mile offshore, a cargo ship was anchored. It had no markings, but a red flag fluttered atop its bridge. The sniper knew what the flag represented, but for now at least, his attention was focused on a Zodiac, its white wake trailing from the ship as its upraised snout pointed toward the beach.

Still another minute, he thought, shifting his attention to a dozen-odd men on the beach. They wore green fatigues and were heavily armed. Even from a distance, he could see the yellow, blue, and red of their shoulder patches. The soldiers were from a Colombian Special Forces unit he knew all too well, a detachment his people thought were the worst of Those Who Know Less. For a moment, his attention drifted: a scenario in which he dropped them one by one. It would be so simple—

He put away the thought and refocused on the Zodiac. He could hear it now, buzzing like an angry wasp. The prow lowered as it slowed and rode up on the sand. Three men rode in it, two in white sailor clothing. The third wore a dun-colored uniform with no insignia but for a red star on the front of his cap. The sniper adjusted his body so the rifle rested securely atop a bone bridge, its stock against his cheek, his eye on the scope. The sailors remained on the Zodiac as the third man stepped onto the beach.

His face was now in the sniper's crosshairs. He was Chinese.

The sniper fired. A startled bird crossed the sniper's sight line. When it was gone, he saw the Chinese lying facedown, a pool of red spreading in the white sand.

The sniper stood and ran up the mountain, leaping fallen trees and entangled roots like the avatar he was: The Older Brother of Those Who Know More.

BENN

I was living on the cheap, and the leftovers from last night's Chinese takeout were this morning's breakfast. *Meh.* At the bottom of the bag was a Chinese fortune cookie plagiarizing Lewis Carroll:

If you don't know where you're going, any road will take you there.

Bull. Not only was the cookie stale, its tidings were false.

Okay, so I had no idea of my precise destination, but I was certain my path led down some rabbit hole to the criminal underworld.

The theme of my life as Benn T. Bluestone, Esq.: a troubling wont that led to trouble.

My suspension had lifted, and once again I was an attorney in good standing of the Bar of the State of New York. On the record, I'd been suspended due to unethical conduct—off the record, because I had been on the verge of being indicted federally. My former clientele were in the wind as soon as my predicament hit the grapevine, reason being everyone assumes a lawyer will flip. Anyway, I wasn't indicted and didn't cooperate—well, not *technically*—but once the word *rat* hit the street, I became a pariah.

I *knew* who'd outed me.

Richard. The mystery man who'd spearheaded my prosecution but was like no lawyer I'd ever known. Sure, he played hardball SDNY-style—Southern District of New York—but he was too rough to be a federal prosecutor. And too smooth to be an agent with the DEA or FBI or any of the other dozens of federal acronyms that can jail one's ass. Richard was the proverbial man in the middle. Best I could figure, the CIA or one of its dozen nameless tentacles ran interference for him . . .

But Richard was history. My problem was here and now. Like, a total lack of business? The irony. A year ago, I was a prince of the White Powder Bar, a solo operator who called himself an "extraditionist," leading jailed narcotrafficking cartel bosses down the yellow-brick road of cooperation. Then I got greedy and got too close to the wrong kind of people, in addition to which—mistake of all mistakes—I followed my dick into the wild blue yonder. Like Icarus, my wings melted, and I became the man who fell to Earth. Hard. I solemnly swore if I were ever blessed with a second chance, I'd not screw up.

Then I got so blessed.

PART ONE:
THE COCONSPIRATORS

CHAPTER 1

I had no work, but I put on my lawyer suit. After Richard had forfeited all my assets, I was left with nothing left worth stealing, but I still double-locked my pad when I left. Force of habit, but being a veritable Paranoid Floyd is how I've survived.

So far.

I caught a downtown express, got off at Chambers Street, and entered the zone. Ever since September 11, 2001, there's been a heavily guarded no-vehicle zone in downtown Manhattan that encloses certain federal buildings, the courthouses, and the MCC—the Metropolitan Correctional Center. I crossed Police Plaza and went down the alley between the old federal courthouse, the MCC, and the US Attorney's office, using the enclosed walkways that connected them. The rat mazes of justice. Nowadays everyone was a rat.

I entered the new federal courthouse at 500 Pearl, went up a floor and down a marbled hallway to the office of the clerk, where I picked up a CJA—Criminal Justice Act—application form. I dreaded the thought of being a court-appointed lawyer for the indigent for a hundred-odd bucks an hour, but I needed the pittance to keep me in mac and cheese.

When I left 500 Pearl, there was a line outside the entrance to the MCC. I spotted half a dozen upper-echelon drug lawyers cupping phones surreptitiously. I guessed a big bust had gone down, and a new platoon of clients-in-waiting had just checked in to the jail. A year ago, I'd have been first in line.

But today and forever after, I wouldn't be repping drug dealers.

See, I'd relapsed into the original reasons I'd become a lawyer.

Standing tall for the very few who were actually innocent, and equally for the guilty entitled to legal representation. That's how I'd started my career a lifetime ago before discovering the wonderland of riches enjoyed by lawyers who repped major narcotics traffickers. Man, I slid into that gig like it was a $5,000 custom-made suit.

But sayonara to all that. It was fun while it lasted. But not funny the way it ended. Now I was just another mouthpiece striving for a buck or three, as long as it didn't come from a drugster.

Not much money in it, but I'd be recompensed in other, better ways. Like, sleeping well. Like, emptying a phial into a toilet and watching a hundred little blue valiums swirl down the flush. No regrets.

Benn Bluestone, ex-extraditionist, recovering moralist.

Anyway, because I didn't have anywhere to go or anything to do, I took lunch at Forlini's on Baxter Street behind the criminal courthouse, a joint leftover from the days when the area had been part of Little Italy. Now it's an oasis in ever-expanding Chinatown. As usual, the place was packed with judges and lawyers and cops, and for sure some robbers. I got a few handshakes and a bunch of nods. I was letting the world know Benn Bluestone was back in town.

After lunch, the place cleared out, but I dawdled over an espresso, considering the CJA form, thinking that I *really* didn't want to be a CJA lawyer . . . when I took note of a news station on the TV above the bar. The footage was video taken from a plane above a sea where rescue vessels aimlessly circled patches of still-burning oil. An off-camera newscaster said something that sent a shiver down my spine and left me on the edge of my seat.

"One vessel was a large factory ship. The others, its satellite trawlers working the rich fishing grounds of the Chukchi Sea. The explosions that sunk them occurred simultaneously, which, according to informed government sources, suggests a terrorist attack . . ."

Informed government? Oxymoronic description.

The camera zoomed to reveal a sprinkle of pepper-size objects amid the burning patches, and in my mind's eye, I visualized dead men with flame-shriveled faces floating in the sea. I gulped what remained of my espresso. The dregs were bitter. I was bitter, too, because I thought I knew all about the so-called terrorist attack . . . but dared not tell a soul.

The screen shifted to a studio. A pretend journalist with a good haircut said, "Russia and China and North Korea have accused the United States of subverting the international waters of the vast Arctic. The fishing flotilla was bound north, through the Bering Strait, and then west in the ocean along the Siberian coast—now ice-free due to climate change—to unload tens of thousands of tons of frozen fish on the far side of the Arctic, in the Russian port of Murmansk. The ships were of low-tax-advantage Panamanian registry, their home port Buenaventura, on Colombia's Pacific coast."

Confirming what I dreaded.

The point being that Colombians don't send factory fishing ships and trawlers halfway around the world; their fishing and shrimping is done close by, in tropical waters. Their long-distance nautical endeavors are limited to one commodity: cocaine.

Mr. Teleprompter was replaced by a trio of hyper ex-jocks talking sports. I ordered a vodka that I downed in a gulp. Shuddered. Resumed pondering Colombia, homeland of most of my former clients.

But Colombia meant doing drug work, so I wouldn't be going there anymore.

Not to mention that I *couldn't* go there anymore.

Reason being: I wanted to live.

Problem: I knew too much.

For instance, I knew that this brave, new northern polar cocaine route serviced druggies from Russia to Portugal. A market snorting powder by the ton. The route had been devised by the kingpin of all Colombian drug lords, a genius who realized no nation had the resources or motivation to patrol the vast, newly ice-free region other than seeking out mineral rights.

Sombra.

Whom the feds—including Richard, my tormenter-in-chief— believed dead. A false assumption I'd corroborated to save several asses, including my own. I had flat-out lied.

Fact of life: *Sombra* wasn't dead.

Fact of death: People who could identify *Sombra* died hard. Which was why I couldn't go to Colombia; which was why I had no Colombian clients; which was why I was the only lawyer in Forlini's during working hours—

My phone rang.

The screen said *Unknown Caller*, but I instantly recognized the asexual, Chinese-accented croon of Albert Woo, owner/operator of the Golden Palace, where he mastered ceremonies for wedding and birthday celebrations in New York's Chinatown. Prior to that, Albert had imported China White heroin from the Golden Triangle, become Federal Inmate 97532-054, and then—under my tutelage—turned into a confidential informant and walked free.

"Oh, Benn, Benn, Benn. Can you come to Golden Palace now?"

I said I could, hung up, crumpled the CJA application, and fast-stepped it out the door.

I was back in the game.

I'd spent too many long evenings in the Golden Palace's banquet hall, listening to Albert, in pink tuxedo and powdered face, sing in Chinese, enthralling his audiences of movers and shakers who ran Chinatown. After I'd cooperated Albert out from under his problem, he'd started sending clients my way. Lots of China White cases—a big industry in those days—and swindlers, murderers, Green Dragon gang boys, and similar ilk.

That was then. Now, Albert hadn't changed much, apart from a chin lift. We spoke in his office. He had on a black suit with a red-star Communist China lapel pin. Didn't mean a thing. Prominently placed on Albert's desk was a photograph of him shaking hands with the vice president of the rival Chinese regime in Taiwan. Albert was a man who loved to please everyone. For a price, of course. Now he hummed happily as he sprinkled food into tanks, where goldfish big as porgies swam.

"Albert? A question I've always meant to ask."

With a red curved pinky nail, Albert lifted a speck of mascara from his lid. "We old friends. Ask whatever you want, Mr. Benn."

My Chinese thieves call me *Mr. Benn*. The Colombian narcos call me *Doctor*. To my Puerto Rican bad guys, I'm the *licenciado*. My Jewish gonifs address me as *Bennie*. I don't care. I'm averse to sticks and stones, but names don't bother me.

"The fish?" I said. "You eat them?"

"Oh, Mr. Benn. They're my *pets*."

"Tsk. I thought you invited me for dinner."

Albert's giggle reminded me of a cheerleader I once had a crush on. The similarities stopped there. Now he leaned across his desk. From my side, I did the same, so his tilted eyes were locked on my round ones. I got a rush of excitement, knowing we were about to talk bad business.

Albert's voice was a susurrus. "Very important case. *Very.*"

I nodded, said nothing.

He said, "Uncle."

I hadn't heard the name in years, but there was no forgetting Winston Lau, better known in the Chinatown precincts as "Uncle." Albert had introduced me to him at a banquet some years ago—*Jesus, Uncle was old then; how old is he now?*—and we'd conversed pleasantly, much about nothing between two guys who maybe might do business. I had hoped so, because Uncle was *the* man in Chinatown.

Nothing had come of our conversation back then. I'd assumed Uncle didn't dig me. Now I realized he'd been sending me cases all along, via his man Albert.

"Uncle wants to see you," Albert said. "Tomorrow."

* * *

My present pad was underwhelming. Instead of the prime real estate I used to inhabit, I now dwelt in a sublet studio in a soulless high-rise. But not for much longer. Because I could feel it in my bones: I had my mojo back. My old blue magic. *Yes!* I fixed myself a Negroni and drank it while puffing a cigarette.

Old-time drink, old-time habit.

Old times were here again.

I was getting a buzz on. Realized I wanted a woman. Photos from my sex life's album ran behind my eyes. My first woman, naturally. Also a memorable one-night stand whose name I forget but whose scent I can still conjure. And, of course, not to disremember—although I try to—my ex-wife, Mady, the love of my life. Nor Jillian Chennault, beautiful Jilly, whose siren song had drawn me into the spider web that had gotten me suspended and prompted my decision to resign from the White Powder Bar.

Jilly . . . I gave a little shiver.

On the far side of the Brooklyn Bridge, there is a cemetery on a hilltop crowded with ornate mausoleums. Jilly was forever locked inside one. She'd been alive when the mausoleum was permanently sealed.

Ach. Forget women. I had another Negroni.

I channel-surfed in search of an old black-and-white war or gangster flick I could lose myself in. No such luck. I settled for the news: a twenty-four seven broadcast out of—*gimme a break!*—Bogotá . . . city of my karmic disaster.

The images sat me up straight:

Night. Rain-slicked highway. A dozen cop cars: red bar lights blinking, blue bubble lights turning. AR-toting cops outlined by blazing flames. A newscaster with bright red lips kissed a microphone as if it was her lover. It wasn't, but it was the next best thing: a massive news cycle that would paste her face on Colombian TV for years to come. A major cartel war.

I'd personally viewed some of the last war's killing fields. Tortures, executions, massacres of innocents. I'd thought the cartel wars were over but wasn't surprised they'd begun again. It was an inevitability because the cocaine on board the sabotaged fishing trawler must have been worth in the hundreds of millions. Meaning it was jointly financed by a consortium of cartels, undoubtedly organized by the boss of bosses, *Sombra*. The loss of so much product had unleashed predictable consequences. People wanted their money back, or someone else's money, or revenge for some old slight. There were plenty of the latter.

The one thing I couldn't figure? What insane desperado had the *cojones* to make a move against *Sombra*? Whoever the idiot was, I'm a betting man, and if I had any money, I'd have put it on *Sombra*'s nose. But no matter who won, there would be blood. People would die simply for knowing people.

I knew an awful lot of people. *Much* too many.

I was *definitely* never returning to Colombia.

CHAPTER 2

It was a squat square building with a tall first floor and two low-ceilinged stories above, topped by a copper dome time-tarnished to a bilious green. The columns alongside the entrance were sooty. The original bronze entrance doors had been replaced by cheap revolving doors made in you-know-where. It was an ugly building on ugly Canal Street, the spine of ugly Chinatown. It didn't have a sign, but everyone referred to it as the Pagoda, although its real name was the Association of Guardians and Trustees of Foochow Tradition. Also known to law enforcement as the New York HQ of the Foochow Tong, a criminal organization of Chinese Americans headed by the man I was there to see, an ancient, mole-spotted, gray-haired man with Buddha-like jowls and a pot belly: Uncle Winston Lau.

I was ushered into Uncle's private office. We shook hands. His was as limp and cold as a dead carp. He bade me take a seat as he plopped back behind his desk, where he sat with his lizard eyes probing mine.

The office was private—a rear room with bricked-over windows—but the meeting wasn't. A third man was there, a young brute in a suit who stood glaring at me. He was tall for a Chinese and might have been handsome but for the ridged scar that ran from a corner of his mouth up his cheek and into his thick jet hair. *Scar.* I knew him from back when he'd led the Green Dragons. For a couple of years, the GDs had run wild in Chinatowns in Manhattan and Flushing and Sunset Park. Extortions. Murders. Drugs. Assorted mayhems. The victims had been too terrorized to complain to the NYPD, so the feds had stepped in and resourced a Southern District indictment that dropped the Dragons quick as a .357 slug to the cortex. I'd represented the head Green Dragon, a then-twenty-year-old nasty beyond his years. That was Scar. I'd gotten him a sweetheart deal because witnesses suddenly had developed bad memories. Of course, the government didn't reveal this, hoping Scar would plead or rat without a trial. Armed with foreknowledge of amnesiac witnesses, I'd declared Scar ready for Freddie: "My client is prepared to clear his name of these accusations." Sure enough, on the eve of trial, the government, the big G, relented, and I'd pled Scar to a flat, three-year bit that equated to time already served. He hadn't even thanked me.

Now Scar had upgraded his clothing but not his attitude. When I entered, he didn't so much as acknowledge me. Guess he figured showing even a dollop of niceness might lower his hard-guy status in Uncle's eyes.

Uncle spoke a few words in Foochow.

Scar translated: "Nice seeing you."

Hmm. Uncle had been fluent in English when I'd met him. Maybe he'd reached a point of forgetfulness.

"Nice seeing you as well," I said.

Scar didn't bother translating. Meaning Uncle's English remained more than passable. He was simply being the same wise, careful man who'd survived a life of crime. Considering the possibility I might be wired, or that the feds had illegally bugged his space—a far more likely occurrence than John Q's think—avoiding English-to-Foochow translation provided Uncle with the ultimate defense: he never was aware of my words.

Uncle said something in Foochow and held his hand out. Instantly, a greenback snapped crisply into Scar's hand, an insignificant single the thug pushed in my face. For a moment, I was tempted to tell him to shove it up his keister, but I didn't because, abruptly, something familiar happened:

My palm itched.

Colombians say an itchy palm is a harbinger of money to come. I'm anything but superstitious but—so help me God—when my palm itched, greenbacks soon followed. This would surely be the case if I again became Uncle's go-to lawyer. Which, I hoped, just might be—hence the token offer of a dollar bill. As his lawyer, I couldn't testify about our dealings. I took the buck.

Uncle spoke. Scar translated: "Now you're my lawyer?"

I nodded. "For this conversation."

Another Uncle-to-Scar-to-Bluestone: "Albert says nice things about you. I made many recommendations for you."

"I appreciate the kindness."

Now Uncle spoke English directly to me. "I have a friend. Just a friend, no business, never. I do this as a favor. You understand, yes?"

I certainly did. It was like asking Groucho if he liked cigars. No doubt Uncle's "friend" was a thief he did monkey business with. Uncle didn't do favors gratis. I just hoped it wasn't a white-powder case, for—tempting as it might be—I'd turn it down.

"My friend need lawyer. I no know why. I just say, talk to Mr. Benn."

"Again, thank you." I meant it from the bottom of my pocket. I was thinking Uncle was into lots of things. Maybe it was an extortion or money-laundering case built on illegal remittances from Chinatown to China.

Or so I hoped. In any case, there was no way I could meet a client in my pad. I needed a lawyerlike conference room . . . maybe in that rent-an-office on East Fifty-Ninth—

"My friend is waiting in next room."

* * *

The next room had bare walls. From atop a small table, an elbow lamp illuminated the room, which was empty but for a chair facing a couch. When I entered, a startled woman stood from the couch. Her eyes were red. For a moment, she was a deer in my headlights. Then she dabbed her eyes, composed herself, faced me.

Funny thing, I didn't feel as if she were looking at me, more like she was *showing* herself to me.

So I looked.

She was the most beautiful sad woman I'd ever seen. How can I recount the ways? Because she had big brown eyes and long chestnut hair and skin as smooth as heavy cream and long legs—I'm a leg man—with ankles slender as a fawn's? As I gaped, I wondered: How had this obviously sophisticated Anglo female come to be a "friend" of a Chinese crime boss?

Didn't matter. What did matter was that I didn't make her as a heroin dealer. And whatever her problem was, she looked as if she could afford me.

I introduced myself, adding, "Just Benn is fine."

She allowed a small nod. "I'm Stella Maris."

Stella Maris? As in, "Star of the Sea"? Was it an alias? Maybe she was a Stella who married a Maris. "Any relation to Roger?"

"Pardon me . . . ?"

"Never mind."

The door opened, and Uncle leaned in. "I go now. You talk, talk, talk."

He left the door open. His footsteps creaked over old linoleum, and the outer door closed. Quiet now. Except for my beating heart.

For on second look, Stella *really* was stellar. As an old-movie aficionado, I put her on a par with Gene Tierney. Her proximity affected me but not in the usual way. Sure, she was beautiful, but I didn't want to bed her. Crazy as it seems, I wanted to *protect* her. Go figure that. I couldn't at all, but no denying the fact.

"I don't know what I'm supposed to do now," she said.

"Sitting down would be a good start." I sat and motioned for her to do the same, and she did. She wore the kind of simple black dress that costs as much as a good used Mini Cooper. Silken with a pleat that parted when she crossed her legs.

"Whenever you're ready, Stella."

She sniffled. "It's difficult . . ."

"Take your time."

She sniffled some more, then spoke softly. "Other than my grandfather, those I consider family are dead. My parents, my cousin, Awn . . ."

"Awn is . . . ?"

Ignoring my question, again she teared up. "My grandfather is too old and sick to get about. He asked me to discuss his situation and then, if you think you may be of help, to meet him."

"Exactly what *is* the situation?"

She wiped her eyes, sat up straight, spoke firmly. "There are disagreements about an estate. Both sides have deep sentiments about custody."

"Custody? You're referring to children?"

"Not children. An esteemed . . . personage. In the past, the disagreements have been unpleasant. Violent, even. My grandfather thinks you may be of help advising him, perhaps even negotiating on his behalf. Will you, Mr. Bluestone?"

"Benn. Tell me about your grandfather."

"His name is Marmaduke Mason, but everyone calls him Duke." She fumbled in her purse, an Hermès croc sans the vulgar golden *H*. She took out a matching croc folder, opened it, and began writing with a silver pen. Cartier.

"I'd be happy to meet your grandfather." I handed her one of my trademark blue business cards. "For now, I'll require a small retainer—"

"Oh. Yes, I'm just now . . ." She tore a check free and handed it to me.

I wanted to look at it, but that would be rude, even for me, so I simply slid it into my breast pocket. "How do I get in touch with you?"

"You can't. My grandfather is . . . reclusive. He doesn't use phones or computers. In some ways, he's still caught in the past. Not that he's senile, mind you. Just that his wartime experiences affected him deeply. He was a fighter pilot during the Second World War. I've been told that when he left home, he was a happy soul. But he returned a changed man. Controlling. Defensive. Friendless except for his wartime friend, Smitty. Smitty used to say—Smitty's dead now, too—that Grandfather still had his fighter-pilot's mentality. That he saw danger behind every cloud. That he was a hunter who felt hunted. May I be honest?"

"Please."

"I came to you because I'm worried Grandfather won't conduct himself correctly. He's . . . aggressive. Perhaps the two sides of the family can't live side by side, but there's no need for us to fight. Hopefully you can represent me and negotiate a solution."

"I'll try to keep things peaceful."

She stood. "Thank you. I'll contact you in a day or so. I *can* count on you, Mr. Bluestone?"

"Benn. You can count on me." I saw her to the door, but she paused.

"Mr. Blue—Benn . . . there's something else you should know. The family . . . *problem* began long ago. There are those who still hold resentments. Some are quite capable of doing . . . bad things. If that's of concern to you, I'd understand if you'd rather not be involved."

Why did I think she was trolling me? Dangling a worm as if she knew I was a fool for trouble? Of course, I bit.

"I have a few capabilities myself."

Abruptly, she moved closer and kissed my cheek. A brief press of pillow-soft lips. Then she left the room without closing the door behind her. Scar was still there, glaring at me . . . and, I thought, at Stella. Couldn't blame him because her rear rated like the rest of her: an eleven.

She passed from view, but I lingered, listening to her heels clacking in the hallway, wondering why I so badly wanted to help her—

Something hard and fast struck the angle where my jawbones met. Knocked me down and blacked me out. When things stopped spinning, I opened my eyes and sat up.

Scar stood over me, rubbing his knuckles. "Been wanting to do that for years."

When I managed to stand, he was gone. My jaw ached as if a wisdom tooth had just been yanked. I couldn't figure it. I'd done well for Scar when he was my client. Why the grudge now? Lord knows I've had serious beefs with violence-prone clients, but I've always been able to silver-tongue a satisfactory resolution. I resolved to try a different tack with Scar. Tit for tat with a bat.

It was raining, and I couldn't bear the rush-hour subway crush, so I dug into my reserves and took a taxi home. Traffic was heavy, and the meter ticked like the second hand of a two-star-hotel clock. I got home sixty-five bucks poorer, but I didn't give a good goddamn.

The check that Stella had given me was issued by a private bank I'd never heard of. There was no printed name on the check. Only my name, as the payee, in the sum of—

$250,000.

CHAPTER 3

Casco Viejo, Panama.

In the predawn hour, the old city was quiet but for the faint clatter of palm fronds stirred by the onshore breeze. The surrounding peninsular waters reflected the softly lit glass towers of downtown Panama City across the bay. The blackness that was the Gulf of Panama glowed with the running lights of ships awaiting entrance to the Panama Canal. The spiderweb span of the Bridge of the Americas was outlined against the lights of the canal itself.

Along Casco's seawall, the colonial row buildings were dark. Their low, eighteenth-century silhouette was interrupted by an unexpected verticality: a phalluslike column framed against the starry sky. A lighthouse?

No. A bell tower.

Whispers emanated from the top floor of the tower, a circular room whose shutters were opened to the night; a room in which a slow-moving ceiling fan cast striped shadows across a man and woman, still entwined and breathing quickly in the aftermath of their lovemaking. The man was a large, heavily muscled American with nicked features and an easy smile. His crew cut suggested military or law enforcement, but he had no title or rank, at least publicly.

He squinted at his steel Rolex, then reached across the woman's breasts to a night table. A Sig Sauer automatic pistol lay there, but instead, he picked up a TV remote. He pointed it at a flat-screen across the room and pressed a button, but nothing happened.

"You're holding it backward," the woman murmured.

Her name was Dolores. She was extremely attractive: petite, perfect figure, striking pale eyes. She had a way about her that drew men like bees to a blossom. A fact she knew. And used.

The man turned the remote around and pressed a button, but the screen remained dark. He looked at the remote and chuckled.

"Wouldn't you know it," he said. "Made in China."

China, yes, thought Dolores, taking the remote from him and pressing a series of buttons, all the while studying the man's profile, musing how suddenly changeable life was. A scant year ago, she'd renovated the bell tower as her sanctuary, and for a while, it had been . . . but no longer. Not since the man had unexpectedly appeared several months ago.

They'd spoken all through that first day. From the very start, Dolores had realized the man knew everything about her, and that his proposal was her only—no, her *best*—path. But she wasn't one to give in easily, so she refused to commit, demanding first that she be told all that was expected of her.

"One step at a time," said the man.

"Not good enough." Dolores had known he had an unspoken goal. And she intended to make herself indispensable to it while pursuing her own ends.

They'd debated for hours. Finally, he'd agreed to verbalize a clue as to his plan, but only if afterward she'd make a decision either way.

As if I had a choice. She'd nodded, and he'd smirked knowingly, confirming her belief that he knew she was bluffing. *Good. Let him think he can read me.*

His clue was vague: "The Orient. Yes or no?"

The Orient, my ass, thought Dolores. *Oh well, let him play his games.* "Hmm." She pretended to consider, then nodded. "Okay, I'm in."

She was already aware of the general shape of his plan, because she'd paid a great deal of money to a black source that had enabled her to access and decrypt many of his discussions with Washington. She'd known about this man for a long time: that he had been hunting her, inching toward this moment. Of course, her information was scanty. But it was enough to confirm what she'd hoped:

That lately, his real priority concerned China.

Which was the same as her own.

Finally, in the early hours, they'd agreed . . . and consummated their partnership. Dolores had known the kind of lover he was the moment she'd met him. Too coarse for her liking, but she'd been abstinent for so long, she didn't mind a bit of rough love.

She set down the remote control. On the roof above, a satellite dish linked, and a Bogotá news station lit up the TV screen.

The images were horrifying. Fallout from the lost cocaine had grown worse: carnage in Cali, truck bombings in Medellín, sniping in Bogotá. Sixteen people executed in Montería. Open warfare waged in the vast Llanos, armored vehicles maneuvering the plains, launching rocket-propelled grenades. Scattered limbs, smoking corpses . . .

"Tsk." Dolores feigned a pout. "Look what you went and made me do."

"I'm kind of pleased about it," he said. "And you? No regrets?"

She shook her head. "None. The opposite. I'm relieved."

This was true. She'd spent many years working toward a deeply personal goal: wreaking vengeance upon the cartel bosses who'd murdered her father, the CFO of the Cali cartel. Many years and murders later, she'd become the incredibly rich, powerful, and reclusive boss of bosses, known only as *Sombra*, or Shadow. When all her deadly goals had been achieved, she'd continued working for no other reason than she took life one day at a time. Did she know she was careening toward an unhappy ending? Yes. Did she care? Didn't matter. She did whatever she wanted to do when she wanted to do it. Call it force of habit.

Until the man had arrived.

"I know who you are," he'd said. "Sooner or later, some DEA moron will manage to do the same." For a moment, she was surprised. *Who was he?* Then she realized he was a different kind of G-man. Not a company man but a singleton. A player.

She knew his point was true: continuing on her present path would end inevitably at a washed-out bridge. But why let him know that?

"Hypothetically speaking?" she'd said. "Even if I am who you say I am, how do you presume to know my future?"

"Sooner or later, everyone goes down. So either you're with me, or waiting for the morning when you never make it to bed that night. Here's my proposal . . ."

If Dolores had any lingering doubts, his proposal had convinced her: in return for her future cooperation, she'd be pardoned for all her crimes by the presidents of both the United States and Colombia.

She'd been amazed. It was a divine intervention that perfectly fit her plans. And so she had agreed to his proposal and, to demonstrate her commitment, added her body to the pact. The sex was enjoyable, but her heart remained with her Logui people: Those Who Know More, a tribe that lived in the shadow of the sacred peak that was the center of the earth, its name her mantra: Anawanda—

"Check that out, babe," said the man.

On the TV was an orbiting satellite view of the North Pacific. Blackness. Then the screen zoomed closer to where a bright disturbance bloomed, rising from the sea, as if from hell.

"Two million kilos . . . *poof*," he said.

Then the screen shifted to a shot from a rescue plane circling an expanse of sea, empty but for an oil slick.

Cut to another shot: a seismograph needle slowly, steadily scratching—then abruptly twitching.

He laughed. "It was the size of a small earthquake. You do things right."

She took the remote from him and shut off the TV. Straddled him so her long black hair caressed the length of his body until her face was inches above his.

"*Sombra* does everything right," she whispered softly.

That she acknowledged her secret identity deeply aroused him. He went to draw her closer, but she held back so they were not quite joined at the hips, and her nipples barely brushed his chest, and their mouths almost touched.

Hovering, she whispered, "Tell me everything."

"C'mon, Dee, I already did."

"You just said it had to do with China."

"Actually, I said the Orient. But, yeah, China. And that's all I'm saying."

Again, he moved toward her. Again, she moved away.

"We discussed the need for a third party," she said.

"I said *a disposable person*, but whatever."

From the bed table, she took her device and typed a word, keeping the screen hidden from him. "This is the third party I have in mind. Type your choice on your phone, and we'll compare—"

"Games? Why don't I just tell you?" He reached for her.

She slid from him. "No writing, no touching."

Sighing, he picked up his device and typed a name.

She held her device alongside his.

The names were identical:

Benn Bluestone.

She'd known he'd choose Bluestone because they both had histories with him.

"The man's an action junkie," he said, "chasing rainbows that end at pots of fool's gold. Which makes him controllable: the old carrot and stick. Funny, how we both thought of him."

"Great minds think alike," said Dolores. Other than her Logui family and only living blood relative, her Uncle Javier, Benn Bluestone was the one person in the world she trusted. He'd first proven his loyalty twenty years ago, on the night of the long knives when her father and extended family had been murdered. Benn Bluestone had risked his life—and taken two others—to save hers. And now she needed him again.

She was well aware that her adopted kinsmen's guerilla tactics against the Chinese troops encroaching on their land would be temporary, that in the long run, this was a no-win strategy for the Logui. Instead of choosing war, they needed to negotiate. But negotiation required leverage. Finding and applying the leverage was her job, but the crucial negotiations would be Bluestone's job, for two reasons:

One, his being in the line of fire shielded her.

Two, Bluestone was a master schemer.

She wondered how Benn was aging. Given his vanity, probably well, and still full of juice. She also wondered—not for the first time—what it would be like bedding him—

"Why the smile?" said the man.

She lowered to him. "I'm happy."

"Second the motion," he said, touching her most sensitive places, the ones he'd learned about earlier.

Dolores would have preferred to lie back and enjoy, but for the man's sake, she passionately murmured his name:

"Oh, Richard . . ."

CHAPTER 4

When I got home, I didn't fix a drink. I wanted to keep my head clear while considering Stella. Her unexpectedly large fee I took as a sure sign she wanted to rent more than my negotiation skills. In retrospect, there was something off about Stella, something I couldn't quite put my finger on. I just sensed that beneath her remarkable beauty was a darkness, that what I'd first mistaken for sadness veiled a deeper anger. No big deal and none of my business. I had myself a big new client, and so what if she was an adorable kitten with a penchant for scratching? But I'd not give her the opportunity. I'd learned my lesson about getting personal with clients from Jilly. I'd simply do my job, starting with some due diligence. I got behind my computer and hit the search engine.

All that came up for *Stella Maris* was what I'd already thought—aka "Star of the Sea" in Latin—plus a reference to the guide star Polaris, and lo and behold, another to Our Lady Virgin Stella Maris, a Brooklyn church around the corner from where I grew up. Maybe it was the thought of my old hood, but I suddenly flashed on my father. He died long before I became a lawyer, but I doubted he'd have been proud of me when I was taking drug-tainted money. Now I had a shot at a do-over . . .

The thought passed, and I got back to work.

As to Marmaduke Mason, I found nothing at all. Stella's alleged grandfather was a cipher. I closed my eyes and reran my conversation with Stella, looking for a clue I'd missed. She'd said her grandfather had been in the Second World War; his pal Smitty had called him a fighter pilot.

Fifteen years ago, I'd have hired a private cop to snoop Mason out. Now, like everyone, I'd gone digital. I have a paying acquaintance with a brilliant geek who'd overcharged me for some exotic software that allowed me backdoor access to certain government networks. Unclassified stuff, but helpful now and then. The Geek, alluding to electronic wizardry about which I hadn't a clue, swore using the program couldn't be traced to me. Being naturally suspicious and a computer-unfriendly person, I had my doubts about that, but being nosy by inclination and experience, I occasionally risked using the software on important matters.

Like the case of Stella Maris.

Why was she important?

Sure, I wanted to help the kid, but no denying another fact: it was the money, stupid. Not to mention that doing well for Stella meant doing well for Uncle, who would then hopefully reintroduce me to Chinatown's ever-profitable criminal underground.

I used the Geek's software to search for Marmaduke Mason in the archival files of what, during the Second World War, had been called the USAAF, or the US Army Air Forces. In them, I visually scanned for his name on rosters, a paltry few digitized, the rest poor copies of the originals. Fortunately, people had nicer handwriting back then. Unfortunately, I found no pilot named Marmaduke Mason.

I left the computer and went for a walk in the night. Clear my mind, maybe. Realize something I'd overlooked, maybe. Have a drink somewhere, maybe.

Few people were out. Strong wind, clear sky, chilly. I was walking west and in the distant sky saw the lights of a jetliner traversing the flight corridor above the Hudson River to LaGuardia. Planes. As a kid, I'd wanted to be a fighter pilot until I discovered the joys of sex, drugs, and rock 'n' roll. Unlike me, Marmaduke Mason had taken the straight and narrow into a fighting cockpit. Or had he? Maybe his name wasn't on the rosters because he wasn't a top gun but an actor.

I was stumped. What to do when stumped? Easy. Go back to the beginning, and give everything thereafter a hard look. So I cabbed to Chinatown.

On the way, my device pinged. A banking alert: Stella's check had cleared. I had the cabbie stop at an ATM while I refreshed my walking-around money. Then I continued on to Albert Woo's place.

Albert was in night mode: incense burning, Chinese music softly playing, a brief glimpse of a boy in white jockeys closing a bedroom door.

"Oh, Benn, you surprised me. Is everything okay?"

"Everything's swell. I was in the neighborhood, so I figured I'd drop by and reimburse your referral expenses." Always on DEFCON One for an unexpected wire, I preferred *expenses* rather than *kickbacks*, a no-say term that could lead to another ethical investigation.

I unpeeled twenty-five Franklins and handed them to Albert, who seemed disappointed.

"Just a down payment," I reassured him. "The client? How did she wind up in Uncle's office?"

Albert's a ninety-ninth-percentile prevaricator, but he never got over on me. His tell was a mini left nostril twitch right before he told a whopper. Now he shrugged and said, "I heard her boyfriend sent her to Uncle." No twitch.

"She has a boyfriend?"

"I heard they broke up." No twitch.

"And after that, Uncle still agreed to help her?"

"So far as I know." No twitch.

I didn't have Uncle's number, so I went over to the Pagoda. No lights were visible from the street. No buzzer. I knocked. No answer.

I cabbed back uptown. In passing, I saw a good-looking blonde woman emerge from a building. From a distance, she resembled Jilly—

An idea came to me, and I hurried home to manifest it.

Just as I had unsuccessfully searched the net for Stella, so had I done after first meeting Jilly, a nickname short for Jillian, whose last name sounded something like *Shenolt*. Much as I'd struck out with Stella, I'd come up with nil online for a Jillian "sounds like Shenolt." But pondering the name *Shenolt* aloud triggered a memory of an old war movie about General Claire Chennault, the real-life head honcho of the legendary Flying Tigers.

Searching for a Gillian Chennault, I'd found my Jilly.

Now the same methodology led me to another find.

Online, I confirmed my memory: that General Chennault's Flying Tigers had not officially been part of the USAAF because they were an American Volunteer Group—or AVG—under Chinese Nationalist government command. I reopened the Geek's software and nosed around the old AVG rosters. And found . . .

Nothing. No Marmaduke Mason.

Disappointing. I rechecked the roster. The pilots had all-American names. Undoubtedly an all-white band of brothers. One of them was named *Marmaduke* Eddington. Coincidence? Possible. I went over the roster still again, and this time saw a *Mason* Peckham. Coincidence? Impossible.

Meaning Stella's grandfather had, postwar, created a new identity honoring his old flyboy buddies Marmaduke and Mason. The rosters showed little crosses next to the names of those who had died, including Marmaduke and Mason. Most of the deaths had been casualties of war back in the forties; the ranks of the survivors had gradually thinned during the seventy-five-odd years since. Now there were a few still alive.

And, excepting one—Milton Peabody—I found neither hide nor home of any.

* * *

Sometimes you get lucky. I did. The next afternoon I drove a rental car to an isolated town four hours north of the big city. Under a white sky in all directions were rolling hills gridded by old stone walls. The cleared land between them had once been pasture but now was reverting to second-growth forest. Understandable. Not many young people want to pull cow udders in subzero weather when they can be in a swivel chair in a warm office cubicle doing whatever it is people do in them. I drove through a small town on the edge of a big stream, crossed a steel bridge, made a hard left, and went up a steep hill that ended at an open plateau of unworked hayfields. In front of the second driveway on the right, a mailbox sat atop a tilted pole. The name on the box was *Peabody*.

The driveway turned out to be a road that a mile later ended at a ramshackle trailer outside of which an old man was whittling a piece of wood. I pulled over and rolled my window down. "Say, could you help me?"

The geezer was bent as a hairpin. Ninety-five if he was a day. More. Without looking up, he said, "Lost?"

"Yes, sir, I am."

"Where you headed?"

I told him the name of the town I'd just driven through. He nodded and snorted a laugh. "The way here is by passing through there. Guess you didn't notice."

"Busted," I said.

"You a writer? Some years back, a fella from *Reader's Digest* wanted to do a story on me. The last Flying Tiger. Don't know if he did . . . least I never saw it."

"I'm not a writer, sir," I said. "Hate to admit it, but I'm a lawyer. Right now I'm trying to track down some ex-Tigers a deceased client of mine left money to."

He looked up. "I among them?"

"No. But there could be a finder's fee for helping me locate them. One fella's named Marmaduke. The other is Mason."

He laughed, showing me his dentures. "Buzzy and Fuzzy. Archie's wingmen. Too bad you didn't check the Tiger old-timer's alumni association, or whatever they call it. If you had, you'd have saved yourself a trip. Buzzy bought it over Burma. Fuzzy made it through the war and wound up heart-attacked in Florida. After the Tigers were disbanded, Archie kept in the fight, even if it meant jockeying transports over the Hump. DC-Threes, loaded to the gills. No picnic. Lots of fellas never made it. Including old Archie."

I nodded. I knew all about the Hump from one of my old fave flicks, *China Girl*, starring Victor Mature. It was about the dangerous India-to-Burma supply route over the Himalayas. Overloaded and undermaintained DC-3s stuffed with food and ammo and illegal booze struggling to clear the gargantuan peaks.

"Archie, he flew like a crazed bird," said Peabody.

"Say again?"

"Man flew on the verge of suicide. Took a lot of Jappos down. Fate, that Archie kept himself alive until the Tigers disbanded, then went and bought it in a damn accident."

Archie. An old-timey name that reminded me of the redheaded comic character who didn't realize brunette Veronica loved him because he was so blindly in love with blonde Betty—

Thinking of twosomes, it occurred to me that two Chinese connections had popped up: Stella coming to me from Uncle, and her grandfather using the names of dead pilots who'd been employed by the Chinese in their war with Japan.

"Archie got shafted," said Peabody. "After the Tigers broke up, he expected to be in the cockpit of a spanking new Hellcat. Hottest pursuit fighter in the air. Instead, some clerk relegated him to Transport. The damn Hump. Coming up on the mountain in bad weather, he realized his bird didn't have enough lift in her. And not enough fuel to turn back. So he came up with a typical Archie solution. *Roll the dice.* Told his copilot to bail, no point both of 'em buying it. Besides, losing the copilot's weight might make the difference between burning to the bone on a twenty-thousand-foot mountain and making it over the top, even if it was just by the skin of his balls."

Peabody shook his head, sighed. "The copilot didn't need to be asked twice. His parachute was floating down when he saw Archie plow into the mountain."

"You in touch with any other Tigers, sir?"

"This entitle me to your finder's fee?"

I reached for my roll.

"I'm joking you. I won't take money for talking about my boys. Far as I know, I'm the last one left. Nice meeting you, and I hope you get whatever it is you're really after."

I thanked him and started home. It was a starry night in the mountains, and I made a couple of wishes—

My phone rang. Its screen read *Unknown Caller.* When I answered, I heard a woman's voice fuzzed by static. Coverage comes and goes in the north Catskills. Missed her name. Asked her to please repeat. She said Lizzie or Cassie or Missy, and she wanted an appointment on . . .

I didn't hear when, so I asked her to please repeat.

Long crackle of static, then suddenly clarity:

"See you then," said the woman, hanging up.

CHAPTER 5

Toungoo, Burma. December 10, 1941.

The girl stood at the edge of the jungle, where she hoped she could not be seen from the dirt airstrip. She was only sixteen but already possessed of the classic beauty of centuries of selective breeding. She wore the black cotton field uniform of the Nationalist Army of the Republic of China. Her family was old money, and she could have lived as a doyenne in Paris, but she preferred to wear a humble soldier's uniform and remain in China to fight her nation's enemies: the traitorous Communist People's Liberation Army, and the atrocious Japanese invaders.

Her name was Li-ang Soo, but an English nanny had dubbed her Kitty, and that's what everyone had called her ever since. Everyone except the man who was the other reason she'd remained.

Ming Chan.

Her superior and her mentor and the man she wanted to spend her life with. Ming called her by her Chinese name, Li-ang, instead of Kitty because he despised everything about Westerners, including their stupid nicknames. When Ming heard someone address her as Kitty, his dark brows knitted angrily, which reminded Kitty of illustrations depicting scowling Japanese samurai. She forced herself not to laugh at Ming's reaction when she'd told him that. To Ming, the Japanese were blood enemies, although deep down, Li-ang suspected war in general rather than any particular enemy motivated him. His warrior predilections troubled Kitty; yet she trusted that, in time, his better angels would prevail.

Like Kitty, Ming was from an esteemed family in which every male between fifteen and fifty was expected to pick up a rifle. Ming's family influence had immediately elevated him to officer status, and he had fought with great distinction on the Nanking front . . .

Until being reassigned to Burma, where he was accorded the great honor of escorting a vital personage of the nation—popularly called Lucky—to a safe place far from the fighting. As Ming's acolyte, Li-ang, now a lieutenant, had accompanied him. But when they'd reached the general area, Ming had forbidden her from continuing to the final destination. Too risky for her, he'd said, although she knew Ming's real reason was that he didn't think a woman worthy of the honor. When she had defiantly joined the detachment escorting Lucky on the last leg of his trip, Ming—*in front of everyone*—had physically snatched her from its ranks.

The utter humiliation. So . . . demeaning.

Yesterday, she'd thought they'd marry.

Today, she didn't love him at all—

A coughing roar commenced from the airstrip, jarring her from her thoughts, refocusing her attention on three warplanes emitting black exhaust, their spinning propellers dazzling in the sun. Technically, they were Curtiss P-40 Warhawks, but everyone called them Flying Tigers because their cowlings were painted with fierce eyes and innumerable fangs.

Abruptly, the engines stopped. Apparently, they were only being tested. Even as their sound faded, another could be heard: from a radio atop a mechanic's bench, a Brit-accented broadcaster read the latest news:

"The United States has confirmed the loss of its battleship fleet at Pearl Harbor. Fortunately, the American aircraft carriers were on maneuvers and unscathed by the attack, which President Roosevelt has called a day that shall live in infamy . . . Japanese forces have landed in the Philippines, but General MacArthur has promised they will be pushed back into the sea . . . Her Majesty's Royal Navy has confirmed the sinking of HMS *Repulse* and HMS *Prince of Wales* with great loss of life . . . Japanese troops are rapidly advancing toward Singapore . . . The Chinese Nationalist government has announced the formation of a fighter force piloted by American volunteers—"

"Turn off the bad news, Smitty," came an American-accented shout, and a moment later, the radio went dead.

That was when Li-ang first saw him. The American. He was so totally unlike anyone she'd ever seen, much less imagined existed: a carefree, shirtless young man standing atop the wing of the lead P-40 while talking to a mechanic seated in the cockpit.

"Just like wing-walking in my carny days," said the young American to the mechanic.

Li-ang wondered what a carny was. The West contained so much she was curious about, and this young American personified its mystique. Slender with corded muscles, his grin white beneath dark aviator glasses, the way he wore his officer's cap, its crushed visor set at a jaunty angle. She saw him not as an aviator, but as a . . . cowboy.

He's beautiful, she thought—

Horrified, she covered her mouth, as if she'd spoken the words aloud.

"Volunteers, they call us?" said the American. "Five hundred smackers for every Nip kill sounds more like bounty than voluntary. Am I right, or am I right, Smitty?"

Smitty, the mechanic who'd been in the cockpit, had climbed from it and was opening a crate of .50-caliber shells, bandoleers of gleaming cylinders the size of a man's index finger. He nodded. "Sure are, Archie."

Archie. Li-ang had never heard the name before. It was so . . . American. It fit him perfectly: *Archie . . .*

Smitty said, "Five hundred, less my five percent."

"Always," said Archie. "How about some music, maestro?"

Smitty turned the radio back on, spun the dial, and out blared big-band swing music: the Glenn Miller Orchestra's hit of the moment, "Chattanooga Choo Choo."

As Smitty loaded the ammo ports, Archie hopped back onto the wing, zipped a shearling-lined jacket over his bare chest, then slipped into the cockpit and began singing along with the radio, *then* turned and pointed toward Li-ang.

Involuntarily, she stepped back. No need, for already he'd looked away, still singing along with the music: *"Choo choo me home . . ."*

Li-ang understood the words but not their meaning, yet she understood she was his audience—abruptly, the music was lost beneath the roar of the three P-40s' engines restarting. The planes started trundling past, bristling with machine guns, laden with bombs. Archie had donned earphones over his cap.

He looks different now, thought Li-ang. Like a man. A warrior like Ming. But she had seen that Archie had another side to him, a playful kind of joyousness she wished Ming possessed.

Archie gave a thumbs-up. He was wearing gloves now. *Of course,* Li-ang thought. The upper atmosphere was freezing cold. *Imagine being up there . . .*

The P-40s turned onto the runway and stopped. Their engines grew louder, and they strained like attack dogs against leashes . . . and then their brakes released, and they started down the airstrip, faster, faster . . .

And magically rose into the air like beasts become birds. In formation, they banked back over the tarmac. The lead plane dived with a sound that shook the air as it barrel-rolled barely a hundred feet above Li-ang—

Briefly she glimpsed Archie's white grin, his extended wave . . .

It was like a snapshot, one she'd never forget.

Then his P-40 was gone, rejoining the formation that quickly diminished to winked reflections in the sun before fading in the distance.

* * *

The setting sun threw long shadows across the airstrip. On the tarmac's far end, a few dim lights shone from personnel huts and supply dumps. On the near end, where the tarmac was streaked with rubber landing marks, Smitty and two other mechanics stood looking at the purpling northeastern sky, where, hours earlier, the three Tigers had flown. Smitty glanced at his watch, shook his head.

Li-ang stood by a fuel shed, which, for safety's sake, was fifty yards away. She, too, peered worriedly at the sky, as she had been doing for the past hour.

Ming had not yet returned from the final concealment of the most-revered Lucky. Kitty, too angry simply to wait for him, had gone for a walk.

And ended up here at the AVG airstrip.

Standing vigil for the American . . .

She admitted it to herself now. She was not only curious; she was deeply attracted to the man named Archie. It was a feeling she'd never before experienced. *A need.* Not that anything would come of it. Yet still she wondered:

What would it be like with Archie? Just once?

And so Li-ang stared into the darkening sky, praying for the American's safe return. Was it too late? Surely, he would be running out of fuel. There were no landing lights . . .

She felt someone watching her. Turned and saw a young Chinese man she recognized as the merchant who operated the base PX. Well dressed in a suit and tie, with neatly parted brilliantine hair and steel-rimmed spectacles, he looked more Western than Chinese. Even his first name was Western: Winston.

Suddenly, Smitty looked up.

Li-ang heard a distant hum. Then, mosquito-size in the distance, two P-40s approached. Li-ang clasped her hands and lowered her head and prayed.

Let him be one of them.

She repeated this over and over as the engines roared closer, tires thudded on hard-packed dirt, and two tiger-toothed warbirds taxied closer. When their engines stopped, Li-ang looked up. Two mechanics were helping pilots out from their plexiglass bubbles. But Smitty remained on the tarmac, still staring northeast.

Kitty was disconsolate. She told herself she was acting like a silly girl, mourning for a stranger while, each day, thousands of her countrymen died—

There came another hum.

The third P-40. *His.*

As it grew nearer, it was obviously in distress. Smoke streamed from its cowling. Its wings seemed weirdly unbalanced—no, one was badly shot up. Its engine sputtered . . . then stopped. The P-40 silently glided toward the tall palm trees beyond the far end of the strip.

Li-ang held her breath. He was too low.

Palm fronds scattered as the P-40 brushed them . . . the plane wobbled . . . then righted itself, and somehow achieved a perfect landing. It rolled down the runway to a stop. The cockpit opened, and Smitty helped Archie out. Even in the fading light, Li-ang saw Archie's grin.

"Took some flak but nailed three of the bastards," he said.

"Drinks on the house tonight, boss," said Smitty, leaving.

But Archie remained, looking around. The Chinese merchant Winston had disappeared. Li-ang shrank against the fuel shed. She relaxed as Archie's gaze passed her—

Or had it? For all at once, he fast-walked toward her, then abruptly stopped, face-to-face with her.

"Evening," said Archie. "My name is Archibald Petrie. What's yours?"

Li-ang, astonished by his audacious bad manners, was too taken aback to reply. Archie's grin was slightly lopsided, as if he were making fun of himself. He reintroduced himself, this time in Mandarin.

"You speak . . . ?" Kitty's words trailed off as she realized how unseemly this appeared. He was an American, and she was a virgin pledged to marry within her race. In English, she replied, "Li-ang . . . Kitty will do."

"Why are you here, Kitty?"

She refused to be bullied, for she had a right to be there. In the harshest tone she could manage, she said, "I am a soldier doing my duty for my country. Why are you here? For money?"

"*Ha!*" Archie grinned. "Earlier? I *knew* you were listening."

Kitty blushed. She wanted to leave—*had to*—but something came over her. Concern. She noticed a dark thin line running from his hairline down his cheek. *He's bleeding.* Without hesitation, she tenderly touched his face.

"You're wounded," she said. "You should—"

"Choo choo me home, Kitty."

What? Oh, that song.

Why don't I leave?

She knew why.

Their mouths met, and she entered his embrace and they lowered to the grass. Moments later, their clothing lay scattered. At first, she tensed, anticipating pain, but he was gentle . . . and then she became the aggressor, pulling him tighter, drawing him deeper . . .

They crested as one.

Afterward, they lay still as, slowly, Kitty's mind cleared. She became aware of the world beyond her lover. Heard insects and night birds chirping in the jungle. Smelled the sweet grass beneath her bare skin. Clarity returned. She'd become a woman with a *gweilo*, a white man. It would be her secret. She had crossed a line and now would step back across it. She stood, turning her back to him as she dressed.

Smoking, he watched her. "Tomorrow the base is moving north," he said. "We won't be seeing one another for a while."

We won't be seeing one another ever again, thought Kitty.

He twisted a ring from his finger and held it up: a silver band crested with gold letters. *AVG.* He put the ring in her palm and closed her fingers around it.

Kitty was nonplussed. *Was this a Western betrothal?*

"Hold it for me," he said. "Until I come back."

In spite of herself, Kitty nodded. Then left.

She reached her quarters minutes before Ming arrived. He said, "Lucky's been made comfortable."

Lucky. Kitty had forgotten their mission, and now, stricken with guilt, she tried to erase the memory of her moment with Archie. There was only one way. She threw herself into Ming's arms. For a moment, he protested—he had been bred a gentleman—but, in spite of his upbringing, he surrendered to passion.

Afterward, Ming allowed a rare smile. "The most fortunate day of my life. To be granted the great honor of possessing both Li-ang Soo and Lucky . . ."

* * *

California. The present.

Lost in her wartime memories, Madame Soo, a wizened sparrow of a woman, fragile as ancient parchment, sat on her balcony overlooking the western sea. It was day's end, and in the last light, the room and all in it—Madame Soo herself, the ornately lacquered cabinets, the vases of ancient dynasties, the likenesses of forgotten generalissimos and long-dead empresses—glowed the amber of a faded photograph.

Ai, those were the days—

A voice pierced her awareness: "Traitorous bitch," said a woman. "I will see to it that she is silenced."

Madame Soo, hearing the faint ebb and flow of waves below the balcony, struggled to return to her memories. For a moment, she seemed almost there, but all at once they disappeared. A light had come on, and she was here, now.

"Wake up, Grandmother of mine."

Madame Soo's lids fluttered open. Her rheumy eyes regarded her granddaughter, Missy Soo. As always, she was struck by Missy's beauty, her perfect face, lithe figure in skintight gym clothing.

"A drink before dinner, Honorable One?"

"No, my dear," said Madame Soo.

Both knew she hadn't touched alcohol in decades. The formal question and reply was a game instigated by Missy, who thought her grandmother age addled.

Not so. The old woman was sharp as ever, although she preferred Missy think otherwise.

Imagine not trusting your own blood.

Yet she couldn't blame Missy. The girl was exactly the way she'd been. Brave and noble-minded, yet subject to impulsive choices that ended badly. *Transport her to 1941, and we'd have been twins—*

Twins.

The word triggered another memory, one that had been in Madame Soo's consciousness for so many decades. A memory so painful yet so beautiful, it was both the tragedy and the beacon of her life. She had a daughter—and perhaps grandchildren—whom she had never met. Meeting her lost child was one of two reasons she'd willed herself to live until she did. The second reason also concerned unfinished business—

"Don't be sad, Grandmother," said Missy. "I promise you'll live to see Lucky again."

This granddaughter of hers was prescient: *that* was her other unfinished business, for which she refused to die until it was accomplished: *Seeing Lucky again.*

CHAPTER 6

Prior to my suspension, I carried three phones, the better to service my many clients. My present circumstances dictated only one device, which rarely rang, anyway. Come the next morning when it shrilled, I hoped it wasn't Stella, for I wasn't ready to share the little I'd learned. It wasn't Stella. It was a woman who introduced herself as Missy Soo.

"Oh yeah," I replied. "We spoke or tried to . . . the connection was bad."

"No matter," she said, her tone businesslike. "I wish to retain you."

Soo? Another case from Uncle? Or the same case? "May I ask who referred you?"

"We have mutual friends."

I let it go at that. The more immediate question was where to meet with her. I'd checked earlier, and the East Fifty-Ninth Street rent-an-office was being refurbished. The box I called home was out of the question.

"My schedule is tight," I said. "We could meet for lunch?"

"That would be fine. Today, if you please."

"Sure." I suggested a three-star Midtown bistro. "Say, one o'clock? You'll be wearing . . . ?"

"Red."

* * *

With few exceptions, my clients range from unattractive ogres to unbearably ordinary. Judging by Missy Soo's Solomon Grundy–like phone demeanor, I expected her to be among the latter. Still, I knotted my best tie and swiped a damp towel across my wingtips.

I arrived at the restaurant half an hour early, figuring I'd have a pick-me-up at the bar before the meet. I was doing so when it happened:

The woman on the stool to my right spoke to me in a voice I both recognized and feared.

"I know you know," she said.

I drew a steadying breath and swiveled to face her. She wasn't wearing red. Her outfit—cashmere and leather—looked as if it belonged on a Loro Piana runway, although she wore it better than any model. She'd altered her look since I'd seen her last. Her dark hair was still long, but blunt cut. Same unreadable expression as always, though. And the same perfectly proportioned, petite body.

"My name is Dolores," she said.

Dolores? I'd known her by many names. Most recently as Laura Astorquiza, antidrug crusader on the blog *Radio Free Bogotá* whose secret alter ego was the drug kingpin *Sombra*, the mass murderer believed dead by all the world except the two of us.

This was the moment I'd been dreading.

Her hand rested lightly atop a shoulder bag. I wondered what caliber of gun it held. A .25 that would ricochet inside my skull? A .357 that would leave an exit wound the size and color of a watermelon?

"You're staring, Benn."

"My petrified look."

She laughed. Exactly the same giggle she'd had when she was seven-year-old Sara Barrera, daughter of the Cali cartel CFO Nacho Barrera, my first Colombian client, the man who'd given me an admission ticket to the White Powder Bar. Until my recent case, in which she'd been revealed to me as *Sombra*, I hadn't seen her—Sara—since the night the cartel's security had rebelled, a coup that killed Nacho and hundreds of the Barreras' extended family and friends. That night I'd saved Sara—no, *Dolores*, I reminded myself—only to lose her again.

I'm not prone to cognitive dissonance, but I felt it now. The girl who'd loved me like family had grown into her generation's greatest cartel chief and now was approaching me, for an unknown but surely nefarious purpose, in the guise of a "Dolores"—

No, I reminded myself. She is *not* Sara. *Not* Laura Astorquiza. *Not* Dolores.

She is, now and forever more, a cold-blooded killer named *Sombra*.

"We have no problem, Benn. I'm no longer in the business."

I'd forgotten how well she could read me, even as a child. I was no slouch at reading her, either. Meaning that I heard her but didn't necessarily believe her. In all her adult guises, she'd become a consummate liar. I signaled to the barkeep: two fingers, a double vodka. If I was to be starring on a tabloid front page under the headline "Criminal Lawyer Gunned Down in Midtown Restaurant," I might as well die drunk.

"It's so strange, Benn. Seeing you now, I remember when you and Papa used to talk. I was always listening. Unless Papa caught me and put me to bed. I learned much from your discussions, but that's really not why I listened. The truth? I listened because I was in love with you."

"You were, what nine, ten?" I threw back the vodka. "I was almost thirty then. Thank you for not molesting me."

Dolores laughed again. "You haven't changed. Always the cynic, always the wise guy, always finding something funny no matter the circumstance."

"I think of it as a survival skill." I signaled for another double.

"I grew up copying you. Treating everything in life like a joke."

"Here's a good one," I said. "Two cynics walk into a bar . . ."

"The prettier one says, 'I joined Team America.'"

Huh? She'd become a rat? "You're kidding."

"What does the other cynic reply?"

"Um . . . you're gonna kill me?"

"Oh, Benn, I *adore* you."

"What do you want?" *Where was that goddamn vodka?*

"Just to say hello. After all, we're on the same side. Take good care of our Stella."

She stood to go, but I gripped her wrist above her purse. Her mentioning Stella Maris as an ally shook me; it was the third leg—Uncle, Stella, now *Sombra*—of whatever the hell I'd stumbled into.

Again, she tried to go, but I held on to her wrist.

"You want me to stay? To take a hotel room, or what?"

"That's not funny."

"Not meant to be." She removed my hand, winked, left. As I watched her go, another woman sat on the stool at my left. An Asian beauty, devilish in a red dress.

"Miss, ah, Missy Soo, I presume?" I smiled.

She didn't. Her almond-shaped eyes had black pupils devoid of expression. Her handshake was firm. Her red-lacquered nails were filed to points that scratched my palm. When the barkeep greeted her, she brushed him off with a curt: "Flat water. No ice."

I said, "Shall we move to a table?"

Her reply was as cold as the ice cubes she'd forsaken. "I've already dined. Let's get down to business."

I shrugged. "Let's."

She said, "Stella's been in and out of institutions all her life. She cannot deal with the stress of everyday life. She refuses to discuss certain pressing matters concerning the distribution of her family's estate. Her recalcitrance is putting the rest of the family's lives on hold."

I raised my eyebrows as if this were all new to me, but I was thinking: *So, another Chinese connection to the exact same case. The other part of the family?*

Stella was Caucasian, but she had a tilt to her eyes that hinted of an Asian bloodline. She wore a small, star-shaped gem at her neck. Ruby red. Could she be pro-mainland Chinese, unlike Uncle, whose

Foochow Tong was allied with the rival Taiwanese Chinese? Was the familial rift political?

I said, "By *family*, you mean?"

"There's nothing you can do to assist her by yourself, but I, together with the rest of our family—and with your help—we can."

Help? Or connivance? They say Mata Hari was a fox. Maybe so. But Mata was a drab Hollander while the exotic Missy Soo was the most beautiful Chinese woman I'd ever been so close to. And I was just a shovel for her dirty work. A shovel she wanted to use to bury Stella. I made Missy Soo as one of those capable-of-anything folks Stella had mentioned, a brat born to wealth who didn't take orders from anyone.

"I'll let you in on a little secret," I said.

She leaned forward eagerly. "Yes?"

"My name isn't Shovelhead."

"Excuse me . . . ?"

"Meaning, let's not continue this discussion."

Her smile was condescending. "If you wish. But I was just about to inform you that I have with me a certified check in your name for two hundred and fifty thousand dollars." She put an envelope on the bar. "For so long as your assistance is required, you will receive an additional two hundred and fifty thousand monthly, for each of the next twelve months."

My damn palm itched. Took an effort, but I refrained from scratching it, then said, "My help? Specifically?"

"Simply arrange for me to meet with Stella. At a place of your choosing. In your presence, of course. If she trusts you, she'll agree."

"You think?"

"I know. Stella has a father-figure syndrome. Understandable, considering she's hopelessly bipolar . . . Forgive my using medical terminology, I meant—"

"I understood what you meant."

Boy, oh boy, did I. I'd been with all kinds of women and found "father issues" to be as common as they were varied: cold, distant fathers; absent fathers; fathers who couldn't keep their hands off Daddy's girl. I wondered how Missy Soo's home life had been. She was so cold, her old man must have been a glacier, but I thought, given the chance, I might warm her up nicely.

I was feeling my old self again.

With good cause. My second double had arrived. Nicely mellow, I was thrilled to learn that Dolores—*Sombra*—didn't want to kill me. I had $250,000 in the bank, and my immediate future promised more. As for Stella's cautionary mention of *risk*, hell, I translated that word to *action*. The fact is, I liked walking the razor's edge. All I needed to do was keep my pole balanced by making certain the game went according to Bluestone's Rules:

Pay me as agreed. Tell me no lies I don't want to know. Instead of CST—Criminal Standard Time—make a reasonable effort not to keep me waiting.

And, paramount among all, the absolute deal-breaker:

Never, ever, ask me to screw another client.

"Mr. Bluestone? What are you thinking?"

I picked up Missy Soo's glass and placed my lips where her lipstick had marked its rim. Her upper and lower lips were the same size. Nicely plump. I drank her water.

Her perfect brow crinkled in a frown. "You're drinking my water."

"I get dry when I'm frustrated," I said. "Your fault."

"*My* fault? Why—"

"Because I'd love to take your money. But I can't. See, you can hire me, but you can't buy me, and in your case, you can't even hire me, because I'm already hired. But I do appreciate your coming out of the woodwork because now I know Stella needs to watch out for a lady in red."

"You're a sad little man," she said. "The kind who get crushed like an ant because no one sees or cares about them. You just lost a lot of money for nothing, because with or without you, we will find Stella, and she will come to her senses."

With that, she left.

I had one for the road while idly watching the TV above the bar. It was tuned to the news. The sound was muted, but the images spoke louder than words. Warships, jet fighters, missiles . . . of many nations. The chyrons on the bottom of the screen provided more details: Six nations bordering the South China Sea—China foremost among them—were threatening military action over sovereignty of the area and its vital trade routes.

Whoa. China? Again?

The envelope was still on the bar. I looked inside and, sure enough, found a bank-certified check for $250,000, made out to me. I drew a fortifying breath, then ripped the check in two, then ripped the halves into little pieces, and set them on the bar. Benn, the alchemist, who turns money into confetti . . . maybe also a bit of a snake, but loyal to only one charmer at a time.

That being Stella Maris.

CHAPTER 7

Now that the two beauties had departed, my thoughts became beastly. Greed is so bitter, it leaves an aftertaste. Wistfully, I stared at the little heap of confetti that had been Missy's check.

"Bartender," I said. "A sparkling water, please."

I needed fizz to clarify my weird reality show. Seeing Dolores had me envisioning charred men in orange life vests in a black sea, a scenario I was certain included her—

My heart tingled. From my breast pocket, I took my device. I had a text from Stella:

I am outside waiting for you.

I supposed Dolores had told her I was here. Whatever. I took a final wistful look at 250 Gs' worth of shredded paper and left.

A black, tinted-window Suburban idled curbside. Its driver—a big-shouldered guy wearing a black suit and an ex-cop face—held a rear door open for me.

I got in the back, and the door closed behind me with the refrigerator-like thud that was a giveaway for armored weight. Behind the tinted glass, the rear compartment was dim, and it took a moment before I realized Stella sat in the corner, bundled in endangered-species fur.

She leaned close to me. Her hair caressed my cheek as she whispered, "My grandfather has a wiretap on her phone."

"Dolores?"

"The *other* woman you were talking to. The one who wants to kill me."

Missy Soo, then. Whose recent proximity suggested she might be following us. I glanced out the rear window but saw only the usual Manhattan traffic through the dark glass.

When the big car stopped at a light, I casually tried the door handle. It was locked. I sat back and didn't enjoy the ride.

* * *

Stella, snuggled in her fur, seemed asleep. Through the partition, the driver was a blurred silhouette, the dash lights a smear of colored control lights. The car had as many gizmos as the Batmobile. Traffic was light as we drove downtown, whizzed through the Midtown Tunnel, and got onto the Long Island Expressway.

Stella remained cocooned.

We turned onto the Northern State Parkway. Half an hour later, we exited onto a winding two-lane blacktop that led to a shell drive that crunched beneath the SUV's heavy, bulletproof tires.

We stopped. Stella's door opened, and a shaven-headed guy in a black parka helped her out, gently as an egg. Then my door was opened, and I got out and took stock of the three men triangulating me.

Professionals, for sure. Brawny lookalikes wearing rubber boots and waxed jackets. I'd have made them for groundskeepers, but their shotguns weren't game pieces, rather sawed-off man-killers. I remade them as ex-IRA or similar former paramilitaries. A shotgun pressed against my back.

"Move, boyo," its owner said.

Yes, an Irishman, or maybe an Afrikaner, but definitely ex-military-gone-merc for the bucks. Having a crew like this suggested that Marmaduke Mason—I assumed it was he who'd sent for me—had a lot to protect.

We came to a guardhouse where two guys held on to a pair of slobbering Alsatians. The IRA guy held a palm up: *Stop.* I stood still as they patted me down. They took my device.

"I get a receipt?" I asked.

"Shut yer damn trap."

We continued on.

Another bend brought us to a view of Long Island Sound. An enormous old mansion perched on a bluff overlooking the water. Impressive place, if you're into Gatsby meets *Bleak House.*

A fourth man waited at its columned entrance. Instead of a shotgun, he had a folding-stock Uzi strapped at port arms. He wanded me from toe to head and back again. Made a detour into my nethers, then nodded. The shotgun guys remained outside as I followed Mr. Uzi inside. As if I had a choice. For all intents and purposes, I was a prisoner.

The interior of the mansion looked like a Deauville resort that had escaped 1910. Not exactly my style, but nicer than most prisons I've been in. I followed Mr. Uzi to a paneled door that clicked open. I entered alone, and the door closed behind me.

The room was large and richly appointed, with a bay window overlooking the Sound. It was artsy in an eclectic way. An exquisite Persian carpet, some fine landscapes I didn't recognize, and two definitely major Picassos. Also, a sheathed Japanese samurai sword; an old-fashioned globe of the world still colored with Brit red; a pair of crossed pearl-handled revolvers, a la George Patton. A glassed-in display of Oriental *shurikens.* The desk was the real standout: massive, four-legged, ornately carved gilded wood that might have been Louis XIV's personal dining table, although the extremely old man behind it bore no resemblance to the Sun King.

"Name's Mason," he said. "Sit down."

I did. Marmaduke Mason was the type of ectomorph that grows ever thinner as he nears his goal line. He had leathery skin and a lionlike mane of snow-white hair. As if unaware of my presence, he watched a flat-screen TV, where a muted newscast's corner logo read *Singapore Times*. On the screen was a map of East Asia and the South China Sea. Then the scene shifted to a Nimitz-class nuclear carrier launching missile-laden Hornets . . . and again shifted to a swarm of Chinese troops bulldozing sand on a low-lying island.

China, I thought. *Again.*

"Arseholes," said Mason, still staring at the screen. "Gearing up for the big to-do. 'China is ours' versus 'No, China is *ours.*' The ultimate 'mine is bigger than yours.' It'll start with an insulting mother joke and end with a nuclear winter. Good for them. Me? I won't be around to see it."

He shut off the TV, then swiveled around and stared at me as if examining a new species of bug. Despite his advanced age, his bearing was one of command, and I had the distinct impression he was evaluating me for whatever mission he had planned.

I seized what little initiative I could muster. "Good evening, Mr. Mason."

My chair was several inches lower than his, befitting a mere courtier to be looked down on. He went on staring at me until I realized he wasn't staring but gone off into an elderly moment, perhaps even a stroke.

"Are you all right, Mr. Mason?"

He coughed like a wet engine wheezing to restart. "Lose the mister," he said. "The name's Duke. As in Ellington."

"And Snider."

His eyes slid out of focus. Suddenly, he shouted: "Keegan!"

The door opened, and a portly man wearing a pince-nez and a harried expression rushed in. He carried a doctor's satchel. From it, he took an ampule, crushed it, and held it to Duke's nose.

After a few moments, Duke's clarity returned. He brushed Keegan's hand away and in a contemptuous voice said, "For the last time, Doctor. Don't *ever* come near me again unless I tell you to."

Dr. Keegan protested, "But you called me—"

"Get the hell out of here, you quack."

Dr. Keegan, bowing humbly, backed from the room. The heavy door closed behind him. It was quiet except for the crashing of waves below the bay window. Funny, I hadn't been aware of them before.

Or, I thought, maybe a storm was approaching.

Duke started to speak, seemed to lose his train of thought, then retrieved it and in a slightly slurred voice said, "Protect my girl, and I'll pay you well. Screw up, and I'll hurt you bad. Clear, Counselor?"

I don't mind being trashed a bit if the price is right. Rudeness comes with the territories I travel. Besides, he was on the kind of meds that loosen tongues. Bank on that. It takes an ex-druggie like me to spot a stoner like him. In a slightly slurred voice, he said, "I don't like lawyers."

"My feeling as well. Protect Stella legally?"

"In particular, I don't like you. You've been hired because I'm told you get results. Stella stands to inherit my estate. Unfortunately, she's had a difficult time of it and is not knowledgeable in the ways of the world. She needs someone to look after her affairs. A trustee, if you will."

Trustee? Man, I *really* had crossed the line into civil law.

He said, "If I was younger, I'd do the job myself. But I'm no longer capable of hands-on maintenance, so you're elected. But understand, so long as I'm still around, you're my puppet, Counselor."

"Sure, Geppetto."

Duke looked at me blankly.

I said, "What did you mean by a 'difficult time'?"

"Stella's parents died suddenly. Murdered. Terrible tragedy. Stella was psychologically damaged. I put her out of harm's way, first in an institution, then in the best boarding schools in the world. Helped her somewhat, but, well, you see how she is."

I shrugged. "I'm not sure I do. Why don't you tell me?"

He spun his chair back toward the bay window. Beyond it, the darkened Sound was sprinkled with running lights. For a long moment, he said nothing, as if again lost in his reveries. The waves crashed, he wheezed regularly, and I thought, *Time to snoop.*

My focus was on an opened envelope on his desk. Made of heavy paper, it had been addressed by hand. The letter that came with it lay open beneath the envelope. I whipped out my device and photographed both.

His back still to me, he said, "The feud that killed Stella's folks is heating up again. I have reason to believe Stella's been targeted for kidnapping. I won't let that happen but don't want to chance traumatizing her again. She needs to go elsewhere. Problem is, it's hard for people like Stella to hide. The way she looks, her sudden mood swings, her behavior when . . ."

"When . . . ?"

"None of your business. All you need to know is that you personally are going to escort Stella to a place where she can't be dragged into, ah, court, or anything like that. She'll be among people I trust. Afterward, you'll return here and continue looking after her interests."

"Which are?"

"You ask too many questions." Duke spun back around, gave a horsey grin, and aimed an automatic pistol at me. Its black-holed muzzle was even with my eyes, although it didn't really matter where he shot me; the gun was a Colt .45 model 1911, the US Army's official sidearm for a century or more. Perhaps Duke's own original service piece. Even a flesh wound from that thing could hydrostatic-shock me from here to eternity.

"I'd like to shoot your nuts off," he said. "Maybe someday I will. All depends on how you behave. For now, you got paid, and you're in the op. Which is strictly need-to-know. And you don't need to know—"

He pulled the trigger.

I flinched, but there was only a dry *click*, followed by his reedy laugh. He put the Colt away, stood, and went to the globe. Spun it so Southeast Asia faced us. Regarded the area for a moment, then said, "The legal matter at hand concerns a certain individual whose presence is desired by both sides. We have custody of an object belonging to the individual, who, I might add, has authorized us to act on his behalf."

"The next time you pull a weapon on me, you better use it," I said. "Because if you don't, I'll chuck it and your old ass out the window."

His eyes narrowed. "Careful, boy."

"*Igual*, old man. What object?"

He reached to a desk drawer. Opened it, paused. "You're retained because Stella insisted, but if necessary, I have no compunctions about overruling her. If you want to earn your fee, keep your trap shut."

From the drawer, he took out a box and set it beneath a desk lamp. The box was a foot-square cube of sturdy metal topped by a lid, otherwise featureless but for a keyhole. He reached inside his shirt collar and took out a heavy silver chain on which a gold key dangled. His hand trembled as he bent into the cone of lamplight; in it, his eyes had the yellowish cast of the deeply ill.

He put the key to the lock, looked at me.

"Ready, Counselor?"

I nodded.

He turned the key, and the lock clicked open. He raised the lid and turned the box so I could see what was inside.

It was some sort of a crown, obviously quite old, made of dull gold inlaid with colored stones—no, not stones. Precious gems: an assortment of diamonds, rubies, emeralds, all huge, undoubtedly rare specimens.

Priceless, I thought. *If real.*

"Lucky's hat," he said. "Stella's unaware of its whereabouts. Unfortunately, certain people believe *I* know where both the hat and Lucky himself are. That's the ransom they'll demand if they kidnap Stella. Only you're not going to let that happen, are you?"

"Not on my watch, as they say."

He squinted at me. "You were military?"

"Not my kind of thing."

"It shows. These people . . . the other side, they're battle hardened. They also believe something else you'd best be aware of."

"Feel free to enlighten me."

"They think you know, too."

"Why would they think that?"

He shrugged. "Wireless in the sky. Ears on the street. Your connection with Stella is known. Like it or not, you're along for the ride."

"You put me in harm's way?"

"A quarter mil bought me that."

"You old son of . . ." I put my balled fist at his face.

He didn't blink. Wearing a self-satisfied smile, he waited for my tantrum to end. He was right. I'd already figured the case was like walking a narrow ledge far above a rocky shore. So I chilled and sat back and replayed what was going down.

On one side, Stella, Uncle, and Dolores were seeking my help regarding someone named Lucky. On the other side, Missy Soo and unnamed others wanted me to turn Stella over, also so as to get Lucky. What could be so important about Lucky that it triggered murders and mayhems?

I don't like not knowing. Damn them all and Lucky, collectively. My big concern right now was *my* luck, since their enemies were apparently my enemies.

"Deal with it, boy," said Duke.

"It's going to cost you," I said.

"Stella's already paid you."

When I was a drug lawyer, one of my credos was, *When the drug dealer's distracted, take the money off the table.* I doubted old Duke was a drug dealer but was certain his secretive lifestyle was both motivated and financed by past criminality, and from the surroundings, I figured he was—or had been—a big player. The kind who survive because everything they do is deliberately planned.

But no way I was getting caught up with violence-prone types unless I got paid a whole lot more. Time to distract.

"I don't charge by the hour," I said. "My bill for incurring enemies is steep. Not sure you can afford me."

"I can afford a thousand of you. How much?"

"One million dollars."

"You got balls."

"In advance."

He brought up some phlegm, rolled it with his tongue, then swallowed it back down, like a cow chewing its cud. Disgusting. The older the criminal, the cruder they get, and the more they hate to part with money. They've been taking so much from so many for so long that they forget, sometimes, that they, too, must give.

"I'll need a few days to raise the money," he said.

I stood to leave. "Let me know when."

"Four days, you'll have it. You'll have to trust me on that. You're escorting Stella on a trip tomorrow. One day traveling, one day there, another day traveling back. Your money will be waiting when you return."

"This trip? Where to?"

He smiled. "Colombia."

Dolores, I thought.

* * *

They escorted me to my room. Nice, comfortable, spacious. Windows with a view of treetops and Long Island Sound. An antique Chinese bed with soft, embroidered cushions. I stretched out and evaluated the photos I'd surreptitiously taken of the letter on Duke's desk. His name and address on the envelope had been written in an old-timey hand. A woman's hand. It was postmarked from San Francisco. Only a corner of the letter was visible, and it, too, was handwritten, although I couldn't make out a word.

I shifted gears to the proposition. I'd be escorting—whatever that entailed—Stella to Colombia, a country that'd been my home away from home for decades. I missed it sorely: the country, the action, the money, the good times. And now that things were again copacetic with Dolores, my previous trepidations about returning there had vanished. Although I didn't dig giving Duke extra time to pay, maybe getting out of Dodge was the smart move. Deliver Stella from her "enemies," then disengage if necessary.

* * *

I must've dozed off, because when I opened my eyes, there was a cover over me and part of it was covering Stella. She was wide awake. Watching me from inches away. I'd been wrong about her resemblance to Gene Tierney. Stella didn't resemble anyone. She was the most singularly beautiful woman in the world. I considered whether I was still dreaming, but before I could crack wise, she put a finger to my lips and made a point of glancing around.

Meaning we were being taped. Probably there were cameras as well, but Stella didn't seem to mind. Or maybe that was why she kept the cover over us as she snuggled closer. But blanket or not, if Duke was watching, I had to get Stella out of my bed, pronto—

But then, as she began unbuckling my pants, I realized she was bare-ass naked. Which provoked a perfect example of balls over brains.

Stella's nipples stood like a baby's thumbs. Her body was silken smooth. She smelled good and tasted better. We moved this way and that, and the sheets tangled beneath us. I noticed something strange: she always made sure to keep one or another part of her body covered by the bedclothes. First, it was her backside, which got me thinking she was hiding some real or imagined flaw. But then the blanket moved, and her ass proved to be as supple and perfect as a newly halved pear. We went on to other things, and she made sure her upper body was under wraps.

Why this need to keep parts of herself unrevealed? Surely, it wasn't the possibility of cameras in the room that made her reluctant to go full body, for if Duke was ogling us, it would be obvious that two pigs were rutting in a blanket, no pun.

We played at being missionaries. Then she got out from under and lowered herself atop me. Her eyes were closed. She looked queenlier than Nefertiti. Me, I was Sir Walter Raleigh, just a cape in a puddle for her convenience. She balanced atop me and pressed harder—"*Oh!*"— and her breathing became more rapid, her lips moved as if she were talking to herself, and she covered all of herself, the blanket a burqa . . . then she slid from atop me and sighed deeply. Her eyes were still closed, but like mercury on a pearl, a tear leaked down her smooth cheek. Her hair was pushed back, and I saw a slight discoloration in her skin below her hairline. A scar? Oh well, perfection is boring—

"Benn?" she whispered.

"Yuh?"

"Pretend this never happened. It's not you; it's me. I'm sorry. You won't leave me, will you?"

"I won't leave you."

"Close your eyes."

I did. And thought how strange our interlude had been. I'd succumbed to her beauty, but it seemed as if she couldn't have cared less about me physically. I was merely a prop for her physical desire, or perhaps some deep need to debase herself by doing the horizontal mambo with a cipher.

When I opened my eyes, she was gone.

PART TWO: THE CONSPIRACY

CHAPTER 8

Guna Yala archipelago, Gulf of Panama.

A speedboat cleaved across the flat sea, weaving between hundreds of islets big and small. From the speedboat, the water ahead was clear as glass. Mantas scurrying from it scattered like dark clouds across the white-sand sea floor.

"I like that one," said Dolores, turning the wheel toward a tiny islet, hardly a bump of white sand topped by a single palm.

Behind her, Richard lay on the cockpit bench, a beer in his big hand, a satellite phone cradled between shoulder and ear, although his gaze remained fixed on Dolores: sun browned, bare breasted, thong bottomed. A sensational woman, no question. Who would do sensational things to further his goals. But the thing about Dolores that really got to him? The way her eyes reflected her surroundings; they were not colorless now but the pale green of the sea.

He was so absorbed in Dolores that he was hardly aware of the woman's voice on the phone. As the speedboat gently nosed onto the islet's powdery beach, he ended his call with, "Sounds like you're doing real good," and put the phone away.

"It's a *New Yorker* cartoon," said Dolores.

"What're you babbling?"

"*This* place. Like in those cartoons of people marooned on tiny desert islands saying funny things."

Richard burped, popped another beer.

"You don't get it," said Dolores. "Have you never read the *New Yorker*?"

"I don't read that commie fag rag."

Dolores drank deeply from her bottle, then closed her eyes and poured the remaining beer over her head. When she opened her eyes, they reflected the white sand.

Reflections always, thought Richard. *Never a hint of what's inside her.*

Dolores finger-combed her hair while looking at his phone. "So?"

"The lawyer was approached."

"What's your take?"

"He's hooked."

"We knew he would be. What's next?"

"You keep asking what's next, and I keep answering that's for me to know and you to find out. So stop asking."

"Maybe I'll stop a lot of things."

"Aw, what the hell, I'll make an exception. I'm thinking it's time for some R and D."

"Been there, done that, but why not?"

He laughed. "Not Richard and Dolores. Research and development. We'll be working separately for a bit. Your first stop is just over the horizon," he said, raising his chin southward.

"Colombia?" said Dolores. "What about it?"

"My people want you to keep the fires burning."

"Oh, I will. You? Where are you headed?"

"Thinking of taking a slow boat to, ah, China."

"China, again. Pray, tell me more, master."

"You've already used your exception . . ."

Richard's voice trailed off as another vessel neared. Not a buzzy speedboat but a dugout canoe propelled by two Indians working paddles. One Indian was young. The other, older Indian was the man who'd sniped the Chinese officer on a Colombian beach. Dolores's Logui kinsmen, watching over her.

"Relax," said Dolores. "They're Kunas who live here. They like tourists."

Richard waited until the dugout was well away before continuing. "We need to code up. From now on, I'm Brutalist."

"I'd say the shoe fits. Who am I?"

"Sangfroid. From the French, meaning—"

"Cold-blooded. Hmm. Why not?"

"The woman from Shanghai? She's Flower."

"A poisonous one, for sure. The other woman?"

"She's the White Tigress."

"Whatever that means."

"The Chinese hold their legends dear. The White Tigress is the lover of the Green Dragon. Together, they represent the power of the Orient. Blah-blah-blah."

"Benn's code name?"

"You dig Benn, or what?"

Dolores didn't reply.

"You fuck him yet?"

Still no answer.

Richard smiled. "Benn's code name is Franklin. As in, the face on the bills he loves so much."

"The mission's code name?"

"Operation Lucky."

* * *

The helicopter followed the northeast Colombian coastline from Barranquilla east over the Guajira Peninsula. Dolores, its only passenger, was enjoying the ride.

She also was enjoying Richard. On a physical level, they interacted as if custom-made for each other. Of course, given the realities, it would be short-term. The way she was. From time to time, when she wanted a man, she took him until she grew bored with his presence. Richard was nearing that point. She'd noted his dyed hair, capped teeth, steroid-enhanced body, and seen a phial of Cialis in his Dopp kit. For sure, he was equally fake beneath his skin, but so were all men . . . well, maybe not so much Benn, a world-class faker, yet at the same time . . . *honorable?* Yes, that was the word.

But, bored or not, she had to stay with Richard.

Thanks to his astonishing leverage within the US intelligence community and military, Dolores was being introduced firsthand to the newest military hardware produced in the arsenal of democracy, a euphemism that amused her no end. Out of necessity, Dolores had become a serious student of weaponry and had already equipped and trained her Logui to defend themselves against the bandits and cartels that poached their lands in the Sierra Nevada de Santa Marta mountains, the northernmost range of the Andean chains that split Colombia like a trident.

The helicopter thrummed along in near silence. It was custom cladded to reduce cabin sound. She made a mental note to obtain a similar machine, a beautiful toy that would be put to ugly use. She'd sent the Brothers of Those Who Know More to flight schools, and they were fine pilots.

Her earphones squawked. The pilot said, "Call for you."

She glanced at her watch. The caller was precisely on time, a trait she demanded of her workers. This worker she knew as Fifty-Five. He'd worked for her father, and now for her. She turned on the Voxal software, modifying her voice to an asexual robotic drone.

"Proceed," she said.

Fifty-Five spoke in clipped sentences while describing the current abysmal state of the Colombian drug business. The Caribbean-coast drug-trafficking organizations—DTOs in DEA parlance—were idled, no product coming through. The vast Los Llanos plains were a cartel battlefield. The southern grow zones were untended. Assassinations had brought business in Cali and Medellín to a standstill. The big guys in Bogotá were locked down, waiting, hoping for the storm to pass.

"Spread the word," said Dolores. "*Sombra* will be arranging a meeting of cartel representatives to discuss reimbursement of their losses."

"When they ask where and when?"

"Say soon. They will be notified."

"It will be done."

"Thank you."

Dolores had no intention of reimbursing anyone, but she wanted to raise expectations, buying time during which the nearly bankrupt cartels would cannibalize one another. This was her part of the deal with Richard, keeping him successful, therefore powerful, therefore *useful*. His masters in Washington would be pleased by the disruptions in the cocaine trade and announce a great success in the war against drugs, no doubt followed by a request for more funds to ensure total victory. Fools. Of course, the drug trade, with its attendant miseries and endless torrents of money, would continue as before. Just as water sought its level, so would the drug trade reappear. It had done so in the lull after Pablo, it had done so after the putsch overthrowing her father's Cali cartel, and it would after she, *Sombra*, was a memory.

So sad. America had saved the world seventy-five years ago, but the sweet smell of that success had corrupted its senses. Now its armies waged wars that needn't be fought and couldn't be won. Vietnam, Afghanistan, Iraq, and the granddaddy of them all, the war against drugs. And all the while the answer was staring in their faces:

Leave the world alone, and the world will leave you alone.

Decriminalize drugs, and the criminals will be gone.

Not that either would happen. The Americans had spent trillions creating military and justice systems that had become lynchpins of their economy: raising and equipping police forces, investigating and arresting and prosecuting and jailing, what, three million prisoners? Most of whom would someday return to society, brains permanently rewired with a con mentality.

It would never change.

If the justice machine were eliminated, it would be an earthquake that devastated the American economy. Jobs lost. Politicians booted. In the end, it all came down to one thing: when money was the fertilizer, there was no uprooting the evils it nourished. Contagious evils. The Chinese were equally infected. She would keep her Logui safe from them—

"Position check," said the pilot. "We're now five miles west of them."

Dolores peered at the panorama. On the right, rising directly from the sea, were the foothills of the Sierra Nevada, and beyond were its snowcapped peaks, the highest of which was Anawanda, which to the Logui was the center of the earth. For Dolores, it was simply home sweet home.

Now she frowned as, on the beach far ahead, she saw rows of prefab buildings and ranks of giant earthmoving machines emblazoned with the red stars of Communist China. Many more than last time she'd been here. She resolved to send the Chinese a message so stunning, it would idle their machines. That was *her* personal mission: protecting the Logui and their homeland, at any cost.

Offshore were anchored a half dozen Chinese cargo vessels. Many small craft moved between them and the beach.

"Two miles," said the pilot.

No point flirting with the possibility of being detected, thought Dolores. Besides, she had seen enough. She ordered the pilot to proceed to their destination, and the helicopter banked away from the sea and flew higher over the foothills that led to Anawanda.

* * *

The Logui village's terraces and mossy walls resembled Machu Picchu, but here was no vista of mountains and sky; instead, the village was surrounded by dense rainforest. Trees lined the grid, and the village's thatched roofs were of live foliage, rendering it nearly undetectable from eyes in the sky.

It was midday, but the place was strangely deserted, except for a youth who resembled a younger version of the Older Brother Who Knows More. The youth, Younger Brother Who Knows More, loped along the empty beaten earth streets, then left the village and continued along a narrow trail that snaked higher beneath the canopy.

He ran easily, his feet barely touching the ground, and stopped where the path seemingly ended in dense green vegetation. Without hesitation, he parted the foliage, revealing a twisty stone staircase. He ran up it . . .

And moments later emerged in the ruins of the long-forgotten city of the Logui, *La Ciudad Perdida,* to which the tribe had retreated five hundred years ago, when the Spanish had invaded the Sierra Nevada.

The villagers were gathered around an old stone building. Two people dressed in white stood in front of the building. One was the village elder. The other was Dolores, although the Logui called her *Alune,* meaning the One Who Knows Most of All. The elder addressed the people in the Logui language, Anchiga:

"*Alune* believes the outside world is approaching a great catastrophe. Increasingly, it is governed by unknowing fools. The wealthiest among them are devising escape plans. Some even speak of finding another planet. We survived our own great catastrophe when the Spaniards came. Again, we survived when the bandits and narcotraffickers invaded, thanks to *Alune.* Now we are faced with an even greater threat from Those Who Know Less. Again, our destiny is with *Alune.*"

The elder shuffled aside, and Dolores stepped forward. The time had come for her to demonstrate her intentions. She nodded to Younger Brother, who in turn motioned to a ruined wall.

A moment later, a dozen people emerged from behind the wall. Two were Logui warriors holding the ends of a chain on which ten young Chinese men were roped. Their mouths and eyes were covered. They wore dun army uniforms. They stood in a row as Dolores slowly passed for the benefit of the villagers, addressing them in Anchiga, although obviously none understood a word.

"You're young men. You come from a great, learned civilization that has disregarded its past and imitated the facile shallowness of the West. You have families you love who love you. Probably none of you ever committed an evil act. You deserve to return to your country and live decent lives. Unfortunately, there is a principle called the Greater Good. Your leaders have sent you to rape our sacred homeland. The Greater Good demands we do what we must to defend it. We need to send a message to your people that they cannot fight us. Tonight we shall pray for your souls."

She paused to regard the prisoners. Poor victims. She looked at her people. *They'll never be victims.*

Again, Dolores nodded at Younger Brother.

Again, he gestured, and a moment later ten arrows flew from the jungle into the hearts of the ten soldiers. They dropped as one.

Dolores said, "Remove your shafts from the bodies. Shoot the wounds where the shafts entered so their people will think the narcotraffickers killed them. Leave the bodies on the beach."

Dolores watched the bodies being removed. The Logui returned to their village. Throughout, Dolores's visage had been grim, but now that she was alone, she smiled, picturing the reaction of the Chinese when they awoke to find their slaughtered comrades. Her smile was brief. She'd murdered innocents in order to protect the Logui. But still . . .

Yes, the Chinese would back off, but only for a short time, and eventually they and the Colombians would attack the Logui en masse. At best, she'd bought her people a respite.

But she knew it would not be for long.

CHAPTER 9

The mercs kept me in the bedroom all day. Its door was locked. They came for me at twilight. They took me outside and put me into another dark-glassed Suburban. I glimpsed them putting Stella into the one we'd arrived in. I thought she saw me, yet she kept her expression hidden.

From them? Or me?

The SUVs navigated the road and got back on a highway. Thirty minutes later, we unloaded on tarmac that reeked of aviation fuel: Long Island's MacArthur Airport, I assumed, yet there'd been no security check.

The power of money.

A stairway led to a sleek private jet. Two cabins. Mine was the rear one. I heard the front fuselage doors closing and Stella's voice—sluggish, probably drugged, I thought—in the forward cabin; then the door between the cabins closed. Within a minute, the jet started taxiing, turned onto a runway, stopped. The engines whined louder, and I felt the powerful machine straining; then its brakes released, and it lurched down the runway.

In twenty seconds, we were airborne. The plane gained altitude, the cowboy at the controls banked hard left, and off we went.

Duke had said an overnight flight, so I settled in for the duration. A couple of hours later, one of the mercs appeared with a tuna sandwich and tepid coffee, then left, shutting the door behind him. I ate while looking out the window. Nothing but ocean below, not a ship's light in sight. I figured we were over the Caribbean, headed south. To Colombia.

It felt as if I were going home.

I awoke when the jet touched down. It was still dark. Passenger jetliners were parked outside a modern terminal. As we neared a jetport, I could see lettering on the control tower—*Riohacha*—a name that spiked my heart like an electroshock. Riohacha was a small city on Colombia's Guajira Peninsula, the desertlike coastal stretch where the Colombian drug trade first went international half a century ago, when weed was king and coca was a ridiculousness chewed by Indians . . . eventually becoming the basis of my vocation.

Again, I wondered: *Why me?* As well as: *Why here?*

I tried not to overthink the possibility of a threat. If anyone wanted to kill me, they already would've. I was safe because, somehow, I was *needed.*

I heard the forward fuselage door open, then voices and footsteps. I inched open the window shade just as Stella was being arm-walked by two mercs across the tarmac to a midsize helicopter—

The jet's rear cabin door opened, and a merc leaned in.

"Your carriage awaits, massah," he said.

He led me to the chopper. It was a big job with a good-size cabin. Two pilot seats up front, four passenger seats in two rows behind. Stella sat in the row behind the pilot, her eyes closed, mouth agape. *Sedated, for sure.* A merc sat alongside her. Another merc pushed me into the seat behind Stella, then sat next to me. The cabin door closed. The main rotor cast quickening shadows on the tarmac. The copter lifted, tilted, then zoomed off.

Something was strange.

Then I realized that, but for a faint whirring, the machine was soundless. I recalled reading something about next-gen weaponry, specifically, the stealth NOTAR—No Tail Rotor—system. Most helicopter noise comes from the tail rotor, so the bright boys of American industry had eliminated it, controlling yaw by blowing air out of vents along the tail boom. Supposedly, NOTAR was not yet in production, but these people, whoever they were, had the collective juice to obtain one.

The merc handed me headphones and motioned me to put them on over my ears. When I did, over them an intercom-altered voice said, "Hello dere, Big Benn."

Altered or not, I recognized the voice. I'd been cursing the memory of its owner every day of the past year. I looked at my seatmate, who wasn't a merc.

He was Richard LNU—last name unknown—the same twisted government spook who'd squeezed my every last dollar as a fine when I was suspended, and then, adding insult to injury, spread the untruth that I was an informant.

What did Richard have to do with this case? It had started as a penny-ante game. Then, first when Duke sat at the table, and again when Dolores took a seat, it had escalated to five-figure buy-ins. And, now that Richard was playing, the game had moved to the big table, where every hand was no limit, all in. That explained the NOTAR, an appliance obviously donated by Richard's befuddled feds. But what was so important that the feds would get involved?

More to the point, who was Richard really working for?
My first thoughts were:
No way it could be Dolores.
Very unlikely Stella.
Very possibly Uncle.
Most probably Duke—
Wrong. They're all coconspirators—

Wrong again. This was Richard's show. He was the big man with the heavy guns and big connections, backed by the full power of the United States.

Bottom line? Whatever was really going on was still hush-hush, with the one exception that I was now part of it.

"Cat got your tongue?" said Richard.

Richard was a strapping guy, but my first impulse was to sock him in the nose, right between his bug-eyed goggles. In fact, I did, or tried to—

I took a swing, but he easily caught my fist. "Easy, *B'wana*," he said. "We're asshole-buddies now."

"One day you'll run out of luck," I said. "When that happens, I'm gonna take a dump on your grave."

His sigh was an electronic rasp. "Change your mode, pally. I've got a proposition for you. I wouldn't call it a matter of your life or death . . . let's just say that if you don't accept it, I can't vouch for your future."

"So speaks a bent cop."

Hard, he squeezed my fist, which he still held. "Can the tantrum, and let me tell you the real haps. 'Kay?"

"Leggo my hand."

He did. "Ready?"

I nodded, and Richard drew what seemed a steadying breath before continuing. "The day the towers got hit? Soon as I heard, I headed downtown, full siren, screw the pedestrians, when all of a sudden I spotted this guy I knew. The kind of guy you can't steal a chopstick in Chinatown without him wanting a piece. You know how guys like that operate, don't you?"

"I've heard stories."

"Don't slide on me."

"They operate according to whatever you want 'em to do."

"That's right. So the day this happened was, ah, 9-11 . . ." For a moment, Richard's voice broke, but he quickly regained his composure.

"Chinatown sits on top of the financial district, so I figure maybe the guy knows something. It'd just come in over the radio that the first tower had fallen, and I was freaking out. I wanted to kill the bastards who did it. Hell, I just wanted to kill *someone*. So I grabbed my guy and asked if he'd seen strangers in Chinatown lately. Unusual money movement. He swore not, but I knew my guy. Had to break three of his fingers before he fessed up. What finally got him talking wasn't the pain, though. It was seeing ghosts—*gweilos*, the Chinks call 'em—powdered-white people emerging from the clouds of dust from the Twin Towers. He took the ghosts as a sign that he should confess his sins."

Wearing the goggles, Richard reminded me of a praying mantis possessed of limitless patience until it struck. Was he really suggesting that today's gig had something to do with 9-11?

"Of course, it turned out my guy knew zip about 9-11," Richard answered my unspoken question. "After the word came it was the towelheads and CIA stepped in—I was DEA Main Justice then—I went back to my regular business. At least my guy had good info on that. He was tight with a big player in Chinatown, whom I could've put into any number of criminal conspiracies, but I let his Mr. Big continue operating because he was my guy's source. Anyway, my guy duped a set of keys to the Pagoda—you know the place I'm talking, right?"

"I know the Pagoda." Clearly, Richard's Mr. Big was Uncle, and his snitch was Albert Woo, whom I myself had made an informant years ago. Not surprising that Albert had graduated to being a paid confidential informant, doing eyes-only stuff. Happens all the time, the government making—sometimes instigating—cases based on the word of professional prevaricators, who get a piece of the forfeited action. No doubt after Richard took his lion's share.

Richard tilted his head so the colored dash lights reflected from his dark goggles like a row of casino slots. Then he looked at me, and his goggles became black bug eyes above his Chiclet grin.

"The Pagoda's owner," he said. "Say the name aloud for posterity."

From the start, I'd assumed Richard was taping the conversation. My intention was to dummy up, but there was the legal doctrine of "conscious avoidance," meaning that deliberately concealing criminal knowledge can be considered as evidence of guilt. And Richard was an ace at bending a word here, twisting a fact there, putting me in a criminal conspiracy.

"Winston Lau," I said. "Uncle."

"Very good. Okay, back in 2006, my guy periodically checked out the Pagoda, looking for financial records, but—can you believe?—Uncle uses abacuses. Also, he never goes to the Pagoda before three, so one morning my guy goes in at seven, and he's snooping around when Uncle unexpectedly shows up. My guy hides behind a cabinet and watches Uncle access a hidden safe, open it, and stare at what's inside, even talks to it. Turns out Uncle opens the safe only once a year, on the anniversary of something or other. My guy only hears part of what Uncle's babbling, but it's enough to get his dick hard. You hearing me, asshole?"

"I know you're excited, but you're spitting on me."

"Just listen and nod, got it? So Uncle bows, closes the safe, leaves. My guy barely glimpses the thing in the safe, but it's enough for him to realize it's worth a fucking fortune. Because Uncle worked the safe's combination slowly, like he was getting off on the anticipation, it was easy for my guy to figure the numbers. So when Uncle's gone, he reopens the safe and steals the thing. Figures it's something Uncle himself stole, so Uncle can't tell anyone he had it; tough titty. My guy knows people who'll pay a gazillion for the thing. *Bingo!* Guess who just hit the jackpot."

"You're about to tell me. And you can call 'your guy' by his name: Albert Woo."

Richard paused a long moment. "Okay, *Albert*, he knew this was too big for him, so he brought it to me. By then I was CIA, but Albert thought I was still a drug cop. The moron acted as if we were partners. But it turned out I was *professionally* very interested in the people Albert wanted to sell the thing to. So I set up a deal with fail-safes and fall-backs. You catching my drift?"

Guys like Richard are world-class manipulators. He wanted my voice on tape. I only nodded.

"So Albert hands over the valuable object to these people while they simultaneously deposit ten million US currency in a numbered overseas account. I had no intention of giving Albert a dime of it, but the yellow rat outfoxed me. The account is fourteen numbers. Before I stepped into the picture, Albert had conned the buyers into showing good intent by giving him the first seven numbers up front. When I took over the show, they gave me the last seven numbers. So I told Albert we're partners, just be patient; one day when things cool down, we'll divvy up the score."

Spittle had gathered in the corners of his mouth, and I realized Richard was speed freaking. *Good.* The more I knew, the better I'd cover my ass and find an escape exit.

He said, "Even if Albert had all fourteen numbers, he couldn't touch the bread. See, in addition to the numbers, there's a security question that needs to be answered. Guess who's the only one who knows the answer?"

"Thou."

"Or, *moi*, as our Dolores might say. Me doing her . . . that bother you?"

"Your presence bothers me."

"How about Stella? You mind sharing her?"

Had the son of a bitch seen our sex tape? I feigned a don't-give-a-crap sneer. "Stella's strictly kosher. She hates pigs."

"You know the *thing* is a hat?"

I nodded.

He mock-slapped his forehead. "Of course you know. Duke told you. Bet you thought Duke was the *man*. Wrong. This is *my* show."

His laugh came over my earphones like milk pouring on Rice Krispies. *Snap. Crackle. Pop.* He said, "I knew what was gonna happen next before it did. The people who bought the hat then wanted to buy the head it sat on. A guy known as Lucky, who never loses a bet."

Lucky again. Was it Duke who'd bought his hat?

"Here's the kicker," said Richard. "The Chinese are *very* serious about gambling. Everything's *auspicious.* This guy Lucky *always* wins. Everyone wants to bet along with Lucky; they'd kill their mothers to find him. Which led to the predictable. A hot war in which a lot of people got killed. As I said, this went down back in 2006. Five years to the day after 9-11 . . ."

Again, he paused, as if choking up at the thought of 9-11. Not surprising. Guys like Richard begin as patriots before eroding to pilferers. Guess he still had a vestige of the old rah-rah left. He gestured at Stella.

"What was supposed to be a strictly business deal turned out to be what I call the War of '06. Stella's parents and cousin were killed during it. As payback, the parents of those who killed Stella's parents were themselves wasted. Eventually people on both sides got tired of killing. By 2007, live and let live had broken out."

"Happy ending. Why are you telling me this?"

"My lab guys did some electronic fiddling with the hat before the sale, so afterward we could track where it went. I put some people together, and they got me the hat back. A little violence goes a long way. And there was nothing the other side could do about it, because they only dealt with me and Albert. Me, I'm just a scrambled voice on a satellite phone. Albert, I put him on ice. Stashed him as a material witness. You're wondering what happened to the ten mil, right?"

"Wrong."

"Bullshit. The ten mil's still sitting in its numbered account until a worthy cause comes along. Like you, pally."

"Like me. Sure. Right."

"Hey, I kid you not. There's a score for you if you do the right thing by me. Getting back to what happened . . . Years pass, Albert's getting older; he wants a comfy old age and starts thinking maybe I forgot about the numbered account. So he makes a deal with Uncle—yeah, *Uncle*—to snatch me and stick acupuncture needles in my balls until I give up the rest of the numbers. Trouble is, Uncle's senile; he can't get his act together. So he hands the deal to his top guy, Scar. A bright boy. Knows you don't fuck with the feds, so he doesn't lift a finger. Tells Uncle it's going slowly, but in fact nothing's going on. You know Scar, right? Your client?"

I nodded, marveling at how figures from the past can suddenly return and kick sand in your face. I waited for Richard to keep talking, but he shut his trap, probably having realized that he'd told me more than intended.

Finally, I filled the silence. "So who is this Lucky guy?"

Richard's mantis goggles turned to fix upon me again. "This whole thing goes back to the thirties, when there was a commie revolution against the Chinese Nationalist government. A very bloody affair, even from my perspective. Whole families were divided."

Families? Both Missy Soo and Stella had alluded to family, but I still couldn't see that picture.

"The fighting ended when the Nationalists retreated to Taiwan and set up their own government, ceding mainland China to the Reds. But there's still plenty of bad blood between the factions. Like over who controls fishing rights and oil exploration in the South China Sea, which they both claim."

"That's what this is all about?"

"What the hell did you think?"

In truth, I didn't know what to think.

Once more in silence, we skimmed the coast, white crests of rollers coming in off the Caribbean in the quarter moon's light. Abruptly, the copter banked right and tilted upward, and once again the outside world turned black.

The control dash panel lights glowed softly. A dial blinked electronic numbers . . . *7,500 . . . 8,000 . . . 8,500 . . .*

We were fast-climbing higher.

With each blink of the altimeter, my understanding grew. The motley crew—Stella, Uncle, Duke, Richard—had been, yes, *evaluating* me as a potential member. Of course, Dolores had already decided I was worthy . . . which made me wonder: *Was the smartest, wiliest woman I'd ever met the real mover behind what was shaking?*

Had to be. I couldn't see her working for anyone else. Or falling under anyone else's spell. Especially not a giant rodent like Richard.

Speaking of the rat bastard, it occurred to me that Richard hadn't chosen to store the priceless hat in a secure government depository. Instead, he'd made Duke its curator. Which begged a question: Was Duke some kind of master spy, or was their alliance based on something else?

There was only one thing that I was sure of: No way Richard would pay me a cent. Good. That spared me the temptation.

The altimeter moved: *10,000 . . . 10,500.* It stopped at *12,000.*

Outside, the blackness was graying toward dawn, and soon I could make out steeply sloped terrain . . . and then, ahead, emerging from mist, an enormous peak whose cone was white with snow that reflected the still-unseen sun. I knew exactly where we were now:

The Sierra Nevada de Santa Marta.

Sombra's lair. I'd been there on my previous misadventure, a much longer journey that I'd been forced to make on horseback. If this was where Duke wanted Stella to hide, he couldn't have picked a better spot.

I got a bit shaky when the helicopter hovered and began descending, for there was nothing below but dense forest . . . but then the big machine tilted, angling, and another vista was revealed: a flatness cleverly concealed beneath overhanging treetops. As we lowered, I realized it was much larger than a copter pad, a soccer-size field studded with well-tended huts shaded by trees. Camouflage city. Again, I watched Stella walk unsteadily until she was gone from view. *Still drugged,* I thought. My turn to deplane.

Gone were the mercs. Instead, my escorts were two copper-colored Indians with long, jet hair ponytailed over their white garments. One was a teenager; the other could have been his older brother, both of them lean, lithe, and graceful. And well-mannered to boot; courteously, they invited me to accompany them.

We skirted the village. Mostly women and children. Cooking pots. Laughter. But also here and there armed men and sandbagged positions protecting antiaircraft batteries. Last I'd been in the village, I'd seen the Logui-constructed defensive positions against incursions by soldiers, paramilitaries, and narcotraffickers; since then, their capabilities had clearly been professionally upgraded.

I heard a whirring: the NOTAR copter rising above the thatched roofs. For a moment, I glimpsed Richard at the window. Then the chopper was gone.

I followed the two Logui from the village up a steep path hacked through the jungle. After a while, we came to steps: weathered stone slabs that wound up the hillside. Up and around we went until I felt like an ant walking up a screw. It got colder by the turn. Once, through a break in the trees, I glimpsed the mountainside below and far beyond it the Caribbean, hazy in the sun. Maybe three vertical miles down and five miles distant horizontally. I was beginning to run out of steam, but my guides kept on keeping on, and I didn't want to lose them. Not up here. They rounded a bend and stopped. I rounded the bed and stopped, too.

"Anawanda," the older said, reverentially.

"Anawanda," the younger softly repeated.

To them, the mountain was the navel of the world. From this perspective, I understood their belief. The mountain filled the horizon: a magnificent, sun-blocking mass, its flanks a hundred shades of green with deeply shadowed folds streaked by mist, threaded by waterfalls rushing from its cap of eternal snow.

"Anawanda," both my escorts repeated as one.

The name echoed as if in a grand cathedral.

I nodded, picturing its high priestess.

Alune, She Who Knows Most of All . . .

CHAPTER 10

Mandalay, Burma. September 1942.

Thus far, it had been both the worst and best year of Ming Chan's life. The worst being the disaster that had befallen Lucky. It seemed impossible. Ming himself had installed Lucky comfortably in a remote jungle in the highland triangle where the French colony of Laos, Thailand, and British Burma converged. Only fierce Shan tribes dwelled there. Despite European fastidiousness, borders were merely lines on a map; no topographers dared venture into a trackless jungle ruled by savages.

But Ming had bravely introduced himself to a Shan chieftain, which led to a degree of respect, which in turn led to a business arrangement in which the Shan received many golden coins in exchange for guarding what Ming referred to as both "Lucky" and the "Ming Treasure," which suggested to the Shan that it belonged to Ming Chan. Ming had no compunctions about dealing with the Shan; for all their ferociousness, they honored their promises.

Yet somehow Lucky, "Ming's Treasure," had vanished without a clue.

The Shan guards were tortured unmercifully but knew nothing; they'd claimed to have been incapacitated by a tincture distilled from poppies, which grew everywhere. For a moment, Ming considered suicide, then angrily punched a tree. Nursing his bruised fist, he cursed his loss of temper. He was not some insane Japanese kamikaze samurai, despite Li-ang's seeming fascination with the latter. No. His race was mankind's oldest and wisest. Somehow he would regain the crate and its precious contents.

He considered his new reality.

Only he and his personal aide knew of the theft. The night after it was discovered, Ming's aide disappeared; just another deserter, hardly noticed. Now Ming alone knew of Lucky's disappearance, and at least for the present, he could return to war joyously—

But what about after the war?

Surely, it would not end for many years; the present struggle was hardly the beginning of the end. Still, the day would come when he'd have to admit his failure.

Lucky . . .

Apart from the legendary father of the Kuomintang, Sun Yat-sen, and its current leader, Generalissimo Chiang Kai-shek, Lucky was the most revered personage in all China. And he, young and upcoming Captain Ming Chan, under whose command Lucky had been lost, risked becoming the most despised man in Nationalist China, his career irretrievably ruined.

He would not let that happen. He would continue his duty with head high. He would protect his beloved country and soon-to-be expanded family.

For this was also the best year of Ming's life.

Li-ang was pregnant. He hoped and prayed she would give him a son.

During her labor, Ming paced, smoking furiously, half listening to the radio, which was tuned to SEAC, the South East Asia Command station. The announcer was an American. Probably broadcasting out of Australia, where the Yanks were pouring in under the command of the legendary General MacArthur, a man Ming disdained as a vain fraud.

The announcer continued.

The Japanese advance had finally been stopped by the Americans at the Battle of the Coral Sea (in reality a standoff, in which both sides sustained heavy losses but the Japanese push toward Australia had been deterred). Now a great battle had taken place near an obscure atoll named Midway, a clash of the American and Japanese main battle fleets, although, incredibly, the ships themselves never engaged. The era of airpower had arrived. Four Japanese carriers had been sunk, and the legendary Admiral Yamamoto had retreated in disgrace on his now-obsolete flagship, the formerly invincible battleship *Yamato*.

From the nursing station, a gaggle of young interns clapped at the news. But Ming was not elated. Following the civilian bombings of Chongqing, he hated the Japanese more than ever and loved China more passionately, but he no longer cared a penny for his Kuomintang comrades, whose corruption sickened him. Not to mention what they would do to him if, when, they discovered the loss of Lucky and the Ming Treasure.

Ming lit another cigarette and went on pacing.

Forget all that, he told himself.

For now, he only wanted a son.

* * *

In the birthing room, Li-ang was crying because at the height of the pain of childbirth, she'd thought of the American pilot, a memory she could not erase.

An hour earlier, she had borne twins.

She'd kissed her firstborn baby, then handed it to her maidservant Aung. "Take her to where she'll be safe."

Watching her firstborn depart, Li-ang wiped tears from her cheeks. When she'd learned she was pregnant, fearing Archie had fathered the child, she'd looked for Archie. The airbase had moved, and the Tigers were no longer independent, now a unit of the Nationalist air force. But Smitty's news had been bad. Archie had died flying the Hump.

The remaining baby began yowling, and Li-ang tried—unsuccessfully—to force Archie from her mind. The past was gone. Forget what might have been. Think only of her new child. The one she still had . . .

* * *

Aung emerged from the birthing room, cradling bunched blankets.

My son, thought Ming. But the maidservant hurried past him.

"Where are you going?" asked Ming.

"Disposing of soiled sheets," said Aung. "Go in and see your child."

Ming entered the birthing room. He held his breath upon seeing the baby in Li-ang's arms. Then the air went out of him. It was a girl.

* * *

Li-ang read Ming's disappointment. As if addressing a child, she said, "Women are more powerful than men. Think of my cousins, the Soong sisters. Ai-lang is married to the richest man in China. Ching-ang is the most powerful woman in Communist China. Mei-ang is betrothed to our President Chiang Kai-shek. Perhaps our little girl someday shall . . . ?"

Rather than swelling with pride and joy at her words, Ming took out a small, ornate medal, a rare honor accorded only to Nationalist China's best and boldest. He put it in Li-ang's palm and closed her fingers around it.

"They said the medal represented my finest moment. They were wrong. *This* is my finest moment. To be with my daughter, who already is as beautiful as her mother."

A tear rolled down Li-ang's cheek.

"Are you sad?" he asked.

"Happy." The baby began to cry. Nursing her, Li-ang let Archie fade from her mind. For long months, she'd feared her swollen belly held Archie's child. But the ancestors had blessed her. One of her two babies, this little girl was a perfect Chinese doll, exactly like the generations of Soo females before her.

"Aung, bring water," yelled Ming. "Where did that good-for-nothing girl go to?"

"To clean herself . . . for our daughter's sake."

But Ming sensed something was wrong.

* * *

Later that night, Ming visited Aung's quarters and told her to come along with him. They walked through the jungle to the edge of an old quarry. In the moonlight, water shimmered two hundred feet below. Ming asked Aung what else besides soiled sheets she'd been carrying. Aung began to cry. He gripped her arm and moved her to the edge of the precipice.

"Another child," Aung cried. "A twin, born dead."

Ming was shaken. "Was it a boy?"

Aung swore it was a girl, and Ming believed her. Now he understood Li-ang's strange mood, and his heart filled with love at the thought of having a wife who chose to bear the brunt of tragedy alone. The shame of bearing two girls, not a son . . . he vowed never to reveal his knowledge to Li-ang.

Aung watched him silently, resigned to her fate. Ming knew little about the maidservant, only that she was a widowed Burmese peasant with a grown daughter, another of the millions who must perish on behalf of the struggle for a new order. A silent prayer for her soul floated through his mind. Then he pushed her, and she dropped like a stone.

She didn't scream.

* * *

Shanghai. 1952.

The car was an old but immaculately polished Russian ZiL limousine. Red flags fluttered above its headlamps. The driver wore sergeant's chevrons. The vehicle drove at a steady thirty miles an hour, passing empty stores on a frigid avenue with few people and no traffic.

From the back seat, Ming looked out grimly. He wore the uniform of the victorious Communist People's Liberation Army, unmarked but for four discreet general's stars. His rank wasn't all that had changed. In the civil war that continued after the Japanese defeat, Lucky had become an afterthought. It had been an ugly war, in more ways than one. Ming had personally killed dozens of enemies but at the cost of a shattered hip—he now limped terribly—and the right side of his face, which had been reduced to an empty socket ridged with burn scars and nerveless muscles that sagged.

But his Li-ang wouldn't care; her beautiful eyes only saw his inner self. And now, home from the wars, he and his family would dwell in the real China.

Red China.

For, incredibly, Ming had switched sides during the civil war.

Although his ferociousness in battle had earned him a designation as a Hero of the People, which was a ticket to the inner circles of the Kuomintang, he'd become appalled at the rampant corruption and nepotism of the Nationalists. They were not the new China he'd envisioned. So he and his little family had crossed the lines into Red territory, where he was hailed as a native son that good fortune had returned to the fold.

As converts to religions and political movements are wont, Ming was now a purist, devoting his life to the communist cause of lifting China from poverty. To that end, he would find the Ming Treasure and personally introduce the auspicious Lucky to the chairman himself.

But not just yet.

For in the national realignments in Southeast Asia following the war, Lucky's hiding place had become inaccessible: Burma was now the isolationist dictatorship known as Myanmar, Laos was a battleground between communist rebels and the colonialist French, and Thailand had become a closed nation ruled by harsh dictators. Thus, the theft was forgotten by all but Ming, who'd carried the memory throughout his many travails as a soldier.

He'd taken part in Chairman Mao's struggle that had expelled the Nationalists to Taiwan. He'd served in the Chinese People's Republic's defense of its sister socialist neighbor, North Korea; under Field Marshal General Ming Chan, the People's Liberation Army's sheer manpower had enveloped a force of American marines at a reservoir the childish enemy lightly referred to as the Frozen Chosin. Ming recalled the images vividly: wind whining over an iced-over reservoir, where blood clotted on new-fallen snow; pieces of Chinese boys armed with trumpets and wooden rifles killed by *gweilos*; dead Americans grotesquely frozen upright . . .

Ming ran his hands over the scarred side of his face, as if trying to wipe such thoughts from his mind. All that mattered now was reuniting with his family. To sleep once more with his wife and listen to their little daughter regale him with stories of her victories at sports and martial arts. So amazing that a girl so young could be so skillful. She knew how to slam a bigger opponent to earth. How to launch a *shuriken* fifty feet into the heart of an adversary.

And Mi-ang indeed was as beautiful as her mother.

He ordered the imbecilic driver to go faster.

His home was in a quarter formerly occupied by diplomats. It was large and elegantly furnished and . . . empty.

Totally empty.

Not in the scattered way that indicated a sudden departure, but neatly, as if no one had ever lived there.

Ming's first reaction was that Nationalist agents had kidnapped his family. A few calls revealed that this was not so. He spoke to neighbors and learned Li-ang and the girl had peacefully loaded their luggage onto a private vehicle and left. Voluntarily. Without as much as a note.

Why?

His wife had never approved of his leaving the Nationalists for the Reds, but she had seemed happy and their lives were good—

Was it because he was so horribly maimed?

In his empty house, Ming Chan, soldier and stoic, sobbed. Then he put emotion aside and got to work. A few inquiries produced answers.

The state car had delivered his wife and child to the main train station. There they had been met by an American national, a nondescript, ethnic Chinese man about thirty years old. Together they boarded a train to Rangoon, where they caught a flight to Delhi. From there, they traveled to the United States. Their precise location was unknown, but the Chinese American man's identity had been discovered:

Winston Lau.

The same man who'd been the proprietor of the PX at the Flying Tiger base at Toungoo, and the scion of a family that had immigrated to the United States in the first great Chinese immigration wave in the 1880s. Worked hard, endured racism, saved money, and prospered. The Lau family was extremely reclusive, rumored to be closely tied with major banks and international criminal Tongs; and they were ardent supporters of the Taiwanese Chinese regime.

Ming wondered: Had he been cuckolded by a shrimpy business-man with a Western name? He swore that someday, some way, he'd regain his honor and his family.

"That's it?" snapped Ming at his terrified aide.

"Yes . . . no . . . well—"

"Tell me all, or I will cut your fucking nose off."

"Yes, sir. The thing is, there's this American law . . . actually, it was only enacted in 1946 and ended a few years after, so it didn't really exist when . . . Anyway, Lau probably lied on the form about the date because he got your wife and child into the United States on what they call the War Brides Act. He lives in New York."

Ming was stung. "She . . . *married* him?"

"A marriage of convenience, I'm told."

"But she's not in New York? Or is she?"

The aide shook his head.

"Answer me, you stupid twat. Where are my wife and daughter?"

"We don't know, General."

CHAPTER 11

The present.

The mountain trail ended at another clearing. Smaller. At first it seemed no more than a grassy outcropping where the jungle gave way to rocky, barren highlands that ended at the snow line, a vast, desolate slope that Andean peoples call *el paramo*. But at the center of the clearing stood an old stone building with a peaked, slatelike roof from which smoke curled. In the slanted morning light, its facing wall—dark and mossy—was marked by a darker oblong. A shadow?

No, not a shadow . . . but a door, half-open. My escorts had disappeared.

What next? Should I enter?

I did, pushing the door fully open. Viewed from glaring sunlight, the interior was dim. I entered tentatively. The door, perfectly balanced, slammed shut behind me. The sound echoed off stone as if the space were a church, although its interior more resembled a pagan meeting hall. It consisted of one enormous room with a fire pit in its center. The only light was from the pit, where burning embers coiled smoke that drifted up through a Pantheon-like oculus. Someone had been here recently, but they were gone. I was alone.

Why was I here?

Then I realized this was the ultimate safe room: the building a harmless stone blip on the outer fringe of satellite camera images, its interior impenetrably thick-walled, its locale far from civilization.

It was a place where secrets were stored.

Here I'd be instructed regarding the heavy lifting that was the real reason I'd been so handsomely retained. I heard a sound—

From the other side of the fire pit emerged a small, dark-haired woman in a diaphanous white dress.

Dolores.

Wordlessly, she approached, stood on her toes, hugged me. As I felt the length of her against my body, a strange cognitive dissonance rose within me: Dolores was still little Sara in my mind, yet now I was all too aware of her womanliness. We fit as if custom-made for each other, yet she was my old friend and client's kid. I shouldn't, couldn't, wouldn't think of her otherwise.

She took my face between her hands. Her pale eyes mirrored the glowing embers in the fire pit.

"I've something to show you," she said.

I nodded. Felt anxiety creep into my gut.

"And something else to tell you."

I swallowed hard, nodded again.

She handed me an old, dog-eared photograph: two unshaven men in hiking gear with arms around each other against a backdrop of a steep, densely wooded canyon in whose vee was wedged an enormous concrete dam, a controlled flow of water cascading down its face. The taller man was an American; the shorter, a bespectacled Colombian.

The photograph in my hand trembled.

I was one of the men. The other was Dolores's father, Nacho Barrera, the long-deceased CFO of the old Cali cartel.

"The dam at Colima," I said. "Near the *finca* where you . . . where Sara kept her ponies."

Tears coursed her cheeks. "Who *am* I, Benn? *What* am I?"

Good question. I might have said she was a natural actor, but maybe she wasn't acting just now. My own emotions were in too much turmoil to judge hers.

I stared at the photograph of me the way I'd been: slimmer and smiling-eyed, footloose and fancy-free. Exactly like the other man in the picture had been . . .

Nacho Barrera. Drug lord, father, friend . . .

Most of my clients are not upright people. Still, a very few, like Nacho, despite their business and its methodology, are honorable men. Of course, the same aberrations apply to their law-enforcing counterparts, who range from purely good to nine-to-five mediocre to the ones who break bad. Like Richard—

Oh, Jesus. Had he been lying? Or were he and Dolores . . .

Dolores took the photograph from me and gently slid it into a worn wallet she tucked into a woven Indian bag. But both our thoughts remained tethered to Nacho, I knew.

Knowing Nacho had changed my life.

I'd lost a beloved wife who couldn't abide my work while my years of living dangerously made me more money than I could hide. Until, many years later, I'd met Dolores, née Sara, now *Sombra*, which in turn had brought Richard into my life. He'd taken me down and left me destitute. The sorry circumstances that had led me here.

Yet these losses were pittances compared to Sara's. In a single night, she'd lost fifty family members and every other person she'd known.

Twenty years later, here we were once again.

"Look at us now," I said. "Cosmic jokesters."

She nodded but didn't smile. "The night I ran away? It wasn't to find my father. I knew his enemies would have killed him first. It was to protect you. When they found me, I told them you'd run away. I assumed they were going to kill me, but they didn't. For a long time, I wished they had, because they used me. Fifteen days shy of my tenth birthday, I lost my virginity fifteen times over. In the morning, they left me for dead, as a reminder for all to see. 'We're the bosses now and . . . this . . . this is what happens to . . . to . . . those who defy us.'"

Her voice had caught. Tears rimmed her eyes.

"A lot of things changed that night," I said. Not just the course of my life, but the face I saw in my shaving mirror: a killer who'd taken two lives to save Sara's. The reason I still swallowed little blue pills before I lay me down to sleep.

"My father trusted very few people, Benn. You were one of them. You proved him right. I trust you, Benn. Prove I'm right."

"About what?"

"The Logui are my family. They would die for me, and I for them. I've armed and trained them to fight off cartels, guerrillas, and paramilitaries. But now a new threat has arisen, one too big for them to fight." She shook her head helplessly. "I've been asking myself what my father would do, and recently I remembered something I heard you tell Papa: 'Forget trying to break a door down . . . just oil the hinges.'"

She moved to within inches of me, stood on her toes, held my gaze. I saw my reflection in her eyes. She said, "The mountain we're on is the center of the Logui world. The land as far as can be seen is theirs. But now a new invader has arrived. The usual reason: plunder. Beneath this land is a vast deposit of extremely valuable minerals known as REE."

"God save me from acronyms. REE . . . ?"

"Rare earth elements that are essential to modern technologies, both military and civilian. Trillions of dollars' worth. Corrupt elements of the Colombian government have leased the Sierra to foreign companies to mine the REE. If this continues, the Logui will be no more."

"Foreign companies," I said. "Chinese ones."

"My Benn, always a few moves ahead."

"We pawns are paid to be sacrificed."

Her laughter echoed off the stone. "You're no pawn. You're my knight in shining armor. Save me, Benn. Save all of us."

I felt a flare of anger. "What can *I* do? Seems like Richard has everything under control."

Her face clouded. "Richard's not what he seems."

"I've already found that out the hard way."

"You don't get it. Richard's a traitor."

"To you?"

"To everyone, and every cause."

"What's his angle?"

"Money. He used me to pump up his cartel body count in Colombia. Now he's America's intel honcho in the South China Sea, and he smells big money."

"So why are you involved in his Chinese caper?"

"I can't save the Logui from the Chinese myself, although Lord knows I've tried. I paid a fortune in bribes to Colombian politicians to have the Sierra declared a World Heritage Site."

"Rendering it untouchable. So then no problem?"

"Yes, problem. The Chinese paid them more. They're going to strip-mine the Logui homeland."

"What am I supposed to do? You can't sue people for outbribing you."

"I don't want you for my lawyer. I want you to negotiate for me."

"Negotiate what? With whom?"

"The situation is . . . fluid. There are a lot of people involved, and they all have different agendas. The only thing I'm certain of is that I'll want your advice."

Her evasive manner troubled me. That, and that she assumed too much. I had myself another boss.

She said, "I'll pay you well. Ten million."

Ouch. Here was the score I'd been chasing when I was a drug lawyer. But I'd sworn off drug money. And this was something else entirely.

"I won't take money from you," I said.

"But you *will* help me?"

I nodded. I'd help her for old times' sake. For Nacho, and for Sara. Besides, I was already part of Team Dolores, on Duke's nickel. I'd committed to watching over Stella, and I would do the same for Dolores.

Not that I had any illusions that the trust in either pact was a two-way street. Stella was dancing to music beyond my frequency, and Dolores . . . well, she was a woman of many faces. Apparently, Richard was familiar with one of them. Also, her $10 million offer matched his. Double money for double trouble?

"Even if you won't take my money, I may be able to do you a favor. I might be in a position to learn about this Lucky person, who's important to Richard. If I do, I'll let you know, and it could be worth a lot more than ten million."

"We'll see how it plays out."

"But you *are* with me?"

"I'm with Sara."

She caressed my cheek. "Go back to New York and wait until you're contacted, then follow your nose. Where you go, I'll follow."

"Contacted? By whom?"

"I don't know. Yet."

"How do I contact you?"

"You can't. I'll find you."

"What about Stella?"

"She wants to stay here until this is over."

"*She* wants . . . or *you* want?"

She smiled. "*We both* want."

CHAPTER 12

An hour later, the NOTAR whisked me to Bogotá, where I boarded an unmarked DEA Gulfstream, undoubtedly seized from some fallen drug lord.

As I have often found to be the case with clients, their absence makes my heart grow colder, and distance sharpens my mind. Forget first impressions. Check out second thoughts.

As my flight droned toward New York, I reconsidered Dolores. Come to extremes, she lapped the field. I like to think I'm hip to all schools of people, but Dolores was a private university of one. Sexy, smart, small woman. Great to look at but difficult—no, *impossible*—to touch, at least for me. Brave and kind to her own, but a merciless killer to outsiders. In public, an antidrug crusader; yet her alter ego was a reclusive cartel kingpin. Whimsy wasn't in her arsenal. She did everything for reasons known only to herself. She was as opaque as a frappe glass of whipped cream.

What did she want?

And why from me?

When beset by puzzlement, I free-associate, tracking random thoughts on paper, then looking for connections. I go through half a dozen yellow legal pads a month. Now I took one from my bag and set it on my lap, then paused for thought, pen in hand.

Okay . . .

As always, atop the page, I doodled a theme to jump-start my brain. This one was a smallish stick figure of a woman with blunt-cut, dark hair . . . actually, the stick wasn't straight but curvaceous.

Dolores.

Richard's comment had gotten under my skin. Hard to believe she'd give herself to the likes of him. Then again, harder to believe she wouldn't do *anything* to win. I willed the distasteful images from my mind and doodled another woman.

Stella.

According to both Duke and Richard, Stella's parents had been murdered as part of a vicious family feud. That feud—which apparently involved Albert Woo, Uncle Winston Lau, Missy Soo, Duke (and, via Duke's letter, possibly Madame Soo, as well)—seemed a small mirror image of the China v. Taiwan conflict itself. Best I could tell, Uncle, Albert, Duke, Stella, Dolores, and Richard were on the side of Nationalist Taiwan—and against mainland Communist China. It made sense: Duke had flown fighter missions for the Chinese Nationalists. Uncle's Foochow Tong was rooted with the Taiwan Chinese.

As for Missy Soo and her hidden coterie, their hostile intent surely meant they were aligned with Red China . . . at least for now. But no telling which way any or all really leaned. Was it to the side that paid them best? Or to their true beliefs?

I doodled on, hoping for inspiration.

Beneath the figures of Dolores and Stella, I drew a line down the center of the page. On its left side I tallied the known downsides:

Dolores: Assume her alliance with Richard was not only a joining of devious minds but also a physical bonding. Next to her name, I wrote: *Liar?* Paused, then wrote, *Definitely.* Then wrote *Goal?* and beneath it *Helping the Logui.*

I paused again, wrote *Lucky.* Thought some more, added *????*

Richard: His $10 million offer was a dangling carrot never to be chewed. Next to his name I wrote, *Thief,* followed by *Traitor?* Then: *Goal?* and beneath that *Money. Glory. Dolores.* I thought a moment, wrote: *Sees me as disposable. Dangerous.*

Duke: I penned, *Dangerous. Untrustworthy. Liar.*

Stella: I wrote, *Client. Unbalanced. Liar.*

Missy Soo: *Red-flagged liar.*

I was playing liar's poker.

Major questions: Despite Richard's braggadocio, who really was in control? Who worked for whom? And, most vexing, how did Lucky—and his hat—link to the Chinese strip-mining the Logui homeland?

Which formulated the downside conclusion:

Liars + danger = get out while you can!

On a fresh page, I tallied the upsides:

Stella had paid me; therefore, I was her loyal fiduciary. But more important, I *wanted* to watch over her, because violence had scarred her in the same way it had Dolores . . . Sara . . . whom I loved.

There were no more upsides.

I reread what I'd written . . .

Decided I was in the thicket.

My usual hemlock cocktail.

I crumpled the pages.

* * *

My longtime driver, Val, picked me up at Newark. Now that I was flush again, I'd rehired my former factotum. Val had buzz-cut white-blond hair, a lined smoker's face, and the pallor of a night person. He was the gentlest man I knew, but although he was in his seventies he had a flip side hard as an anvil. His family were central European Jews who somehow had resettled in postwar Berlin in the '50s, and young Val, the

Jew boy, had both taken and given many lumps. Yet he had managed to remain an essentially kind and good person.

"My heart is filled," said Val, hugging me, pinching my cheek. "My Bennela is back."

He'd upgraded from a Flex to a big Rover. I climbed in the back and told him to take me to the East Side hotel where I'd phoned in a reservation. No more sublet studios for Bennela. Not to mention it was a comfortable place to hole up. Like they say, eat, drink, and be merry; die fast, and leave a good-looking corpse.

The Jersey side of the trip to NYC was ugly and industrial. Val turned the radio on. A news commentator delivered the latest. It wasn't good. Humanity was another day closer to the end of days. An emergency meeting of the UN was vainly trying to defuse the Asian crisis. Six nations, foremost among them China, were claiming rights to the South China Sea. Already, the Chinese had crossed wakes with the naval forces of Taiwan, Australia, Vietnam, Malaysia, and the Philippines, although these lesser powers, confronted by the far more powerful Chinese forces, were warily skirting the conflicted areas. Uncle Sam was making noises about getting into the act, reminding the world that his navy was nuclear. In response, the Chinese spoke of their own nuclear capabilities and their new carrier-killing missiles.

The station played part of a speech by the Chinese ambassador, his words translated:

"In the near future, the People's Republic of China will provide conclusive proof that the disputed islands of the South China Sea were settled by the Ming Dynasty, which long ago established China's exclusive sovereignty over the entire area."

Conclusive proof? Whether the phrase was propaganda or the truth, I had a feeling that Richard would not only be aware of the game but also playing in it. It was what he did. That, and his link to Duke, and Duke's links to Uncle.

Which included me. *Why?*

I needed to find out.

The Rover hummed through the Lincoln Tunnel, its strip of overhead lights flashing by hypnotically. But when we emerged on the New York side, my gears began meshing. Just being in the Apple was like smoking crystal, speeding my brain waves, provoking inspirations. By Forty-Second Street, it came to me.

The realization:

Doodle time. I pulled out my legal pad and drew a man's figure: bulging biceps, full head of hair, too-bright grin. Richard. Forget which of the many characters in my personal drama was truly in charge—or thought they were. Richard was the hub around which the others orbited.

I drew a cobra and a mongoose. Mortal enemies. Richard was the serpent. I was the small mammal, who seemed overmatched. Unless the snake got sloppy. As Richard would. His mix of drugs and ambition had given him absolute faith in his own infallibility. In his arrogance, he viewed me as weak; ergo, I was no threat; ergo, he'd be loose-lipped around namby-pamby me.

Hmm . . .

I checked in to a five-star hotel—$900 a night—and hit the lobby bar. While imbibing a Bison Grass, I found myself in conversation with my stool mate, a gorgeous woman I guessed cost more than the room for the night. I politely declined, then went up to my posh room and opened my device.

First search: REE. Rare earth.

I let my fingers do the walking and soon learned it was an amalgam of seventeen materials collectively known as "rare earth elements." REE was essential for building high-performance magnets and batteries used in consumer products like TVs and smartphones. Dolores hadn't been exaggerating—the REE deposits could be worth trillions. I read on and realized much more was at stake.

It's not just the money, stupid.

REE was crucial to building global-positioning, satellite-imaging, and guided-missile systems and new, Columbia-class nuclear submarines.

Recent discoveries along the entire Guajira Peninsula had confirmed the presence of huge REE deposits and prompted the Chinese to make a massive investment to secure mining rights in a remote area far from prying eyes. According to the articles—which cited unnamed sources—there'd been a bidding war between the Chinese and an unnamed entity. Undoubtedly, Dolores.

I used the Geek's software to have another look at the Flying Tigers roster, two of whom had bestowed their names to Marmaduke Mason, alleged fighter pilot, known deceiver.

No Smith, aka Smitty.

Ah, but the roster was a scan of an old, typed document that began with a list of pilots only. I moved to a second page and saw the AVG Tiger ground-crew rosters.

There he was: Smith, William E., Corporal, USAAF.

With an X alongside his name and his date of death in November 2006. I segued to the newspaper archives and read about an auto accident that had taken place on Thanksgiving weekend that year, just outside Duke's place on Long Island. Six victims, including an unnamed driver, a teenaged girl named Katrina Mason—Duke's granddaughter?—a Mr. and Mrs. Gilbert Maris—most certainly Stella's parents—and a Mr. and Mrs. William E. Smith. Smitty?

Was this what Richard called the "War of 2006"? The newspaper didn't call it murder, but Duke, Richard, and even Missy Soo had hinted otherwise.

Had to be. I needed to learn more about Smitty.

I called the Geek and told him we had to discuss a matter. He understood not over the phone and invited me over. His pad was a fifth-floor walk-up in Hell's Kitchen that perpetually reeked of quality pot. Hydro. I took a toke to upgrade to his level and communicated what

I needed. It was a lot, but he seemed unfazed. Simply told me to have another toke and relax. He handed me a pair of wireless earphones. I put them on and to my surprise heard classical violins. I closed my eyes as sweet weed carried me into sweet music—

A minute or an hour later, the Geek woke me.

"Mission accomplished," he said.

It cost me a grand, but I learned that after the Flying Tigers were disbanded, Smith, William E., Corporal, USAAF, had joined a USAAF cargo unit. When the war was over, he'd been honorably discharged. The following day, he'd filed a request that his new Burmese wife, Ky Aung, be accorded American citizenship under the War Brides Act . . .

Burma. The name jump-started a stray thought, one I considered for a while, then stashed for later reference.

Smitty's request had been approved. He and his Burmese wife had bought a home in LA's then-remote San Fernando Valley. As LA prospered and expanded, so did the Smiths. Their home became a hillside compound surrounded by fifteen acres of extremely valuable land. But despite huge offers from developers, the Smiths kept the land intact.

The Geek even had satellite photographs of the property: set amid the Valley grid, the fifteen acres of green formed an outer barrier around a gated compound where a grand house sprawled.

The home's title was in the name of his wife: Ky Aung Smith.

I took out my roll and peeled off Franklins for the Geek. "An advance for whatever you can dig up on a certain client, and everyone and everything about him." I told him Duke's name and location.

He held out a joint. "One for the road?"

"I'm already high on life. But you go ahead. Stoke your warped brain and find out about this guy. He may have a Southeast Asia connection . . ."

"What's that mean?"

"You'll tell me. I also need the skinny on the deaths of a Mr. and Mrs. Gilbert Maris." I gave him the details.

I took the stairs down two at a time, ordered up an Uber, went back to my hotel, hit my device, and searched Southeast Asian languages. Myanmar, formerly Burma, had its own language and an alphabet that to my eye was indecipherable squiggles. Incredible what information lurks in the net. There was even a phonetic guide to Burmese pronunciation.

Aha . . .

In our first meeting, Stella had mentioned a name that sounded like *Awn*. Smitty's wife had been named Aung, but in the Burmese language the final *g* was silent.

Meaning *Aung* was properly pronounced *Awn*.

* * *

For many people, Los Angeles conjures up visions of Malibu, Beverly Hills, and other enclaves, where palms sway above luxurious homes owned by plastic-perfect people. Experience had left me with other impressions of the City of Angels: razor-carrying Mexican cartel workers, the trash who haunt Hollywood Boulevard after midnight, the remote desert canyons in which cultists dwell, the brown smog that more often than not veils the sky.

But the day I arrived, the sky was crystalline, the city green and orderly, outwardly a nice place to live. The Smith place was on a hillside in Encino. The ornate gate was opened and unmanned, so I drove through and up the driveway. The grounds were in need of a shave and a haircut, and the house could have used a dab of face powder, but you had to love the isolation. When I stepped out of my rental, everything was quiet except for birds chirping and the distant murmur of some freeway. Not a soul in sight. I pressed the doorbell and heard a faint *ding-dong* from within. I waited. Pressed the bell again. Flashed on Philip Marlowe, snooping among the LA rich—

The door opened.

From within the house, a woman regarded me calmly through light-blue eyes. She was barefooted and wore a simple white smock. No jewelry, no makeup. Despite her pale eyes, she was blessed with the delicate eyes and cheekbones of a Southeast Asian. Hard to tell her age, but one thing was certain: she wasn't the Ky Aung Smith who'd married Smitty. Even if it had been a May-December marriage, Aung had to be at least eighty-five, and this woman wasn't a day over fifty.

"Sorry. I'm looking for Aung Smith."

"You found her," she said kindly.

I introduced myself, said, "Guess I'm confused."

"Or maybe you're looking for my mother. Her name also was Aung. Family tradition. My grandmother's name also was Aung. The family refers to us as Aung One, Two, and Three. I'm Aung Three. You seem troubled. Can I be of help?"

"Actually, I'm not sure what I'm looking for."

"Well, if it has to do with Aungs, come on in."

The house was grand but like the grounds needed some loving care. I followed her through it to a rear garden, where we sat in the shade of an old magnolia, its delicate fragrance citruslike, its fallen petals carpeting the grass. In the daylight, it became obvious that Aung Three was quite ill: her color was bad, she was much too thin, and she seemed to have difficulty walking.

"I've been waiting for you for a long time," she said.

I double blinked but didn't interrupt. She wanted to speak, and I needed to listen.

She said, "After my father's death, I began divesting myself of all he'd accumulated. You'd think it would be easy giving things away, but there was so much . . . anyway, all that's left is the house, and your people are welcome to take it."

"I don't understand. My people?"

"You're a policeman, aren't you?"

I laughed aloud. "Definitely not. Why would you think so?"

She smiled benignly. "Because my father was always looking over his shoulder. He was a criminal. Well, you can still have the house, anyway."

"What? I don't—"

"Now you're *really* confused. I'd best explain the rest. My mother and father *passed* in 2006. . ." The way she said *passed* was a tip-off that she knew her parents had been murdered. "Soon I'll give this house away, and my family will be forgotten."

"You can't just give this house away. It's your home."

"I'm a Buddhist. I won't live among ill-gotten gains."

I felt as if a hidden door had just opened; probably because I have a nose for ill-gotten gains. I was configuring a polite way of digging deeper but needn't have bothered, because whether I was a cop or not, Aung Three had been waiting to tell her story for years.

It blew me away.

* * *

Aung Three said, "My father was a sweet man who got mixed up in something he shouldn't have. It started during the war, when he was a mechanic with the Flying Tigers. Are you familiar with them?"

I nodded, and she continued:

"Father partnered up with a Tiger pilot. I never learned the pilot's name or any details, but obviously, there were illegalities involved. They amassed a great fortune after the war, until they finally decided enough was enough, although there was one thing that they always regretted never being able to bring home."

She paused, reflecting.

I said, "That was . . . ?"

"They called it the Ming Treasure. In any event, they parted ways. Father had married a Burmese woman, my mother, Aung Two. Father liked California, but his pilot partner preferred the East Coast. If he's still alive, I imagine the poor man must be tortured by his past."

I didn't respond, although the thought befitted Duke.

She said, "I know my father was anguished. I don't want to be. I don't want things bought with tainted money. Neither did my father. He couldn't live with it and eventually drank himself to death. Soon afterward, my mother committed suicide. My grandfather—everyone called him Smitty—he raised me. I'm told my grandmother—Aung One—was more assertive than my mother or myself, and had she been alive, she might have prevented any of it from happening. I have no children, so I'm the last of the Aungs—oh!"

"What is it?"

"I just remembered, I still have my grandmother's little box. It's quite a lovely box. I want you to have it."

"There's no need."

"I think there is."

"Why?" I asked, but she was already padding inside the house, leaving me with more questions than when I'd first entered.

She returned moments later, cradling a small, ornately carved wooden box. She set it down and opened it. There were bits and pieces of cloth with Chinese characters and a pincushion pierced with gold needles, all atop a lining of old, yellowing newspaper.

"These are acupuncture needles," she said. "The Chinese characters are instructions for using them," said Aung. "My grandmother was a great believer in alternative medicine. Perhaps it's what you're looking for."

"I'm not ill. But I'm sure it helped your grandmother."

She shook her head. "The acupuncture wasn't prepared for my mother, or my grandmother. It was for the woman my grandmother worked for. A wonderful woman she adored. They called her Kitty, although her Chinese name was Li-ang Soo. Have I helped your understanding?"

"I'm not sure."

She took my hand. "You didn't come here by mistake, Benn. Everything happens for a reason."

"Trouble is, I don't know what it is."

"You're not the only one. Another man whom at first I thought was a policeman came to speak to me. Turned out he was a journalist. I told him what I told you."

"What was his name?"

"Richard."

CHAPTER 13

Richard's father was a USAF flyboy during the Cold War, stationed with his wife and young Richard at Wheelus AFB in Libya, on the edge of the great Sahara. Richard was a curious child who was impatient with his classmates. Frequently while school convened in an aircooled Quonset hut, his classmates playing and engaging in nuclear attack protocol—"Under the desk, children"—Richard would sneak out and explore the sunbaked base by bicycle. The lawns in front of the personnel bungalows were painted green, the streets crisscrossed with the shadows of overhead wires imprinted by the blazing midday sun. Sometimes he'd pedal to Tripoli, where he'd hide his bike, cover his school clothing with a white robe, and wander the souks and bazaars. With his dark eyes and hair, he resembled a native. He had a natural aptitude for languages and quickly learned Arabic. In the bazaars, he'd listen to merchants making small talk and voicing their feelings about the country's despised King Idris. It came as no surprise to Richard when the king was overthrown by the military and a Colonel Gaddafi became the country's new ruler.

Richard reveled in his secret knowledge.

Sometimes he biked out to the old Roman ruins, the sunbaked, crumbling arena at Leptis Magna. Soaking his scout bandanna with canteen water, he'd wrap it as a cap and climb to the top of the spectator section. He'd sit there for hours in the blazing light, looking down at the pit of the arena and reimagining how it had been when blood was spilled: animals devouring people, gladiators fighting to the death.

He pictured himself as Richardus, Roman viceroy of the Carthaginian provinces, who alone could signal thumbs-up or thumbs-down. He promised himself that someday he would possess that same power of life or death.

The walls of the family bungalow were thin, and from his bedroom he could hear his parents at night: drinking, arguing, making love, and best of all, exchanging secrets they'd overheard during the day. The major's wife was having an affair with a pilot. Washington was planning to close Wheelus shortly. He knew the secrets in the souk, too, the fakers and the thieving.

Richard *loved* secrets.

When he came of age, Richard enlisted. Assigned to intelligence training, his knowledge of Arabic and ability to blend in with Middle Eastern people proved invaluable, and he was quickly promoted. He was dispatched to other posts, at one of which he met a Chinese American woman named Jeannie, whom he fell in love with and married.

His home life secure, his ambitions grew.

He volunteered to operate as a civilian behind enemy lines in the first Gulf War. Afterward, he was transferred to Somalia, where he sniped those who'd shot the Black Hawks down.

In 2000, Richard's life altered when he was made chief of the DEA special operations unit investigating Taiwanese renegade troop involvement in the heroin trade in the Golden Triangle. He and his wife resettled in New York. He worked around the fringe of Chinatown, staying in the shadows, listening, watching. His wife became a securities trader who worked in the World Trade Center.

She was lost in 9-11.

Richard grieved for a month. Then he continued going after the top players of the Golden Triangle. Eventually, he identified an American air force vet named Archie as the big guy. But instead of taking Archie down, Richard flipped him: in exchange for paying a tithe to Richard and cooperating—so copiously that Richard devastated the entire Golden Triangle junk trade—Archie was allowed to keep his money and given a new identity in the States. He selected the new name himself, a twisted tribute to his lost buddies Marmaduke and Mason. Back in the United States, Archie had only one obligation: stay the hell out of the heroin business. Which he happily did, having already accumulated a Midas-like fortune.

In 2006, an interfamilial war broke out in a prominent Chinese American clan whose allegiance was bifurcated between mainland Red China and Taiwan's Nationalist China. By then, Richard had moved on to CIA and become a singleton, a lone-wolf operator who had the keys to the henhouse.

It was what he'd always yearned for. Not just for the power and the glory but for the money. There was money to be made in the war of 2006, whose combatants were willing to spend unlimited funds to win. The stakes were enormous: to the winner went the resources and control of the vast South China Sea.

In the aftermath of the family feud, Richard met another Chinese woman combatant he fell in like with. He knew Missy Soo was a Red spy, but—pun intended—preferred keeping his enemies close.

He traded secrets and money with Missy. Missy begged him to find the whereabouts of the man who harbored the estranged family members she'd sworn to destroy.

Richard had contacts, but witness protection secrets were not easy to come by. He was still trying when again he was transferred, becoming the CIA top dog on the old Spanish Main, the Caribbean Rim that arced from Cartagena around the Antilles back to southern Mexico. In these tropical climes were old cities—Cartagena, San Juan, Santo Domingo, Havana, Panama City—where the drug war was heating up. Richard loved the action and the sense of history . . . here, in the name of Christ, native populations had been exterminated, African slaves freighted and traded, and local populations raped and pillaged by pirates. Once again, the rim was nonstop action: the money spigot was turned full on, and tons of cocaine were pouring through it. Richard had a blast; he missed Missy, but there were plenty of loose women waiting to be picked up. He lived *la vida loca*: nights of salsa on Avenida Sexta in Cali, thousand-yard sniped assassinations by day, HALO drops into narrow valleys. Bullfights and cockfights.

And, most of all, *secrets*: drugs, money, people.

Analysis and counteranalysis. Coca production estimates. Refining sites. Routes. Different aspects having different analysts. Richard was the funnel that law enforcement's collective knowledge passed through. Only he saw the big picture. The patterns. His targets were careful but paid no attention to patterns. Richard's methodology was simple: he made use of PACER—Public Access to Court Electronic Records.

He created his own algorithm. For example:

A big dealer on the north coast in Barranquilla, or some such town, loses several *lancha* loads of coke. A day or two following the busts, a certain lawyer puts in a notice of appearance as the big dealer's attorney. The lawyer's a top guy in the White Powder Bar. Richard waylays the lawyer and whispers sweet nothings into his ear:

"Help us get the big guy behind your client, and you're cool with us. Hell, we don't care if you represent the boss after he's down. Of course, you don't have to do anything, but before you decide . . ."

And then Richard would proceed to remind the lawyer of other drug attorneys who had gone down in recent years, most of them still doing hard time in US penitentiaries. Invariably, the lawyer would agree, the result being that Richard had gained another BFF who told him secrets.

One day, Richard, pondering a string of recent takedowns so massive, they had to have come from the same DTO, applied his algorithm.

It came up with Bennjamin T. Bluestone, Esq.

Richard set up a meet with a double CI: a deep-cover confidential informant who specialized in informing on cheating informants. Which most all were. The double CI came up with a former Colombian cop who now was a bagman for an ex-CTI—elite Colombian cop—who sold information to extradited guys cooperating their time down. A thriving enterprise. Richard found the ex-CTI, a guy named Helmer Quezada, in a whorehouse in Cúcuta, a shithole border town between Colombia and Venezuela. Quezada flipped before putting his pants back on. Still another source for Richard and, far more importantly, a name for the big guy paying Bluestone:

Sombra. Shadow.

Richard followed *Sombra* from afar through interconnected cases—all defended by Benn Bluestone—until the final denouement, when *Sombra's* true identity emerged from the—no joke—shadows.

Which was how Richard met *Sombra.*

Now calling herself Dolores.

Which in turn led to Richard—in exchange for Dolores's Colombian cooperation—inadvertently allowing her a window into his Chinese investigation, which was now ripening to a full-blown crisis.

In one fell swoop, Richard would destroy the Colombian drug trade, kick the Red Chinese in the nuts, steal an untraceable huge fortune, earn the grateful thanks of his Washington bosses, lock up an irritating mouthpiece named Bluestone, and own himself a piece of ass named Dolores.

Hail, Richardus!

CHAPTER 14

I caught the red-eye back to New York. Beneath dimmed cabin lights, I looked out the window. In moonlight seven miles below lay a pale patchwork of fields and occasional lights of a farmstead. Normal people leading normal lives far from their cares and woes. Sometimes I wished I could be among them. But then I'd tell myself, *Forget about it. It'd be like going cold turkey every day. You need your daily fix of action.*

I looked from the window and thought about Aung. We walked different paths. She accepted death as another phase of life. Me, I thought it was all over once my time was up, and I wanted to go out fast, before my brain registered the fact. Considering my predilections, I'd most likely get my wish.

Ahead, dawn was a sliver of gray between dark land and sky.

I'd flown first class: seat 1-A, my own private corner office, offering first-on, first-off access. Ten minutes after touchdown in New York, I climbed into the back of Val's Rover. A tray was lowered; on it, a cloth napkin laden with bakery-warm bagels, three kinds of smoked herring, and an electric coffee setup. I told Val to take me directly to Duke's seaside mansion.

We arrived at Duke's place late that morning. It was quiet except for a pair of terns screeching at one another. The house stood tall and dark against the mist layering the Sound. Two goons were at the front gate. One made a call, nodded, and the other opened the gate.

Despite our agreement regarding payment, I half expected Duke to have a delay in store. That was the way he was wired: *As long as the money is in my pocket, it's still mine.* I was wired the same way: *That's my money in your pocket.* I'd renounced accepting drug money, but Stella's fee was clean, and I wanted it.

I found Duke in his study with Dr. Keegan—in tails resembling a penguin—doling out his pills. Today Duke was a country gentleman in a vested tweed suit.

He swallowed the pills. "Get out," he said to Keegan, then hooked his long thumbs in the vest pockets and leaned back in his chair. "Speak."

"Stella's safe in the Sierra, so it looks like my job's over."

"Actually, your job's just beginning. You *do* want to get paid?"

I got in his face. "I *will* get paid, and you'll drop the attitude, old man. Bet I can throw you through the window before you get your gun."

He raised a leathery palm between us. "I strongly advise you never to threaten me again. The unfortunate fact is that it's difficult for me to accumulate bank funds. I considered payment in cash—"

"On second thought, cash is fine. I'll just need your information to fill out the IRS 8300 form." I figured that advice would cut the knees from his manipulations.

"Some advice, Counselor. Two things you never screw with a man about. His money and his woman." He gave me a horsey smile. "Actually, I don't have cash on hand, anyway. What I do have is this . . ."

He opened a desk drawer and took out a gold ingot he placed on the desktop in front of me. "One kilo. Worth fifty thousand, give or take."

"One million *dollars*," I said. "Bank-certified check."

"I'm on the gold standard. The kilo and Stella's check together total three hundred thousand dollars. I'd say that's a fair down payment, demonstrating our good faith."

"Pay me my *money*."

"I'll guarantee you an ingot every month until you're paid in full. Take the deal. If not for my sake, then for Stella's."

Duke's using my duty to protect Stella as leverage was detestable because it worked.

Sensing me acquiesce, he said, "Shoulder your cross, brother."

"Who pays me after you're history?"

"Richard and Dolores," he said. "Because of Richard, you're under the US government's aegis. Meaning no forfeitures. And kilos of gleaming aurum, all yours."

I shook my head. *How do I extradite myself from this?*

"Take the kilo."

Kilo was a potentially bad word. I imagined Richard and some government tech geek manipulating my recorded words. My paranoia meter needle was in its red zone.

A small framed photograph stood on a ledge behind him. A beautiful teenage girl who had a strawberry birthmark on her forehead just beneath her hair.

Duke followed my gaze. "My other granddaughter, Katrina."

"*Two* granddaughters. You're a fortunate man."

"Katrina's dead," he said, bitterly. "Auto accident. 2006."

My hand had found its way atop the ingot. Its surface was uneven. There was a faint imprint, a maker's mark on it. I'm not a braille reader, but the marks didn't feel as if they were in English language; yet they seemed familiar. Made me curious. Yet I hesitated. I guessed the gold had been converted from dirty money, but a guess was a far cry from knowledge. And not taking it seemed a meaningless act. Besides, it was payment for legitimate legal services . . . well, quasi-legal, considering.

"No," I said, refusing the gold for recorded posterity, but I took the ingot and left.

* * *

I directed Val to West Forty-Seventh Street between Sixth and Seventh avenues, told him to wait until I returned. The street, hub of the Diamond District, was crowded. Orthodox Jews, variously shaded Asians, rappers, and drugsters bling shopping. I threaded through them to a drab building with a heavy steel door above which half a dozen cameras blinked. I turned my face to them and pressed a buzzer. The door clicked open, and I entered.

Over the years I'd done business with H. Farberman & Company. Buying gold coins as a hedge against the deluge, selling them back at a loss when I was broke, selling gold watches I'd gotten in lieu of fees. Now my purpose was assaying the ingots. One of the Farberman sons filled an eyedropper with some chemical, dripped some atop the ingot, grunted.

"Pure gold," he said.

I pointed at the imprint. "That?"

He screwed a loupe into his eye and bent closer. He grunted some more, said, "Never saw that mark. Don't even know what alphabet it's in. Have a look."

I did. Magnified, the mark was a series of squiggles. I made a pencil rubbing of the mark. Palmed the assayer a couple of Franklins and left. I wanted to catch some shut-eye but instead had Val take me to my bank. There, I descended to its lower-level vault, where safe deposit boxes lined the walls. One of them was mine. At various times it'd been stuffed with Franklins, but now it was empty, or at least it had been, for I now stashed the ingot in it.

When I got home, I turned on my device. It took a little searching, but I found what I was looking for.

The maker's mark alphabet was one used by the Shan peoples who inhabited the area where Laos, Thailand, and Myanmar (formerly Burma) converged, an area infamously known as the Golden Triangle, where poppies were transformed into China White heroin.

Where, decades ago, Duke, née Archie, had made his fortune.

The Triangle was the source of opium refined to heroin. Despite my best intentions, I'd blundered back into the drug game. I considered this and gave myself a pass. Ignorance of my self-imposed law is a valid excuse.

I researched the Shan a bit more. After the Chinese Communist People's Liberation Army won the civil war in 1948, most Kuomintang troops had fled to Taiwan and set up a rump state, but sizeable Nationalist units moved south and established alliances with the Shan: providing protection for their poppy business by killing thousands of wannabe rivals.

In my mind's eye, I saw blood. Blood pooling on jungle floors. Blood filling hypodermics that were emptying liquid dope. *Blood dripping from gold ingots . . .*

Now I understood how Smitty's past had ravaged his family.

And remembered how the drug business had savaged me.

Just when I thought I was out, they were pulling me back in.

* * *

Six hours later I awoke, slumped in front of my computer screen. I took a shower and shaved and unpacked my overnighter—

And saw Aung One's box.

I'd forgotten all about it. For no reason, I looked inside again, took out the pincushion, and plucked its golden needles, admiring their glow beneath the desk lamp. Clearly, I'd been bitten by the gold bug. These beautiful slivers deserved a proper nest. The newsprint lining the bottom of the box was tawdry but adhered to the bottom as if glued. Little wonder, it was ancient. I looked closer and saw it was the front page of the *Bombay Times*, dated October 20, 1942, its boldface headlines: "Germans Engage Soviets at Stalingrad" and "US and Japanese Forces Battle for Guadalcanal."

Beneath the headlines were the news stories, most of them bad: the Japanese were still advancing into south China; Rommel, the German general known as the Desert Fox, was battering Allied forces in north Africa; an American convoy carrying aid to the USSR had lost six of eight vessels on the Murmansk run; another DC-3 supply plane hadn't made it over the Hump—*ah!*

Aung Three said everything happens for a reason. I'd dismissed the thought, but now I knew she'd been right.

Gently, I unpeeled the newsprint and read the account of the surviving DC-3 copilot. When the pilot realized his craft was too heavy to clear the Himalayas, knowing he lacked fuel enough to turn back, he'd ordered the copilot to bail. No point in both of them buying it, and hopefully the lost weight would lighten the plane enough to clear the Hump. Didn't happen. From his floating chute, the copilot saw the plane explode just a few feet below the crest of a twenty-thousand-foot peak.

Same story as I'd heard from Milton Peabody, plus an additional fact:

The copilot was Smith, William E., Corporal, USAAF.

CHAPTER 15

As always, the Geek produced. He had nothing on Duke himself. Archibald Petrie and his alter ego remained blank slates. But he did come up with copies of newspaper articles, police, and Emergency Services Unit reports, birth and death certificates, and even photographs of graves of the six people who, in November 2006, had perished in an auto accident within a mile of Duke's Long Island mansion. The casualties were a licensed-to-carry Aussie driver named Ian McKay; a Mr. and Mrs. William E. Smith; Duke's granddaughter Katrina; and Gilbert and Emma Maris, née Mason, the parents of Stella Maris, the sole survivor. All of which I already knew.

But something seemed hinky. I said, "How were the IDs made? Dental records or visually?"

"The bodies were cremated the day after the accident. Kinda unusual, right? Wonder why?"

"There's a reason for everything," I said, palming the Geek more green for another job. Ten minutes later, he'd accomplished it. I stood behind him, looking at the results on his computer screen.

Then I beelined back to Duke's seaside palace.

The guards waved me through. I found Duke on the back lawn. He looked quite the country gentleman today: wearing corduroy, leaning on a heavy blackthorn walking stick, walking a pair of short-legged corgis.

"Damned rude of you, just walking in on me," said Duke.

"Wanted to see two sausages and a beanstalk. Nice."

"Careful. My stick can take your face."

"I'm tired of it, anyway. Let's talk."

Duke's eyes swiveled around the lawn. Beyond it was second-growth forest where a man with binoculars and a penchant for lipreading could do a good day's work. That was what Duke was thinking, as was I. Can't be too careful.

Duke lifted his chin toward the house, but I shook my head and said, "That glass-roofed structure adjoining. It's an indoor pool?"

Duke picked up on my concern and gestured us toward the pool building.

On previous occasions when I'd felt the need for extreme secrecy, I would meet with cartel and Tong emissaries in otherwise empty steam baths. But Duke and I skinny-dipped in a gorgeously tiled pool. I pride myself on staying in reasonable shape, but despite Duke's age and illness, his long body was as toned as mine.

"Nice pool, Mr. Petrie. Or may I call you Archie?"

"Nice catch, Counselor. How'd you make it?"

"You were sloppy from the get-go," I said.

He blinked in surprise, frowned.

Gotcha, you old fuck. I said, "Your sentimental tribute to Marmaduke Eddington and Mason Peckham was the first giveaway. The clincher was the identity of the eyewitness to the DC-Three that *supposedly* crashed on the Hump. Not a copilot but a mechanic? Your buddy who just *happened* to be along for the ride? You had *Smitty* verify your death? Give me a break."

He smiled. "Good old Smitty."

I needled him again, adding some torque. "Your granddaughter Katrina died in an accident in 2006."

His face hardened. "So I said. You finished?"

"Far from finished, Archie."

"*Duke.* There is no Archie."

"Whatever you say. I was wondering where you waited out the war after playing MIA. My guess is your DC-Three never went north toward the Hump. It went somewhere else. Let's go to your study."

We dressed and walked there in silence.

Using Duke's old globe, I pointed out the possibilities. "North of Burma was Japanese-held territory. South of Burma, the Andaman Sea was patrolled by the Japanese. West was British India, where a draft-age civilian Yank would stick out like a sore thumb. That left east as your only destination, although not too far east, which was Japanese-ruled Indochina. Just slightly east. Say . . . in the Shan hills. I hear the Shan women are pretty. You and Smitty must've had a helluva war."

He showed no surprise. "That we did."

I hesitated, unsure of the wisdom of saying more. But tiptoeing around Duke was meaningless; the only communication he understood was in his face.

"I bet," I said, "when it came to China White heroin, you and Smitty were the men. Made enough to buy this place a hundred times over. I'm guessing that Uncle Winston Lau, who referred me to you, was your money launderer."

He looked at me mildly, as if I were a fruit fly not worth swatting. I wanted to provoke him into hitting me so I'd have an excuse to rip the heroin-dealing prick's head off.

"You blackmailing me, Counselor?"

"Your style, not mine. Just know that everything I said and more is in another lawyer's office, in a sealed envelope to be opened in the event of my untimely death or disappearance."

"Counselor, I have deep regrets—hell, fucking *scars*—from the consequences of my actions. I quit the business, but you . . . you still suck from narco teats. You're totally amoral. For you, it's all about the money."

I felt no need to correct his misconceptions. I just wanted to stick needles and draw blood. "Stella's parents didn't die in an accident. It was homicide, and . . ."

"And?"

"You had the bodies immediately cremated to ensure no criminal evidence remained. Very clever."

"You know some things. None of which amount to diddly-shit."

"Could be. For example, I don't know what happened to your daughter, Stella's real mother."

"She died," said Duke tersely. His face was pale. He reached for Keegan's button but hesitated. Instead, he opened his gun drawer and put his other hand inside. But then he paused, as if wondering which was better: summoning Dr. Keegan to stabilize his heart, or putting a .45 round into mine.

Truth or dare. I said, "There's no statute of limitations on murder for hire . . . a conspiracy that originated here. Meaning US law applies."

"You said this wasn't blackmail."

"Blackmail's just another word for everything left to lose. How many Shan ingots do you have, Duke? Five thousand? You're not going to live long enough to spend a fraction of it. Be smart. You really want someone to watch over your granddaughter? Give to charity. With a little luck, you might wind up in limbo instead of hell."

I pointed to the framed picture of his granddaughter on the shelf. "That photograph shows a strawberry birthmark on Katrina's forehead. After you made Katrina into Stella, you had it removed . . . but Stella's got a little scar right where the birthmark used to be."

He dipped his head, then looked up at me, anger and something else, perhaps fear, showing behind his eyes. "Enough. No cash, no gold. Instead you'll get the deed to a property in Phuket. Ever been there?"

The old criminal still thought I was trying to blackmail him. I shook my head. "I'm allergic to tsunamis."

"The Phuket property's worth more than twenty-five mil. Title's clear and legal. Right now there's a bidding war for it between two major hotel chains. I'll give you the information. You check it out for yourself, all expenses paid."

More bullshit. Nor did I want his Thai resort, even if it were real. Yet refusing him outright might get me canned, which meant I'd be abandoning Stella to his mercy. Best to let him think I was like him. I said, "As long as it's clear that it's payment for my work with Stella."

"Whatever, however. So you're in?"

"Not yet. For now, I'm just taking an all-expense-paid vacation to Phuket."

"On your way back from Phuket, I need for you to meet with some people."

"Not happening. Stella's my only client."

"These people may very well determine Stella's future. If she has one."

From a drawer, he took out a Redweld file. He unspooled the string and opened the flap and took out documents that he set in front of me. They were written in dense legalese, for me a dead language. When my work requires such a document, I subcontract the task to a paper lawyer who gets off on *wherefores* and *in the event of said occurrences*. In fact, the reason I chose criminal lawyering over civil litigating was to exercise my tongue instead of my typing. Still, atop the documents I recognized the first page of a deed conveying the Phuket beachfront property to Bennjamin T. Bluestone—for the princely sum of one dollar.

If this wasn't a con, it was a no-brainer. A bank-certified deal for $25 million-plus—I'd need a Trumpian accountant to figure a tax-free angle—was a ticket to a cleaner, better life. I paused for thought: I'd sworn off getting involved in drug work, but maybe this wasn't drug money, and besides, if you trace it back far enough, *all* money is dirty—

I was kidding myself. Duke's money was dirty drug money, and I'd sworn off taking any, whether in the form of greenbacks, gold ingots, or a beachfront hotel.

I continued thumbing through the papers. Beneath the deed were glossies of the property—impressive if you're into huge resorts—and purchase offers from lawyers representing both hotel chains he'd mentioned. There was also $10,000 in cash, which I assumed was to cover my trips to Thailand and the people he wanted me to meet.

"You'll enjoy Phuket. The people you'll be meeting afterward are in California. The Bay Area. By way of introduction, personally deliver this"—he handed me a sealed envelope—"to a certain older woman. You'll know her when you see her. Actually, you'll be dealing with a younger woman—a fine piece of ass, but enter at your own risk."

The envelope was made from expensive stock. It felt heavy, as if it held something else within.

"Always a displeasure," I said as I left.

That night I drank. In the brief acuity following the first sip, I understood the irony of my situation: All my lawyering life, I'd sought the ultimate score that would allow me to retire and find myself a real life. But now that I'd vowed not to accept tainted money—*Bingo!*—I'd hit the proverbial jackpot.

Well, I wasn't going to take the money and run.

A strangely unfamiliar statement.

It made me feel, um . . . *clean.*

CHAPTER 16

Rangoon, Siam. December 1942.

The Tigers had been disbanded as an independent unit and integrated into the USAAF, becoming another of the many squadrons the United States war machine was churning out twenty-four seven. All the AVG unit, young Tiger airmen and gruff old sergeants alike, had descended on Rangoon for a farewell gathering. The milieu was a private party in Mrs. Ting's whorehouse. Tears and beers flowed. The dearly departed were solemnly toasted. Guys got drunker.

Smitty and Archie, nursing warm beers and smoking foul, India-made cigarettes, were the only two sober guys in the place. Archie loved the Tigs as a group but wasn't tight with his squaddies. He'd lost too many friends and decided it was better he kept a personal distance. Except, of course, for Smitty, who hated the Tigers but considered Archie a brother.

Archie had no more stomach for war. Against all odds, he'd aced his missions, earning a row of departed-Jap flags on the fuselage below his cockpit. He'd loved the fight until his closest buddy, a kid named Vito out of the South Bronx, couldn't shake a Jap Zero off his tail. Vito's P-40 flamed as he jumped ship. Archie circled Vito's parachute as it floated down.

He's gonna make it, Archie had thought; luckily, the territory below was controlled by friendlies—

But a stray spark from the spiraling P-40 had found its way to Vito's silken parachute. The chute burst into flame like the *Hindenburg's* final moments.

Horrified, Archie watched as Vito, already engulfed in flames, saluted Archie beau geste . . . then smashed to earth. Archie circled one last pass, looking at the still-smoking char who'd minutes ago been his good buddy. Afterward, he'd muttered a mantra to himself during the flight back to the base:

No more. No more. No more . . .

With the Tigers disbanding, Archie and Smitty had decided to insulate themselves from danger—at least combat-wise—by joining a cargo squadron that operated far from harm's way. But to their dismay, they soon learned they'd stuck their necks in a separate but equally dangerous noose. The cargo birds were underpowered, overused DC-3s. Overloaded with supplies, they flew between India and Burma over the Hump, the top of the Himalayan spine. If the weather went bad, things got dicey. A lot of DC-3 jockeys rolled double sixes.

The whorehouse farewell party moved to the sing-along drunkenly stage.

Smitty didn't join in the songs; his eyes were wet.

Archie sipped his beer. A bitter brew, befitting the way he felt. Unimaginably insane as it was, he was still madly in love with Kitty. He'd just turned seventeen but looked and acted twenty-five and had been with many women. For him, sex had been something often desired, easily obtained, quickly forgotten. He and Kitty fit so perfectly, but the reason he loved her was because she was strong-willed, yet prone to gentility. Ethereal *and* pragmatic. Kitty, she was like . . . like . . .

Fresh air in the stink of war.

Yes, that was it. Kitty was an immaculate being in a filthy world. He'd been in her company for hardly an hour, yet he knew beyond certainty that she was the love of his life. He drew deeply on his lousy cigarette—

"Hey," said Smitty. "You know that guy over there?"

Archie didn't reply. Despair gnawed like a rat in his belly. He'd wanted to see Kitty again so desperately that he'd been on the verge of deserting. That changed when he learned she had married a Chinese officer and borne him a girl.

"You know him, Arch," said Smitty. "The guy who owns the base PX."

Archie glanced up. He recognized the PX guy, some Chinaman.

But the Chinaman had seen them and for some reason wended through the revelers to their table. He wore a suit and tie and a flower in his lapel; among the drunken, vomit-stained airmen and whores, he looked as if he'd entered the wrong movie set, a Charlie Chan look-alike gone astray.

He reached Archie and bowed politely. But then, astonishingly impolitely, he sat close to Archie and whispered:

"No need to worry. Your child is safe."

"What're you talking?" said Archie.

Smitty stood. "I'll leave you two lovebirds. There's a piece of nookie at the bar I'd like to know better."

The Chinese took a handkerchief from his lapel and mopped his forehead, refolded it fastidiously, and tucked it back in his pocket. He spoke looking down at the table so no one could read his lips.

"The child was given to the nurse," he said. "But the poor woman didn't have any resources. So I took the child and my cousin transported it safely to India. Sadly, the nurse has disappeared. I fear the worst. But the important thing is that they're in the United States now. Please accept my apology for intruding into your life, but it was a thing that needed to be said."

"What? Say it again," said Archie.

But the Chinaman had gone.

That night Archie lay awake. Instinctively, he made the Chinaman as honest, yet his story was too fantastical to believe. Kitty had had a baby girl by her Chinese officer; it was pure nonsense that he, Archie, had fathered her child. Besides, how could the child be in the States if Kitty was living with her family in Chongqing? A fact Archie had checked and rechecked before finally surrendering to despair.

It was growing light out when a thought came to Archie:

The Chinaman had spoken of a child, not of a girl. And he hadn't mentioned the nurse by name. Nor the mother. So . . .

Was it possible the Chinaman had mistaken him for someone else? Another man who connected to a different matter?

Yes, obviously that was it—

The door burst open.

Smitty was back.

Archie figured Smitty would collapse in his sack and snore away the day. But Smitty wasn't drunk and tired. The opposite: he was sober and energized.

"I had some kind of night shooting craps," said Smitty. From his pockets he emptied American bills he tossed atop his bed. Tens, twenties, fifties, hundreds. The pile grew as he emptied his jockeys, his wadded socks, a sheaf of hundreds tucked in his cap.

Archie was astounded. "You stuck up a crap game? Nobody wins that much money."

Smitty grinned. "I did, brother. Nine passes I went seven or eleven. Over three thousand bucks."

"I'm glad for you. But just now—"

"I met this girl, Ky," said Smitty.

"Go to sleep, goddamn it."

Smitty yanked Archie's pillow from beneath him. "Listen up, Arch. Ky is from Burma. The Shan hill country. Hates the Japs, hates the Chinese, for some reason loves me. Instead of slam-bam-thank-you-ma'am, after we did it, she begged me to stay all night. For free. She wanted someone to talk to. Me."

"If you don't shut up, I'm gonna rip your tongue out."

"Do that, and I won't be able to save your ass *and* make you rich."

Archie sat up. He lit a smoke and listened to Smitty relate Ky's tale.

Last December, a few days after the Americans had entered the war, a contingent of Chinese Nationalist troops appeared in Shan country and cut a rough landing strip in the jungle. They hired Shans for the grunt work. One of the Shan workers was Ky's third cousin by marriage. He'd told Ky the construction work concerned both a Chinese antiquity and a man they called Lucky.

The evening after the strip was finished, a Chinese Nationalist plane— two-engine, cargo—landed there in the jungle. Ky watched as the soldiers unloaded a wooden crate they set next to a big hole they'd bulldozed, as if they were going to lower the crate into it. But then the Chinese officer in charge yelled for them to stop, and for everyone to clear out.

Only a shaven-headed, orange-robed monk remained as the officer used a bayonet to pry open one side of the crate.

"Guess what's inside?" said Smitty.

Archie flicked an ash. Shrugged.

"Gold and jewels," said Smitty. "Tons of it. The officer and the monk stand there like they're praying, then they bow and close the crate. Then the officer yells for the Shan to return. Chop-chop, the crate gets lowered into the hole, which gets covered with dirt. Rolled flat like it never was. The soldiers pack up and fly away. Like Porky Pig says, 'That's all, folks.'"

Archie considered, then said, "Your girl's relative actually saw the gold and jewels?"

"Not just *saw* 'em. Was practically blinded by them."

Archie considered. "Okay. There's a fortune waiting to be stolen. How do we get it out of there, and where do we take it?"

"That's your job, boss. Figuring the details."

Archie winked. "Consider them figured."

Archie worked out a timeline. First, Ky had to show them where the crate was buried. Second, Smitty had to make certain arrangements via some Aussies he was friendly with.

"Ky will do it for me, no problem," said Smitty. "But how'm I gonna pay the Aussies?"

"With your crap game score, Einstein."

Third, they needed a crew of Shans.

Smitty nodded. "Ky's got sixty-seven cousins."

Fourth, they'd have to fly the Hump.

* * *

Two days later, their heavily laden DC-3 took off bound for the Hump, Archie at the controls, Smitty false flagging as his copilot. Within minutes, their base was gone from view in the expanse of greenery behind, at which point Archie changed course from northwest to due east.

Two hours later, Smitty looked at his watch. "I'd say by now the big mountains would just about be dead ahead."

Archie nodded. "Carry on, Mr. Smith."

Smitty got on the radio and called in a mayday: "The wind's bad. No way we can clear the Hump. Low on fuel. Request permission to abandon."

Air Control Center granted permission. "Good luck, guys."

"Affirm—" said Smitty, turning the radio off and looking over to Archie.

"So," Archie said, smiling for the first time in days. "How does it feel being dead?"

"Not bad at all. Hey, Arch, I didn't tell you. Knowing Ky was a bar girl, I didn't believe she was for real. But then she proved herself by telling me her full name. Ky Aung—"

"Can it." Archie didn't want to talk about true love.

* * *

It was nearly dark when Archie expertly set the DC-3 down on the newly constructed jungle strip. The Shan waiting there got immediately to work. One crew offloaded the DC-3's military cargo while another crew unearthed the crate. It took ten men to lift it aboard the DC-3. Archie asked everyone to leave the cabin because he wanted to personally lash the crate, make sure it was balanced. When he was alone, he saw the marks on the crate where the Chinese officer had opened it. Using the same marks, he pried a plank open—

And stared in amazement.

Inside the crate was a mass of solid gold glinting with a rainbow of large precious stones. There was some sort of hat-shaped item as well, also made of gold and studded with jewels.

Archie removed the hat, crown, whatever. It was heavy. He stashed it beneath his pilot's seat, then closed the big crate and lashed it securely. He told Smitty to pay off the Shan, have them get rid of the offloaded military cargo, and prepare for takeoff.

Half an hour later, a parallel line of flame pots ignited along the borders of the strip. The DC-3's engines coughed to life. They revved higher, and the plane lurched as its brakes were released. It gathered speed and took off into the night.

Equipped with supplemental tanks, the DC-3 had a range of about 900 miles. More than enough for what they'd planned. Keeping low to avoid Jap fighters, they threaded low mountains into the triangle formed by Burma, Siam, and Laos. As dawn broke, they saw the gleaming surface of the South China Sea two thousand feet below. On the far horizon appeared the faint outline of the Chinese shore.

"Let China sleep," said Archie. "When she awakes, the world will shake."

"What?" Smitty kept glancing at his watch, then at the fuel gauge.

"Napoleon," said Archie. "Short guys are smart."

"I'm kinda short," said Smitty.

"Why we're pards, pard."

They did not speak for the next several hours. Then, through the heat haze, in the flat sea ahead, appeared a tiny white speck of land. An atoll. Hardly a few irregular acres: a horseshoe of white sand and brush surrounded by a shallow lagoon, which was enclosed by a reef where the deep ocean waves smashed whitely. Archie throttled back and pointed the DC-3's nose at one end of the horseshoe—

The starboard engine sputtered and died.

Running on only the port engine, they were losing altitude much too fast. Archie pulled the stick back. The atoll was extremely close now, but they were barely skimming the drink.

"Holy Mary, mother in heaven," said Smitty, covering his eyes.

"Stay up, you fucking goony bird," said Archie. "Stay *up!*"

The plane disobeyed Archie's orders. It hit the water short of the atoll. But with its nose up, the tail struck first, acting as a brake. The plane shuddered to a stop. As its fuselage slowly sank, water began leaking into the cockpit.

"Dunno if I mentioned it before," said Smitty, "but I can't swim."

"You got to be joking. Everyone can swim."

"Not in Oklahoma. Where's my life vest?"

Archie opened his window, looked down, laughed. "No one drowns in five feet of water."

Archie grabbed the jeweled hat, and they got out and waded ashore. The plane had settled with only the tip of its tail protruding above the surface. Archie cocked an ear. A moment later, there was the buzz of a boat engine, growing louder.

"God save the Queen," said Smitty.

An outboard manned by four leathery, bearded Aussies appeared. They unloaded tools with which they dismantled the DC-3's tail, leaving no part of the plane showing above water.

"Like it never was," said Smitty. "Jeez, Arch, *smile*. We got it all now."

Archie just fired up a smoke. *No, I don't have what I want most.*

They climbed into the boat. It crossed the lagoon, exited it slant-ways through a break in the reef, and once in open water headed for a tramp steamer a few hundred yards offshore.

Archie spoke quietly. "Smitty? Can we trust these guys?"

"Of course not. I told 'em we were deserters hiding booze. Maybe they don't buy that, but next week they're shipping to the Solomons. Gonna be kind of a big fight. The few of them who make it through will be too nutso to remember us."

After the war, Smitty and Archie made their way to the States. They bunked together in San Francisco, getting by with odd jobs, of which there was no dearth, most Johnnies still not having come marching home, resulting in a labor shortage. They'd spent the war with the Shan. Smitty had married his Shan girl and was arranging her entry to the States under the War Brides Act. They kept the golden crown wrapped in a blanket stashed in their refrigerator.

"On ice," said Smitty.

Archie didn't think about the hat, or the statue. He'd resolved to take things day by day, adding a pint of bourbon to his routine. He hadn't been at all interested in the Shan women, nor was he now interested with the glut of single American women: WACS, WAVES, US Navy nurses, Rosie the Riveter types. Most of all, he avoided war widows. He neither wanted to hear nor discuss angst. So he simply worked and slept.

And dreamed of Kitty.

Although Archie was content to wait many months before retrieving the treasure, the Chinese civil war between the Reds and the Nationalists proved so ferocious that the months became years, during which scarcely a week passed in which clashes didn't occur in the South China Sea. No way could he mount an expedition to the atoll.

And so Archie went on waiting for diplomacy to defuse the war.

Smitty went on waiting for his bride. Bureaucratic SNAFUs.

One day Archie found himself in San Francisco's Chinatown having a drunkenly foolish conversation with an old man. Speaking Mandarin was both a painful and pleasant reminder; the last Mandarin conversation he'd had was with Kitty.

The old man excused himself, going off to gamble. "Wish me the same good fortune as Lucky," he said.

"Who the hell's Lucky?" asked Archie.

"The gambler who never loses."

"Yeah? I'd like to meet him."

The old man looked at him oddly.

By 1952, Smitty was happily married with two kids and a third on the way. Archie lived alone in a two-room flat with a calico cat that apparently came with the place. He labored in a rail yard, frequented a rough saloon, occasionally got in a brawl—generally winning, for he'd added muscled heft to his lanky frame and had a need to vent anger at his fate. Very occasionally, he hired a woman, afterward always regretted having done so, for it made him feel as if he were cheating on Kitty. Every day he devoured the newspapers, but the news was not encouraging:

The Nationalists had retreated to the big island of Taiwan, from which they continued their war with the mainland Reds. The South China Sea remained a hot spot, and the United States, still feeling its oats as the champion of the newly freed world, was deeply involved. Which meant the Soviets were, too. Which meant mankind was a button touch from nuclear war.

Which meant Archie might never retrieve the treasure.

Still, he and Smitty had found another way to make money. Using their Shan contacts, each week they had a kilo of heroin dispatched to the States. They dealt it to wholesale middlemen only, wisely limiting contact with potential informers. Archie saved most of his money, except the $200 he forked over every month in the Tenderloin office of a private dick. The dick's reports were always the same: nothing new to report about Kitty.

But then there was.

The dick heard from people in New York who'd themselves heard a rumor that Kitty and her daughter had abandoned her husband and fled Red China and were now living in the States.

All of which Archie had learned from Winston Lau in Rangoon. He had no idea of what his daughter's life was like, but although he yearned to meet her, he was no longer worried.

Thank God, she's free, he thought. Archie, until that moment a staunch atheist, now believed there was a God presiding over love and war.

His immediate reaction was to hop a train to New York and find Kitty. Bags at his side, he waited on a station platform.

"All aboard!"

But Archie hesitated, reconsidering. It would be dangerous, but he thought soon he might safely mount an expedition to retrieve the treasure. The operative word was *soon.* He'd have to wait a little longer until things settled down. He told himself they would, for soon the Reds would win, and the war would be over.

Moreover, it was a mission he could not leave undone. For several reasons:

For some inexplicable reason—love being blind—he was sure that the treasure was important to Kitty. In their few moments together, more than a decade ago, she'd mentioned the word, but abruptly cut herself off. He'd asked what treasure. She'd just shaken her head, and he'd let it go at that. But he'd remembered every second of their time, every word, and knew the treasure was important to her.

Good. He had a fortune of his own stashed.

The treasure would be his gift to her.

Problem was, he knew Kitty would be repelled by his heroin trafficking. All right. He'd give up the business, but . . .

There was another complication.

The Chinese had claims on the treasure superior to his. Which led to the inescapable fact that Kitty would be dragged into the mess if it was revealed he had found the treasure. He was willing to risk his own life—if the Chinese busted him, he was a dead man—but he couldn't expose Kitty to their fury.

"All aboard."

Best to wait until circumstances improved. Then he'd sail to the atoll, where he'd pry out the precious jewels and cut the gold into small pieces. Just as he'd downsized tons of white powder to kilos.

"Last call . . ."

Archie told himself everything was copacetic. There'd be more trains. One would be his. The engine huffed steam that washed over him. It was like being in a cloud. But the cloud would pass and the sun would return, and the air would be as fresh as Kitty . . .

Please wait for me, my darling girl.

He was certain that she would.

That moment in the grass . . .

When Archie returned home, Smitty was handing out cigars. His wife had just given birth to a girl, whom he'd named after his wife. Archie was puzzled when he heard the baby's name.

"I thought your wife's name was Ky?"

"Ah, that's what I call her, sort of our private joke about the phony bar girl name she first told me. We named the kid after her real name, Aung, the same one all her female ancestors went by. Sounds like *Awn*, but in her language, the final *g* is silent. In English, the name is pronounced without the hard *g*—"

"The point being?"

"We call her Awn."

CHAPTER 17

The present.

I steam-opened the sealed envelope Duke had given me. Inside it was a smaller envelope of heavy stock on which a shaky hand—*Duke's?*—had written a name: Kitty.

I considered opening the smaller envelope but decided not; it was securely shut, and I feared it would show tampering. I replaced it in the larger envelope, which I reglued shut.

Duke and his machinations. In the unlikely event Phuket happened the way Duke promised, I'd refuse to accept title. Say so to Duke and Richard's hidden recorders and in writing by registered mail, return receipt requested. Say so loud and clear that I was clean as an Ivory Soap baby.

I liked that image of me. A far, far better image than the old me.

But for now, I had to continue. Duke expected me to be Dirty Benn, and I *needed* his approval to continue lawyering on behalf of Stella Maris.

I visited a reputable security firm—not too many of those, trust me—and overpaid an ex-NYPD Detective One turned private investigator to enjoy a week's vacation in beautiful Thailand.

"What's the catch?" he said.

"Just snoop, baby."

The cop's name was Steivler. I'd met him when he worked under-cover on a joint city-state-federal task force, an experience that had imprinted suspicion as his first and foremost thought. I was curious about Phuket but dared not stick my nose into the deal. I needed a stand-in to do the work.

Next, I retained a young rising star at a 150-lawyer firm. Serious young man with ambitions. So straight he wouldn't use an office post-age stamp to mail his home electric bill. I gave him a check for $5,000 as an advance against his $500-an-hour fee and told him to check out the Phuket deal.

"Verify the purchase offers from the big companies," I said. "Then reduce your work product to a *Real Estate for Dummies*–type reader like me."

"I'll make everything perfectly clear."

"The smell factor is important."

"Pardon?"

"I want to know if the deal smells."

"Of course, we do due diligence."

"Not the *look*, the *stink*."

Was I being overcautious? *Ha!* No such thing. I learned the hard way that the best defense was a good offense, and I wanted dirt in case I needed to leverage Duke.

"Yes, sir."

The lawyer's firm was in the older part of the downtown Financial District, where majestic old edifices loomed above narrow sidewalks and roadways, cutting off the sunlight so the streets lie in perpetual gloom. No cabs or Ubers around, and Val was home in bed smoking menthols, his way of nursing a cold.

So when I left the lawyer's office, I walked.

The crowd at the corner of Wall and Beaver was so thick and slow-moving, I had to move sideways. Which was a good thing. Because that's when I noticed I was being tailed, much as I'd anticipated. Actually, all I saw were people waiting for the light to change, but one was a guy in a Brooks Brothers raglan raincoat who too abruptly averted his eyes and pretended to amble away down Beaver Street. The confirming tell was that immediately, a middle-aged woman with green cat's-eye glasses slid into the curbside space he'd vacated and made a point of not looking at me.

So. If there were two of them, I was seriously being tagged. But by *whom*? Duke was the prime suspect. An equally prime suspect was the crooked agent Richard. Or Dolores. Or Missy Soo.

I rode the subway uptown. Another pair of snoops—black gentleman wearing glasses and a bow tie; a tattooed white boy carrying a skateboard—took over the surveillance. As the train slowed at the stations, I picked up on their tensing in anticipation at the possibility I might dash out just before the doors closed.

I didn't.

Instead, I casually got off at the East Sixty-Eighth Street stop, enjoyed a pastrami on rye at PJ Bernstein on Third, then strolled the few blocks to my hotel. They were still behind me.

On my way past the front desk, I glanced sideways. They were outside the entrance, although now Skateboard was partnered with Brooks Brothers. I continued on to the hotel restaurant, which operated within the hotel but was open to the public via its own entrance. I didn't even bother looking that way because my watchers were cover-all-exit-type pros. Instead, I scooted into the kitchen, hurried by white-aproned people too busy yelling at one another to notice me, and left by a back door.

I found myself in an alley rank with overflowing garbage. The alley's far end was midblock around the corner from the hotel entrance.

I went through the alley. On the street I walked against one-way traffic, then stole a cab from the little old lady who'd hailed it. I directed the driver to Midtown, got out, hailed another cab.

"Take me to Newark Airport. Take the Holland Tunnel."

"Lot of traffic that way. Lincoln Tunnel's much better."

I pushed crumpled bills into the plexiglass receptacle. "The Holland. Fast."

The route to the Holland Tunnel ran down the West Side Highway, where it'd be easier to spot a tail than in the heavily trafficked Midtown entrance to the Lincoln. Same deal in the tunnel. Only two lanes Jersey-bound, curved, allowing a long hindsight view.

Not a suspicious vehicle in sight. Looking good.

I flew west, napping a couple of hours to ward off jet lag, then reading the latest Earl Swagger novel. Ol' Earl was a stand-up marine who fought his way across the Pacific toward the South China Sea . . .

China. Figured.

In San Francisco, I checked in to a boutique hotel on Nob Hill. Small number of guest rooms, small lobby, the easier to spot strange faces in.

The next morning I rented a Mercedes convertible. The price was ridiculous, but I wanted to convey a well-heeled impression. Then, wearing wraparound shades, I crossed the Golden Gate, then drove north, paralleling the Pacific Coast, keeping the speed down, enjoying the beautiful scenery.

The highway narrowed and became the main street of a prosperous village. At the far end of town, just before the highway began again, I turned left. The roadway ran narrowly between high hedges, an occasional ornate estate gate. The ocean came into view where the road ended.

There, a gate fronted a long driveway at whose end was a bluff occupied by a sprawling house, towers, and terraces, all white stucco and red tile in 1920s California style. Not quite San Simeon but impressive.

The gate was unguarded. There was an intercom alongside, and I pressed the buzzer. Nothing. I waited a few minutes and pressed the buzzer again. Still nothing. But I had a tingly feeling in my neck, as if I were being watched. I got out of the car and made like I was checking my tires while sideways looking at the house. For a moment, I thought I saw a wink of sunlight reflecting behind a window, but it was quickly gone. Was I being watched? Only one way to find out. I reconsidered the gate, wondering if I could climb over. Waste of time.

It was ajar.

I took my time driving up to the house, as if I belonged there, much like the cars parked near the main building: a highly polished old Rolls, a station wagon, and a red Ferrari.

I got out of the Mercedes and lugged my attaché to the entrance. I pressed the bell and heard chimes deep within the house. The door clicked open.

"Hello?" I said.

No reply.

I entered the house. The entrance hall was high ceilinged, decorated with expensive-looking antique Chinese furniture. I called out:

"Hello? Hello?"

No response.

I went deeper inside to a great room dominated by a sweeping marble staircase. From somewhere, Chinese music played softly, not the screechy kind Albert Woo sang; this was easy listening, sort of a symphony of wind chimes. I followed the music up the staircase.

"Hello . . . ?"

Nothing.

The staircase ended at a landing. The music was coming from a door that was ajar. "Hello?"

Nothing.

I went through the door.

It was a large room, dim and clouded by smoke from incense burning in a large stone bowl. The walls were lined with antique Chinese furniture set beneath old framed photographs. Double doors opened to a balcony, the sea *shushing* below. For a few moments, I thought the room was unoccupied.

Then I saw her.

An old Chinese woman sat with her back to me, gazing at the sea. I walked around to face her. Age had stolen her flesh and bones: parchment skin, rail-thin, bent. She was still as death or, if alive, showed no inkling of my presence.

I said, "Terribly sorry to walk in on you unannounced, but—"

"Quite all right, sir," said the old woman in a surprisingly refined upper-English accent that reminded me of the actress Maggie Smith. Although sunken in her time-ravaged face, the old woman's eyes were beautiful, and in the dim light her high cheekbones shadowed her cheeks. I tend to be struck speechless by a great beauty, and no doubt she'd been one—

"My name is Kitty," she said. "You are . . . ?"

"Thomas Brownstone. I came here to—"

"Brownstone, my ass," said a woman from the doorway. She was slender but curvaceous in a formfitting exercise suit. Perspiration beaded her brow. She pushed hair from her face, and I recognized Missy Soo. Behind her was a man with a gun.

"Murdering an intruder is legal. Why are you here, Mr. Bluestone?"

"I had the impression I was expected."

Her laughter trilled. "They sent you?"

The old woman perked up, clearly interested now. Missy noticed and wasn't pleased. "Time for afternoon nappy, Grandmother." Then she looked at me—*Gad, she was beautiful*—and said, "Come, Mr. Bluestone."

Missy motioned for me to leave with her. So I followed her superb glutes down a carpeted corridor where fresh-cut flowers leaned from exquisite vases. We passed an inner courtyard in which butterflies danced. Missy walked briskly, long black ponytail dancing between bare, tanned shoulders.

Another corridor, shorter, ended at a door with a number lock. Missy punched in a code, the door opened, and the two of us entered.

Unlike the rest of the house, the room was sparsely furnished. A pair of computer stations. A studio-quality radio. Phones hooked up to jammers and recorders. One wall dominated by a map of Southeast Asia. From the north China coast, a red-dotted line circled a vast area of ocean that came near to Vietnam and the Philippines and totally enclosed Taiwan before curving back to the south China mainland. The setup looked like Espionage Central.

"Pay attention," said Missy, placing her palm within the dotted line. "This is called the South *China* Sea for a reason. Europeans were painting their faces blue and killing one another when China's peoples controlled the sea. And its bordering nations. Those were peaceful, prosperous days. The People's Republic of China intends to restore that. The West must understand we do no more than they do. The Americans, by virtue of their so-called Monroe Doctrine, consider the Caribbean to be theirs. They react violently if others think differently. Witness Cuba, Panama, and Grenada. So, just as the Americans exert hegemony over the Caribbean, so shall the People's Republic reign in the South China Sea. Do you see, Mr. Bluestone?"

I'd been studying the contours of Missy's torso. I looked up, nodded, said, "No arguing with that."

"How would America like it if we armed and defended Puerto Rico as an allied communist nation, around which we paraded our navy close to your shores?"

"Not very much, I'd say."

"Don't condescend."

"Can't even spell it."

"You're CIA."

"I dislike acronyms."

"Stop the word games. Our message for you to convey to your compatriots is simple. We do not want to repeat the tragedies of 2006.

We're ready to negotiate in good faith . . . *if* Mr. Marmaduke Mason is also prepared to do so. Is he?"

I shrugged. "I'm just the messenger. In fact, I have a message to personally deliver to your grandmother."

"Is that so?"

"That it is."

"Come."

The old woman was napping. Missy leaned over and rearranged a stray wisp of gray hair, then kissed her brow. The old woman stirred. The tenderness left Missy Soo's expression as she turned to me.

"You must stress to your people that any agreement must acknowledge there exists only one China. The mainland People's Republic. That fact is nonnegotiable. Is that abundantly clear, Mr. Bluestone?"

"Copy that. Abundantly."

"All right, tell Grandmother the message."

The old woman's eyes opened. She said, "There are many Chinas—"

"Please, Grandmother, do not speak."

But the old woman ignored her, pointing a bony finger at the sea. "China is across the water." She placed her hand over her heart. "I am a Soo whose ancestors rest there."

I handed Duke's envelope to the old lady. It shook in her grip as she tore the flap open. She took out the smaller letter, addressed to Kitty. Seeing it, she gasped, then opened it—

I suppose Missy had expected a verbal message and for some reason disapproved of a written, private communication. Missy snatched the letter from her grandmother's hand. "You're not wearing your glasses, Grandmother. I'll read it for you."

"I'm perfectly capable . . ."

Too late. Missy's eyes swiveled across the paper. It was a brief letter, and a few seconds later she smiled. "Oh, Grandmother, you still have male admirers. It's a letter from a gentleman promising his undying love. Must be an old admirer, he still calls you Kitty. Ugh! A *gweilo* name. You properly should be addressed as Madame Soo."

Missy thrust the letter at Madame Soo, who read it avidly. From where I stood, I saw a few columns of handwritten Chinese characters. I hadn't an inkling of what it said. Old story. Once I got some Chinese guy acquitted on a minor beef. The win made the local Chinese paper, which ran an article and my picture: post-trial and proud, sucking it up for the cameras. I hung the clipping in my office for a couple of years until some Chinese gang boy told me I'd cut and pasted the wrong text: under my picture was an article on herbal remedies for male sexual problems.

Come to think of it, that gang boy had been Scar.

"Your head's on backward, dude," he'd said.

A hint of rose tinged Kitty's cheeks. Whatever she'd read had affected her profoundly. I had the feeling that Duke's real message lay beneath the lines, that the communication wasn't simply a love letter. Or maybe the proof of love was the fact that there *was* a communication.

The old woman looked at me. "Forgive me for not introducing myself properly. I am Madame Soo. Please inform the sender that I appreciate the letter."

"I shall."

Madame Soo reached beneath the incense bowl and took out a long wooden match, struck it, and held the flame to the letter. When it began burning, she dropped it in the incense bowl and watched the paper darken and curl to ash.

Missy hooked an arm through mine. I felt her breasts against me as we went down a corridor to a home gymnasium larger than the one I pay $300 a month not to go to.

She gripped a barre and stretched one long leg and spoke without looking at me, although I couldn't take my eyes off her.

"Tell Mr. Mason the primary matter is nonnegotiable. Lucky's custody is to be transferred to the People's Republic. Got that?"

I nodded. "Abundantly and clearly."

"Are you always so goddamn flip?"

"Most of the time, I'm afraid."

She clenched her jaw and continued. "In return for the People's Republic receiving certain geographical concessions in the South China Sea, and the return of Lucky, the People's Republic will renegotiate trade agreements that are very favorable to the United States. Over time, a concession worth *trillions*. Clear?"

Clear, *if* it was the truth. It seemed absurd that Missy, despite all her adorable bells and whistles, seemingly was representing China in a trillion-dollar deal. Meaning at the very least, she was a go-between to the top people in China. Or maybe she was top-ranked herself, one of those referred to as a *princess*, a daughter of an influential big shot, a Westernized brat who played at spying. Still, even more absurd than Missy's participation was the insane fact that *I* was negotiating on behalf of the United States.

Which meant I'd just knowingly violated the Logan Act, which forbids private citizens from negotiating on behalf of the US government.

"I have a nonnegotiable matter as well," I said. "Stella Maris is to be left alone."

Missy smiled. "How sweet. Tell me, was Stella that good?"

I gave her a half-lidded look of disdain.

"I'm better," she said, slipping into a mock-pidgin English persona. "I'm number one girl, *gweilo*. When you come back to see me, maybe I allow you a taste. Maybe I even make you rich. Maybe you work for me? What you say, *gweilo*?"

I refrained from responding to her insults. See, I wasn't done horse-trading. The first offer in a negotiation is never the final offer. The comeback to it has to be a way-upward demand, an opening gambit for something that will surely be refused but will later serve its purpose as a bargaining concession.

"I appreciate the offer, but let's stick to business. We need one other thing: your bosses in Beijing will get rid of the fat midget who runs North Korea."

"You're joking . . ." Her smooth face quilted into frown lines. "You have the authority to propose that?"

"I'm here, aren't I? You have the authority to reply?"

"I need to speak to . . . I'll let you know."

"Sure. I'll be twiddling my thumbs."

"It will take some time. I mean, your proposal would require an extraordinary effort. Maybe it could be . . . I don't know."

"Well, then," I said. "Find out."

She crossed to the door and held it open for me. As I started out, she put her finger beneath my chin and turned my face toward hers. "Do you want me, Benn?"

An offer hard to refuse, but I wasn't a whore. I said, "I can't afford you."

"You can't *afford* . . . ?"

"Morally speaking."

Her smile became a sneer. "Go home. Wait until you're summoned."

CHAPTER 18

Upon returning to the Apple, I updated my personal profile. Rented a floor-through in a good brownstone on a Central Park side street. Signed a month-by-month office rental in case I needed use of a conference room. Ordered stationery and business cards. Overnighted to Miami and got my yearly physical from Doc Concierge. Filled his script for Valium. Flew back to Barney's New York to refresh my wardrobe. Hit the gym for real. Got massaged, pedicured, a shave and haircut. Ate and drank in fine restaurants, and refrained from pursuing temptations.

Which doesn't mean I didn't think about them.

Came a night I staggered home drunkenly.

Fell into bed and fixated on Missy Soo . . .

Despite her stern veneer—or perhaps because of it—she emanated sexuality, a bouquet promising a garden of delights. But even thinking about bedding Missy was teasing the devil—

I went into the bathroom and vomited.

Went back to bed; visualized Stella . . .

Despite her ravishing beauty, I viewed her simply as a client. In retrospect, I regretted our brief encounter. She'd avoided eye contact throughout, and I felt as if I'd abetted her debasing herself by our acts, which were clearly not motivated by any lust for me, but rather to hurt another man, or perhaps herself.

Was she still with Dolores on the slopes of Anawanda?

If so, it was disturbing that Richard knew about it.

Now Dolores had entered my mind.

And she stayed there . . .

The next day, my real-estate lawyer reported, saying he was the bearer of good news. I asked what it was. He replied that it had been difficult to obtain, requiring trips to DC and Boston. "As agreed, we'll amend our costs to your bill."

I didn't remember agreeing, but screw it. "The news?"

"I'm fortunate enough to have colleagues who take me into their confidence. Everything you showed me is accurate and truthful. Both the competing companies who bid are profitable international conglomerates. Their attorneys are from major firms. The competing offers are both twenty-five million US. The bank being used is Panama-based and specializes in tax-friendly LLC transactions. Independent appraisals value the property at thirty million. Summing up, I'd say it's a good deal."

"In your considered opinion." I know lawyers. He was eager for me to proceed whether it was a good deal or not; big transactions generated big legal fees.

"Another thing? The Thai government is considering legalizing casino gambling. If that happens, the property value will double overnight. Please keep me advised, as there are certain minor aspects to the agreement I'd like to renegotiate."

"Thank you. Along with your bill, please put your findings and opinions in writing."

"Absolutely," he said agreeably. "Anything else?"

I glanced at my watch. We'd spoken for fifteen minutes. Just long enough for him to bill me for a quarter of an hour. "Thanks for your counsel, Counselor," I said, and hung up.

Shortly after, I met with the PI. He had a post-Phuket tan. His report was positive, too, not top-down but bottoms-up.

"You would not believe the ass there, Benn. Girls, girls, girls, and women that still look like girls. Thousands, drop-dead gorgeous. And thousands of old bucks with big bucks chasing them. Big cars, big boats, big houses. The hotel on the property was packed. Cost a fortune. Afraid that'll cost you."

"I was afraid you'd be afraid."

I rented a car and drove out to speak to Duke. My nocturnal worries about my client, Stella, still nagged at me. I wanted to know if he'd been in touch with her.

I found Duke amid a field of scree on the cliff-side. Dr. Keegan, huddled in an overcoat, stood fifty yards away. Weird sort of doctor-patient relationship. Duke's anger was so ingrained, he despised the man who kept him alive. Probably paid Keegan a fortune to surrender his dignity.

Duke sat with his arms around folded knees, looking out to sea. He must've heard my shoes scrunching but didn't look up. I sat on a rock alongside him. His left hand cupped small pebbles. His right hand plucked one that he squinted at, then flicked into thin air above the sea.

"I smell a deep thought coming on," I said.

"Fook yourself, you fooking fook."

"I'd rather do one hundred push-ups, sir."

He shook his head in disgust. Then tossed a pebble and spoke without looking at me. "God takes people from me."

Seemed strange for Duke to mention God, but maybe Aung Three had been right. Maybe Duke was tortured by his shameful past and knew he was nearing a reckoning from on high.

He hurled the remaining pebbles into the sea except for one, which he dropped into his pocket. His eyes were wet, but whether from the sea air or his thoughts, I did not know. Nor did I care to know.

I said, "Let's talk business."

"Business? Sure." A grin split his coarse face, and for a moment, he looked like the young man he'd once been. "Phuket's beautiful, isn't it?"

I was sure he knew I hadn't wasted my time in Phuket, but why admit anything to him? I shrugged.

"How was California?" he asked quietly, his expression sober.

"Nice weather. The old woman appreciated your note."

"I see." He paused, then, "And the younger woman?"

"Missy's a fox," I said. "A beautiful fox."

"Missy's a bitch. She's red as they come."

"She mentioned her support for mainland China, but many, if not most Chinese Americans feel the same way."

"She's no supporter. She's a *spy*."

"I wouldn't know anything about that. She asked me to convey the message that the United States withdraw support for Taiwan's claims in the South China Sea."

"Same old," he said. "Then she demanded Lucky, right?"

I nodded. "In return, she promised the People's Republic would make trillions of dollars' worth of trade concessions to the United States."

"Until they find a reason to rescind the concessions."

"I thought that, too. So I upped our demand. I said no deal unless Beijing cuts off North Korea."

For a moment, his expression froze but for a vein throbbing in his temple. Then, very slowly, he allowed a small smile, which became a big smile, which became a full-throated laugh. "You're one ballsy son of a bitch. Dolores was right." He paused as if considering something. "You doing Dolores?"

"Sorry, but I don't do and tell. If you're curious, ask her."

"I did. She said to ask you. The old woman . . . she's well?"

"Sure. As sharp as a tack."

"That's one fine woman."

"My impression as well."

"You're satisfied with the Phuket property?"

"Still considering it. You heard from Stella?"

"We don't need to speak to communicate." He tapped his forehead. "She's my blood."

"Really? I don't think she seems like you at all."

* * *

I drove the rental back to town. Nice little car but not for me. I walked off the street into a Jaguar dealership and leased a top-of-the-line full-option model, on the condition it be delivered tomorrow. I figured might as well live large on Stella's money.

The dealer gave me a ride home in a floor model. "We aim to please," he said. "Time comes, I'll give you a helluva deal on a trade-in for next year's model. What're you driving now?"

"I'm between vehicles. Say, you can drop me here."

He pulled over, and I got out.

It was the twilight hour, and the East Side was slowing down, its outdoor cafés humming, the evening promising. I felt like getting a glow on. A pair of giraffe-legged models got out of a Maserati and crossed in front of me, tittering like I didn't exist. My feelings weren't hurt. I've had my share of kid models . . . now I was drawn to real women. Not women, a wo*man*.

Dolores.

Funny, that. It felt good thinking about her, but I didn't want a relationship. Too many other fish in the sea. Case in point: As I neared a café where candles glowed on outdoor tabletops, I spotted a pair of gorgeous crossed legs whose owner I recognized as an important *Vogue*-ish magazine editor. She was so pretty, she could have been a model, most probably once had been. I felt an urge coming on, so I palmed the maître d' a Franklin and sat at the adjoining table.

I tend to be a man of few words. In court, I skip the bull and go straight for the jugular. With women, I go straight to introducing myself and asking if I might buy them a drink, or some such lameness. I was just about to do that when—

A man sat at my table, interposing himself between me and my intended.

Richard spoke quietly. "Missy Soo's some piece of ass, right?"

I didn't reply.

He said, "A little birdy informed me you're about to be seeing her again soon. A word to the wise? She's trouble. By that, I mean if she crosses a certain bright line she's ending up in a courtroom. She may be a US citizen, but she's also a bird colonel of the People's Republic Ministry of Security. I don't give a rat if you mess yourself, but I don't want you shitting on my op. Got it, *Benn*jamin?"

"Processing," I said.

"Do not touch her."

"Scout's honor."

Obviously, Richard wanted to keep me away from Missy Soo. It was almost as if he were jealous. More probably, he worried she'd outbid him for me.

Richard stood, smiled at Ms. *Vogue*-ish, and left. As he swaggered out, to my dismay, she displayed definite interest in him.

I leaned toward her. "I'm Benn. Buy you a drink?"

She looked at me. "No, thank you."

CHAPTER 19

I knew my real-estate attorney would pad my bill, but not triple what I'd expected it to be. He'd traveled first-class up and down the eastern seaboard, ostensibly to obtain the skinny on the Phuket deal. I was of a mind to dispute the bill, but the last thing I needed now was to litigate a litigator; I'd have to hire a lawyer whose fee would eclipse those gratuitously phony add-ons.

My old bud, the PI—for whom I'd gotten some nice scores—also went greedy on me. His voyage to Phuket was a daytime-TV game-show-winner's dream, with all the trim—his pun, not mine—covered under "Miscellaneous Investigative Hours." Him, I just wrote a check; the guy deserved a fantasy memory.

The ink on the check had scarcely dried when I got a call. A summons, actually, from Missy Soo. Not delivered personally, rather by a Chinese woman who spoke English almost perfectly, but for a trace of the *L* problem, addressing me as Mr. "Bruestone."

"Good day," she said. "On behalf of the manager of the People's Republic Trade Mission, you are pleased to be invited to business conference this afternoon."

"I'm expected halfway around the world in eight hours?"

She laughed daintily. "The Mission's in Manhattan."

"I'll be there."

I immediately replayed her words in my head: *The Mission's in Manhattan.*

And thought: *Oh shit.* I doubted my phone was tapped but was sure the Trade Mission's lines were. I had a hot flash: a change-of-life scenario; a bomb goes off in Manhattan, and the Chinese, hoping to curry spy-swapping, give me up. The proof of my guilt would be in my own words:

UNKNOWN FEMALE: *The Mission's in Manhattan.*

B. BLUESTONE: *I'll be there.*

And, bingo, I fall into the hands of an overly ambitious federal prosecutor trying to inflate an indictment to bolster his resume. Dirty lawyers' scalps were worth many rungs on the bureaucratic ladder.

I quickly covered my ass. "Please inform your superiors I'm honored to attend the meeting. I'm committed to explaining the legalities of the textile trade between our nations."

The Mission was in a neighborhood of five-story walk-ups, originally second-rate tenements for workers exiled east of the long-defunct Third Avenue El. Now the tenements were garden-gated, multimillion-dollar condos whose ever-escalating prices never failed to astound me.

On the corner of Second Avenue, NYPD Midtown South had erected barriers, behind which stood a ragtag group of protesters, all carrying signs: TAIWANESE PEOPLE AGAINST PEOPLE'S REPUBLIC AGGRESSION. REPUBLIC OF VIETNAM PROTESTS CHINA ISLAND CLAIMS. MALAYSIA OPPOSES CHINESE LAND-GRAB. There were a few more similar signs supporting other countries on the rim of the South China Sea. There was even an American presence, an angry old escapee from the '60s waving a cardboard sign that said US IMPERIALISTS OUT OF ASIA in Magic Marker. A burly NYPD sergeant halted the Second Avenue traffic, and I crossed the street.

The Trade Mission building's neighbors had preserved their quaint brick-and-mortar exteriors, but the Mission's facade was smooth gray granite and tinted windows. Discreet lettering identified the Mission in

English and Mandarin. The front door was a steel slab with no handle. No bell—

Yet the steel door slid open. I touched my brow as a thank-you to the camera-watchers. In the doorway, a Chinese woman in a blue dress bowed.

Then she waved a metal-detection wand over me.

The conference room was an interior space—windowless and bug-proofed, its decor functional, featuring an oval table. I sat on one end. Four middle-aged Chinese gentlemen in ill-fitting suits were seated in pairs on both sides of the table. Missy Soo sat on the opposite end, but we didn't touch eyes. Her attention was on one of the gentlemen, probably her superior, as he went on and on . . . and on, in Mandarin.

When he'd finally finished, Missy addressed me.

"The manager apologizes for the space, but it is necessary for security. My country and Russia get the headlines, but I assure you that they are dwarfs compared to American cyberintelligence."

I said, "Not that we're doing anything illegal here."

"Many things I admire about America. Your constitution's guarantee of separate branches of government breeds competition between them. Smart politics. My country and Russia prefer having a single massive organization. At last count, your government employed eighteen separate intelligence agencies and probably an equal number unknown. So many information-gathering tentacles."

"The manager said that, too?"

Missy smiled. "The comment regarding intelligence services was mine. A prelude for my again asking what agency you are with. I assume Richard's your fellow agent, so my guess is CIA."

She paused to study my reaction to her knowing, or knowing of, Richard, but I kept things in neutral. "You asked me here. Why?"

She said something in Mandarin. As one, the four gentlemen stood, gave me a stiff bow, and left. Missy opened a drawer and removed a small device that bristled with buttons and dials. She pressed a button.

Small green lights winked on the device, and it emitted a barely audible electronic hum. She set it on the table between us. I figured it was the latest in bug-killers, no doubt equipped with a recording option, now turned on.

Missy got up and sat next to me, and I sniffed her perfume. Comes to women's luxury items, I'm all too knowledgeable, having spent hundreds of hours and hundreds of thousands of dollars gifting women on mornings after. Missy wore Turbulence. Figures.

She said, "Politically, we respect the integrity of the Democratic People's Republic of North Korea. Even were we to cut them off completely, they would continue their present course."

I wasn't surprised.

But then I was.

She said, "That is not to say there doesn't exist an element among us who believe the North Koreans will eventually pose a threat to China, just as it now does to the United States. The *element* who believe this have certain . . . resources. If our deal is completed satisfactorily, this element might be willing to employ those resources. There will be repercussions. Including, perhaps, the emergence of a new North Korean leadership."

She was bullshitting a bullshitter, and we both knew it. I said, "A bloodless coup of a leader whose finger is on the nuclear button? Nice work if you can do it; not so nice if you fail."

"We won't fail. China possesses codes that will freeze the DPRK's launching communication systems. Simultaneously, their public television will be jammed. A special detachment will arrest the present leader. The television will resume, introducing the new leadership. And, of course, the new leader's finger will not be poised above the nuclear button. Convey this to your superiors at Langley."

Either Missy Soo was a genius at a quick reaction or maybe, just maybe, she was being truthful. *Hmm.* I, who earned his keep as a criminal mouthpiece, was actually negotiating a coup that might alter the course of humanity.

Humbling thought.

Missy crossed her legs. Silken. Nice, but her next words were not:

"Do not betray us. At any moment, I could have you exterminated."

"Save you the trouble. I'll cross Second Avenue against the light."

"I believe the world would thank me for killing a mass murderer."

"You don't think well of me, but I never mass-murdered a soul."

"Not personally. You just give orders. Isn't that so . . . *Sombra?*"

Wow . . . I hadn't seen that coming. But it figured that somehow, openly or subversively, Missy had learned Richard was working with *Sombra*. And Richard—perhaps with Dolores's connivance—had passed along word that *I* was *Sombra*.

How, why, did Dolores doing so relate to the whole megillah?

The answer had to be in the basic motivations. Missy and Red China wanted unfettered reign over the South China Sea and for the United States to recognize Red China as the sole legitimate Chinese government.

The pro-Taiwan China lineup was larger: Uncle and Duke wanted to protect Stella and brought Richard in to help them. Richard wanted money and power. Richard used Dolores to destroy the cartels, thereby elevating his position with Washington. Dolores wanted to conceal her *Sombra* alter ego and most of all wanted the Chinese out of the Logui homeland.

"Prove that you have Lucky," said Missy.

Lucky, again. Lucky was the key.

"Like a DNA sample, or what?"

"Richard knows what."

PART THREE:
2006

CHAPTER 20

Long Island. November 2006.

On a crisp evening a few weeks before Thanksgiving, Duke—against his doctor's orders—poured himself a superb port, lit up a genuine eight-inch Havana, and sat in his den by his fireplace. The exotic wood filled the room with its rich aroma, reminding him of the smell in the Burmese hills following the rainy season, the sweet aroma of new flowers that carpeted everything. After they'd blossomed, his Shan workers plowed them under and in their place planted fields of poppies.

So many years . . .

So much money.

And look what it had bought him: a new identity, a magnificent home, and a lonely old age. It was hard on him, and each year grew harder. His body was beginning to decay; his mind dwelt on the past; his only human contact, Dr. Keegan. He not only hated Keegan's weaknesses, he hated himself for the way he treated Keegan.

Christ, all I want is to love . . . and be loved.

He inhaled his cigar deeply, as if wanting to hasten the corruption of his body. Ashes to ashes, dust to . . . no, not dust, white powder. He chuckled for a moment, then refilled his glass and went on brooding.

Waiting for . . . what was the name of that play . . . ? Ah, *Waiting for Godot*—

He chuckled again. He was turning into a damned existentialist. Doing nothing but waiting for tomorrow.

But then everything changed.

It began when outer security buzzed. Duke growled, "What the fuck is it?"

"You have a visitor, sir. A gentleman who says he's a relation, but if you don't mind my saying so, that's unlikely because he's Oriental—"

"His name, you cretin."

"I don't know, sir. He just said to inform you that he's your uncle."

"Let him in."

"Yes, sir."

When Duke saw Uncle, his mood abruptly changed. It was as if the unexpected visitor had jolted him from his bourbon-induced malaise. Last time they'd met, Uncle had spoken of rescuing Kitty and her daughter. Had something happened to them?

Uncle nodded as if they'd seen each other yesterday. His appearance shocked Duke: Uncle had been slender, fastidious, but age had diminished him to slabbed piles of fat. Duke's attention quickly shifted to the extraordinarily beautiful adolescent girl, who introduced herself—most properly—as Katrina, accompanying him.

Within minutes, Duke was attracted to her—not sexually, but because of who Uncle said she was:

"This is your granddaughter, by Kitty."

"Wait," said Duke. "My daughter?"

"She became ill. It was terminal."

Duke felt a pang for the death of a daughter he'd never seen. Yet that pain was diminished by a sense of wonderment. *It's incredible!* Katrina, a Caucasian, bore no resemblance to Kitty; yet she had his own long limbs and thick brown hair. And, he thought, his own strong personality.

The girl Katrina spoke, as if by rote.

"My grandmother raised me and my cousin, who's my age . . . actually, I'm not sure she's really my cousin . . . you see, our family has a history of problems. My so-called cousin plans to kidnap me and demand you pay as ransom something called Lucky's hat. My grandmother says it's part of the Ming Treasure, a priceless, long-lost antiquity. They say if the Red Chinese acquire it, it will embolden them to proceed to expand the Greater East Asia Co-Prosperity Sphere."

"How do you know all this, child?" said Duke.

"Grandmother instructed me to tell you."

Uncle stood. "Goodbye, old friend."

"Goodbye, Winston."

They knew they'd not meet again. Duke's regret was brief. Katrina fascinated him. Her movements, her boldness. It was like seeing part of himself. During dinner, they spoke of many things, none of which concerned her predicament. Duke was further impressed by her poise, her worldliness. She was mannered, patient.

After dinner, Duke asked if Katrina's grandmother had sent him any other message. Katrina nodded. "She said my being here explained everything."

Yes, it does. It means Kitty trusts me.

When they'd left the table, Dr. Keegan carefully wrapped Katrina's glass in a linen napkin he sent to a laboratory for DNA testing. The result was 99.9 percent conclusive:

Katrina was the living proof of his union with Kitty.

Katrina moved in. He had her homeschooled and shielded her from the outside world. Despite the clandestine nature of things, he was happy.

He was no longer alone.

CHAPTER 21

Manhattan. November 2006.

When Ming Chan shaved, he avoided looking in the mirror full-face. He found it abhorrent to see himself as a hideously disfigured old man who needed naps and had to avoid certain foods and was subject to the lingering aches and pains of a lifetime's accumulation of wounds and injuries. Nearly all the comrades with whom he'd fought were long dead. He had no friends and, except for the daughter and wife he hadn't seen since they'd disappeared seventy years ago, no family.

He was rich, powerful, and honored among the masters of the People's Republic, but he didn't care. Only one thing kept him from total despair.

Seeing his wife once more before he died.

He would. He was Ming of the Chans.

So, come a warm late-autumn morning, he awoke feeling spry as a young man. He washed his still-sturdy body but, most pleasantly, did not bother shaving. He planned to cultivate facial hair, hopefully to partially mask his well-known disfigurements during the mission ahead.

One week later, he entered the United States illegally from Canada. The next day he arrived by bus in New York's Chinatown. He wore an old baggy suit, yellowed white shirt, worn-down shoes. In his pocket were his papers: a false US passport and Medicaid card, and a scrap of Chinese-lettered coded phone numbers.

He ate in a noodle shop on Bayard Street where codgers his age babbled in Cantonese. In that dialect, he made an inquiry that led to his checking in to a jerry-built hotel in a ramshackle tenement. The hotel rented tiered bunk beds by either half a day or a six-hour night. Ming rented a day bunk and instantly fell asleep.

That night he ventured out. He followed memorized directions: four blocks east, two blocks north, half a block west to a bus stop. Buses came, but he didn't board any. Just stood there, chain-smoking, amazed that this all-Chinese neighborhood existed in the heart of the de facto capital of the American empire.

A big black vehicle slowed. Winked its lights. A rear door opened.

Ming Chan climbed in and found himself gaping at . . . *Li-ang*?

She was still as young and fresh as he remembered. It . . . she, was an impossibility: if he was dreaming, let him never wake up—

"Hello, Grandfather," said Missy Soo.

* * *

Earlier that day, Missy Soo had been reclined on a chaise, smoking opium with her lover of the moment, a handsome but boring clerk at the consulate. When her phone rang, she answered in a haze that immediately cleared when she realized whom she was talking to. The conversation was brief. When Missy hung up, she told her lover to get out. When he protested, she cursed him, raked her opium pipe across his face, and threw him out. She spent the next several hours alternating between a sauna and ice baths. Her clarity restored, she went to meet her legendary grandfather, whom she'd fantasized about meeting all her life.

He was all she'd thought, and more.

She saw his disfigurements as badges of honor. To her, he was a pillar of strength and wisdom whose eyes, determined yet loving, matched her own feelings. There were so many things to say, yet they no longer needed to be spoken. Each instantly knew they belonged to each other. Always had belonged and forever would belong. They were Chans.

"Your mother?" said her grandfather.

"Dead. Grandmother raised me."

He blinked, said, "Talk, girl."

Missy related the proposed deal that included Lucky's return to his homeland. Ming asked who had approached her.

"A piece of shit who'll do anything for money," said Missy. "I demanded proof. He agreed to get me Lucky's hat for ten million dollars. Afterward, I'll get rid of him."

"One step at a time, girl. Where's the hat now?"

"Winston Lau of the Foochow Tong has it."

* * *

Ming's frown deepened. He knew Winston Lau had been Kitty's enabler. He remembered his Burmese days and the meek coward who'd years later facilitated his family's escape from China. From his bag, Ming took a thick leather braid, snapped it like a whip, then tied it around his waist beneath his long shirt. He'd killed with the braid and would again, if need be.

"No negotiation," he said to Missy.

"No? But I thought we—"

"Just take the damn hat."

CHAPTER 22

Manhattan. November 2006.

At his advanced age, Uncle Winston Lau had survived so many dangerous situations, he'd developed an almost uncanny knack for detecting the presence of warning signs well before they appeared. Over the years, he'd groomed a network of hundreds of loyalists: extended family, workers both legal and illegal, assorted allies of the Foochow Tong. Not to mention he had ears in the NYPD's Fifth Precinct, hardly a stone's throw from the Pagoda on Elizabeth Street, and several sources in NYPD HQ over on Police Plaza, which he frequently passed while walking to the Wah Wing Sang funeral home on Mulberry Street. *Too frequently,* he thought. One by one, the last of those who'd shared his lifetime were dying. Just last night, he'd learned his old bodyguard Hong Fat had passed.

And so, on a rainy afternoon, Uncle walked through Police Plaza. Always when he ventured out, he was protected, but today his men had already gathered at Wah Wing Sang, so Uncle walked alone, untroubled by his lack of security. He felt good being alone.

Danger? Pah!

He was in clear sight and shouting distance of NYPD HQ and SDNY security personnel; there were dozens of other kinds of police all over, and crowds of people shielding from the rain beneath the arch of the municipal building. All in broad daylight in Police Plaza. In this area, no one would dare attack him.

He went down Saint Andrew's Alley between the US Attorney's office and the federal jail. Places he'd managed to evade. He gave a little shudder, then quickened his pace. He hurried by the old federal courthouse and the new one at 500 Pearl, and moments later emerged from the no-vehicle zone, entering the brightly jumbled maze of Chinatown. Wah Wing Sang lay just ahead—

Uncle never got there.

A gloved hand covered his mouth, sturdy hands lifted him up, and he was put on the rear floor of a car that drove off.

Frail as he was, Uncle remained an iron-willed pragmatist. Never mind *why or who*, all that mattered was surviving—

The car lurched around a corner, tossing Uncle an inch away from a large pair of smelly shoes. The man above them spoke:

"We killed Hong Fat to draw you out, fool. Where is Lucky's hat?"

Uncle thought the voice eerily familiar. Could it possibly be . . . *him*? But his orderly mind shelved the thought. It didn't matter. Whether *him* or not, *they* knew he had Lucky's hat. Deny it, and he was dead. Give it to them, and maybe he lived. During the ride to the Pagoda, he counted his abductors: Six. *Lucky number.* Two remained in the car. The three who escorted him inside the Pagoda and to his private office had the expressionless demeanors of Red security. The sixth man—*him*—who had spoken in the car watched from a shadowed corner.

Uncle spun the safe's dial. Once, twice . . . but then he paused, not yet able to ultimately commit, still desperately seeking a way out. Hopeless. He spun the dial to the third number. A *click*, and the lock was undone; at the same time, he suffered a wave of self-revulsion, for the coded number was Kitty's birthday. He felt as if he'd somehow besmirched her.

He opened the door to the safe—

Which, to his stunned disbelief, was empty. *How could . . . ?* He viewed Lucky's hat once each year. On Kitty's birthday, of course—

Forget that. *Think.*

Uncle was shoved to the floor. The man who'd been in the shadows pressed a filthy shoe atop his cheek. "Where's Lucky's hat?"

It is him, Uncle concluded. He was doomed, for without the hat, he had nothing with which he might barter for his life. It was as if a shadow had fallen over his soul; not because he was about to die, but because he'd been determined to outlive both Ming Chan and Marmaduke Mason. But damned if he'd go out a coward.

"I do not know," said Uncle. "If I did know, I would not tell you."

The man laughed. "A mouse that roars. It's good that we'll be rid of you." Slowly, he increased the pressure on Uncle's skull—

A deafening explosion reverberated in the windowless room. Even as it rang in Uncle's ears, he realized it was a pistol shot, followed by a volley of gunfire. The foot left Uncle's head. More shots. One of the Reds fell across Uncle; another dropped nearby. More shots. The third Red fell. Then . . .

Silence.

Uncle lay still, pretending to be dead. But the cordite stink made him sneeze—

Footsteps approached, then a voice: "Are you all right?"

It was Scar and a pair of his former Green Dragons, all crouching carefully as they looked around.

Uncle found his voice. "I'm here, Grandson."

"Three of them down," an ex-Dragon said.

"The two in the car as well," said another.

"There was a sixth man," said Uncle.

But the sixth man had vanished.

"I'll find him," said Scar.

Uncle respected his grandson's abilities but doubted he was up to outwitting Ming Chan. He gingerly felt his bruised face. Scrapes and lumps were the least of his worries. The inescapable fact was that Ming Chan was still alive—*the old fox would never die*—and Uncle would never sleep well again.

Scar helped him to his feet. Looked from the empty safe to Uncle, brows raised in a question.

"Not important," said Uncle. "Clean up this mess immediately."

Scar motioned, and the Dragons began wrapping the bodies in canvases. Uncle realized Scar had brought the drop cloths for just such a need. "You've been watching over me, haven't you, boy?"

Scar allowed a rare smile. "Like a hawk."

"From now on I will live here, in the Pagoda," said Uncle. "See to security measures. No one is to enter without my personal permission."

"It will be done at once."

Uncle retreated to his office. Closed the door. Sat, thinking:

Albert has clearly stolen Lucky's crown. What to do? All right. Do not kill him . . . yet. He might prove useful.

CHAPTER 23

Long Island. November 2006.

For the first time in many years—*hell, in his whole life*—Duke enjoyed a family Thanksgiving, introducing Katrina to his old friend and partner, Smitty, and his wife; a son-in-law and daughter by a wife long dead; and their child, his granddaughter Stella. On the Sunday evening following Thanksgiving, Duke, ordinarily hyperaware of strangers, was lulled to relaxation by the weekend and did not notice the three dark SUVs cruising nearby Duke's estate but avoiding the road just outside it.

* * *

The SUVs were in radio contact with one another and with Missy, who waited in the woods across from the mansion. She was dressed in black fatigues, wore a shoulder-holstered 9mm automatic, and held powerful night-vision binoculars to her eyes.

She had been doing the same thing every night for weeks, waiting for the right opportunity. This night she'd stood there for hours, watching the house, which for the first time was brightly lit. Some kind of gathering finally seemed to be ending. She watched people leave the house . . . she counted seven people, two of them smaller, young adults.

A bullet-headed white man got behind the wheel. The others climbed into the rear of an extended Suburban festooned with antennas. Doors slammed, headlights came on, and it started down the driveway.

Missy gave orders to her SUVs.

The three vehicles each had a task: part of a plan to block the Suburban, grab Katrina at gunpoint, and spirit her off. A ransom would then follow, and Lucky's hat would be theirs, and eventually Lucky would be, too.

So much for carefully laid plans.

When the SUVs suddenly blocked the road, the Suburban driver, a former mercenary, spotted the setup and put the big car into a skid that stopped so his side faced the SUVs. A moment later, his window was down, and he was emptying a clip at them.

His first salvo tattooed one SUV's windscreen, and that vehicle veered off the road and rolled over. By the time the driver had reloaded, the other two SUVs were returning fire. The Suburban was armored, but a round went through the opened window. The driver slumped, his foot came off the brake, and the big truck rolled forward and tumbled down the side of the steep hill.

The attacking SUVs stopped above, and its occupants got out. One hundred feet below, the Suburban lay upended, its cabin crushed. Nearby, the bodyguard/driver sprawled where he'd been ejected.

"All dead," said one of Missy's men.

"Let's make tracks," said another.

"Call the boss," said a third.

The call went unanswered.

From her position, Missy had watched the opposing sides converge and, quickly realizing what would ensue when they met, immediately ran toward them, leaping down the embankment when she saw the Suburban flip.

When she got to the scene, there was a strong smell of gasoline; a stream of gas poured from a ruptured tank. The sight stunned her. Joyfully.

They were all dead.

"Better than kidnapping," she said aloud, thinking that the death of Marmaduke Mason's granddaughter was a message that would make him shit his drawers.

But then Missy frowned.

Although the Suburban appeared crushed flat when viewed from above, its roof had come to rest between two small knolls and remained intact . . . and Missy could see people moving inside. She watched them and thought of bodies floating in the Yangtze in the civil war, when her grandfather and his comrades had fought for, and won, their country. The bodies in the Yangtze were innocent peasants, victims of Nationalist cruelties. But the bodies in the car were whites whose country still supported the Nationalists.

Missy's radio crackled. She ignored it. She reached into one of her cargo pockets, her nimble fingers searching for something among her tools and weapons.

She found it.

A waterproof canister of matches. She opened it and took out a match and tossed it atop the pooled gasoline.

Poof!

CHAPTER 24

Long Island. November 2006.

Albert Woo and Richard were alone in the rear dining room of a Pell Street restaurant when Albert's phone ding-donged. Albert looked at the phone, then paused, glancing at Richard.

"Recognize the number, do you?" said Richard.

Albert shrugged. "Just a friend of mine."

Richard twisted Albert's ear. "Who?"

"Little Ching. He's Uncle's man."

"Take the call."

Albert took the call, listened, hung up. "The Reds tried to get Lucky's hat from Uncle. Fortunately, Uncle was able to convince them he doesn't have it."

"Convince?"

"Five dead Reds. Uncle . . . he wants to see me."

"Worried, are you? Tell me everything, Albert. If you lie, I'll hurt you so badly, you'll spend the rest of your years in a prison hospital."

Like sinners, scammers were relieved to confess their sins. And so Albert told Richard he had stolen Lucky's hat from Uncle's safe. Then he'd reached out to Missy Soo. "I thought she'd be interested in buying it because of her mainland sympathies."

Richard smacked Albert hard. "Shove your thoughts. The facts."

Albert cleared his throat. "We agreed on a price. Five million."

Richard leaned in, put a hand to his ear. "Say again."

"Sorry," said Albert. "Ten."

"You just used your last free lie. The next one will cost you your life. How was the price to be paid?"

"Deposited in a numbered account they'll give me when they get the hat."

Richard considered taking the hat from Albert. But the Reds were its only potential buyers, and Richard couldn't risk personally dealing with them. He gripped Albert's collar and yanked him close. "Three things you're going to do: First, tell Missy Soo you have the hat. Second, tell her when the money's in place, you're ready for the exchange. The third thing? Tell Missy Soo I want to screw her."

"But Missy Soo, she's . . . I can't just say that."

"I know exactly who she is. Say it, or—"

"She'll want to know who you are."

"Just say I'm your partner in crime."

Albert whined, "Uncle's angry with me."

Richard shrugged. "Good luck with that."

CHAPTER 25

Long Island. November 2006.

Duke stood on the roadside, looking down at the still-smoking wreckage. The night smelled of burned flesh. He'd led a solitary life, but that seemed to have changed. But as quickly as it had come, so it had gone: in an instant, he'd lost Smitty and his wife, Aung; his daughter and son-in-law; and both his granddaughters, Katrina and Stella. Duke did not cry. He internalized his grief and used it to steel his resolve. He knew his adversaries were Reds and that he needed help, big-time.

He called his old handler, Richard.

"On my way," said Richard.

Duke awaited in his den.

The den door opened.

"Richard, thank God—"

It wasn't Richard.

It was his granddaughter Katrina. Her clothing was grass-stained. Like Duke's now-dead mercenary driver, Katrina had been thrown free from the vehicle. Everyone else had been burned alive.

"I heard one say they wanted to kidnap me," she said, sobbing.

"It's all right now." Duke saw everything clearly. The Reds would try to snatch Katrina again in exchange for learning the whereabouts of Lucky's hat. The goddamn Ming Treasure business. *Jesus, what fools.* Gripping Katrina's shoulders, Duke spoke hard and low.

"Hear me. Katrina is dead."

"No, it was Stella in the—"

He shook her again.

"It was *Katrina.*"

"I don't under—"

"*You're* Stella."

After a long moment, the girl wiped a sleeve across her eyes. Nodded. "Stella's parents are dead, too. And your friend Smitty and his wife."

Duke hugged her. "But Stella's alive."

Duke hoped that as "Stella"—whom the Chinese did not know was his granddaughter—she would be free from danger. Katrina's death would appear in the local papers. The girls had been nearly the same age and physical type. No one would realize "Stella" was Katrina.

The girl composed herself. "I saw the one who started the fire. I saw a photograph of her when we were very young. But I recognized her as Missy Soo, my cousin. I ask only one thing. When the time is right, help me kill Missy."

Duke nodded. She was just like him. "When the time is right."

When Richard arrived shortly afterward, Duke filled him in on everything but the switched identities.

"Cremate the bodies immediately," said Richard. "If the bodyguard is autopsied, cause of death will be murder. We don't need that complication."

"I don't have the right to have the bodyguard cremated—"

"Sure you do. If the price is right, you can buy anything."

"Right. I . . . I'm not thinking clearly."

"Never fear, Richard's here."

Their course of action was planned immediately. Bribes would be paid, the remains then quickly cremated and death certificates issued, the legalisms would be accomplished. Richard upgraded security to form concentric rings around the house. Years ago, after Duke—at that time Archie—had operated while cooperating with the DEA, he'd kicked back 15 percent to Richard. Now Richard was on Duke's payroll again.

"Your price?" said Duke.

"Duke, you dildo, I'd work for you for nothing," said Richard. Not that he planned to. Before the gig was over, he'd be deep in Duke's wallet. Then he'd close Albert's $10 million deal for the hat. Thinking of which . . .

The Reds had forsaken negotiation for aggression. That ran contrary to their style. It was almost as if one of them had taken the mission personally.

Fine. He was in the mood for a hardball game.

* * *

One week later, Richard orchestrated the double assassination of Missy Soo's mother and father. In Shanghai, no less. After rendering Missy's parents helpless, he'd doused them with gasoline and set them on fire. He'd used his device to record the scene and anonymously e-mailed the video to Missy.

The following week, Richard texted Missy a message:

End the fight and we'll do the deal as promised.

Her response:

Who killed my parents?

His reply:

Not me. Deal?

Her final text:

Deal.

And so, despite nearly interminable delays dictated by caution—one step at a time, a dozen fail-safes to ensure neither side could cheat—the deal was done. The Reds got Lucky's hat and Richard, cutting out Albert Woo, got $10 million parked in a numbered account.

Only it wasn't over.

Richard had a bug implanted in Lucky's hat, tracked its movement, and unleashed a team to steal the hat back—an item that Richard had been eyeing for himself.

His plan worked, but not quite as he'd hoped.

Albert—correctly fearing Richard would cut him out—had schemed sole possession of the first seven numbers of the numbered account in which the payment had been deposited. It was a secret no amount of threats from Richard could overcome. Albert made it clear he'd prefer dying to revealing his numbers. Richard wanted to accommodate him but decided there was no hurry. Richard anonymously took over the negotiations and gained sole possession of the last seven numbers. Moreover, in order for the money to be released, it was necessary to answer a security question posed by the banker—an answer only Richard knew.

Satisfied that the $10 million was secure, Richard was in no hurry to get it. He had lots of other action in play; afterward, he'd break Albert. Besides, moving and hiding that kind of cash was dangerous, even for Richard, who knew every trick of his trade. One day, when Richard had wearied of government service, the numbered account would be his golden parachute.

He had a backup chute as well. Later for that.

Richard recognized that—despite his age and infirmities—Duke was a formidable man. He also knew that Duke needed his help, which he was happy to provide, for he wanted to stay close to the man with the serious money. As a gesture of solidarity, Richard allowed Duke custody of the hat.

* * *

Duke was staring at the hat—*the source of so many troubles and woes*—when Katrina entered his den. She saw the hat, then turned to Duke, her face a question.

He shook his head. "Not yet, darling."

"If not now, then when?"

"Soon, child. Soon . . ."

"I stopped being a child when she burned them alive. Every day I live with a stone in my heart. A stone I want to use to bash her head to pieces."

Duke smiled.

CHAPTER 26

Manhattan. December 2006.

Ming seethed. *The duplicity!* It was beyond his ken that anyone would dare steal the hat after he'd paid for it. But his true fury derived from the revenge killings in Shanghai. Given the audacious murders—in *his* country—he knew he was up against a strong, resourceful foe. CIA, or some such. A pragmatist, he realized that for now, nothing could be done to regain the hat. Missy Soo was all for going to war, but Ming calmed her.

"China's strength is derived from patience, girl."

"But for how long, Grandfather?"

He smiled. "In my lifetime."

CHAPTER 27

California. December 2006.

Although ensconced in her private world, Madame Soo had her ways of knowing what was going on. Only a few days after the Thanksgiving incident, she knew the particulars: what was, what wasn't, what lay behind all. There was no trick to this faculty; she simply knew nothing ever changed. People stole and killed. Same as nations. After so many years, it almost seemed funny, watching all these people so blindly rush around. Yet in the end, none of it mattered.

She pictured Ming's anger, how he would be scowling like one of the Japanese samurais he so despised. In fact, the entire scenario reminded her of her favorite Japanese film.

Rashomon.

In which the same story—either the seduction or the rape of a beautiful woman—radically changed when told by different eyewitnesses. Each of their stories was a mix of self-serving lies and half-truths.

Yet, despite her cloistered life, Madame Soo knew the real truth.

Her white granddaughter was still alive.

A tear coursed down her withered cheek.

PART FOUR: OVERT ACTS IN FURTHERANCE OF THE CONSPIRACY

CHAPTER 28

The present.

Richard and Duke and I spoke on a deck facing the Sound. Chilly night. Misty. From afar, a ship's horn bleated, but from the deck, the sea shone black beneath heavy fog that blocked overhead surveillance. No way our conversation could be memorialized, excluding the listening devices I was sure both Duke and Richard wore. I, too, wore one beneath my shirt, its mini-mike disguised as a button.

No surprise we whispered close together.

Duke smelled of illness and medicine. He leaned heavily on his blackthorn stick. The shaft was thick, its nobs wet black. Even a glancing blow would do serious damage. Old Duke was old-school weaponized.

Funny thing: it wasn't cold enough to see Duke's or my breath, but when Richard spoke, his breath hung whitely, as if he were some sort of spectral presence. His breath stank of weed, but that didn't account for his pinpointed pupils, and it occurred to me that Richard was more of a hardcore stoner than I'd thought.

"Spit it out," he said to me.

I related my conversation with Missy Soo at the Mission.

Although I privately believed Richard a traitor, I described my role as being under his aegis, as if I believed I was assisting our government.

If it ever came to my being indicted, my defense would be that I was following orders.

Just like the Nuremberg defendants.

All of whom were executed or committed suicide.

Duke and Richard said nothing about my North Korean add-on, as if it were so implausible, it wasn't worth discussing. Their sole interest was in how Missy Soo had replied.

"She wants proof you have Lucky. Says you'd know what the proof was."

Duke said, "As if any of it matters. Whether in the next week or next year or ten years, it's all over. An accidental incident becomes a major confrontation ending in nuclear holocaust. I couldn't care less because I'll be gone by then."

A breeze came up and the fog lifted, and an anchored yacht became visible a quarter mile offshore: a customized 450-foot super-craft. I wondered whether it belonged to Duke.

"All right," said Duke. "We delay until Lucky's ours. Find an excuse for the delay. You're going to deliver partial proof, Counselor. You will formally present it to Madame Soo. Tell her soon they'll have Lucky himself."

"Missy will ask when, where, and so on," I said.

"Madame Soo will know," said Duke.

CHAPTER 29

After our meeting, I replayed the theoretical surveillance tape of my discussion with Duke and Richard. Nothing overtly illegal on my part, but proof positive I was doing business with them. *Not good.* If the situation turned into a chess game with the feds—not Richard, the *straight* feds—I'd have to deploy my Stella defense: that I was pretend acting to save my client. It wouldn't be easy.

I needed to reexamine the entire situation.

On my trusty yellow legal pad, I drew a vertical line. One side for each list. Plus and minus. I started with the minuses:

Minus: Missy Soo might easily kill me on a whim.

Minus: Duke's way was killing his enemies.

Minus: Richard was a stone-cold killer.

Minus: Dolores. Killer accomplice.

My murderous (alleged) partners in crime. All of whom, with the possible exception of Dolores, wouldn't deign to spit on my grave. I sighed. Mine was a lonely road.

Okay . . . now for the pluses:

Plus: Should Missy Soo get what she wanted, she and China would no longer pose any danger. A good incentive to keep our negotiations on track.

Plus: Duke's Phuket hotel deal might be clean. If it were, I'd sell the place, give up drug lawyering, donate the money to a worthy charity like rebuilding Puerto Rico, keep a few bucks to buy a big-boned black Lab and a tricked-out F-150, and drive wherever my dog's nose pointed.

Plus: Richard killed people who got in his way. So I'd not get in his way. He knew I was ignorant of the big picture, and professionals don't kill unless necessary. Or so I told myself. With an asterisk denoting a footnote: If I sensed Richard was about to make a move on me? I'd kill him first.

I gave a little shudder at the fact I was ready, willing, and able to kill. When I'd represented killers, I'd always been careful to keep above their frays. But, inevitably, some of their ways had rubbed off on me . . . Amend that: not *their* ways, but Dolores's ways. Good God in heaven, I was smitten with a mass murderess. I wanted to make Dolores happy. I wanted her to make me happy. I wanted Dolores, period.

Plus: Stella was my client, and I owed her. She was so obviously traumatized—PTSD, if you will—that I couldn't abandon her.

It was a total no-brainer.

The pluses had it.

CHAPTER 30

I bided time while things played out. Both Richard and Missy Soo had been schooled in tradecraft before the dawning of the Age of Technology, and predictably, both returned to the old ways: messages were carried mouth-to-ear by messengers.

Not an hour passed without at least one messenger passing over North America, going to or from San Francisco and New York. It took several days for the important details of the exchange to be negotiated. Many minor issues remained, pending resolution.

Duke was pleased by the delay. "We're not quite ready to give them Lucky. All you need to know is that it's been agreed that the first exchange—Lucky's hat—will occur under rigid, multicontrolled circumstances in Madame Soo's home. Pack your bag, boy, you're about to travel."

"As long as it benefits Stella," I said.

Duke studied me. "Why aren't you asking for your gold?"

"What gold is that?"

Duke laughed. "Johnny Straight Arrow here. Take the hat."

The hat was now nestled inside a heavily wrapped, foot-square wooden cube. I had some trepidations about taking it—what if Richard had planted an incriminating kilo in the package?—but talked myself out of that worry with the rationale that Richard had bigger things in store for me.

I took a night flight, my third trip to the West Coast in a week. *Bor*ing. I set up in first-class seat 1-A, walling off the adjoining seat with my headrest wing and propped pillows. I adjusted the box beneath my feet, chugged a minivodka, swallowed a blue valium, and slept until the captain announced final descent into San Francisco.

A car was waiting for me at the airport. Its driver, holding a sign with my name, was an older Chinese man. He offered to hold the box, but I declined. I followed him to the parking lot, where a dark BMW idled. The driver held the rear door for me. I got in, and the driver got behind the wheel.

We drove in silence.

When we arrived at Madame Soo's seaside manor, Missy Soo—wearing a skintight orange and purple tiger-striped jumpsuit—greeted me pleasantly.

"Like your colors," I said. "Hermès meets the death of a pope."

"You're the only one who understands your humor."

Wrong, I thought. *Dolores does.*

Missy led me through the house to a sitting room, where a table was laden with drinks. We sat. The box at my feet, I accepted a glass of sparkling water but only pretended to sip, well aware of the possibility of Missy Soo spiking me with some sort of truth-talking pill.

I sensed another presence in the next room; felt a not-unpleasant tingle of anticipation deep in my pits. I was about to take a giant step toward knowing my destiny. Thrill of victory or agony of defeat. Added to which, Missy's dazzling presence—the devil wearing Prada spandex—further heightened the moment.

She excused herself but returned a few minutes later wearing a tight black dress, high-collared and slit-legged and buttoned-up one side in the Chinese style. Auspicious, all right. For the Chinese, black was neutral, slightly allaying my fears of a doomsday scenario.

"I've decided you're not *Sombra*," said Missy. "Richard is. I received a vulgar personal message befitting an arrogant boss like *Sombra*."

She waited for me to reply. I didn't.

"Are you jealous?" she said.

"No, I'm not even zealous."

"I'll have the package now."

"I'm to deliver it directly to Madame Soo. After which I will deliver another personal message to her."

Missy seemed unconcerned by my requests. "To be clear, *I* am in charge, but for now we'll play your little game. Come along."

Madame Soo's chair was swiveled from the sea view to a TV, whose screen was bright with a blazing office building. A breaking news chyron described the scene: *Chinese Embassy in Bogotá, Colombia, Bombed.* Then the scene shifted to a newsroom. A newscaster spoke:

"There is a growing anger in Colombia, a backlash against the country's environment being exploited. Threats of further violence have been received, and the Colombian armed forces are on alert."

Dolores's doing, I thought. *No doubt.*

"Meanwhile, on the other side of the world, threats and demonstrations are occurring in the six nations disputing China's claim of sovereignty over islands in the South China Sea. The Chinese have said they will defend their islands. The United States is sending naval forces to the disputed area to demonstrate what they term 'freedom of the seas' . . ."

Missy lowered the volume and made a call. Listened, frowned, hung up. "For unknown reasons, the Bogotá embassy attack was conducted by narcotics traffickers. Which leads me to believe *Sombra*—Richard—was behind it."

I shrugged. Whatever chaos Dolores was sowing in Bogotá, I couldn't see it helping her overcome the Chinese mining deal. Were my meetings with them intended to find leverage for Dolores to save Anawanda?

Madame Soo turned the volume back up.

The scene had again shifted, from the newsroom to the street. Offscreen, the newscaster said, "The well-known antidrug activist Laura Astorquiza, popularly called Colombia's *La Pasionaria* and rumored to be the blogger behind *Radio Free Bogotá*, has described China's increasing investments in Colombia as corrupt enterprises that are disastrous to the country's environment."

On the screen a woman wearing a black ski mask was exhorting a crowd through a bullhorn. I recognized her voice:

Dolores, posing as her alter ego, Laura.

Missy turned off the TV. She nodded for me to proceed. I approached Madame Soo, bowed formally, offered the box, and said, "The person who sent it says it is your decision what to do with it."

"Open it for her," said Missy. "She's about to drool."

Madame Soo showed no sign of hearing the remark. She sat with her hands in her lap as I removed the outer wrapping and opened the wooden box. Then reached in it and took out Lucky's hat. Madame Soo's expression remained unchanged, but her hands shook as she took the hat and held it before her eyes, as if mesmerized.

I couldn't blame her. The hat was something else.

Actually, it was more like a crown. Dull gold embedded with huge emeralds and rubies and topped by a diamond that could have given the Hope a run for its money.

I said, "I am to inform you that soon China will have Lucky himself as well."

Madame Soo spoke softly, as if to herself. "I never stopped believing."

Then she closed her eyes, as if shutting windows to her soul.

But Missy's eyes remained wide open. "How soon?"

I shrugged. "As I said, I'm just the messenger."

CHAPTER 31

When I returned to New York, Val drove me to Forlini's for a late bite. Baxter Street was blocked by vans carrying inmates from the state criminal court back to Rikers, so Val let me out at the corner. Halfway to Forlini's, something caught my eye. I stopped and stood behind a lamppost from where I surreptitiously peered into a Chinese fast-food restaurant.

There, two men sat at a table. The man with his back to me was a big old frazzled guy. The man facing me was Scar. They were deep in conversation, the old man doing most of the talking, Scar nodding agreement. By their demeanor, it was obvious that Scar respected the old man.

Made me wonder.

Scar worked for Uncle in a business where you respect only one boss. *So who was this old guy?*

I waited until they left. Scar trotted off into Columbus Park, in the direction of the Pagoda. The old man—gray-bearded, seeming even older than I'd first thought—shambled along old, original Chinatown, crossed the Bowery, and continued into newer Chinatown, a neighborhood of tenements where, one hundred years ago, Italian ladies had strung clotheslines and Jewish men had daily entered shuls whose Stars of David were still cut into lintels above the entrances to Chinese shops.

I caught a glimpse of the old man's face as he turned a corner. A large patch covered one eye. The flesh below was horribly scarred.

I followed him to an illegal hotel that rented beds by the hour. When he entered, I stood aside, watching as he climbed steps—

"Hey, Mr. Bluestone, what you doing here?"

I turned and saw a man whose name I'd forgotten but whose face I recalled: a former client who'd been a snakehead, a transporter of illegal immigrants from China to the States.

I shrugged. "Thought I knew a person was all."

"That man? *Gweilo*, he's the great Ming Chan."

"Not the man I thought, then. Thanks."

I stopped in a shop and, over coffee and steamed pork buns, searched my device. I got a hit on Ming Chan immediately. Impressive. He was a living legend, a Nationalist soldier, then a Red general proclaimed a hero of the Revolution, married to Li-ang Soo, daughter of a venerable family—

Soo? As in Madame Soo . . . ?

Man, talk about who's on first? Was Scar's dalliance with Ming Chan a betrayal of Uncle? Was Uncle even aware of Scar's meeting Ming Chan? Or was Uncle betraying Taiwan China? And since Ming Chan was too old to be a field agent, what the hell was he doing in the States? I ground my gears on that, and then it came to me: if Ming had married Madame Soo, then his granddaughter was Missy Soo.

I decided to go to the Pagoda and get Uncle to clarify.

It was dark and drizzly, and the steep, narrow alley called Mosco Street was deserted as I neared the intersection of Baxter Street . . . as Scar came round the far corner. There was some construction going on, and the partially blocked sidewalk was too narrow for two people, meaning one or the other had to step aside.

Only neither of us did.

I wanted to talk it out.

So did he: "Eat shit, *gweilo*."

This from a guy who'd sucker-punched me. Got my blood up. Skillful as I am parrying verbal thrusts, deep down I'm still an uncontrollably nervy street kid. There were only two fight rules in old Brooklyn: "Just win, baby," and "No mother insults."

But rules were made to be broken, so I said, "After I'm done screwing your mother."

Nah-nah-nah. Yeah, juvenile, but I wanted to push Scar's button. Bad idea. I had no idea he was so quick. Gathering himself like a big cat, he sprang at me. Lifted me right off my feet and threw me atop a wooden barrier, which splintered apart and left me on my ass.

The blow put me down but not out.

I got back up and went at him.

Mistake. I ran into a left jab.

Followed by a leg sweep.

I was on my ass again, but this time in no hurry to get up. No way was I going to take this kid, who was half my age and obviously knew how to handle himself. There were a lot of guys like him in the East Flatbush of my youth, but they knew better than to fight a known crazy guy: a nutcase who kept on fighting until he was dead . . . thereby setting the killer up for a homicide arrest. I was one of the crazy guys.

I held up a palm, like, *Truce?*

Scar's smirk said, *Pussy.*

Still on my ass, I put my hand on a piece of the wood from the smashed barricade. It was maybe a foot and a half long, narrow, and wet-heavy. I got up slowly. Using the wood as a makeshift cane, I summoned up a groan.

Scar smiled. Then chuckled. Then laughed—

I whipped the wood across his face.

He dropped like a rock and lay stunned, blood oozing from his reopened scar, his glazed eyes begging: *Okay, you win. Please, no more.*

But *I* needed more. I whacked him on the arms as he raised them to defend himself, then gave his torso a couple more blows. I laid off his legs because I wanted him able to walk away. I didn't want to leave him helpless, after which EMS and cops would be looking to lock me up.

Scar was now a ragdoll. I wiped my prints from the wood with my suit coat—*I should make the jerk pay for the dry cleaning*—then flipped the club away, now just another piece of broken wood left by some vandal.

"What's going on, Scar?"

He spat at me.

"Tsk. Germs."

I kicked him again and again and a few more times while he mewled like a lost kitten. I left him like that. My nose hurt where his jab had landed, and the club had left splinters in my palm, but there was a jauntiness in my step that I hadn't felt in far too long.

CHAPTER 32

That night, Duke, Richard, and I watched the world going mad on TV. The US Pacific fleet was on DEFCON Two. US intelligence reported the Red Chinese forces were likewise. The opposing leaders—China's fat-cheeked, thin-eyed Sing and the out-of-his-league US president— were communicating like teenagers via tweets. The radioactive *n* word was uttered and responded to in kind. Scary, yet I felt oddly detached. I have this theory: one's fear of imminent death is diminished if one knows no others will be left behind. At least mine was.

The screen cut to footage of a hydrogen bomb test.

Richard laughed. "All is well, sire."

"Shut up," said Duke. *"Listen."*

Voice-over, a newscaster said, "Meanwhile, in Colombia, Laura Astorquiza, *La Pasionaria,* has termed the recent Chinese investments in the Sierra Nevada a *rape.*"

"So clever, my sweet baby," said Richard.

She's not your baby. Or so I hoped.

"Duke, shut the TV off," said Richard. "The word is still *delay.* We can't give what we don't have yet, so we fill their heads with crap we say comes directly from the White House. They'll buy that, for sure. Counselor, you're on standby. Incidentally, no more ingots; your check is in the mail.

"And I *will* come in your mouth," said Richard.

I looked at them. "You invited me to your coffee klatch to toss sixth-grade insults? I suppose next you'll tell me the news is that there is no news?"

"Invited you here to make sure you're keeping your head in the game, Counselor," said Duke.

"Zero hour's a-coming," said Richard.

Zero hour? Sounded like a movie I didn't mind not seeing. But, as I again reminded myself, I was already in a front-row seat. "Meaning?"

"Today's L-Day minus fourteen," said Richard.

L? For Lucky? Best not to ask.

Duke said, "Now you boys have a drink, and let an old man watch his nightly porno in peace."

Richard helped himself to a full tumbler of aged Scotch. Opened the bay doors facing the Sound, stepped onto the terrace, lit a cigarette, and smoked it while gazing at the sea. But the door was slightly ajar, and I knew his lizard brain was focused on listening to us.

Duke knew, too. He swiveled, reached to the door, slammed it shut. When he turned back to me, his face was beet red. He pressed a button on his desktop, and a moment later Dr. Keegan entered. Wearing a white smock, he carried a doctor's satchel. Using its contents in short order, he injected Duke, forced him to swallow a half dozen pills, inserted oxygen tubes in his nostrils.

Beyond the terrace door, I saw Richard's shadow. Cigarette glowing, watching.

Abruptly, Duke sat up. Blinked. Looked at Keegan. "Get out."

When Keegan was gone, Duke cast a glance at the closed terrace doors, then spoke too quietly for Richard to hear. "I've met my share of bad cops, but that son of a bitch is the bottom of the barrel. Asshole doesn't have any idea of whom he's dealing with. I've been there and done that against the best of them. Oh yeah, I'm onto this dude. When he makes his move, I'll be ready. Asshole will suffer the ultimate shame of being wasted by a ninety-five-year-old dying man."

From their deeply hollowed sockets, Duke's eyes were burning pinpoints. Whatever Dr. Keegan had injected had whacked him out of his mind. He rapped his knuckles atop a manila envelope on his desk; then spoke, loudly, as if wanting Richard to hear. "I got him on paper. His posterity's gonna be a potter's field. It's all in here, from the beginning."

"Interesting," I said. So interesting I wanted to grab the envelope and run.

"The bastard was eyeing my Stella. Oh, he's gonna die very, very slowly."

Richard reentered. "Gosh, were you fellows talking about me?"

Duke sniffed. "You wearing perfume?"

"Aftershave," said Richard.

"What kind of a man wears perfume?"

Richard smiled. "Does it attract you?"

"You're a goddamn arsehole."

"Love arseholes, do you?"

I wanted out of there. While they stared each other down, I slipped Duke's envelope that allegedly contained the dirt of Richard beneath my jacket and left.

Actually, I had the odd feeling he *wanted* me to have it.

CHAPTER 33

The envelope from Duke's desk was thin. It held half a dozen pages, most a transcript of a speech given by an assistant professor of the People's Republic of China's Ministry of Culture. The topic was the lost Ming Treasure and Lucky: believed, if not revered, to be fortuitousness incarnate. Were China to finally become the world's sole Eastern power, it wanted Lucky as its image, bestowing his blessings. Got me to wondering:

Was Lucky part of the Ming Treasure?

If so, maybe he wasn't a man . . .

Was he a bejeweled artifact?

A preserved, embalmed body?

I respect Chinese traditions, but luck wasn't in the curriculum of my school of thinking. As a child of the West, I was expected to make my own luck. Sadly, too many times I'd tried and failed to grab the gold ring. But now I was like, *What ring?*

Besides the transcript, the envelope contained an old black-and-white photograph, purportedly a close-up of the Ming Treasure's surface: a light-colored metallic landscape pebbled with precious rocks. The jeweled surface of Lucky's hat looked identical to that of the Ming Treasure. Was the hat *part* of the same treasure?

Or was "Lucky" actually the Ming Treasure itself? They shared so much in common. Both lost to posterity. Both awesomely auspicious. Both sought by opposing factions.

Duke had implied that the file had to do with Richard. But I didn't see anything remotely connected to Richard. Had he said so because he, knowing Richard was listening in, wanted to worry him? If so, *I* was worried about the implications of Richard knowing I had the envelope. Perhaps I'd made a mistake in taking it. But no going back. I owned it now.

Rechecking the envelope's contents, I found beneath the photograph another document I hadn't noticed: an old, yellowing typed statement on the letterhead of one Colonel G. W. Rogers-Smith, medical doctor in chief of the British Royal Burmese Constabulary. It described a rare medical occurrence that—

Ping! I received a text.

It was from Uncle:

Come now!

CHAPTER 34

I used to have a concealed-carry permit, but it was revoked when I was suspended. In my new apartment, I'd discovered a crevice behind my stove that I could plausibly deny knowing existed. There, wrapped in oilcloth, I kept a battered old Starr revolver whose handle had been taped when it was the throwaway weapon of a bad cop.

I'd nearly killed Scar, and I had the uneasy feeling that this was payback time. Sure, I had an option. I could simply ignore Uncle's summons, but sooner or later he—or his minions—would catch up with me.

The hell with it. I'd face the music.

As long as it wasn't "Taps."

The Starr was a .38 caliber. Its barrel had been sawed short, probably to use it as a backup belly gun. It smelled of rust but dry-fired perfectly. Loaded, it weighed heavily in my hand. And on my mind. The NYC penalty for possessing an unregistered weapon was a minimum three. The first year in the Devil's Island known as Rikers, the remainder in an upstate medium-security lockup overcrowded with buttholing lifers—

I shuddered at the thought.

But six in the chamber might prevent my being six feet underground.

I stuffed the pistol beneath my belt. Slugged a Bison Grass vodka.

Then went to the Pagoda.

Turned out I'd read the situation wrong. Uncle had no beef with me. His anger was directed at Scar.

Bandaged and swollen, Scar bowed his head as Uncle shamed him in Mandarin, tossing in furiously broken English.

"Stupid boy! You allowed them to penetrate the Pagoda."

"They had credentials from the electric company—"

"I'm ashamed to call you my grandson."

Right now Uncle was furious with the kid, but odds were he'd turn his anger my way because, in the end, blood always rules.

I said, "Mr. Lau, I apologize, I didn't know—"

"Not necessary. You acted like a man. Not like this *boy*, who can't even control his woman. Go now, boy, leave us."

Eyes averted, Scar left.

Uncle sighed. He'd reverted to perfect English. "Derek is a good boy. I can't stay angry with him." He sighed again. "I asked you here because I'm concerned. The meter readers were feds. The signs are foreboding. Soon I am going to be arrested. Promise you'll be there for me."

"I'll be there for you." I'd considered this broke my promise about repping heroin dealers. But my better angel whispered that Uncle's drug activities had been so long ago, there was no way proof beyond a reasonable doubt existed. So if he had problems, they'd be recent, likely money-laundering or illegal-immigration based, or any of the other scams he ran. Crimes that remained in my moral ambit.

And Uncle was a very wealthy man.

If he were arrested, his retainer would partially offset the fees I wasn't going to refuse, enough to keep me operating in style while I rebuilt my practice.

"Drink," said Uncle.

He filled two tumblers with Hennessy XO. It was late, and I wasn't in the mood to tie one on, but as a sign of respect I took a sip—

Agh. The high-octane stuff burned my esophagus.

Uncle poured refills. He gulped his and refilled again. He was mellowing now to a side of him I hadn't seen. Solicitously, he said, "How is your wife?"

"She's fine." I'd been married when I'd first met Uncle.

His eyes suddenly grew watery. Not from the booze.

"A man's life," he said. "There's but one chance for love. Fail, and you live a solitary existence."

I nodded sagely. Pretended to take another sip.

"My grandson you beat up very bad," he said.

Very bad? Uh-oh.

"Derek, he jokes with his friends. I overheard him saying that I suffered a condition he calls 'babe paralysis.'"

"Never heard of it," I lied.

"I never was afraid of any man, but Derek's right. When it comes to women, it's true. I'm . . . shy."

He offered another toast. As he drank, I dumped my drink in a plastic shrub. He tottered and plumped into his chair, his expression oddly vulnerable. Boozed, he'd just confessed a deep-down secret. I figured it was a good time to learn another.

"Lucky," I said.

He looked up.

I said, "I don't understand why he's so important to so many people. Years of revenge killings, and now, talk of war. Just for a lost treasure?"

His voice was slurred. "Lucky is not a treasure. Lucky is a holy man."

"Sort of like the Dalai Lama?"

"Lucky is a monk who is the greatest gambler ever, the always auspicious one who never loses."

Wrong again, Bluestone. Lucky wasn't part of the Ming Treasure. He was a man. A monk.

"Scar—Derek, I'm sorry—he and I, we had an altercation."

"He knows he deserved it."

"I saw Derek with a big, very old, one-eyed man whose face was disfigured. Who was he?"

Uncle paused. Shrugged. "I know you will do your best for me. Please, protect Stella as well. Whatever your fee, it is not a problem. Money is shit. What matters is the legend."

"The legend?"

"The White Tigress and the Green Dragon. The White Tigress possesses Tao knowledge passed by generations of her female ancestors. Only the Green Dragon has the ability to be guided by her inner wisdom, so together they create the ultimate perfect union."

"I see," I said, although I didn't.

"Stella and Derek are meant."

Puzzle solved. Stella was the reason why Scar—Derek—had punched me. So Stella and Derek were, or had been, in a relationship. That bond suggested that Duke's using Stella to contact Uncle was part of their mutual friendship pact with Taiwanese China.

"Thank you so much for your kind hospitality." I stood to leave—

"Most called her Kitty, but to Ming, she was always Li-ang."

Hmm. Earlier, he'd ignored my inquiry about Ming Chan.

"Now she's Madame Soo. But to me, she's always my *gweilo.*"

Confusing. *Gweilo* was a reference to a ghostlike personage, or to a white person. Yet Madame Soo was Chinese. Did Uncle call her *gweilo*—a white—because of her Western ways? Uncle was the top boss of the Green Dragons, and clearly, he cared for Madame Soo. Or, rather, "Kitty." Was I mistaken about Uncle referring to Derek and Stella with the White Tigress–Green Dragon rap? Did he see *himself* as the Green Dragon who should have been joined with the White Tigress—Kitty—long ago?

But why ponder the prattling of a drunken old man?

Uncle was sleeping as I started from the office—

From outside the room came a *thud.*

Then the lights went out.

CHAPTER 35

Federal agents are trained to react according to threat levels. When there's a possibility of a violent arrest, they come in hard with battering rams. Perhaps because of the Green Dragons' history, the feds had opted to use a door-breaker tonight. Uncle's office door splintered, and three men wearing FBI-stenciled windbreakers entered.

I knew the one who too-roughly patted Uncle down, a field agent named Ianucci. Word was that he was dirty, and he looked it: a perpetual five o'clock shadow and dour puss. He plastic-cuffed Uncle's hands behind his back. Gasping with pain, Uncle bent double, trying to ease the strain in his neck and shoulders.

"For Chrissake," I said. "He's an old man. Loosen the cuffs."

"Shut up, Counselor, or I'll cuff you, too. For obstruction."

I clenched my jaw to keep from retorting. I remembered Ianucci better now: he'd killed two men during a money-laundering bust. As per standard operating procedure, the shooting had been investigated. As per the usual conclusion, the shooting was ruled justified. Rumor had it that Ianucci had even received a commendation. The money in question had never been recovered, and another rumor was that Ianucci had swiped it.

The second agent was a young guy in jeans and sneakers. I'd seen him before, too, working DEA-FBI task-force cases. He held up a warning palm for me to shut up but loosened Uncle's cuffs.

"Your hands are the least of your problems, Uncle," a third agent said, chuckling. Then he winked at me. "What's cooking, Benn boy?"

Beneath his peaked cap and shades, I recognized Richard.

He grinned. "Judgment Day comes to the ancient one."

I couldn't parse the situation. I had no doubt Richard had been truthful during our helicopter conversation when he'd spoken about allowing Uncle to continue operating because Albert Woo was feeding him all kinds of inside info on Uncle's business in Chinatown. So why take him down now?

Ianucci read Uncle his rights, ending with the standard, "Do you understand?"

Uncle glanced at me. My eyes swiveled from side to side. Uncle didn't respond.

Ianucci said, "You're getting bad legal advice, Uncle—"

"You're not to address my client, Agent," I said.

Ianucci grinned. "Your turn in the barrel soon."

"You don't talk to a man who's lawyered up."

Ianucci ignored me. "You're gonna talk to us eventually, Uncle. Make it easy on yourself. You know what we want. Start talking *now*."

Ianucci was a dumb dick. He'd just given me advance notice that they wanted Uncle's *immediate* cooperation regarding something *specific*. One or more of the usual suspects whose common denominator was *China*.

And, by extension: Lucky.

Although I knew I'd find out the particulars later, during the case's discovery process, it was nice knowing from the get-go that Uncle had some leverage.

"Mr. Lau," I said, "do not respond."

Richard said, "Uncle, you're looking at wire fraud, mail fraud, and extortion. If you don't want to die in jail, tell this lawyer to wank off." He looked at Ianucci. "You patted down Little Boy Blue?"

I took my device out. "I'm recording this. I'm not a defendant, nor do I pose a threat. Any agent who lays a finger on me can kiss his buzzer goodbye."

Ianucci was torn. "Richard, I can't . . ."

Richard laughed. "Forget it. He's harmless."

Uncle said nothing as they led him away.

The Pagoda was messed up. Broken doors, shattered glass, trashed cabinets. Derek and his boys were there.

"What do we do?" Derek asked.

"Whatever I say, period."

"Something you should know," said Derek. "Albert Woo's dead. Took two days to ID him because they cut half his face away."

The dead snitch explained Richard's decision to bust Uncle now. I had not an ounce of pity for Albert. In fact, it was good knowing he wasn't going to be what I'd assumed was the government's main witness against Uncle.

I looked at my watch. It was 1:00 a.m. I told Derek, "Contact every politician, every important person that Uncle knows. Get signed letters attesting to your grandfather's good character. Make a list of his bank accounts and any property holdings."

Derek nodded sullenly. "Why?"

"Bail," I said. "Get moving. Uncle will be arraigned this afternoon. Meet me at two o'clock, 500 Pearl, fifth floor, Magistrate's Court. Bring as many of his supporters as you can."

When I left the Pagoda, I ducked into a noodle shop and went into the men's room, where I ditched my pistol beneath an overflowing can of crumpled hand towels. If Ianucci had searched me, I'd have been busted.

The next morning I went for a run, then showered, shaved, put on a court suit, and went to 500 Pearl. The fifth floor was as familiar to me as the back of my hand. On one end were the new-arrest pens, where pretrial service interviews were done. In the middle of the floor was the Magistrate's Court, where new arraignments were made. On the other end was a private suite of offices, where rats regurgitated. Over the years I'd accompanied many clients along the route: arrest to court to rat room.

I saw lawyers I knew and guys I knew were lawyers. Some nice, some nasty; some sharp, some dull. I'd worked with hundreds of lawyers but never been friends with any. The weird truth is that I dislike lawyers; maybe that was why sometimes I didn't like myself. I needed to find another life. Maybe become a monk; spend my days cross-legged atop a mountain.

Acting on my advice during his pretrial interview, Uncle only stated his personal details, including his congestive heart problems and his substantial net worth . . . or, at least, the part of it that was legal.

I went to the clerk's office and requested Uncle's charging instrument.

The clerk gave it to me. Had it been a criminal complaint, the evidence would have been laid out in a timeline affidavit signed by Ianucci. But Uncle had been arrested on an indictment, a three-page bare-bones statement simply citing the criminal statutes he was alleged to have broken. I'd guessed right about no heroin, but there were a host of other allegations: wire fraud, extortion, money laundering, to name a few. Enough to upgrade the charges to a RICO indictment, a conviction that carried a twenty-year minimum sentence.

Richard's decision, I was sure. Putting the pressure on Uncle to flip on his coconspirators. I doubted Uncle had an inkling Dolores even existed, but the possibility of his cooperating didn't bode well for Duke or Stella. There was a hidden link between them, I was sure.

Derek showed with his letters and financial documents at 2:00 p.m.

By 3:00 p.m., Magistrate Court was filled. Derek and several dozen Chinese, young and old, sat in the spectator seats. Richard and Ianucci sat at the government table along with a line AUSA, a serious young woman named Lacy Goode. I sussed her out as a newbie flattered to have been selected to prosecute a major case. Could well be that Richard had selected her, thinking because of her inexperience, he'd have no difficulty calling the shots. As for Ianucci, despite the often bitter rivalries among different federal agencies, he clearly was pleased to be working with a heavyweight CIA guy like Richard. It was also clear that he was as dirty as Richard.

The presiding magistrate was Leah Weyser, whom I'd known since she was a young AUSA like Goode. A stickler, but fair.

The arraignment took less than a minute. On behalf of Uncle, I waived a reading of the indictment, entered a plea of not guilty, and requested an immediate bail hearing.

"Very well," said Weyser. "I'll hear from the government."

Lacy Goode spoke briefly. "Your Honor, this case has been under investigation for years. The government possesses a massive number of intercepted conversations that clearly indicate criminality. More important, there is testimony from a close associate of the defendant, more than enough to prove the case beyond a reasonable doubt. Many of the predicate acts include violence. Moreover, the defendant is financially independent and ostensibly possesses dual citizenship: he is a naturalized American but has never renounced his Chinese citizenship. Should he flee to China, there exists no extradition treaty to bring him back. Therefore, he fails to meet the bail standards concerning both risk of flight and danger to the community."

"Mr. Bluestone?"

"First and foremost, my client is a very sick man. He needs to be cared for at home. There's no way the Federal Bureau of Prisons can provide adequate care."

"That's why we have hospital prisons," said Weyser.

Ianucci chuckled. A small sound that pushed my button. My rule of thumb is never to say things I can't back up but—*the hell with them all*—this was an exception to that rule, and my reply was a doozy:

"Your Honor, the government claims this was an ongoing, long-term investigation supported by a lot of evidence, so it seems strange that only now has my client been indicted."

"Happens all the time," said Weyser impatiently. "Government's discretion."

"Actually, maybe it's not so strange," I said. "Considering the fact that certain members of law enforcement are committing a fraud on the court, for they not only allowed but abetted what they now claim was his criminal activity."

Goode leaped to her feet. "That allegation is offensive—"

"Mr. Bluestone has the floor," said Weyser. "But before he continues, I want to warn him that I will not tolerate baseless accusations against government employees. Meaning he'd better be prepared to prove his statements."

I glanced at the government table. Goode was furious. Ianucci's face flushed with anger, but I saw worry in his eyes. As always, Richard was cool.

I had no idea as to whether I could back up my words, but no turning back now. I'd already ridden into the valley of death. So I played my ace in the hole.

I said, "Although the government refers to a 'close associate' of my client who provided testimony, I have reason to believe that person is dead. *And* that the government is aware of this, and is now deliberately misleading the court."

I heard Ianucci frantically whispering to Goode, but to her credit, she motioned him to be quiet. For a long moment, no one spoke. My thoughts were bifurcated. On the one hand, I'd taken a risk by letting Richard know I was potentially dangerous to him; on the other, I was elated at having thrown down my gauntlet at his feet, warning him that this dog had some bite.

Weyser stood. "Ms. Goode, tomorrow morning you and I shall meet ex parte so you may respond to these allegations."

Ex parte meant I was excluded. I said, "I'd like to be present."

"I've already ruled. For today, that's enough."

Black robe swirling, Weyser left before I could reply. *Ruled? Enough?* I'd been shut down because some candy-assed magistrate was nervous about presiding over a case involving government illegalities.

I glanced at Richard, who let his blank gaze lock on to mine without moving his head. Reminded me of a cobra again.

More than one. Ianucci looked as if he wanted to kill me.

CHAPTER 36

I went to the marshal pens to speak to Uncle before he was taken to a cell in the MCC. While waiting for him in a small attorney-client visit space, I thought about Stella, who'd first enticed me into the scenario. As beautiful as she was screwed up, she needed someone to watch over her. I was only a temporary trustee, but now I knew she had Derek, whom I found myself liking. He had been smart enough to put our differences aside and accept that I was running his grandfather's defense.

The door behind me suddenly opened.

Richard entered. "You're a real fart smeller, pally," he said. "You have no idea of what's going on, yet you run off at the mouth. Truth is, you don't have to worry about me . . . *yet*. You still got plenty of things to do, starting sooner than you think. Do them right, and you live, maybe even get a taste of green. Do them wrong, and—"

He reached over and twisted my nose. Just a pinch but so excruciating, my nose felt afire. Then he let me go and slapped my face hard. Flashing his capped grin, he left.

Talk about shock and awe. Unbelievably, Richard had been allowed entry to the strictly monitored interview area, meaning he carried even more weight than I'd feared. Which in turn meant that sooner or later,

I was going to pay—perhaps with my life—for upsetting his applecart. Mental note:

Move on him before he moves on you—

A door opened, and Uncle appeared on the other side of the screen. Through the mesh, his pixelated face was gray, as if he were an old back-and-white cartoon.

Only there was nothing funny about it.

"My heart," he said.

I alerted the marshals that my client needed medical assistance. Half an hour later, medics arrived. As they wheeled him into an ambulance, he crooked a finger at me. I leaned over his face. Through an oxygen mask, his voice sounded like Darth Vader's brother.

"The White Tigress and the Green Dragon," he said. "No forget."

I said I wouldn't. Then he was in the ambulance, taking him from MCC to Bellevue Hospital's penal wing. I watched the ambulance disappear into Chinatown, its siren dwindling.

My device pinged. A text from Duke:

IMPORTANT YOU COME NOW.

Christ, I was a human emergency room. First Uncle, now Duke. Oh well, that's life. Mine. Ten minutes later, I was in my new Jag, zooming from the city. I feared Duke had summoned me because of Stella. Had something happened to her?

Richard. It had to be his doing—

Again my device pinged.

Another text, this from an unfamiliar number, although no doubting who'd sent it, or its obvious meaning:

WE WANT THE THING THAT HAT SITS ON.

Missy's convoluted verbiage got me wondering. Why hadn't she said *man* instead of *thing*? It gave the lie to my latest conclusion, that Lucky was a monk, a living man. Uncle must've been drunkenly fantasizing.

And so I reversed my thinking yet again.

Lucky was *not* a man. Lucky was a *thing*.

Also known as the Ming Treasure.

CHAPTER 37

A USN warship. The present.

The cabin's inch-thick metal walls were covered with a polymer that blocked electronic transmissions. Fresh air came from an interior recycling machine; the space had no ducts, electrical outlets, or other conduits, and it lay deep within a complex of larger, similar rooms, all of which were off-limits to everyone but those possessed of top-secret clearance. The room was a Sensitive Compartmented Information Facility, or SCIF.

A spy room.

Most of it was taken up by a gray government-issue table. The shirts of the six men at the table were patched with perspiration. Their combined breath and body heat made the room stifling. Two of the men were US Navy: a rear admiral and a ship's captain named Starski, who sat as stiffly as an Annapolis midshipman on graduation day. Three others were civilians: one from the State Department, one from CIA Langley, and the president's personal envoy.

The sixth man, who sat atop the table, had the floor.

It was Richard. His demeanor was different here—no brashness or smirks or off-color jokes—it was absolute military.

"Summing up, gentlemen," said Richard. "I alone make all decisions. I act directly on behalf of the president of the United States."

This was true. He'd bypassed CIA and gone directly to the White House, convincing an insecure president who liked acting macho around fighting men that the upcoming show needed to be run by a single individual. The president invited Richard to a round of golf. After the eighteenth hole, he and Richard spoke in the clubhouse. The prez drank Coke. Richard followed suit. "Make mine a Diet, please."

The president had soundly beaten Richard and was pleased. His perfect grin got Richard to wondering if they had the same dentist. He'd said, "I like you, Richard. Do right by me, and I'll do right by you. It's called *loyalty*."

Richard looked around the room. "Any questions?"

There were none.

"Nevertheless, I repeat . . . The chain of command stops at *me*. If I say go, you go. Stop, you stop. Shoot, you shoot. Any questions?"

The man from State looked skeptical about a CIA singleton being granted absolute power over a situation that was a flash point that—literally—could jeopardize mankind's future. But he was a career veteran who knew not to query above his pay grade. He said nothing.

The president's personal envoy said, "I can confirm the orders come directly from the Oval Office. The president hopes force will not be necessary. Supposedly, negotiations between the parties are nearing fruition. However, if not . . ."

"The navy will have an opportunity to put its new toys to use," said Richard.

The rear admiral chuckled, but Captain Starski remained silent, although his expression said it all: he didn't like a civilian overlord in his domain.

There was a long moment of silence as the men in the SCIF brooded over the fact that two nuclear-armed nations were on the brink of war. Then Starski said, "Are our orders in writing?"

The rear admiral silenced Starski with a glance, then said, "The navy's ready, willing, and able."

Richard looked at his watch. "It's presently twelve forty-five hours on L-Day minus ten . . . synchronize your watches, gentlemen."

The men did so, grimly.

"We cast off at oh three hundred hours on L minus five," said Richard. "That's all for now."

When the others were gone, Richard dry-swallowed three pills, his customized blend of amphetamines and relaxants that would sustain him for the day. Then he left the SCIF, navigated a maze of long, narrow corridors, got into an elevator, and pressed the topmost level button.

The elevators slid open to the bridge of a ship. Beyond its forward windows was the awesome sight of the prow of the USS *Corregidor*—known in the service as a "commando carrier"—a spanking-new Wasp-class amphibious assault ship: 843 feet long, armed to its alloy teeth. Phalanx batteries of multibarreled Gatlings capable of unleashing three thousand rounds per minute of radar-guided M61 Vulcan 20mm cannon shells. Dozens of long- and short-range cruise missiles. A squadron of vertical takeoff Harrier fighter jets; another mixed squadron of Sea Stallion and Apache attack helicopters.

It was a baby aircraft carrier.

In fact, it had been named after the original USS *Corregidor*, CVE-18, a Casablanca-class escort flattop that had been in the thick of the South Pacific campaigns, decommissioned during the postwar era. Richard knew that history, as well as each and every millimeter of the present vessel. He drew a deep breath of salt air, exhaled, grinned. He was both master and commander.

Goddamn. He'd actually pulled it off.

Bolstered by his previous string of successes in conflicts all around the world, Richard had insinuated himself into the latest hot spot: the Chinese-American dispute. As was his habit, he'd embedded himself in the place through which all information funneled. He alone knew all of the players and all of their intentions.

The president had recognized this. He'd said, "Many Indians but only one chief, right?"

"Well put, sir," Richard had replied. "But, with all respect, this situation is not a time for dilly-dallying over a proper response. The *only* response is an instantaneous ass-kicking. Think of Grant at Shiloh."

The president, ignorant of Grant, let alone Shiloh, had said, "Go get 'em, son."

At the memory, Richard felt light-headed. Like his childhood fantasy figure, the Roman governor Richardus, he was possessed of the power of life and death.

Now, from the deck outside the bridge, Richard watched supplies being loaded from a wharf to the *Corregidor*, his thoughts wandering. He thought of Dolores. He thought of Missy. He thought of Stella . . .

Then, from his pocket, he took a plastic envelope holding a two-square-inch piece of something that looked like dried leather, marked by blue stenciling. The sight stirred a memory, and he smiled.

Upon learning of Uncle's impending arrest, Albert Woo had panicked: without the information he'd been stealing from Uncle, he had nothing to offer Richard. To calm his anxieties, he'd washed several Xanax down with rice whiskey. Stoned, he'd felt the need to remind Richard: "Accessing the numbered account requires both of us."

"Indeed it do, Albert," Richard had said. "But I got to tell you, I've been thinking . . . how do I know you really have the first seven numbers?"

"Of course, I do."

"Prove it."

"I deliberately haven't memorized them so no one can force me to give them up."

"Don't game me, Albert."

"I had them tattooed."

"Where?"

"Where no one can see them."

"Where?"

"Inside my cheek."

"Smart," Richard had replied. "Very smart."

Now Richard watched as munitions cradled in steel netting were loaded aboard the *Corregidor*. He was impatient to cast off and jump the starting gate. Gain the element of surprise by arriving at the transfer point first. Make sure all went well, then reap the harvest he'd sowed:

Collect $25 million for delivering Lucky to the Reds.

Quit the CIA. Live in luxury with his wicked China girl.

Richard had a thing for Chinese women. He loved their smooth skin, hairless but for a wisp below, their instinctive intelligence. In that order. He'd thought that Jeannie, the wife he'd lost on 9-11, was the most beautiful and brightest Chinese woman he'd ever known, but that changed the moment he'd met Missy Soo.

He'd tracked her down in person soon after the 2006 incident. From afar he'd admired her beauty and her haughty carriage. He'd finally approached her at a sidewalk table in a Beverly Hills café just off Rodeo Drive, half a dozen designer purchase bags at her feet. She'd seemed more interested in them than in the handsome young Italian man seated with her.

Watching, Richard had thought, *She's absolutely perfect.*

"Pardon my interrupting," he'd said, joining them.

"Sir, you're being rude," the Italian man said.

Ignoring him, Richard addressed Missy: "Luck, be my lady tonight."

"Go, Paolo," Missy Soo told her date.

Once alone, Richard and Missy Soo spoke for ten minutes. She immediately realized he was the American agent who had sent the message that he wanted to bed her. Until now, he'd been her shadow opponent. Her lovely features darkened.

"You killed my parents," she said.

"Duke's people did. As I previously communicated, I had no knowledge of the incident before the fact. Had I known, I would've prevented it. My mission is to *end* the violence. I am authorized to act on behalf of the United States. We wish to assist China to retrieve her lost treasures."

"And in return, you want . . . ?"

"Twenty-five million dollars."

"Payable to . . . ?"

"Me."

"So that's the way you are."

He nodded. "Just like you."

Ten minutes later, Richard hung a **Do Not Disturb** sign on the entrance door of a Beverly Wilshire hotel room. When he turned, Missy was already naked.

They'd bonded spectacularly. Now, their mutual future would soon be secure: lovers, best friends, accomplices. Total honesty, no secrets . . . well, just two.

Missy Soo didn't know he'd killed her parents.

Nor did she know that, in her absence, he'd cheated on her. And not only with Dolores. With Stella as well. It had been a strange interlude. No small talk, no flirting. He'd just reached beneath Stella's blouse and squeezed her breast, and she had closed her eyes and let him proceed. Kept them closed throughout the act. Shown no response but lain still, as if acquiescing to a rape. Richard thought she was acting out a fantasy. Crazy girl. Next time he'd screw the bejesus out of her, make her beg him for more. Stella was still hiding with Dolores. He'd enjoy a farewell fling with both of them—a threesome, *yes*—before joining Missy Soo for good—

The *Corregidor*'s foghorn moaned.

The loading was complete.

Almost time to hunt.

CHAPTER 38

At twilight, Duke and I walked along the bluff overlooking the Sound. He leaned heavily atop his blackthorn shillelagh. As we walked, he idly swiped the stick across a stunted pine that sprouted from the scree. The stick was blunt, but the speed with which he wielded it so fast that the sapling was severed. He stopped and turned toward me, one eyebrow raised in a silent question.

"Glad I'm not a tree," I said.

"Quick mouth, fast death."

He took the stick from beneath himself, raised it, as if to smite me. I shifted my weight so, if he swung, I could duck the stick instead of backing away and throw myself at his legs. In his day, he probably could've punted my ass through the Brooklyn Bridge's towers, but his day was long gone. In fact, Duke looked sicklier than ever. He was noticeably gaunter, and his elevens were up: the parallel tendons on the back of one's neck that, when protruding, are a harbinger of death.

"You and my granddaughter," he said. "Tell me why I shouldn't kill you."

I shrugged. "Welcome to the club. Lots of people want to kill me."

He lowered the stick. "Richard sure as hell does. He thinks you're no longer necessary to the op. Not to mention he plain doesn't like your face. The vain son of a bitch thinks Dolores has a thing for you."

Words that would have uplifted me some other time, but not now. "Why are you telling me this?"

"Because you need to know. You're *necessary*."

"After I'm not, you feed me to Richard?"

He smiled. "By then, Richard's dead."

"When is *then*?"

He took out the gun he'd threatened me with before, although this time he didn't point it at me. "If sidearms could speak, this one has a helluva story. It belonged to Generalissimo Chiang Kai-shek's personal executioner. A murderous bastard. I intend to add a notch to the gun by shooting Richard."

"Right. What's next on *my* agenda?"

He tapped his stick atop my shoulder. "I hereby dub you Sir Curious George. All right, I'll tell you this much: the clock is at L-Day minus six, and counting."

"*L* as in *Lucky*, I presume?"

"Stop asking and start listening. I've got a cadre of bad types. Ex-Legionnaires, former IRA hit men; in short, a small army of highly skilled killers. But all of them together aren't nearly enough to ward off both the Chinese and the Americans."

"The Americans?"

"Richard. When I was cooperating, he was my case agent. A thieving snake I paid a fortune to over the years. Made a lot of cases for him, too, enough for him to work his way to the position he holds now. Against him, no way we can stand our ground."

"Then what do we do?"

He smiled. "Go to sea."

"When?"

"Soon."

As I left, a jeep was parked nearby. It hadn't been there when I arrived. The rear door of the house was ajar, and as it closed, I glimpsed Dolores inside. Which led to two unpleasant thoughts:

One, for some reason Dolores was avoiding me.

Two, which side would she take, come L-Day?

CHAPTER 39

That night I came across the document from Duke's file I'd been about
to read when Uncle had summoned me. It was written seventy-five
years ago by the chief medical doctor of the British Royal Burmese
Constabulary and, although yellowed and fading, was clearly legible. It
was a typewritten description of a rare medical event that he'd learned
of in September 1942.

Very enlightening, although I didn't understand how it related to
the scenario. Still, Duke had thought it important enough to include in
his file, so I warehoused its content until its significance surfaced—if it
did—and hit the sack. My last waking thought was why Duke had let
me glom the file. We abhorred each other, and yet . . . I had the feeling
he was trying to help me . . .

My phone awoke me. I'd been dreaming of my pa, Louis.

But, as some dreams do, it quickly faded from mind.

I picked up the phone. "Who's this?"

"Derek Lau." His voice broke; he cleared his throat, said,
"Grandfather passed overnight."

"Sorry to hear that," I said. "My condolences."

"I've texted you my address. Please come to my place as soon as
possible. From there we'll go to the funeral home."

"Today? Isn't it customary to wait—"

"It has to be *now*. Please, hurry."

He hung up, leaving me wondering: what possible importance required Uncle's funeral service to be immediate?

I went to my garage to retrieve my new Jaguar, but it no longer was factory fresh. The tires had been slashed and the windshield shattered. There was a note beneath the wiper that said, *Have A Nice Day*, with an extra-large smiley face beneath it. Richard.

I cabbed to the address Derek had given me.

There'd been an accident on the Williamsburg Bridge, so from Houston Street south, the streets were a parking lot. I got out and started walking down the Bowery. In my long years of drug lawyering, I'd driven the Bowery a thousand times, always with my thoughts focused on my next stop. Only now, while walking, did I fully appreciate how the city was so rapidly changing. I'd still thought of the Bowery as flophouses for drunken bums. But that was then. Now there were no slums in Manhattan proper. The richest city in the world had transformed its Bowery to a plethora of new condos and renovated lofts and *très* cool shops and restaurants. It was as if I'd been wearing blinders for years and only now had removed them. Blinking, I looked around, thinking:

Oh, Benn. Where have you been?

But I already knew the answer:

To hell and back . . . and forth.

A far better question:

Where was I going?

Derek's address was a wide three-story building, formerly a plumbing-supply discount outlet, now with an upgraded face: freshly pointed bricks, new windows, and a sturdy steel door on which a stenciled sign said **Yellow Submarine**.

It seemed Derek had bootstrapped his way up in the world, but some things never change. Like a sense of irony. Obviously, the name Yellow Submarine was an homage to the old Green Dragon lair. That had been a damp cellar below a fish market on Pell Street the gang boys had dubbed the Green Palace. Now this multimillion-dollar structure was a Beatles song. Imagine that.

"Benn, my man," said a familiar voice.

I turned and saw a young black guy getting out of a stretch limo. I did a double take. *Him, here, now?* I'd known Billy Shkilla since the ethnicity of my mother's Brooklyn hood had morphed from white to black. After my ma died, young Billy helped keep an eye out for her old, lifelong friend, Bea, a childless widow who lived across the alley. After Bea died, Billy got into a serious jam. He was lead man of a rap group—the Shkillas—whose act featured brandishing guns and boasts of having used them. Never mind that the guns proved to be stage pieces, the local precinct dicks made Billy as the hitter in a gang killing. Another case opened by an ambitious prosecutor whose progress was measured by his body count.

Billy's jam coincided with my own tiff with the feds, the same that nearly led me to jail. Ultimately, over the long course of negotiation and giving up every hard-earned dirty penny I had, I'd managed to include in my agreement with the government that Billy's state case be tossed.

The initial response to my demand had been, "We're federal. We have neither the desire nor the ability to interfere in the New York State courts."

"Sure you do. Just make one goddamn call," I said.

The prosecutor had shaken his head. "I can't—"

"Do it," said the fed honcho. "Do it now."

The call was made. Arrangements were made. A ranking DOJ—Department of Justice—prosecutor would call his equal at the Brooklyn DA's office. A *request* concerning an unnamed investigation would be made. The Brooklyn DA, who aspired to be a federal prosecutor, would agree. The fed honcho who'd started the ball rolling was the indomitable, string-pulling Richard.

I hadn't seen Billy since. "What the eff you doing here at seven in the morning?" he asked.

"I was about to ask you the same thing."

He sighed. "Friend of mine was buried yesterday. Heroin. I drank the night away."

Heroin. I'd sworn to remove it from my world but had blundered into working with—for, whatever—one of the biggest players in that filthy game.

"You okay, man?" said Billy.

"Fine," I said.

The Yellow Submarine door opened, and Derek emerged, then stopped short. "Billy, what're you doing here?"

Billy grinned. He'd had a diamond implanted in his white teeth, and his grin sparkled in skin so black, it seemed blue in the hazy morning light. He said, "D, you my yellow bro, right?"

"Right," said Derek. "Like, separated at birth."

"Benn here? He's the lawyer who saved my ass. My white bro."

Derek cocked his head, reappraising me. Then he and Billy did some extended, secretive handshake.

"Later, Shkill," said Derek. "Benn and me got business to discuss."

"Go to it, my friends," said Billy and got into his limo.

Derek and I entered the Yellow Submarine, whose theme was neither psychedelic nor Asian. The interior was sleekly modern: exposed brick, wide-planked floors, leather and glass furniture. There was plenty of art, too, not absurdly splashed canvases or meaningless installations but tastefully classic landscapes, and what looked like a real Hopper of a woman framed in an opened window, her face half-shadowed. For a moment, she reminded me of Stella; then I realized she *was* Stella. Amazing how similar they were. Or maybe I just thought so.

"What is this place?"

"Sometimes I help Uncle out, or at least let him think I am. Truth is, since you got me off, I've been on the straight and narrow. I'm in the software biz. My boys have become expert, ah . . . techies."

"Hackers?"

He shrugged. "You might say so. But only for the big companies. That's where the money is. Follow me."

He led me up a curved stairway to a mezzanine partitioned behind shoji screens, antique originals probably worth a small fortune. Again, I thought Derek had come a long way since being Scar. It occurred to me that, had I bothered to look at him instead of just his case, I probably would've picked up on his hidden potential. Man, I could hardly wait to quit lawyering and start living in the real world.

We sat at a carved teak desk. He said, "Any news of Stella?"

I shook my head. "As they say, no news is good news."

He nodded. "Listen, about you and her, I bear no grudge. She's got issues, and when I disagree, she gets crazy. Tries to hurt me by hurting herself. You catching my drift?"

I nodded. Stella's anger always simmered. Just like Dolores's.

He lit a joint and passed it to me. One hit, and I was not only lightened but enlightened, having noted that his matchbook was from a bar in the town near Madame Soo's California estate. It seemed I wasn't the only one who'd been carrying cross-country messages. The difference being, I'd been there for Duke, and no doubt Derek had been there on behalf of Uncle.

He saw me looking and made a dismissive notion. "Yeah, I visited Madame Soo and Missy. I negotiated between them and Uncle."

"And Duke."

Derek evaded my comment, said, "We need to move fast."

"Explain."

"The other side is about to jump the gun as soon as they clean up here. By *cleaning*, I'm talking about you. When your buddy Richard gets high, he gets sloppy. Instead of his texts that self-delete in one minute, his delete in five minutes. More than enough time for my boys to snatch 'em."

He slid a paper across the desk. It was a transcript of a texted conversation.

The text read, *I'm waiting for him alongside the funeral home.*

The response was, *I'm across the street by the park.*

The response was, *Send the pet to the vet and get.*

Derek said, "That was Richard and this FBI lapdog, Ianucci, one hour ago. *Him* means *you.*"

Another twist in my road that opened to a new vista. *I had proof that Richard and Ianucci were conspiring to kidnap me. Maybe.* "How can I be certain this was them, talking about me?"

Derek smiled. "People think Chinatown's a ghetto of uninformed people who converse in harmless gibberish. It ain't. Like everywhere else, Chinatown's wired to everything. It was child's play for my boys to capture the fed phones. We've been listening to them for a while. Sometimes they call one another by their names. Arrogant assholes. We ran the old and latest conversations through an oscillograph. Richard and Ianucci? Their match is as good as fingerprints."

I took out my device.

Derek picked up on that and forwarded me the conversations. In turn, I forwarded them to Richard, along with a message: *YOU TALK TOO MUCH.*

"You want them knowing their nuts are in your hand?" said Derek.

"Yep. Now they won't dare touch me."

"I wouldn't be so sure. Maybe it only gives them more reason to snatch you. Or off you. I'd understand if you didn't want to go to the funeral."

"I'm going," I said. "They'll back off."

He smiled. "Want to get in their faces, huh?"

I nodded. Now that Richard knew I had him cold, he wouldn't dare touch me. Would he?

"The funeral," I said. "Why so quickly?"

"Because there's no time to waste."

"Why do you say that?"

"*It's* about to start."

"What's *it* mean?"

"The countdown."

"To what?"

"L-Day."

CHAPTER 40

Derek's ride was a Bentley driven by one of his boys. The morning rush hour hadn't begun, and we quickly entered Chinatown. Derek got a text. Concerned by it, he said, "Richard's moved to Worth Street, just across from the Wah Wing Sang funeral home on Mulberry. There's more feds watching from Columbus Park. Benn, maybe you should reconsider."

I already had and decided instead of entering, I'd first scope out the scene.

Even if they spotted me, I wasn't worried. Wah Wing Sang was a fixture on the corner of Mulberry Street, in a direct sight line to the federal courthouse on Worth Street, which was guarded by uniformed and plainclothes cops twenty-four seven. Even if Richard figured he could delete the texts, he wouldn't dare snatch me in plain view of law enforcement, not to mention the many mourners come to bid farewell to Uncle.

We were nearing the funeral home. Derek said, "You sure?"

"I intend to pay my respects to your grandfather."

"Your call. Get out at Bowery and Worth. Walk west on Worth. Just before the corner of Mulberry, there's an unmarked back door to the funeral home. It'll be open. Go in that way. At the same time, I'll distract Richard by going through the main entrance."

"Sounds like a plan."

A minute later, the Bentley pulled over, and I got out. I walked up Worth and—

Stopped short. Richard had moved and was now in the lee of an underground garage that allowed a direct view of the back door to Wah Wing Sang.

Fortunately, his attention was focused on Mulberry Street, where a flower-bedecked hearse and half a dozen Town Cars and a pair of NYPD cruisers were double-parked in front of Wah Wing Sang. Unfortunately, Richard's pocket was bulged with a gun's long outline . . . *too* long. A silencer, which meant . . .

Richard intended to kill me.

I understood his reasoning. Shots fired. The crowd panics. Cops all over looking for what, who? Richard, his badge hanging from his neck, calmly leaving the scene.

Just as I surmised, an unmarked car with a whip antenna was at the curb, a few steps from where Richard stood. Its engine was idling, and it had a wheelman. His getaway car.

Now that L-Day—whatever it was—was nearing, he no longer had any use for me. I knew too much about him . . . And then there was Stella. Duke had said Richard had his eye on her. Jesus, I couldn't leave her to his untender mercies—

Stop! First things first.

Number one on my non–hit parade was getting my ass elsewhere. I considered turning back toward the Bowery but realized Ianucci's men could be stationed there. Best to keep heading toward the side entrance and try to get inside without Richard seeing me. Providence came along in the form of an NYC Transit bus. It stopped at the light, blocking me from Richard, and I entered through the rear door.

It led to a dim corridor that smelled of formaldehyde. I went down the corridor and through another door that opened to the funerary services.

An urn sat on a pedestal that was the hub of a circle of shuffling mourners wearing white duncelike hats, chanting their respect for the deceased. Irreverent asshole that I am, I flashed on a KKK sing-along.

I put a hat on and joined them.

I'd been to Wah Wing Sang often but always kept my visits brief. I have a deep respect for Chinese culture, but their traditional funerals are too spooky for my taste. After a few shuffling circles, I wanted out of there—

"Right behind you," said Derek.

"All respect, I'd like to get out of here."

"You can't. Richard spotted you. They've got both exits blocked now. Maybe I could slip you into the hearse?"

"I've got a better idea." I explained what it was.

Derek grinned. "I like how you think."

I stepped from the circle, went back down the corridor, and called Val. I knew he had a morning customer he ferried to downtown Manhattan and hoped he was still in the area. He was.

I told him where to meet me.

Then I returned to the mourning circle and waited. The room grew crowded. Uncle had known a lot of people, and it seemed every fishmonger and banker in Chinatown had come to pay their respects. As the chanting grew louder, I checked my watch:

Twelve minutes had passed. *What was taking Derek so long?*

Then it happened: a series of explosions from outside. The mourners paused. Another ripple of explosions, and en masse they made for the door. I inserted myself into the thick of the crowd, and moments later emerged on Mulberry Street.

The NYPD cruiser doors were ajar, the cops inside them now flat-footing toward the federal courthouse, across from which a pall of smoke rose from the shrubbery lining Columbus Park. I caught a glimpse of two of Derek's boys, casually walking away from the scene, ignoring the SWAT team that emerged from the courthouse, heavy weapons drawn. Then I saw Richard with gun in hand—the silencer now removed—racing toward the explosions, no doubt fearing another 9-11-style attack in downtown Manhattan.

Only it wasn't.

I'd just orchestrated one of my all-time great irresponsible, not to mention illegal, acts. At my direction, Derek's boys had walked along the shrubs, casually dropping time-fused cherry bombs—there are *always* firecrackers available in Chinatown. True, there was always the possibility of an innocent pedestrian getting hurt, or dropping dead of a heart attack, but come to self-preservation, it's every man for himself.

I hurried back to the Bowery, took a final look at the chaos behind, then crossed the Bowery and walked north on East Broadway, where sidewalks crowded with people jabbering about what had occurred.

Five minutes later, I spotted Val's Rover parked beneath the Williamsburg Bridge overpass. I got in and told him to drive uptown fast. We made it as far as Delancey Street, where more NYPD cruisers blocked the roadway, a rapid response unit making sure suspects weren't fleeing the scene of the explosions.

"Make a U," I said.

Val didn't ask why. Without hesitation he jammed the brakes and turned the wheel, and we skidded full circle and headed back downtown—

Ahead, an ESU team blocked the street.

Devil or deep-blue-jumpsuit time.

Neither. I said, "Stop here."

I got out and started walking, skirting the main streets, staying on the tenement blocks where Chinatown blended into the Lower East Side. My objective was the Delancey Street subway entrance, but then I spotted Ianucci standing there.

I needed another way out of Dodge.

I walked vaguely north and east toward Union Square and its super-size subway terminus. I was nearly there, but when I glanced around to make sure the coast was clear, I spotted Ianucci a block behind, fast-walking after me.

Son of a bitch was crazy glue.

I ducked into a Best Buy and beelined down aisles lined with laptops, slipped into a men's room, went into a stall, and locked its door, then crouched atop a seat.

None too soon.

A moment later, the entrance door slammed open. I sensed a man there, heard him breathing heavily. Then the door closed, and it was quiet. I waited five minutes before cautiously venturing back into the store.

No Ianucci.

I headed down an aisle lined with game consoles, turned into another offering TVs, and exited the store via an exit to Fifteenth Street—

Ianucci and another agent were at the corner, looking around.

I crossed Park Avenue South, entering Union Square Park.

"Stop," a voice cried from behind.

I entered the big old Barnes & Noble, one of the few bookshops that hadn't succumbed to the online-reading onslaught. I navigated the aisles, plucked a book from the shelves, and hunkered in a corner. Out of the corner of my eye, I saw Ianucci and buried my face in the book.

I turned pages for ten minutes—primer or not, there were things I didn't know, not that I cared to—then checked around again. Ianucci was gone, at least for now. I called Val and told him where I was. Five minutes later, I was in his Rover.

It wasn't until we were uptown that I felt home free.

Trouble was, where to? Richard knew where I lived—the defaced Jag proof of that—so my apartment was a no-go.

"Not to worry," said Val. "I know a safe place."

CHAPTER 41

Val took side streets into the financial district, then exited at the Battery and entered the tunnel to Brooklyn. The tunnel had two lanes, and when it doglegged, I could see the traffic behind us. Not an unmarked in sight. I finally relaxed.

Not Val, though.

His usual taciturn but easygoing demeanor was replaced by an exaggerated hyperawareness. He kept glancing in the rearview and reaching beneath his seat, as if reassuring himself that something was there. When we exited the tunnel, he turned in to Red Hook, where we rumbled over the old cobblestones, occasionally squaring a block to ensure that we weren't being followed.

"It's okay," I said. "They're gone."

"*Them,*" Val growled. "They're *never* gone."

We left Red Hook. Still keeping to side streets, we drove through neighborhoods—Sunset Park, Park Slope, Carroll Gardens, and the rest of brownstone Brooklyn—before entering Greenpoint. The old Polish neighborhood was unchanged from last I'd been there: old men playing cards on stoops, women wearing babushkas. A smoked fish grocery that sold Bison Grass vodka. I was a particular drinking man then. Eventually, I discovered a liquor shop on Columbus Avenue that stocked and *delivered* the vodka, minimum one case at a time. I'm still a drinking man—although, come to think of it, I hadn't touched a drop since the day of the meeting with Uncle. Hadn't the craving. Maybe because my guardian angel was whispering to me to stay sober and be cool because I was nearing the beginning of something big.

Yes, it was. Maybe the beginning of the end of something, or maybe the end of its beginning. The space between whichever was purely *action*. Aka Bluestone's addiction. I felt good because I knew what was coming up would be *bad*.

Val turned into a side street lined with well-kept bungalows, then pulled to the curb just short of a commercial avenue. He turned the ignition off. Started to light a Gauloises, then paused.

"Okay if I smoke, Mr. Benn?"

"Give me one. Where're we going?"

"I already say where. To safe place."

I'd never seen Val wear a hat, but now he took a wool cap from his glove compartment and pulled it low over his ears. I'd never seen him wearing glasses, either, but now he put on a pair of shades.

"Wait here," he said and got out. He pointed a remote, and the Rover's locks snapped shut. I sat there waiting and smoking his killer tobacco, feeling its toxicity metastasizing in my body. I could smell myself—an odor like that in a Port Authority Bus Terminal restroom—and liked the smell. I was thinking Val *really* seemed different. He was angry as hell and wasn't going to take it anymore, but he didn't want to yell it out a window; no, he wanted to *kill*.

Trust me, I know this. I've seen men in that state before and witnessed the things they do. Another memory I wanted to erase; another reason for me to get out of the game. Not just criminal law. Law. I'd gone from being an extraditionist to being a trustee, and in the end, it was the same. Slimy characters and side-street deals. No. I wanted *out*. I was done with people's problems. I—

The rear door of the Rover opened. Val. I hadn't seen him approaching because he came from behind, having gone around the block. He carried a shopping bag he deposited on the front seat. A bottle of Bison Grass vodka protruded from the bag, and I remembered it was Val who'd first turned me on to the green magic. I smelled smoked fish and fresh bread.

"For enjoy later," he said with a gap-toothed smile that made me realize that, despite the ever-present twinkle in his eye, I'd never seen him grin. He was enjoying the action. "For now we keep on waiting."

"For what?"

"Ah, Mr. Benn, a man who lives like you do, I am surprised sometimes you don't understand the, how you say, *basics*? These men who hunt you, they are professionals. You think this is the first time they follow you?"

"They've been on and off my ass for days."

"Exactly. They see my license and look up my registration, presto, they know the address my car is registered."

"Your home?"

Val grinned again. "I am not a stupid man. I learned early never trust authority. I grew up where there were many men like the ones following you. Nazis. I know their ways. When Sonia and me come to this country, she thanks God we free. I thank God, too, but I know here, too, are plenty men like those we run away from. So I take precautions. My mail goes to post-office box. My apartment is under another name. My automobile is registered to brother-in-law who lives above grocery."

"They—the men—they're there now?"

"Two of them. By the door, next to the mailboxes. The one who looks like he needs to shave and one who looks like a Hitler Youth."

"What are we staying here for?"

"Soon it is dark. Stores close, people go home, streets are empty. Then I gonna talk to these men."

"*You?* Val, stay out of this."

"Trust me, Benn."

That was the first time Val called me by just my first name. For some reason, he now radiated determination. Besides, he was right. I had to trust *someone*, and no way would Val hurt me.

We ate and drank a little vodka and smoked a lot of cigarettes. I got a nice buzz on, though my mouth tasted like cat shit. When it was full dark, Val put his cap and glasses back on, this time adding a pair of thin surgical gloves. He reached beneath his seat and took out something I couldn't see. Then he handed me a cap and glasses and gloves and told me to put them on.

"What the hell for?"

"Time now. Come."

We got out, and I followed him around the corner. The shops were closed, the streets empty. When we reached the door to the stairs leading to the apartment above the grocery, he quietly gripped the knob, then paused and looked at me.

"Stay," he said, and yanked the door open.

It slammed against the wall with a crash that startled Ianucci and the young fed. Before they could react, Val was beating them with a tire iron. I supposed it was the item he'd been feeling for beneath his seat, but I hadn't realized his intentions.

Holy crap!

Ianucci's fed took a blow to the ear and dropped. Then Val worked Ianucci, who went to his knees, blood spurting.

"Jesus, don't," I said, trying to pull Val off.

He shrugged loose from me and hit Ianucci some more, grunting with the effort, repeating a phrase I didn't understand:

"*Zoll zelmer shyner menschen . . . zoll zelmer shyner menschen . . .*"

Spittle flew from Val's mouth, his normally pallid face bright red. Finally, when they both lay still, he stopped. Val was breathing heavily, whether from exertion or emotion I wasn't sure. I grabbed his arm, and we left the vestibule.

The street was empty. The whole episode had taken less than a minute. We went back to the Rover and drove off.

My heart was pounding. No matter their bad characters, the beaten men were feds. If we were busted, at best we'd both die in federal prison.

"Val, they were *federal*—"

"Federal, schmederal," he said bitterly. "They were bad men no different from Nazis. My family were Jews who fought back. All my life since I was a boy in Berlin, I wanted to be the hunter, never again the hunted. *Never again.*"

"*Zoll zelner shyner menschen.* What's that mean?"

For a long moment he didn't reply. Then, in a quavering voice, he said, "It's Yiddish. It means . . . *they* were good people."

I didn't ask who *they* were, knowing Val meant family and friends lost in the Holocaust. His postwar life in a nearly *Judenfrei* Germany must have been a living hell.

Insanely, I, too, had no regrets. I'd spent my professional life being careful not to cross the line, but now I'd deliberately stepped on and over it. It was almost a relief. I'd turned a corner in my life. I'd broken the law but had administered justice, for I agreed with Val that dirty cops were no different from SS storm troopers. Ianucci was a Nazi, and I was a Jew.

And now I'd joined the Resistance.

As we cruised over the Pulaski Bridge, he stuffed the tire iron and glasses and gloves and caps and gloves into a paper bag. He lowered his window, edged the Rover closer to the bridge wall, then hurled the bag into the black waters of the Gowanus Canal below.

He nodded grimly. "End of problem."

As we crested the bridge, the Manhattan skyline appeared: a fantastical jumble of towers, diamond-bright in the night. Saddened me. Would it ever be safe for me to return to New York? Probably not.

Crazy.

For Chrissake, I was a lawyer. Not a Waco fanatic or white-trash Aryan. Yet I'd participated in an act that only crazies like them aspire to. Then again, I was no longer a lawyer.

To borrow a phrase from Val:

Never again.

CHAPTER 42

Val lived in a walk-up in Bushwick. The exterior of the building was sooty and graffiti-scarred, but Val's railroad flat was freshly painted and spotless. It was dimly lit by a single night light.

Val put a finger to his lips, whispered, "Sonia sleeping. She get up early for work."

Something brushed my leg, and I jumped.

"Arthur," Val said happily, picking up a white cat that purred in his arms. "Arthur gonna guard us, yes, Arthur?"

Arthur purred again.

Val led me to a small bedroom mostly taken up by a neatly made bed. "Sleep now. Gonna need rest before."

"Before what?"

"It starts."

Before it starts . . . Derek's words when we parted. But how did Val know I was about to embark on . . . *it*? Had my so-called allies reached out to Val?

Val picked up on my thoughts. "I only know you must leave because you are in danger. Miss Dolores tell me, but I ignorant of details."

I'd seen Dolores briefly at Duke's estate. Now she'd been here and talked with Val as well?

Why was she avoiding me?

"Miss Dolores, she remind me of the good German lady who hid my parents. I think maybe we need another vodka. For sleep, yes?"

"Yes."

We had more than one vodka. Between the pale-green booze and my adrenaline come-down, I was beat. I staggered to my little bed. The glowing minute hand on my watch touched twelve, then ticked to 12:01 a.m.

L-Day minus four.

That night I dreamed. I saw myself back-to-back with Val and Derek, a gladiator triad bracing against a host of aggressors . . . gray-uniformed *Sturmführers,* led by *Oberleutnant* Richard. The three of us—no, the *seven* of us, for Dolores and her Logui brothers and Duke had magically appeared, standing against the advancing forces of the Third *and* Fourth Reichs.

CHAPTER 43

I was deep asleep when something disturbed me. Not a sound, a movement. As I came awake, a hand muffled my mouth, lips moved against my ear. A woman shushed me.

Dolores?

A red-capped flashlight dimly illuminated the room. In its cherry glow, I saw Dolores crouched alongside me. From combat boots to watch cap to cargo-pocketed bodysuit, she wore all black.

"Don't speak," she whispered. "Get up. Pass by the window on your way to the bathroom. Stay in there a minute, then pass the window again, and lie back down."

Was Dolores only being super careful? Or, despite Val's precautions, had Richard found us? A midnight shuffle to piss would explain the small sounds we were making . . . if indeed Richard's vigilantes were listening via window-vibration sensitive receiving devices.

I carried out Dolores's tradecraft as instructed.

When I returned to bed, she was already in it. Naked. She reached across me—her small, perfect breasts pressing against my body—and turned the clock radio on. She fiddled a moment until she found Coltrane, set the volume on low.

She said, "At dawn, we're leaving."

"Now? It's still L-Day minus—"

"That's Richard's lingo. Forget Richard, Benn. It's *you* I want."

I, a veteran of a thousand one-night stands, was too stunned, too conflicted to react. She'd been Sara, my old friend and client's little girl . . . I was old enough to be her father . . . she'd been *Sombra*, a murderous narcotrafficker . . . and Laura Astorquiza, the phony antidrug activist who'd deceived me . . . now she'd morphed into Dolores, horny and hellbound and inviting me along for her ride—

She fitted her mouth to mine.

Her lips were soft and sweet.

I, ah, rose to the occasion.

While Coltrane's sax crooned "My Favorite Thing," I lost myself dancing with Dolores doing the leading . . . until "Blue Train," after which I led our coupling.

Spent, we lay entwined, silent until daylight seeped through the shade seams.

Dolores turned so we were face-to-face. As a child, she'd had the enormous dark eyes of a kid in a Keane painting; yet somehow they'd never revealed her thoughts. Her gaze, then and now, reflected only those things she chose to see.

Now, in her eyes, I saw myself.

Abruptly, the image was gone, her gray eyes again opaque, as if her thoughts had transported her elsewhere.

"Richard." She whispered the name disparagingly. "He now thinks of me as he does you: disposable, since he got his merit badges for my destroying the cartels."

I won't let him hurt you, I thought. *Or me. Us.*

I left the bed, flattened against the wall, inched the shade away, looked at the street. The streetlamps were still on. Beneath one a dark sedan was parked. Its steamed-over windows were cut by the shadowed arc of a hood-to-tail antenna.

"Hard to believe," I said. "I knew the feds broke rules, but . . . *assassinations?*"

"A few, but Richard's too smart to trust the suits with doing wet work. He's using his own people now. Men blooded in Eastern Europe and Africa. We can deal with such scum. It's the others that concern me."

"Others? You mean Missy and the Chinese Reds?"

"Them. No matter. Together, we're unstoppable."

I sat on the bed and gripped her arms. *"Together?"*

"For the long run, Mr. Bluestone. Think of me as your personal Plan Colombia."

I laughed. "Plan Colombia" had been the highly publicized joint effort by the United States and Colombia to eliminate the cartels. It began in the '90s, when Colombia legalized major miscreants extraditable to the States. Didn't matter. Despite the billions spent breaking cartels, they'd quickly reconstituted. The only real benefactors of Plan Colombia had been those who lived off its largesse: the employees and collaborators of the American criminal justice system, the Colombian politicos and generals who diverted funds their way, and of course, lawyers like myself. Plan Colombia would have been a joke were it not a tragic failure that to this day leaked blood and money.

But maybe Plan Colombia wasn't the proper analogy; from its inception, it had been rife with secrets and betrayals. But Dolores and I *truly* were on the same side . . . weren't we?

In her gaze, again I saw my own reflection.

"Together," I said, and kissed her.

CHAPTER 44

The clock alarm went off at 5:30 a.m. The tiny bathroom was neat as a pin. Sonia had set out two new toothbrushes. Hmm. Not only did Val know I was into something fraught with peril, but he had also known Dolores was coming. It didn't bother me. Val's instincts for people were unerring, and he'd chosen to trust Dolores.

Dolores bathed first. She came out finger-combing her wet hair and zipped into her black bodysuit. I had an urge to unzip her but remedied it with a cold shower. Business before pleasure. When I came out of the bathroom, Dolores and Sonia were seated on the edge of the bed, drinking coffee.

I was surprised. "Sonia? You're with them, too?"

"Who is them? I'm with *you*, Mr. Benn."

"Ditch the paranoia," said Dolores.

The bedroom door was open. I could smell Val's Gauloises and hear a TV newscast about an incident that had left one FBI agent dead and another grievously wounded in a vestibule in Greenpoint.

I hit the bathroom. In the mirror, my face looked the same as always. Why shouldn't it? Nothing special had happened. I'd conspired to kill men. Again. I had no choice. I had no choice. And I *wanted* them dead. I had nothing else to say.

I joined Val. He lit a fresh butt from the stub he'd smoked down.

The world news came on next: stock footage of atolls in a tropical sea, a voice-over: "In the South China Sea, a Chinese frigate passed within yards of an Australian patrol boat, which that country's government has called a provocation. Both nations have lodged formal protests and warned of armed responses. The Secretary of State has just reaffirmed that an attack on Australia will be considered an attack on the United States. Pundits have noted that this is the first confrontation between nuclear powers since the Cuban Missile Crisis."

"Oy vey," said Sonia.

Two Logui appeared from the fire escape: the ones Dolores called Older and Younger Brother. They too wore black outfits, their cargo pockets stuffed with banana clips. They set down two duffel bags, then left me alone with Dolores.

From the one duffel, Dolores took a black bodysuit and tossed it to me. I took off my boxers—*Jesus, I'd been wearing nothing but rumpled, stained underpants while talking to Val's wife.* Dolores tossed me pairs of heavy socks and lightweight combat boots. I laced them up. Also in the duffel was a Dopp kit . . . and two hard plastic cases whose shape betrayed their contents: a long gun and a handgun.

I stared at them. The killing wasn't over. It had just begun.

The newscaster's voice jarred me back to the present:

"This just in: North Korea has warned of a preemptive strike if US warships interfere—"

Dolores shut off the TV. "Let's go, Benn."

A window was open to a fire escape, the blank wall of the adjoining building beyond. Dolores tweeted softly, like a night bird seeking a mate, and Older Brother again appeared in the window.

Following Dolores's lead, I handed him my duffel. Sonia kissed my cheek. Val kissed the other cheek. Older Brother disappeared down the fire escape, and Dolores and I followed. He scrambled down and stood below, waiting for us. He wore faded work jeans, a corduroy jacket with a fake fleece collar, and shitkickers with run-down heels. If I didn't know otherwise, I'd have made him for a Mexican laborer seeking day work.

He wasn't a laborer but had been working. I knew there were probably cameras in the surrounding backyards, then realized he'd somehow scrambled up sheer walls and covered their lenses with duct tape. He'd also cut a flap in the chain-link fence enclosing the yard. We went through the flap into an alley lined with garbage cans, then stopped when Older Brother held up a palm just short of the street around the corner from Val's place.

There, another dark sedan idled at the curb.

Dolores spoke quietly. "The next shift. In another minute, the guys in front of Val's apartment will leave. These guys will take their place."

"Li'l Abner's Freaking Fearless Fosdicks," I said.

She stifled a giggle. "So many years, and you still make me laugh."

I wasn't trying to be funny. God help me, I was *amped*.

The sedan's headlamps came on. It pulled from the curb, drove to the far corner, turned from view. Immediately, from the opposite side of the street, an old Nissan appeared. It pulled over, and the three of us got in and it pulled away. We turned at the corner and went in the opposite direction of the watchers. The driver was Younger Brother.

He and Dolores conversed in Anchiga, their soft, avian-sounding language.

We drove crosstown west before turning south. Instead of taking the West Side Highway downtown, we stayed on its parallel side streets. Younger Brother had the same street smarts as Val. If somehow the watchers had learned we'd fled, they'd put out an alert on the major byways, which, knowing Richard's resources, would be heavily enforced. Short of the Battery, we turned east, looped the tip of Manhattan, and emerged parallel to FDR Drive, heading north, uptown—

At the last moment, Younger Brother swerved onto the Brooklyn Bridge ramp. He kept at a steady 45 mph, so as not to chance a random traffic stop. Still nothing suspicious behind us, but the tension in the car remained palpable. We exited the bridge, drove side streets to the LIE southbound, drove around the wide bulge of west and south Brooklyn—the Heights, Cobble Hill, Carroll Gardens, Gowanus, Bay Ridge—slowed in Fort Hamilton, and from there swooped onto the Verrazano-Narrows Bridge that crossed to Staten Island.

Across the wide sweep of Upper New York Bay, Manhattan's downtown towers glittered in the morning light, but to my eyes, they'd never be the same. Not since 9-11, when the Apple's two front teeth had been so foully knocked out. The world in general and mine in particular had changed since then. Gotten far more dangerous and much too dumbed down . . .

I wondered if ever I'd see New York again.

Was I leaving someone dear behind? Nope.

Was I leaving a career behind? Nope.

I had nothing left to lose. I was free.

Once in Staten Island, it was the same routine: avoiding the major thoroughfares, staying on sleepy side streets. After a quarter hour, Older Brother, who was riding shotgun, whistled. A word or a signal? Whichever, Younger Brother pulled to the curb. We were in a deserted zone of empty buildings, an industrial park devastated by Hurricane Sandy and never rebuilt. Already, it was being consumed by marsh grass.

Younger Brother got out carrying a long plastic case like the one Dolores had put in my duffel. He disappeared in the tall grass. Older Brother resumed driving.

"Stay aware," said Dolores.

It's begun, I thought.

We turned onto another empty street. Suddenly Older Brother stood on the brakes, simultaneously turning the wheel. As we skidded sideways and turned around, headlights came on at the far end of the street.

Searchers.

I hadn't the slightest idea how Older Brother sensed their presence, or how they'd found us. Then something flickered above.

They had a drone.

CHAPTER 45

We burned rubber back the way we came. The searchers were gaining ground. One leaned from the shotgun window. He held something—

A moment before it flashed, I yanked Dolores down—

Our rear window shattered; glass pebbles hailed.

Dolores spoke in Anchiga, her voice calm, as if neither surprised nor concerned. The damn woman never failed to lift my spirit. Given her manner, I figured this was her preplanned move.

Older Brother pulled over near where we had left Younger Brother, who was nowhere in sight. I was astonished. We're *surrendering*? But then Dolores winked at me.

I'd figured right: the woman who'd risen from obscure poverty to the throne of the mighty *Sombra* wasn't about to be undone by a small-time shooter on a desolate roadside.

The searchers pulled over twenty yards behind us. They had a loud-speaker that boomed:

"Everyone out! Hands up high—"

Two shots rang out. The searcher's windshield shattered. Where it had been, two men slumped.

Younger Brother reappeared, long gun in hand. He went to the searcher's vehicle, fired a head shot to both men, then climbed back into our car cool as the underside of a pillow. Older Brother drove off.

"What about the drone?" I asked.

"Relax, little boy," said Dolores.

"You're not my mother."

"But you're my baby."

Comfort amid chaos. True that I needn't have worried about the drone, for another few blocks ahead was a Yellow Cab garage. We drove beneath its entrance canopy, out of view of the drone camera. The driver shifts were changing. We got out of our car and got into a cab whose driver was about to start his long day's work. His Taxi & Limousine license was inserted in the plexiglass dividing the front from the rear seats. It was upside-down on purpose, the better to deter customer complaints. I cocked my head and made out his name—Mohammed Chaudrey—an NYC generic cabbie moniker if there ever were one.

He blinked as Dolores handed him five Franklins.

"That's for starters," she said. "Now *go!*"

And off we went, just another anonymous cab among dozens streaming from the garage, indistinguishable to the drones—there were multiple drones now—buzzing aimlessly behind, like mosquitoes searching for prey.

We went down a lightly trafficked highway.

Dolores, ever possessed of the ability to control her emotions, relaxed. Leaning her head against my shoulder, she closed her eyes. Me, I was anything but relaxed. I knew Richard would manipulate the facts so the dead men became federal employees whose killing during the commission of a crime was punishable by death. Not that it mattered, for Ianucci was enough for them to fry me.

But then Dolores's hand squeezed mine.

And just like that, my fears vanished.

We drove through a neighborhood of small frame homes in need of paint and whose patches of lawn needed trimming. One home appeared abandoned. In another's dirty window was a fading MAKE AMERICA GREAT AGAIN sign.

The cab wasn't old, but the city's potholes had taken their toll, and the ride was not smooth, although Chaudrey was doing a good job avoiding the big axle-breakers. Younger Brother hand-signaled directions.

He pointed at a darkened house.

Chaudrey pulled over in front of it. We got out. Dolores leaned into the driver's window and spoke to Chaudrey:

"You aren't going to record the trip, because why split five hundred bucks with the boss, right?"

"Right."

"Say goodbye," said Dolores.

"Goodbye," said Chaudrey.

Still again, I marveled at Dolores's machinations. She'd set up a win-win situation. If Richard's searchers found the cabbie—and they would—no doubt he'd immediately vomit everything up. Including us being in a place we weren't any longer.

When the cab was gone from view, Older Brother whistled. A moment later, headlights came on in a parked Honda. It started up and drove to us. The driver was another Logui who could have been the brothers' cousin. He drove us onto a main drag. The Honda was a small SUV. Not new, not old. Needed a wash. Younger Brother up front with the driver. Older Brother behind the driver, Dolores in the middle, me behind Younger Brother.

Again, Dolores rested her head on my shoulder. I took that as a sign that all augured well for the immediate future. Yes, a *fact*, for I was now convinced—that whether by witch- or tradecraft—Dolores possessed a third eye. Uncanny.

Or maybe not uncanny, considering she'd grown up in constant threat of attack. Yet this woman of steel was sleeping on my shoulder like a kitten. I admit to having narcissistic tendencies, but it was difficult to accept I was the man she'd loved since she was a girl.

The punch line was not that I wanted to believe her . . . but that I did.

We drove to the west end of Staten Island. Not exactly God's little acres. Old warehouses, rotting piers. We crossed the Bayonne Bridge over the oil-sheened Kill Van Kull. Wended through industrial Jersey, then got on I-95 headed north. Here and there on the roadside were still patches of swamp grass that had survived the great pave-over creating parking lots and malls. We passed the Meadowlands Racetrack and MetLife Stadium, both in their own ways temples of mass dementia.

Traffic our way was light; the city-bound lanes crawled. We exited I-95 at Washington Avenue and drove north.

It began raining as we passed a sign: WELCOME TO TETERBORO AIRPORT. No one asked to check our creds, and we drove directly onto the tarmac, stopping at the boarding steps of a gleaming Gulfstream. Much as I was impressed by Richard's seemingly endless capabilities, I was starting to think he didn't have much on Dolores. I mean, *No airport security?*

Again, Dolores read my mind. "Three things about business my father told me. Both money and power are the keys to success. The third thing is the most important. Money *always* trumps power. I have a lot of money, Benn."

None of this was a news flash. Dolores was loaded, and everything and everyone had a price tag. Complication being, that for better or for worse, she'd bought me.

We and the Logui boarded the Gulfstream and buckled up. Quickly, we were cleared for takeoff. Scarce minutes later, we pierced the morning awakening murk into the new day's flawless blue sky. The sudden change felt as if I my life were starting over.

Dolores and I had a private rear compartment. We sat side by side.

After a while she said, "I went along with Richard to protect the Logui homeland from the Chinese. If I didn't cooperate, it was only a matter of time until I was captured, and without me, the Logui . . .

well . . . In dealing with Richard, I learned about his Chinese mission, which provided a way for us to save my people."

"*Us?*"

She took my face between her hands. "I slept with Richard. Maybe that makes me a whore. But the currency passed both ways. Richard and I used each other."

I opened my mouth to speak, but she put her finger to my lips.

"He meant nothing to me. You did it with Stella, didn't you?"

I nodded. "Yes, but that was before we—"

"Richard was infatuated with me. Maybe because he knew I was as ruthless as he was. Doesn't matter. What did matter was that he got careless with secrets. Or perhaps it was intentional, his way of boasting. Doesn't matter, either. What does matter is that through Richard, I learned enough to gain a foothold in the game."

"Whatever that means."

"It means I've never stopped loving you. It's not a girlish infatuation, because I'm no longer ten years old. So store that fact in your hard drive and listen."

"I'm all big ears. Runs in my family. My pa had ears like an elephant."

"*Listen,* you jerk. Richard's been a traitor to your government since he met Missy Soo. He intends to give her Lucky and receive a fortune from China in return."

"One part I still don't get: Why is an old monk so important?"

"At this moment, that old monk is the key to keeping peace on earth. There's so much more to it, but best you digest things as they come."

"Sure. *If* I choose to believe you." Words of regret even as I spoke them; I had already chosen to believe her, yet a smidgeon of false pride had twisted my tongue.

To my remorse, she winced as if bee-stung and looked away.

For now, our conversation was over.

CHAPTER 46

It was late afternoon when we set down in a city whose modern skyline I recognized: Cartagena, Colombia. I'd had some wild times in the new city's nightlife, as well as in the adjoining old city's maze of dark streets.

Dolores continued avoiding my eyes. She was looking out, too. She had her memories as well. Was she now regretting having slept with me? Letting me know it wasn't going to happen again?

Again, no customs or immigration before we boarded an almost noiseless unmarked copter that immediately rose, tilted, then zipped east, flying low above the Guajira Peninsula's white-sand beaches and dark, jungle interior. I estimated about another hour before we turned toward what I assumed would be Anawanda—

The copter slowed, hovered, landed on the beach.

The pilot—another Logui—spoke in Anchiga.

Dolores translated. "The Chinese have air cover up now and have installed their top-of-the-line radar. Actually, their top-of-the-line is what they copied from you Americans ten years ago. They'd shit if they knew the stuff your country has now."

"I'm not '*you* Americans' anymore."

"Wrong," she snapped, "gringo."

"Very observant, muchacha."

"Eff you, Benn."

"Love to."

For a moment, I thought she was about to laugh. Instead, she turned away. "Let's get going. I want to make the village by nightfall."

The hike up the foothills was a more difficult route than the one that had led from the now-Chinese-occupied beach. It was a long, hard trip. Dolores and the Logui walked fast, and keeping up with them was exhausting, but I didn't want to find myself alone at night. Besides, I liked hiking behind Dolores's butt, the way it flexed as she moved. A few times we paused for canteen water. Ate energy bars while still walking. Blistered feet, insect bites, scratched faces.

We reached the Logui village at dusk.

Things had changed again. Defense positions were now entrenched in sandbagged bunkers. The population went about their tasks silently, with purpose. A man was videotaping three bullet-riddled bodies. I realized they were Chinese soldiers—

Dolores spoke, and I turned.

A kerchief covered most of Dolores's face. She was talking to the man's camera. The videographer was about my age: trimmed beard, silvering at the temples, a distinguished bearing. For a moment I was startled, for he strongly resembled Dolores's—Sara's—father, Nacho Barrera. But then I thought, *Nah, impossible.*

"Good seeing you, my old friend," he said and winked.

It was his voice that awoke the memory and his beard that had thrown me. I knew this man as "PF"—Benn-speak for *Permanent Fugitive.* For ten years or more, he'd been my client, a Colombian on the lam from an American extradition warrant. A soul stuck in limbo. His case was a no-win trafficking beef with a mandatory thirty-to-life sentence in the Southern District of Florida. His only out was to cooperate, but the government wanted him to point at heavyweights who were keeping PF's wife and kids sequestered as a hedge against his ratting. He was well known in Colombia, which fairly crawled with informants who'd give him up for a few pesos; consequently, he'd spent the last decade hiding out in the Central American boonies. PF was an erudite, educated man who loved reading and music, neither of which were available in his moveable abodes. For years he'd been waiting, hoping the witnesses against him—his codefendants, themselves doing long sentences—would die or be deported, and the case against him would fall apart. Once every year or so, he'd satisfy his need for contact with civilization by paying me to go meet him. We'd dine and drink wine from sunset to sunrise in a Honduran shithole named San Pedro Sula, whose sole distinction was being the world's murder capital. Our last meet had been in Caracas. I remembered it well.

"My name is Javier," he said. In his indictment, the feds had listed him as FNU LNU—First Name Unknown, Last Name Unknown.

"Bennjamin T. Bluestone," I said formally.

Then we laughed and embraced, kissed cheeks Latin-style, shook each other's shoulders. In retrospect, despite the scary trips to see him, I'd enjoyed our meetings immensely as well. In the birdcage of my life, Javier was a rara avis: a friend. Not that I trusted him.

"Didn't recognize me because of the beard?"

That's when I realized it: Javier was the brother of Nacho I'd never met. Nacho had always worn a beard. Javier's made the resemblance striking.

"Jesus, you're practically his twin."

Dolores hugged him. "My Uncle Javi." She went on cold-shouldering me, telling Javier, "Let's get to it."

Javier pointed his camera at her, and she raised a microphone to her mouth. Her expression projected gravitas, her voice thrummed with fervor, and I thought:

La Pasionara, yes.

She said, "Although Colombian authorities will not *publicly* comment, informed sources have confirmed these men were *Chinese* soldiers killed by *Colombian* Special Forces, following the *Chinese* kidnapping of an *American* tourist."

Colombian Special Forces? Chinese kidnapping a tourist? Stella?

Dolores said, "The Chinese claim the tourist was trespassing on their property. *Their?* The Sierra Nevada de Santa Marta are and always will be part of the *Colombian* homeland. The Chinese, offered an opportunity to surrender, chose to fight. *Our* forces shot them dead . . ."

Dolores pointed at the bodies; Javier moved his camera to tape the corpses, this time zooming in on the bullet wounds.

"This is Laura Astorquiza, *Radio Free Bogotá*, in the Sierra Nevada de Santa Marta. *Viva, Colombia.*"

She made a cutting motion, and Javier stopped taping.

"Release it to the usual media," she said, then motioned for him to start taping her again. "Wait an hour, then release this."

When Javier resumed taping, she said, "The identity of the American tourist has just been confirmed. She is a botany student named Stella Maris."

My heart stopped. The thought of Stella in captivity was sickening.

"This is Laura Astorquiza. Good night, and God bless Colombia."

She made another cutting motion, and Javier ceased taping. Dolores motioned for us to walk with her. As we passed the corpses, I saw their wounds were the standard 5.62mm rounds of automatic rifles: small, puckered entrance holes, gaping, meaty exit wounds.

But something caught my eye. Only momentarily, but long enough for me to note that each entry hole was rimmed by four symmetrical cuts in the surrounding flesh. I'd seen the Logui arrows: hand-hewn shafts of local wood, steel-tipped blades with steel vanes rather than feathers. The vanes were razor-thin and sharp, and I'd bet my fee they perfectly fit the cut marks around the entry holes . . . as if the killing wounds were made by bow-launched fléchettes; then, after being removed, obscured by bullets fired into the wounds.

Bullets, according to Dolores, fired by a Colombian Special Forces unit. Maybe it was true. Equally possible, Dolores's claim was one the

CSF unit would hesitate to deny; doing so would indicate they were unable or unwilling to confront the traffickers. Turned out, I was right.

"How the hell did you bring in Special Forces?" Javier asked Dolores.

She shrugged. "I didn't. But the Colombian populace will approve of their soldiers fighting back. No way will the government deny it."

The three of us gathered in the stone hut. Cool there. She sat close to Javier, across from me. She said, "How was it being me, Benn?"

I said, "Sorry, am I missing something?"

"Missy Soo doesn't believe you're just a messenger. She thinks you're the decision maker. She thinks you're me. *Sombra.*"

"So she told me. Which makes me a disposable cutout."

"Yes, it does. Missy's very beautiful, isn't she?"

"There was a deal. Why'd she grab Stella?"

"Why don't you ask Stella?" said Javier.

"Wrong time for bad jokes, Javi."

"I'm not joking," he said.

"I'm chilly," said Stella.

She'd been in a dim corner all along. Wrapped in a white shawl, face as angelic as ever. She came and sat close to the fire.

"Time for you to earn your fee, Mr. Bluestone," said Dolores. "The president of Colombia has ordered the military to full alert. They took four of the last cartel bosses yesterday. You and I are going to destroy the remainder."

"Right," I said. "Destroy? *How?*"

"My thought exactly," added Javi.

Dolores said, "I'm confident Mr. Bluestone will find a way. He has a knack of finding things the way a pig does truffles."

Javier laughed. "You're your father's daughter."

Dolores shrugged.

"*Knack?*" I said. "Why am I here?"

She smiled. "The art of the deal."

CHAPTER 47

That night I lay alone in a hammock in the hut. I tried making sense of things but couldn't. I closed my eyes and fell into a heavy, dreamless sleep. When I awoke, daylight shafted through the oculus. The faint sound of engines murmured from outside—

As I processed the fact that a helicopter had awakened me, Older Brother entered, motioned me to follow him. In the clearing, a small NOTAR helicopter waited like a resting insect.

Dolores was already inside. To my surprise, she wore a suited skirt, and her hair was neatly pinned up. She pointed at a bag on the floor. I opened it and saw one of my court-going outfits: navy suit, pale-blue shirt, dark-blue silk tie.

Astonished, I said, "How did you get my cloth—"

"Not important. Turn yourself into a lawyer."

The chopper took off as I changed clothing.

Using a compact, Dolores applied eye shadow. It enhanced her beauty even as my spirits sank. I wanted this unique, incredible woman, but she didn't want me, at least in the same way.

Our chopper lifted and sped south, away from the Caribbean and toward the interior of the continent—the same route it must have used to reach the mountain stronghold, avoiding Chinese radar and weaponry on the Guajira Peninsula. We threaded between the green, lesser peaks, far beneath the looming snow-tipped cone of Anawanda. Older Brother had become a hell of a pilot.

Dolores's eyes were closed, but I sensed that she was not asleep. Wide awake, I stared below. Colombia is the most beautiful country I've ever seen: snow-topped ranges, long miles of rolling hills dotted by small towns, patched by green fields. Rushing rivers uncoiled below, their white foam visible even from our height. We saw no other aircraft for we remained above the countryside, well away from towns and cities. We crossed the high Cordillera Central, where glaciers shone whitely, then followed the Cauca River valley south between the Central and Cordillera Oriental, and I began glimmering our destination:

Cali.

The city I knew so well: the city where my Colombian adventures had begun long ago. Danger was a constant in Cali, lurking in both its mean streets and grand boulevards. And yet, incredibly, we were off to destroy the worst of it. The cartels.

If I could find a way.

Dolores touched my thigh—intimately, I thought, spirit soaring—but she was just indicating to me to tighten my seat belt, for we were descending.

Below, surrounded by thick jungle, lay an enormous green lawn next to a modern, steel-and-glass building I recognized as the training facilities of America de Cali, the city's beloved soccer team. It was here that I'd often met with Nacho, when the old Cali cartel owned the franchise.

We landed and exited the copter. Groups of armed men stood in clusters apart from one another. They were armed. Dolores—*Sombra*—had invited me to a convocation of the remaining cartel bosses.

Like filings drawn to a magnet, the groups converged, circling us. Among them were a few men wearing suits and square-toed shoes: cartel lawyers, a couple of whom I recognized. Others were bandoliered *sicarios*, the cartel chieftains' personal Praetorian Guard. I didn't personally know any of the bosses, but I'd seen their photographs on wanted posters. All in all, a motley crew of desperados, grimly waiting for Dolores to address them.

"Thank you all for coming," she said. "I invited you here on behalf of *Sombra*, who wishes to assure you that your losses incurred in the recent ship sinkings are about to be reimbursed."

There were a few exclamations of approval but more expressions of doubt. Then came a chilling comment:

"I recognize your voice. You're *La Pasionara*."

"Why should that surprise you? You gentlemen and I want the same thing . . . the complete and utter withdrawal of foreign soldiers from Colombia. Not only the Chinese, but the Americans."

"*Sombra* keeps assuring us, but nothing happens," said a boss known as *el Carnicero*—the Butcher. "Now *Sombra* sends a woman. We want to speak to *Sombra*. We want to hear it from him. We want proof."

There was a grumble of assent. This wasn't going well.

"Here is your proof," said Dolores, turning to me. "This man is the American lawyer who was a go-between for Nacho Barrera and the Escobar family during the Cali-Medellín war. He was trusted by both sides with good reason, for he speaks the truth, whether it is good or bad."

All eyes turned to me.

I hadn't the faintest idea of what to say. Yet Dolores had gambled our lives based on her confidence in me. Uplifting.

Oh, baby, you know me so well.

Much as I'd done countless times in court, I conjured up a compelling untruth, then improvised from there.

I said, "My clients are a conglomerate of the insurance companies that insured the sunken ships. I am authorized to reimburse you for their losses."

"Is this a joke?" said a burly man whose wanted poster referred to his nickname: *el Diablo,* kingpin of the murderous combined

Colombian-Venezuelan *Cartel de los Soles*. "The damn ships were worth a fraction of the lost product."

"I assure you my employers are well aware of that," I said. "That is why *Sombra* has added significant monies to the insurance settlement, a sum that will provide you *complete* reimbursement."

"When do we get it?" asked a man I knew ran the Pacific cartel.

"As I'm sure you can understand," I said, "the insurance companies need time to, ah, *justify* the reimbursements on their ledgers—"

"How much longer?" said another boss.

Bad question. If my reply was soon, they might keep us here until they were paid. If my reply was vague or too long, they might keep us here permanently, maybe six feet beneath the soccer field.

Hmm . . .

As if there were no problem, I looked around the circle, smiling. Briefly, my gaze paused on a man among the *Cartel de los Soles*. Strangely, his features seemed to have an Asian cast, but I decided he must be part indigenous Colombian.

"When, woman?" asked another boss.

"When, Doctor?" he asked, using the Colombian term for lawyer.

Good question, no answer. But then an idea blossomed: Duke had created a timetable, one that Dolores had bought into. Today was what, L-Day minus three? Dolores was operating according to it, so I assumed three days was enough time for Dolores to keep Richard at bay. I added another couple of days, just in case.

"Six days."

They grumbled among themselves, then the man from the Pacific cartel said, "Five days and not one second more."

El Diablo added, "Until then, you shall remain here."

"Impossible. I *must* be in New York to finalize the transaction."

"Then the woman remains," said the Pacific Coast boss.

"Unacceptable. She *must* return with me. The reason is rather . . . delicate. She has, let me put it this way, a *close* personal relationship with the head of the insurance conglomerate."

For a moment, there was silence. Then one man laughed, and the rest joined in. They were shrewd negotiators, but all Colombian men understood one thing:

The spellbinding power of a woman.

"All right," said *Diablo*. "But should you fail, we will find you. The woman will be passed around. You, Doctor, will be spread-eagled between four horses and pulled apart. Maybe you'll be lucky and before your limbs are yanked, you'll choke on your cock and balls."

"Thank you for your time and consideration," I said.

The cartel circle opened, and we returned to the helicopter. My mouth was dry as alkali, but Dolores was fairly spitting anger.

"*Maricones,*" she cursed. "*Cabrones.* They won't see a peso."

I like a woman who curses. What I didn't like was that for a brief moment, I'd thought she'd exchanged knowing glances with the *sicario* who looked to be of Indian blood. *What means that?* And now, as the copter lifted, the man doffed his fatigue cap—a silent signal?—and as his jet hair shone in the sun, his eyes appeared dark and narrow above prominent cheekbones.

He was not a Colombian native. He was Chinese.

What had passed between them?

More important were the consequences of the events we'd set in motion. When *Sombra* disappeared, a new round of cartel wars would result, which would trigger the reemergence of anticartel paramilitaries, sparking a new war for control of the drug trade.

More blood would stain me.

We flew in silence to a *finca* fifty or so miles east of Cali. There, in the midst of an otherwise empty field, a pickup was parked. Next to it a generator hummed and lights glowed on a dial atop a fuel drum. The hose that snaked from it was held by an older man in white peasant garb. A Logui. Dolores's preferences were clear; her trust was limited to her people.

Where does that leave me?

The Logui fitted the hose to the copter's fuel intake, and the drum began pumping fuel. Minutes later, we lifted off. Our flight path took us half an hour west to the Cordillera Central—the middle ridge of the Andean ranges that trisect Colombia—then turned north and followed the spine of the range. After an hour we veered east, and slowly rural Colombia gave way to towns that grew larger, and I realized where we were headed next:

Bogotá.

CHAPTER 48

Bogotá is set on a nine-thousand-foot plateau partially ringed by steep mountains—eight million people living and working in a mostly low-story grid that runs for miles across the concrete and beaten-earth streets of a once-lush savanna.

Dolores looked straight ahead, unmoved by the city that wasn't her Colombia.

I decided it was time to defrost the situation. Between the altitude and Dolores's attitude, I felt breathless and deeply heartsick. Maybe I was better off keeping my yap shut. Maybe if I opened it, Dolores would tell me to buzz off. Permanently. Then again, at least I'd know where I no longer stood.

I took her hand in mine. She didn't resist but wouldn't look at me, only stared at the passing landscape below. Gently, I turned her face to mine.

She was crying. Mascara streaked her cheeks.

I said, "I'm sorry for what I said."

"I'm not crying because of you," she said sternly. "It's because this will be the last time I see my country again."

"Me?" I said. "I'm crying . . . because of *us.*"

Her lower lip quivered. She spoke softly. "I'm lying, Benn. My tears *are* for *us*. I know you're angry with me. At who I've been and what I've done . . . and my not trusting you. Look in my eyes. What do you see?"

I looked and saw and said, "I see . . . myself."

"I love you, Benn."

We kissed for a long moment before she took her lips from mine. "Back there, I needed you to help me stall the cartels. When they finally realize *Sombra* is still lying about reimbursement, they'll go on a feeding frenzy, devouring one another. Until that happens, Richard will leave me and my people alone. And soon after that, Richard will no longer matter."

Meaning Richard would no longer be *matter.*

I considered the implications. If Richard lived, I was dead. I'd already decided I'd kill him. Now I had an ally. I hoped.

Abruptly, she laughed. "You should have seen your face when I put you onstage back there."

"It was a hairy moment, I must admit."

"I knew you'd find a rabbit in your hat."

"No rabbit," I said. "I just freestyled."

The chopper was slowing. We were above downtown Bogotá now. "So," I said. "Our next chapter?"

"Yes. Act as you did in Cali. *Freestyle.*"

The copter was circling lower toward a large building topped by a heliport. We set down on the bull's-eye and got out. White-helmeted cops in dress uniforms escorted us from the helipad inside the building.

Its corridors were marble-floored. The elevator was shiny new and fast. It opened to an expansive, deep-carpeted anteroom. On a paneled wall was the gilded seal of the *Fiscalía General de la Nación*, the nation's national prosecutor. I was up-to-date on the vagaries of the Colombian governmental structure, and although the national prosecutor supposedly answered to half a dozen cabinet members and ultimately the president himself, I knew the current prosecutor was an ex-general and current spymaster who wielded the true power.

He didn't keep us waiting. His secretary—at the least a Miss Colombia runner-up—came to fetch us. We followed her into an inner sanctum.

The prosecutor of the nation was a tall, distinguished man with a courtly manner, his desk bare except for a tidy stack of papers and a rack of ornate pipes. His name was de Braun, and although he was thought to be a hard-liner with the narcos, in truth he was inclined to leave them be as long as they behaved well with the citizenry at large. An arrangement that I'm sure included anonymous cash donations to his reelection campaigns from certain connected Colombian lawyers. It wasn't corruption; it was their culture. Say what you will about it but know that it's no different in the States. Big people engaging in conspiracies of silent compliance to their benefit, maybe throwing a smidgeon to the populace and magnifying it by fake news. I reminded myself that Dolores was one of them.

The prosecutor of the nation greeted Dolores with familiar warmth and gave me a firm handshake. Then he sat, looked at the stacked papers, sighed, and said, "At this point, there's nothing that can be done, Doña Laura. The president has signed, and the senate ratified the mineral rights treaty with the Chinese government."

Dolores said, "Despite UNESCO having declared its support to designate the Sierra Nevada de Santa Marta as a World Heritage Site in which mining is strictly prohibited."

"There were other realities to consider," said de Braun, not unkindly.

"Only one, señor," said Dolores. "The Chinese outbribed me."

De Braun frowned, his voice rising as he said, "*Bribe* is not the word. It was—"

Dolores stood. "Whatever it was, it will no longer be. *Radio Free Bogotá* has a dossier—think WikiLeaks—of who received what, when.

Your name appears, sir. That dossier will be made public unless the mineral rights contract is terminated."

"Unilaterally? Colombia would be a pariah in world trade."

I said, "Not if the alternate proposal was considered."

De Braun looked at me. "Forgive me," he said. "I don't know who you are or why you are present."

"My name is Bluestone. I'm an American attorney whose specialty is trade agreements. I take it that among that stack of documents is a map of the Guajira Peninsula delineating the boundaries of the mining area?"

"Of course, but why—"

"Show it to me," I said.

Again, de Braun studied me.

I held his gaze a moment, then snapped my fingers impatiently. "Time is a factor. I take it the people who accepted bribes—"

"Campaign contributions," he corrected.

"*Bribes,*" I repeated. "These people must realize their actions have serious consequences, not only for their careers, but for their families."

"You dare come here and threaten me?"

"Not a threat, a reality. Unfortunately, as you no doubt are aware, in your country violence often plays a part in negotiations."

"We . . . these congressmen are not narcotraffickers."

I said, "*Radio Free Bogotá* can prove otherwise."

De Braun fell silent for a moment. Then he removed a document from the stack and placed it atop the desk. It was a map of the Guajira and its adjacent mountain range. I studied the colored lines, then the map's legend. I put a finger atop a snowcapped peak. Anawanda.

"From here to the sea," I said. "It's the area the Chinese leased?"

He nodded.

I moved my finger west from the border of the Sierra Nevada along the rest of the Guajira Peninsula, stopping at the city of Riohacha. "My researchers inform me that the REE deposits extend to Riohacha. The solution is simple. Move the mining area to Riohacha."

He shook his head. "It's too late. The Chin—"

"It's never too late." I stood and cupped Dolores's elbow. "Thank you for your time, sir. For the good of all concerned, I hope you and your cohorts rethink your decision."

For a moment he glared full macho at me. Then his expression became abject. "I will bring the matter to their attention."

"Do so quickly. The *alternatives* . . ."

He nodded. "I understand."

We did not speak until our copter lifted from the pad. It was a NOTAR, and beneath its low thrum, Dolores's voice was audible. "I can't believe you threatened him."

"Nothing I said he wasn't already hip to. Pipe smokers tend to be old-fashioned. This one has been around long enough to know that theft invariably leads to violence. He wasn't surprised. Besides, I doubt it will come to that. The Chinese have already begun deploying, but I think they'll be open to renegotiating the contract and move their mining rights well away from the Sierra Nevada."

"Why would the Chinese agree?"

"Maybe they'll get a better deal."

"From whom? What kind of deal?"

"You. And your secret plans."

"Don't put it like that, Benn."

"How should I put it?"

"This is something I need to do on my own. Much as I value your insights, I don't want to be distracted from my own. Each day the coming events shift, and I don't have time to consult. Just to react. Trust me, please."

I sighed and flipped a mental coin. It came up heads. I said, "I trust you."

Beyond the copter's plexiglass bubble, a brassy sun was sinking into the west. The Sierra Nevada lay due north, but we were heading toward the sunset. I said, "We're not returning to the Sierra Nevada?"

"No," she said. "We're going far, far away."

"I've always wanted to visit Wonderland."

Dolores smiled, and my heart melted.

CHAPTER 49

The chopper's muted rotors lulled me into a half sleep, an indistinct haze between reality and daydreaming. Dolores slept with her body imprinted against mine, the faint, sweet smell of her perspiration dizzying, her breath soft against my ear.

Was it true that she loved me?

Or was I only her cutout?

To negotiate with killers.

Threaten a prosecutor.

Dispose of Richard.

It didn't matter.

Dolores snuggled closer, and I put an arm around her. Protectively. That's when it came to me. I wouldn't have to steel myself to kill Richard.

I *wanted* to kill him.

CHAPTER 50

Below was trackless green jungle. Far ahead, sun glittered off a distant sea. The Pacific. The copter descended to a small airport. A single runway cut through a mangrove swamp, its terminal a cluster of old buildings outside which *amarillos* were parked: the ubiquitous, small yellow cabs that careen recklessly throughout the country. There were half a dozen small prop-driven craft parked, and several large jets tethered to gates: Copa and Avianca and LAN and an unmarked 737 that I figured was a cartel craft. The airport was named Tobar López, servicing Buenaventura.

I'd been there before.

Not a pleasant trip, for Buenaventura was a sore on Colombia's beautiful Pacific coast. Its port was fringed by ramshackle slums that were the de facto capital of Pacific narcotrafficking to Central America and Mexico. I'd had a client who'd once been the big man in BV, raking in tens of millions by charging the cartels a tax on each kilo shipped from the city. A week after he was arrested on an extradition warrant, he'd been found dead in his cell, cause of death being dead men tell no tales. That same day his attorney barely escaped being kidnapped.

Me.

Until now, I hadn't returned to Buenaventura, which, following my client's death, had become a sporadic battleground for would-be kilo-tax collectors. Both the local and the Colombian National Police had been accorded a piece of the action for them to ignore the drug trade. Murders and kidnappings were the norm. Unlike in Bogotá, Medellín, and Cali, here gringo lawyers were not immune from violence—

Hold on! Was Buenaventura Dolores's "faraway place"?

The copter door opened, and we stepped out into wet heat tinged with the stink of aviation fuel. Immediately, I was sweating, not just from the climate but from the bad vibes. By the terminal, a squad of soldiers eyed us, as did a crew loading a two-engine prop plane, a craft undoubtedly short-hauling product up the coast to Central America, where its cargo would be transferred to trailer trucks bound north on the Pan American Highway.

An airport cop car appeared, headed toward us.

It stopped, and two cops in fatigues got out, followed by an officer. The cops carried automatic weapons, the officer's holster flap unbuttoned.

"Señora Astorquiza?" said the officer, gravely.

Was this the end of our road? Surely Dolores didn't expect me to freestyle our way out of *this* predicament. She was unknown as *Sombra*, but her face was well known as Laura Astorquiza, *La Pasionaria*, the voice of the people in the streets who opposed corrupt officials—the same officials who were their bosses.

But, still again, I'd underestimated Dolores, for the officer cordially welcomed her to Buenaventura, expressing regret that her short stay deprived him of an opportunity to take her to dinner. His disappointment was assuaged when Dolores handed him a thick envelope. He peered inside—I glimpsed a $10,000-size brick of Franklins—and smiled to myself.

Even as the officer's car pulled away, the unmarked 737 began trundling toward us. As it rocked to a stop, its door opened, and the soldiers rolled boarding stairs to its fuselage. Dolores, both brothers, and I climbed aboard. Immediately, the door closed, and the big jet resumed moving.

Ten minutes later, we were airborne, headed toward the last sliver of daylight. West, over the darkening Pacific.

Dolores and I were alone in the rear cabin.

"Don't ever leave me, Benn."

"I've got your back forever."

A discreet knock interrupted us, and Younger Brother entered. He'd ditched his farmworker persona for a bodysuit like ours. Only he had on the trop-weight white version, so I figured we were headed somewhere warm. Or hot. Unlike the cross-county copter trip, this leg wasn't an instant coffee run, for he carried a silver tray loaded with what appeared to represent the entire IHOP breakfast menu, then left us alone to enjoy it. Yet again, I marveled at Dolores's influence and timing. We'd not passed through security, had been in Buenaventura for hardly a quarter of an hour without filing a flight plan, yet she'd arranged for catered food.

I didn't realize I was so hungry until I began stuffing my face, but there was so much food, I couldn't finish my serving. Dolores ate all hers, including the chocolate croissants.

She offered me one. I shook my head.

"Just have one. Do it for . . . me?"

How could I resist? And the croissant was delicious, down to the last crumb. Made me smile like the little kid I still was. I reflected on that thought, which segued into an unrelated observation, and then still another. I wondered why this kaleidoscope was playing—realized why—and turned to Dolores.

She was curled up, asleep again. Beyond her window, the sun was dipping in the west. Nothing out there within the 737's range but Hawaii . . .

Pearl Harbor. From Here to Eternity—that's when it hit me:

Movie memories? I was stoned out of my mind.

The croissants were laced with pot: top-quality sinsemilla, according to my sensory perception index. Too mucking fuch. Me and my girl—yes, *my* girl—were made for each other. We'd both grown up liking our weed. Me, because I'd been a wild kid who'd loved toking what was then street-known as *boo*. Dolores, because the first wave of Colombian drug exports was dubbed Colombian Gold, which was grown in the Sierra Nevada, where, as a fugitive from her father's killers, she'd been raised by the Logui, who simply viewed the stuff as an herbal stimulant. And she liked weed for all the right reasons—not to giggle stupidly but to amplify awareness, or perchance to dream.

Dolores chose to dream.

I chose to enjoy whatever came along and looked at the Pacific shining in the sunlight seven miles down. I reclined my seat . . .

Time passed, a reverie of good vibes.

I was bound for an adventure.

Me and my girl and my guns.

Minutes or hours later, the 737 began descending, and I glimpsed Diamond Head as we touched down. The airport was crowded with jetliners and the private chariots of billionaires. We taxied by them to an unmarked DC-10 parked at the head of a runway.

We left the 737 and boarded the bigger plane. Apparently, it had been a cargo craft, for the interior was unfinished but for a bulwark dividing its cavernous interior. Another half dozen Logui came aboard. They and the brothers staked out the forward cabin, their duffels on its bare floors their seating. Their plastic gun cases were open, and they were cleaning their weapons. Among them were bow tips jutting from woven tubes. Higher than any kite, I stared at them, thinking:

Bows and arrows? Why not? David took Goliath down with a stone.

Dolores's voice pierced my clouded mind. "Sit in the back, Benn."

"You segregating me? Y'know, gringo lives matter."

She smiled. "Just go and enjoy your head."

So I did. A pair of spacious seats had been bolted to the bare floor. I eased into one, but Dolores remained forward. From there, I heard voices: Dolores and a man, an official of some sort, although I couldn't make out their words, only their tone. Familiar as hell. A bribe. Dolores gifting an official with a brick or three of Franklins. We then took off without having filed a flight plan.

My Dolores, always thinking ahead.

She sure had it down right.

Money trumps power.

Man, I was stoned.

CHAPTER 51

Dolores remained forward. When Younger Brother brought me a snack through the opened door, I glimpsed her seated behind the pilots, headphones clamped over her ears, animatedly speaking into a mike.

The snack was a smoked tuna sandwich on a fresh-baked bun, sweet, newly cut pineapple on the side. I wondered if it was spiked with weed. I hoped so. Pot was the perfect kick-starter for thinking out of the box . . .

The snack was laced, all right.

Set me to wondering if Dolores was fueling me to go berserker on whomever our weapons would be pointing at. But then I bipolarized and decided to trust Dolores: she was protecting me; keeping me chill, ready to freestyle. After all, I was a negotiator, not just another killer. Right . . . ?

The grass shook off all my cares and woes, and I perked up, remembering that I was on one kind of great adventure. *Westward, ho!* The outside range of the DC-10 would be the Philippines.

Luzon, Bataan, Mindanao, the Battle of Leyte Gulf . . .

At age sixteen, my father had enlisted in the marines and fought his way through the Pacific—including a memorable interlude in the Philippines—toward the Japanese homeland. Pa had been a carefree street kid when he'd left Brooklyn but returned a moody vet who kept mum about his war. Yet, despite this, he was an avid fan of war films, getting a kick out of watching Hollywood poseurs who'd avoided the draft and waged phony wars in front of moving-picture cameras.

Poor Pa. After he'd come marching home, he'd muted his memories for thirty-five years until they caught up with him, and he swan dived off the Brooklyn Bridge. I was only fifteen at the time but street-schooled enough to consider his motives. Was he finally unable to resist going into the nether to rejoin his dead buddies? Had he waited so long to be sure I was wise enough to care for myself?

Both, I thought. But *was* I wise enough?

We were still racing the sun west, but it had gained on us and, now through pink-streaked clouds, it glowed mere inches above the horizon.

Strange, that. The sunset was off to the left . . . meaning we were not headed west toward the Philippines . . . but northwest into a vastness devoid of airfields—

Some minutes later, the plane banked and again headed due west.

I wondered why we'd circled northwest. Perhaps to deceive Manila air control as to our destination. Dolores at work. Again. In any event, now I knew our next destination was indeed the Philippines.

Bataan, Corregidor, the Battle of Leyte Gulf . . .

Again, I flashed on Pa—funny, how often I'd been thinking about him lately after rarely thinking about him at all. Him and me seated amid a scattering of Sunday *Times* sections and *Post* sports pages, Pa smoking his beloved Old Golds, me spooning pistachio ice cream to sate my weed high, both of us glued to the screen of our ancient Zenith—black and white, but so was the flick we were watching— *Wake Island,* starring William Bendix as Pvt. Smacksie Randall, son of Brooklyn, wheeling a water-cooled machine gun at strafing Zeros.

Oh, mein Papa.

Pa had played his hand to the bitter end. And now, long years later, his prodigal son was headed into the seascape of his old man's past. A remake?

Didn't matter. There was no turning back.

CHAPTER 52

Manhattan. The present.

"Lucky," said Ming Chan in his gravelly voice.

"I can hardly wait, *yeye*," said Missy Soo.

Suppressing a sudden stab of pain in his innards, the old man smiled. This granddaughter of his was a true believer. *Just as I was,* he thought. *Once.* "Actually, *sunnu*, I was referring to . . ."

He pointed at the Air China jet they were about to board, its silver fuselage and nose bright with red swirls.

Missy nodded understanding. "It's painted lucky red, as if Lucky himself beckons us."

The old man agreed. It was true. The monk who personified good fortune at last was drawing them to him. And he and Missy were obeying the monk's bidding. Ming believed the day he met the monk might well be his last on earth, for by sheer force of will alone, he'd refused to die until then, although his predicted life span had long since expired.

They were at a departure gate in San Francisco International Airport. Beyond the window was the red-swirled Air China flight they were about to take to Shanghai. But Ming's good eye—veined and yellow—was fixed on the craft's nose. Its swirls seemed to him a mouth and an eye, reminding him of the Flying Tigers . . . and the American who had ruined his life.

We will die together, my old enemy.

With the thought came another stab of pain. He wished he could sit but feared he would not be able to get back up. Better to stay hunched over his half-good leg. And a thousand times better than requesting a wheelchair, as so many of these American travelers had. Such a sickly, complacent people, and yet they'd ruled the earth for nearly a century. But now China's turn was nearing. In his youth, that thought would've swollen his chest with pride; but now it was just an observation he cared naught about. Governments were all the same. Ruled by would-be saints quickly becoming drunk with power and morphing into monsters.

Scum. All of them.

On a TV screen, a yellow-haired newswoman spoke. Ming had lost much of his English over the years, but he understood most of what was said, the rest clarified by a map behind the newswoman. The news was grave:

Warships of seven nations were converging in the South China Sea. There were reports of near-collisions and low flybys. A simple miscalculation would set off a war.

Not to be outdone, the North Koreans were threatening preemptive nuclear strikes to support their own territorial claims of sovereignty over much of the Yellow Sea and Sea of Japan. In response, the United States was reasserting that Japan and South Korea were protected by the American nuclear umbrella.

Missy spoke into Ming's good ear. "The North Koreans *really* are crazy, *yeye*. As part of the deal for Lucky, we asked them to tone down their rhetoric. Instead, they escalated it."

"Not crazy. Smart. They escalate so when the deal is concluded, they can lower the temperature back to where it is now. They please their patron China. China gets something for nothing."

"Except losing the twenty-five-million-dollar payment to the American traitor."

"No, *sunnu*. Lucky is sacred. China does not pay for her legacy. Your American will be paid with a bullet."

Missy Soo smiled prettily. "I hope to see his face when he learns that. But what if the North Koreans push the Americans too far? What if they go to war?"

"Then they destroy one another. Leaving the field for China."

Missy squeezed his arm. It hurt. She said, "It is our destiny."

Oh, my naïve sunnu, he thought. *The only destiny is death.*

Their flight was called. He shook off Missy's helping hand and hobbled aboard. She'd booked a sleeping compartment for him, and he gratefully lay down. The jetliner's engines came to life, and it left the gate and taxied toward the runway.

Ming squinted at his watch—*getting hard even to see the damned time*—and saw that it was six o'clock. The flight would take fourteen hours. It would arrive on September 20. Then two days of travel—not nearly as luxurious—until the matter was concluded . . . on September 22.

His left lip curled in what for him was a smile.

September 22 . . . an auspicious day.

The date Li-ang had left him.

CHAPTER 53

I dreamed of my father, Louis Abraham Bluestone, aka Kid Louie when he was a Golden Glover. Ma had told me that, in the Glove quarterfinals, Pa had knocked a kid into a coma he never woke from. The day after the kid passed, Pa had enlisted. At first, I thought enlisting was Pa's way of doing penance, but I was wrong. Ma said that boxing match was the moment when Pa understood the extent of his anger and figured the best place to let it out was in the service. But my dreams were of Pa's gentleness, the soft touch of his big hands, those long evenings smoking Old Golds . . . when no war flicks were showing, he read poetry—

I was jarred awake as the plane touched down. I was still alone in the rear cabin. Beyond the windows an airport was unlit except for a small terminal whose sign said **PUERTO PRINCESA INTERNATIONAL AIRPORT, PALAWAN**.

Palawan.

Pa *really* was guiding me. The doctors had said otherwise, but I knew Ma had died of a broken heart. In her last days, she'd told me about Pa's wartime experiences. As a hardened veteran of the Pacific Islands campaign, he'd been assigned to the elite unit accompanying MacArthur's heralded fulfillment of his promise to return to the Philippines. After the Japanese invasion, MacArthur had abandoned his forces and escaped via a PT boat to Australia. When he made his triumphant return, he carefully crafted his image—crumpled campaign hat, dark shades, corncob pipe—heroically wading from a landing craft onto Philippine soil. MacArthur hadn't been satisfied with the first take, so they'd shot the scene several more times, before each of which Doug had smoothed his comb-over and changed to deliberately rumpled, dry khakis. When Pa couldn't help but laugh at the travesty, MacArthur had shot him a look. The next day Pa had been transferred to the front line in Palawan. In December '44, Pa's unit had been captured. One hundred sixty-one guys herded into a gulley where they were raked by Japanese Nambu machine guns, then set afire. Eleven guys survived. Pa was one of them. At least for the next thirty-five years . . .

Like Pa, I had come to distrust authority. Why I became a defense lawyer, I suppose. My proclivity for going all-out fighting the government had introduced me to some strange people and places. Some were good, most were on the bad side, but they all provided what I craved. *Action*—

The plane gave a little shudder as it stopped in a far corner of the airport.

Dolores entered the compartment. Behind her, Younger Brother carried a tray. Coffee, bread, fruit. He set it down and left. I was hungry but too curious to eat just yet.

"Why Palawan?" I said.

"A brief pit stop. Food."

"More weed?"

She laughed. "No more weed from now on. The next leg is the second to last to our final destination."

"Which is?"

"A beach."

I sighed.

"I'm not being secretive, Benn. Truth is, I'm not sure what happens next, other than it's on a beach somewhere. I know what I want to happen then, but it's your job description. Bullshitting the bullshitters."

"Well said. You should've been a lawyer."

"You shouldn't have been a lawyer."

"I don't think I am. Not anymore."

"Well, maybe *once* more."

From outside came the rhythmic thudding of a helicopter. Then its landing lights appeared—a huge twin-rotor craft—and set down fifty feet from the DC-10.

Dolores left the compartment.

Through the window I watched her cross the tarmac to the copter and climb inside. Older Brother leaned from its doorway and motioned for me to follow her.

It was hot and humid, and I was sweating by the time I reached the copter. Up close, it was even larger than it had seemed. I followed the brothers up its boarding stairs.

Dolores sat behind the pilots: the two brothers.

Behind them, the passenger compartment was stacked with gear and duffels, atop which a dozen men sprawled. Filipinos. Reassuring. Ma had said Pa thought the Filipinos were the bravest, toughest soldiers in the war.

But when I found a seat and my eyes adjusted to the dimness, I realized they weren't Filipinos. They were a combination of Logui, and—was it possible?—*Green Dragons.*

Yes. The one giving me a thumbs-up was Derek Lau.

I wondered if he was here for Stella or for Uncle. Or both. I wanted to speak to him, but the PA squawked for us to hold on, and the helicopter lurched, then rose. On the eastern horizon was a seam of orange, but then the copter turned west, where only darkness lay ahead. And China—

"Almost there, Bennjy," said Dolores.

Bennjy. Pa called me that.

CHAPTER 54

Madame Soo unquestionably was feeble, yet was stronger than she let on. Each day, when alone, she did her own age-limited mix of tai chi and yoga. She was building a reserve of stamina for what she knew would be her final journey. This was one of many secrets she kept from Missy Soo.

At 2:00 a.m., long after her bedtime, Madame Soo left her bed and dressed in an outfit whose possession was another secret. It was a black jumpsuit. She tried on the accompanying black combat boots, but they were far too heavy. Instead, she improvised a sock-and-sandal foot covering. She caught a fleeting glimpse of herself in a moonlit mirror that had once been in the boudoir of a Ming empress. Madame Soo was not at all vain; yet now she paused before her image.

I'm dressed the way I was that day. When I last was Kitty.

Then she unlocked a red-lacquered cabinet. Wincing with the effort, she took out a silk-shrouded box, cradled it like a baby, and carried it out onto the patio. She'd lived in this home for many years and knew its hidden amenities. Behind what appeared to be a rosebush stood a gate.

Below, the dark sea smashed against rocks, its rhythm repeating itself. She saw things more clearly than she ever had before. Like the relentless waves, her life had been repetitious, a riddle alternating between pure joy and tragic sadness for reasons she did not comprehend. But now the last few pieces of the riddle were revealing themselves, and at last, she visualized the completed puzzle.

Carefully carrying the silk-wrapped box, she went through the gate and down a narrow stairway cut into the cliff face. The stairway ended at a small stone landing.

A Zodiac bobbed there. Two men inside. Both were lean and dark, but she didn't think they were local Mexicans, who did most everything the neighborhood's .01 percenters were too busy golfing and drinking to do. One man offered his hand and assisted her into the boat. Solicitously, he helped her sit and fastened a seat belt around her. Then the two men paddled from the landing. Some distance from shore, they started an outboard, and the craft bounced over the chop. Madame Soo wasn't afraid; to the contrary, she laughed like a little girl on a carnival ride.

She knew it was almost over.

PART FIVE: TRIAL

CHAPTER 55

By midmorning, the helicopter cabin was stifling. The big machine droned deeper into the South China Sea. I'd have thought that, given the naval presences below, we'd be skimming the deck, staying beneath radar. Instead, we were a mile high, well within radar range of missile-bearing ships of half a dozen nations, all on high alert. Dolores unfolded a map. Here and there, clusters of small islands sprinkled the blue sea.

Dolores pointed to the northwest quadrant.

"This is where we are now," she said.

I peered at the map. Saw nothing but ocean. Her finger moved northwest to nameless reefs and tiny atolls.

She said, "This is where we're going."

I raised a questioning brow. Why were we going to such a remote destination? More important, the route brought us near the Spratlys, an archipelago in which the Chinese had already created artificial islands large enough for airstrips, declaring sovereignty over all of them.

Dolores picked up on my thoughts. "They won't bother us. This helicopter is owned by an exploration firm contracted to Chinese oil companies."

"I thought the Chinese were the other side."

Dolores smiled. "They are."

The reefs and atolls she'd pointed out were easily several hundred miles past the Spratlys. Even if we were equipped with supplementary fuel tanks, our destination seemed well beyond the copter's range.

Again, reading my thought, Dolores said, "We'll make it."

I felt a familiar sense of anticipation. I was again tiptoeing atop the razor's edge, and it felt *good*. And I knew why.

Dolores. She Who Knows Most of All. She, who as a child had copied my ways, and now was my copilot on the route less traveled, she who disregarded the journey and focused on the future, she whose blood, like mine, sang when there was *action*.

Below was another cluster of atolls: broken strands of white and black pearls amid turquoise lagoons, much like thousands of other atolls scattered across sixty million square miles of water.

Still again, I thought of Pa. This was his hallowed place. Somewhere over the horizon was Tarawa, where a major World War II SNAFU had deposited the invading Second Marines on a tidal reef hundreds of yards from the beach, forcing gyrenes loaded with sixty-pound rucksacks to wade through chest-high water while Japanese 99s spat green tracers that blotched the turquoise water with American blood. Pa had survived that day physically but left his spirit floating among his dead comrades.

I didn't want to end like Pa.

"Iron Bottom Sound," I said aloud.

"Translate, please," said Dolores.

Without realizing it, I'd muttered the name of another Pacific slug-fest that had left a hundred warships, Japanese and Allied alike, forever rusting on the bottom of Tulagi Harbor. Dead men floating.

Like the dead marines by the reefs of Tarawa.

Like the drug runners in the icy Bering Sea.

I said, "Seventy-five years ago, we fought the Japanese here. Now we're on the verge of war with the Chinese here. The more things change, the more they stay the same."

Dolores didn't reply. She knew I wasn't finished.

I said, "It was you who sank the fishing fleet."

For a moment, she seemed disinclined to answer, but she changed her mind. "My role was to convince the cartels to send the load. Richard and his people did the wet work. But since you mention it, yes, I'm responsible for killing hundreds, perhaps thousands, of people. I thought you were over it."

"Not quite. Not until Richard's dead."

Dolores smiled. "My man emerges."

Below was a large container ship. And then another and another, and oil tankers and cargo vessels and tramp steamers. From above, they looked like a vast convoy of water beetles, all headed southeast.

"The shipping lanes," said Dolores. "From here, they're funneled through the Strait of Malacca. Whoever controls the strait controls a third of the world's trade."

Among the ships, smaller, sleeker vessels left white wakes.

"Mostly Chinese navy on patrol," said Dolores, "and a scattering of warships from the other six Southeast Asian countries who also claim the area, although they stay well away from the Chinese—"

A huge roar erupted, quickly grew louder, louder, then a pair of fighter jets streaked past, so close I could see the red stars on their wings.

The intercom squawked: "We just were advised to turn before we enter Chinese airspace over the Spratlys."

Older Brother turned, looked at Dolores.

Dolores nodded, said, "Reply . . . Red Lucky."

"Copy that," said Older Brother.

"No response," said Younger Brother.

"Go straight over the islands," said Dolores.

The brothers glanced at each other but stayed on course. Below, the Spratlys appeared: reefs and islets, some already reclaimed from the sea and lined with airstrips and dotted with buildings on whose roofs were painted the ubiquitous red star of Communist China. Dozens of ships were anchored offshore: cargo vessels, dredges, a pair of frigates.

The intercom crackled: "Their radar's locked on us."

Dolores's face turned grim. I sensed the Logui and Green Dragons were equally concerned. Dolores took my hand and squeezed it, hard.

Long seconds passed.

Then the Spratlys disappeared behind us and ahead lay only empty sea. Dolores released my hand. The Logui and Dragons had visibly relaxed.

"Red Lucky?" I said.

Dolores didn't reply. She didn't have to because now I understood, remembering the Chinese *sicario* at the cartel confab outside Cali. I'd thought something had passed between him and Dolores. Now I was sure. The man was there because Dolores had something going with the Chinese. A side deal? Was I about to reprise my role as the Great Negotiator?

With them? Or with Richard?

If my adversary was Richard, I needed to prepare. I said, "I'm going to be dealing for what, for whom?"

"With everyone who wants Lucky. For an old woman who needs your help. You met her. Madame Soo."

"Madame Soo has Lucky?"

"Not exactly."

"Don't make me pull teeth."

Dolores laughed. "Madame Soo has a male admirer who's going to tell her where Lucky is. Look there."

Dolores pointed, and when I followed her gaze, I made out a small speck in the distance. Another atoll?

No. A cargo vessel, gray-painted, flagless.

As we lowered toward it, I realized its rear deck was flat and uncluttered. A helipad? Yes. Atop which a flagman guided us in. As we neared the pad, I glimpsed the vessel's stern. Beneath the gray, the lettering of the vessel's name was faint but visible:

Kitty.

CHAPTER 56

When we left the chopper, I realized the ship's hull and superstructure had been painted in different shades and patterns of gray. Irregular blotches and splotches, as if halfhearted attempts to conceal rust. They seemed random at first—dull leaden areas, black-and-white striped patches, Jackson Pollock–type drippings in ashen shades—and then I realized the vessel was deliberately camouflaged. Professionally. From a nautical mile away through heat haze, she'd be an old freighter. But the vessel was anything but.

It was a man o' war.

Gray tarps covered radar-controlled air-to-air missiles, state-of-the-art CWIS batteries, other deadly toys. Made me wonder what force or power had such resources. The vessel and its armaments must have cost many hundreds of millions of dollars. The Yanks and the Reds could easily afford that. And perhaps a consortium of Vietnam and Taiwan and other, lesser nations making claims in the South China Sea.

Had Dolores made a deal with one of them?

The thought was short-lived for I realized beneath gray paint, the deck was not the riveted sheet metal of a warship but was intricately inlaid hardwood. And beneath their drab finish, the knobs and fixed hardware were mahogany-ringed titanium. I laughed aloud.

The ship was Duke's yacht. The very same I'd briefly seen emerge from the mist on Long Island Sound. *Kitty.* Clearly, Duke was the "male admirer" carrying a torch for Madame Soo.

The crew was a mix of Duke's mercs and Filipino merchant mariners. Dolores spoke to the Logui in Anchiga, and they went below.

Dolores turned to Derek. "Get your boys ready."

Derek nodded. "G'night, Ms. Dolores."

Dolores took my arm. As she led me below deck, the copter was being refueled. My worries about its range were misplaced. *Miscalculation* wasn't in Dolores's vocabulary. Obviously, Dolores had been aboard before, for she knew the way to the master cabin. Duke wasn't there, but no mistaking his presence.

The cabin befitted a wealthy dilettante. Paneled walls, brass porthole fittings, a nice area rug—Chinese, I noted—and a big, soft bed. Like Duke's den, the space was filled with the odds and ends of his memories . . . but these photographs were much older. Taken together they were a visual autobiography of Duke, from when he was Archie Petrie. Fading black-and-whites: a shirtless Archie standing atop the wing of a P-40. Archie and a dozen Shan men. Archie and a tough-looking short mug—Smitty?—lying atop a pile of money, beers in hands, laughing. Archie holding a little girl . . . Smitty's child?

From outside, we heard the copter cough to life. Its rotors thudded too loudly for us to speak, so we waited until it took off and its engine faded to distance.

"Tell me about Duke," I said.

"I met Duke through Richard. We agreed that, although our individual agendas were different, by pooling our resources, we could help one another."

"So then you and Richard pooled?"

"You need to get past that, Benn."

"I need to get past Richard."

"Nothing to get past. He's a creep old enough to be my father."

"I'm old enough to be your father."

"And immature enough to be my son. I helped Richard break the cartels. In return, although he doesn't know it, he's going to help me save the Sierra Nevada. But since you want the gory details, here's how it was. Richard learned I was *Sombra*. He offered me a deal: full pardon for all my crimes. In return, I'd help him break the cartels."

"You believed him?"

"Of course not. But he opened the door for me to save the Sierra. That's how I know he's a traitor. Because he used me to carry messages between him and the Chinese. Which suited my purpose, that being to deal with the Chinese."

"What's Duke's game?"

She shrugged. "I wonder about that myself. He doesn't need the money, and he sure doesn't want the publicity. He wants to spend his last days peacefully. My take is that he's doing it for a personal reason."

"Stella."

"Yes, and more."

"Kitty."

"Yes."

"Richard and Duke make an odd couple. What's up with them?"

"Richard's using Duke to get Lucky. If, when, he does, the Chinese will reward him with a fortune. My moves in Colombia are making him a big man in Washington. Maybe he wants to go into politics. Maybe he wants to launch his own security consulting firm. Maybe it's about money, or power. Richard doesn't care what or whom he hurts as long as he gets what he wants."

"But how's Richard gonna be a hero in Washington if he gives Lucky to the Reds?"

"Because Washington won't know."

"But someone will have to answer."

Dolores smiled. *"USA v. Bluestone."*

"Not funny. So Duke has Lucky?"

"He knows where Lucky is."

"What's your plan A?"

"For you to react accordingly."

"Chinese checkers."

"Yep. So jump me."

We spent the next hour or three dreamily making love. We were getting to know each other. Our first time had been fast and furious. Now we took things slow and easy. I nibbled at her ear. There was a thin gold wire in her lobe that had been hidden beneath her hair.

"You gave it to me," she whispered. "Remember?"

I remembered. What do you give a kid who has everything? Twenty years ago, my answer had been this gold wire, one we'd pretended was an antenna connecting our thoughts when we were apart. Then a realization came to me:

All my life I'd been waiting but never knew for what. Now I knew. I'd been waiting for Sara to grow old enough to be with me. Of course, now Sara was Laura and *Sombra* and Dolores and She Who Knows Most of All . . . but a rose by any other name . . .

"White picket fences, lots of kids, and dogs," she said.

Is she for real? I desperately hoped so but even more desperately feared being let down.

"I love dogs," I said. "Fences? Not so much."

"My wonderfully weird Benn. I so love you."

I saw myself in her eyes. "Double ditto."

The PA squawked: *"Battle stations!"*

CHAPTER 57

Openly armed now, the crew rushed about, their footsteps clattering. When I emerged from the cabin, two of Derek's Dragons stood in front of the next-door cabin. I'd forgotten their names but knew them both, but they gave me the cold shoulder. Some things never change. I remained the *gweilo* lawyer who'd taken their boss's hard-stolen money. Obviously, Derek had told them that no one—including me—was to enter the cabin they guarded.

I wondered who was inside. Was it Duke, resting, girding his old bones for whatever lay ahead?

Or was it Lucky?

On deck, the weapons were still shrouded, but the crew stood ready to uncover them. The vibes were tangible, electric. I followed Dolores onto the bridge and saw why.

We'd caught up with the cargo traffic headed for the Strait of Malacca. Moving at flank speed, a sleek Chinese frigate cleaved toward us.

Older Brother handed Dolores a pair of binoculars and a radio phone. Looking up at a man on the flying bridge, she spoke into the radio phone:

"Captain? Signal 'Red Lucky.'"

Our captain, a stocky, unshaven Filipino, gave a half-assed salute, then leaned into the bridge house, took out a mike, spoke into it.

A moment, then the Chinese frigate sharply turned away, rejoining the convoy.

"Magic words," I said to Dolores. "You *are* working with them."

"No . . . sort of."

"*Sort of?*"

"Mind control, Benn. They won't touch us because they *think* we control Duke, and they *think* Duke knows where Lucky is."

"Why don't they just follow us to him?"

"I told the Chinese that Duke's in the process of bringing Lucky to them at a position two hundred miles due west of us. We're headed east so, for now at least, they're not interested in us."

"So, then, where are we going?"

"To see Duke." She handed me the binoculars and pointed to the horizon, away from the convoy. "There's another reason the Chinese won't bother us."

I looked through the binocs and saw in the far distance a large amphibious assault ship, actually a small aircraft carrier. Its flight deck was occupied by the wasps and bees of copters and VTO—vertical takeoff—Harrier fighters.

"That's a US Navy ship," I said.

"That's Richard," she said.

"He's shadowing us?"

She shook her head. "You can bet your last buck that Richard's broken the Chinese secure communication system. He's been tagging along, knowing it's a ruse that Duke's elsewhere, knowing we're on our way to meet Duke."

"To where Duke won't be."

"Oh, he will be. Later. Come."

I followed Dolores to a cabin just below the bridge. A windowless space lined with electronics and monitors. Dolores sat at one, pecked some keys, and a wall-size screen came on.

It was a map.

Its optics were in color. On a white sea, atolls were small blotches ranging from black to pale gray. I recognized the black outlines of the Spratly Islands.

Dolores said, "The black areas are where the Chinese have already established bases and are constructing airstrips. The paler areas indicate atolls in the process of being reclaimed. The palest are those earmarked for future development."

She touched the keyboard, and the screen magnified, the white sea now speckled with small brown dots.

"These are the ships in the trade routes with us. As you can see, the route circles the black areas, so already the newly constructed Chinese islands have created a new status quo."

Dolores's fingers danced over the keyboard, and a green cursor blinked.

"That's us," she said. "*Kitty.*"

Her fingernails clicked some more, and a red spot appeared alongside an almost colorless atoll that must have been at least a hundred miles ahead. Again Dolores tap-tapped, and a yellow line appeared between our green cursor and the red spot.

"That's our course," said Dolores.

She worked some more magic, and the image reformed: from off-screen, beyond the red spot, a gray arc appeared, enclosing the red spot within it. Even as I watched, the gray arc jittered and grew fractionally larger, like a weather map depicting the approaching eye of a storm. It reminded me of the late-night war movies I'd watched in my bad old days—namely, near the end of *Patton*, when the German command worriedly contemplates a map on which rings indicate the range of allied bombers. The arc on the screen represented fighter-bomber range, which *Kitty* was rapidly approaching. But did the fighters belong to China's one dated, refurbished carrier? Or the amphibious attack ship Richard somehow had commandeered?

Dolores was hunched over the keyboard, bringing up images and numbers beyond my ken. I said, "The red spot? That's Lucky?"

Concentrating, she ignored me. I left the room.

The wind was up and bow spray showered the deck, salting me down, so I went to Duke's cabin and showered. His medicine chest was essence of Duke: mixed hints of leather and manly astringent and a dozen-odd phials of prescription meds.

Refreshed, I kicked back and turned on the TV. To my surprise, we had Internet and a BBC-clone station showing emotionless Asian commentators. On-screen was stock footage of a large US Navy warship, a copter-equipped amphibious landing craft. The commentator said, "In keeping with United States policy, Washington has announced that US Navy ships are again patrolling the South China Sea, a vital waterway though which passes one-third of the world's cargo. The United States says that it will not allow the shipping lanes to come under Chinese control. China has ordered a general mobilization. The US Seventh Fleet reputedly is steaming to the South China Sea."

I felt a not-unpleasant tingling.

It was happening.

CHAPTER 58

Late day. The sea glassy flat, the sky pale blue. But the weather changed as quickly as my moods. We entered a squall, and my thoughts coalesced to a landlubber's knot in my gut as I held on for dear life while *Kitty* bucked and plunged beneath my feet. A dense fog spat blinding sheets of rain that seemed to endlessly worsen—

And then, in an instant, we emerged from the squall line to low sun gleaming off calm sea, and in the far distance ahead, I saw white waves smashing against the outer reefs encircling a small atoll. From *Kitty*, the atoll seemed as pale and insubstantial as it had appeared on the war-room screen. A godless half acre of white sand crested by a green ridge.

Skull Island?

Kitty slowed. The crew was active now, their vibe resonating anticipation. A pair of Filipinos stood on the flying bridge, peering through binoculars. The captain barked orders in Tagalog; at each, *Kitty* slightly altered course. As we neared the atoll, more reefs appeared. Dangerous waters, but our captain was a master seaman, and soon we were past the outer reefs. The atoll was horseshoe-shaped, and *Kitty* slowly proceeded to its open end, where it dropped anchor.

The sun was nearing the horizon, the sky a pastiche painted by a Renaissance genius, a canvas of spirituality. But at the moment, I wasn't into religion, rather what I saw on the atoll:

An old tramp steamer was anchored, bow facing the sea, stern close by a dredge fifteen feet from shore, powered by a generator on the white sand beach. Men working there guided the dredge as it scooped sand from the shallows.

I hadn't an inkling of what was going on, nor did I try to make sense of it. My attention was fixed on the small ridge of greenery in the center of the atoll, where light shone through the windows of an old tin hut. Above the hut flew a flag.

The red field of the People's Republic of China.

And again, I wondered: was I Dolores's lover, or her tool—

There was a sudden flash of green—I turned and saw the sun had dipped below the horizon. Night had fallen. A moment later, the lights went out in the hut, and another moment later, *Kitty* went dark.

The only sound was the sea gently lapping against the hull.

I stood there in the black tropical night, thinking that this time I'd really fallen through the cracks, into a hole so deep, I was still tumbling. No rabbit hole, no Wonderland, a hole to eternity. I remembered how fervid Missy had been:

How would the United States like it if China patrolled the Caribbean, staking mineral rights, and arming anti-US factions in other countries?

The undoubted answer was that Washington would go ballistic—depending on the specific president and his generals, possibly literally.

Was this December 6, 1941, redux?

If so, the world was about to change, and if I were to survive, I'd have to adapt. No more playing in criminal sandboxes for me. I was at the no-limit table now, where only a few won. I was determined to be among them. To survive.

With Dolores.

* * *

That night Dolores and Javi and I dined by candlelight. I'd located Duke's liquor cabinet and liberated a $1,000 Petrus, with which we washed down a surprisingly good dinner. The Filipino crew cooked for us and served us. In their white jackets—undoubtedly pillaged from Duke's storeroom—they resembled USN officers' mess boys. Got me to thinking how Filipinos had fought and died side by side with Americans during the Second World War, and how so many Filipino medical professionals had immigrated to the States, forming a seemingly unbreakable bond between the two countries. Yet now the Philippines—like most Southeast Asian nations—faced tremendous pressure from China's growing stranglehold on the region and looked to the United States for help.

"To Lucky," said Dolores, lifting her glass.

"To *la vida salvaje*," said Javier.

Salvage? "Al buen vino," I said.

We touched glasses.

After dinner, Dolores disappeared into her war room, and Javi and I went up on the bridge, where we sipped Duke's superior brandy—

Suddenly, there was the growing roar of jet engines, and a moment later, two fighter jets flashed overhead, streaking shadows against the starry sky.

"Chinese," said Javier.

"Auspicious," I said.

"Checking us out. Trying to figure out what's going on. A month ago the only things here other than the old fishing shacks were a palm tree and some rocks, half a speck in the middle of one hundred seventy million square miles of water."

So Javier had been here before. And wanted me to know it.

"No secrets, Benn. You're like family to me."

"I felt that way about your brother."

"I'm not talking about Nacho."

I just looked at him.

"Dolores," he said.

"I love her," I said.

"I know you do." He poured another brandy and drank it in a swallow. "That's why you're going to save her."

"Sure. Benn, the Great Negotiator, to the rescue."

"Killing Richard's the key. Sleep tight, blood."

I left Javier with the brandy and went into the electronics cabin. Dolores was at the computer, looking up at the big screen. The green cursor that was *Kitty* was now well within the gray arc, and at the arc's center a blue ship-shaped image had now appeared.

"Tell me that's the American navy," I said.

"That's Richard's command."

"He'll easily catch up to us."

"He won't. He just wants us to lead him to Duke."

"And then what follows?"

"You earn your pay."

CHAPTER 59

That night I slept alone. Dolores wanted to keep tabs on Richard's amphibious assault ship. In the morning, I found her slumped asleep at the computer. On the big screen, the gray ship was about a hundred miles away, unmoving. I woke Dolores gently. When her eyes opened, she seemed startled by my presence, but then she hugged me close.

"Be right back," she said, leaving.

I waited, but she didn't return.

So I went out on deck.

The atoll was humming. Even as I watched, three fast boats appeared from behind the old freighter and started toward us. As the first vessel neared, I realized the men crewing it weren't Chinese but Dolores's Logui. Made sense. By another name, the fast boats were called *lanchas*, the go-fasts that ply the Caribbean cocaine routes from Colombia and Venezuela to Puerto Rico and the Dominican Republic. The Logui must have done their share of runs.

But why the Chinese flag atop the hut? Was it one of Duke's fake-out moves? Had Dolores known?

But Dolores cheerfully cried, "Ahoy!"

She had climbed partway up the mast above the flying bridge. The sun behind her formed a halo around her ink-black hair. Her silhouetted figure was a Greek goddess in alabaster. One elegant arm was pointed.

I followed it to the third approaching go-fast.

Three men on the boat. A mechanic at the triple outboards, a wheelman, and a man gripping the prow rail. All were sun-darkened. The mechanic and the driver looked like Filipinos but might have been Logui. But no mistaking the tall man on the prow.

Duke.

Barefooted, Dolores nimbly climbed down to the foredeck. As the fast boat came alongside, she leaped across open water onto it and embraced Duke. His sour face split in a smile. Dolores had expressed her disdain for Duke, so I perceived their familiarity as a case of the enemy of my enemy is my friend. Not to mention that Dolores knew she could mold sour Duke like clay.

Duke called out, "Benn. Javi. Come, I'll give you the guided tour."

Laden with his video gear, Javi leaped onto the go-fast. I waited until it bobbed closer, then boarded the small craft one leg at a time.

Duke's laugh was raspy. "No sea legs, Benn?"

"I don't know," I said. "Check my website."

Perched on the prow, her hair a black flag in the sea breeze, Dolores was dazzling in her white sarong. *Dorothy Lamour,* I thought. *No, better.* The go-fast took off, and I fell into a seat and held on as it made for the atoll.

"The dredging is nearly done," said Duke loudly over the engines' roar. He looked better than when I'd seen him in New York. Maybe the ocean air. Maybe the action. He said, "According to my ground-penetrating radar, we've got two feet left to pay dirt."

Javi braced in a shooting position, videotaping the atoll.

"Include the flag," Dolores told her uncle. "Then do another version without it."

Always thinking, this one.

Duke pointed his cane at the freighter anchored by the dredge. It was an old, sturdy vessel, its aft deck flap lowered, open to the water, nothing inside the cargo bay.

"I figure maybe one more day," said Duke.

Go-fasts were buzzing between *Kitty* and the atoll. I spotted Derek and his Dragons in one, a pair of Logui in another—

A sudden ear-splitting roar as another pair of fighters flashed by low overhead. I caught a glimpse of them: stubby crafts with overlarge intakes and short wings laden with missiles and fuel tanks.

"Harriers," said Duke. "Tough little birds."

"Richard's," said Dolores. "He's just over the horizon. Close enough to fight from a distance, far enough for deniability."

Fight? Against the Chinese? Deniability?

Impossible. The world's infested with secret proxy wars, but direct combat between nuclear powers cannot be denied, much less concealed.

We passed close by the dredge. It had already excavated an enormous pile of sand from the shallows, piling it high on the beach. Visible beneath the crystalline water, a fifty-yard square had been cut in the sea floor, maybe ten or fifteen feet deep. The bottom of the square was still thinly layered with sand. The excavation had partially exposed the geometric outline of something that lay below the sand. There are no straight lines in nature, so the hidden object had to be man-made.

But what was it?

We went ashore. Duke and Dolores remained with Javier, who was now busily videotaping the excavation. On the green ridge, the Filipinos and Logui were filling sandbags, setting up defensive positions against an assault from the sea. For a moment, I froze, seeing a squad of dun-uniformed, red-star-capped Chinese soldiers setting up machinery and electronics.

Then I realized they were Derek and his Dragons. I was still digesting the implications when something else caught my attention:

The go-fasts were being driven almost to the point of recklessness, but one was ever so slowly nosing onto the beach. A canopy covered those aboard. As the crew got out and secured the go-fast, it drifted in the current so that the sun was behind it, and I saw, clearly, the silhouettes of two passengers beneath the canopy.

Even at a distance it was obvious that both were small and bent. Oldsters. The crew splashed back to the go-fast and transported one of the old people ashore in a sedan chair. It, too, was shaded, but the person within was silhouetted against the sun. A woman. *Madame Soo?* Had these two been inside the guarded cabin on *Kitty?* Another foursome transported the second passenger into another sedan chair. This time a puff of wind raised the curtain, and I glimpsed the passenger.

He was a beyond-ancient Asian man so bent, he barely measured four feet tall. He wore an orange monklike robe fastened over one bony shoulder. His bald pate shone in the sun. Despite his age, his face was unlined and tranquil. For a moment, our gazes met, and I thought he smiled, a smile so radiantly benign, it made me smile in return.

Then the curtain descended, and he was carried off.

I stared after him, wondering, thinking, *Monklike?*

And now I knew that I'd finally seen Lucky.

CHAPTER 60

The Logui, gleaming like wet seals, were diving in the dredged square, using handheld vacuums to gently excavate the submerged object. Gradually, it became clearer: a waterlogged old DC-3, lost in some forgotten mission. As I watched, the top of its fuselage was removed; its hold contained a time-darkened wooden crate, ordinary and insignificant.

But obviously, Dolores and Javier thought otherwise.

From the opened aft bay of the freighter, Javi videotaped the excavation, occasionally pausing for a still shot with the Leica hanging from his neck.

By now, I'd become convinced that what lay beneath the sand somehow was—literally—of earth-shaking importance. In the glaring heat, I watched the excavation from the beach, feeling nutty as an Englishman in the noonday sun, waiting for the mystery to finally be revealed.

I didn't realize Duke was beside me until he spoke.

"You're not as dumb as you look, Counselor," he said. "I must admit I was surprised when you busted me on my Golden Triangle days. Jesus, they were wild. There we were, in a jungle in the middle of nowhere, producing product that was changing life on the far side of the world. There was even a film, *Panic in* . . . ah . . . ?"

"*Panic in Needle Park*," I said. "The seventies. Al Pacino. No heroin in the streets."

"The seventies, yeah." Duke laughed raspily. His eyes were pinpoints. Painkillers? Possibly. Despite his tan, up close, he looked awful: gaunt and worn.

"What the H slowdown really was?" he said. "Me and Smitty took a break to set up new routes, get rid of some people the feds had turned."

Get rid of. The moron was owning up to murders, a crime that has no statute of prosecutorial limitation. Painkillers had transformed Duke from taciturn to loose-tongued.

He laughed again, this time a high-pitched cackle. "The panic didn't last long. We opened this amazing route through Vietnam. Shipped the product to the States inside GI coffins."

The same scam used by Harlem drugsters like the infamous Nicky Barnes. I felt like punching the son of a bitch. I had been in high school in the '70s and watched the H epidemic destroy my friends and their families' lives, those who'd survived the needless Nam sacrifices engineered by monsters like Nixon, Kissinger, McNamara, and Johnson. Bastards.

Duke said, "In the eighties, we unleashed a freaking heroin blizzard. Man, those were the days." He sighed happily at the memory, but then, strangely, his smile faded, his voice morose. "I'm going to go to hell, Benn."

I'll meet you there, I thought.

Duke said, "I was so greedy, I gave up the one woman I ever loved because I knew she wouldn't tolerate my business."

I thought of my ex-wife, Mady. "I share your pain."

"But all good things come to an end. My business did when Richard came along."

I gave him a raise of the eyebrows but didn't respond.

"You must've been wondering why I told you about Lucky," he said.

I shrugged.

"In case I died, you'd know the real deal."

Right. Everything's crystal clear, old man. Thanks so much.

"Well . . . soon enough, it'll all be over."

"What's that supposed to mean?"

"Read your bible. Armageddon."

"How about an eye for an eye?"

He hesitated, said nothing.

An eye for an eye. I'd verbalized a random thought, a stab in the dark, but struck a target. For Chrissake, I'd been looking for a mystery when all along it had been a romance novel. Uncle had drunkenly mentioned Ming and Kitty, emotion in his rheumy eyes. And Uncle had led to Stella, who led to Duke, who wrote love letters to Kitty. Lucky was a sideshow that would've been long forgotten had it not been for one-eyed, humped, old Ming Chan versus one-lunged, bent, old Marmaduke Mason, both vying for Madame Soo's favor.

Wind blew Duke's hair behind him like the strands of a witch riding a turbocharged broom. I wondered which had come first: his evil or his insanity?

I couldn't bear his presence and distanced myself, walking along the shoreline. A stray wave washed across my boots. I took them off and laced them in a sling over my shoulders. The sun felt good on my pale feet. I unzipped the top of my bodysuit and let it hang from my waist, luxuriating in the soft wind cooling my sweaty body. I fought down an urge to go skinny-dipping. That option seemed off the charts of protocol, disrespectful even, for fifty yards from where I stood, something was happening that might evolve to a conflict that might plunge the earth into the fires of hell. As a wise man who built the first atomic bomb said upon gazing at the mushroom:

Now I am become death, destroyer of worlds.

The sun was making me dizzy. In search of water, I trudged to the hut on the green ridge that crested the curved spine of the atoll.

Derek and his Dragons had commandeered the old, tin-sided shack, which probably had been built by itinerant fishermen years ago. It was stifling hot inside, and they'd stripped down to their skivvies but were still sweat-sheened as they rushed about, fiddling with rat's nests of wires and assorted doodads. Derek nodded at me and went on working. I drank a gallon of tepid water, and my senses cleared. It seemed to me they'd already set up and accomplished what they'd intended, and now were disassembling.

"We're leaving?" I asked.

"Few more things, then we're out of here," said Derek. He glanced at his watch. "Speaking of which, the time has come."

"Time for what?"

He didn't reply. Instead, he donned earphones and opened a laptop and ran his fingers over the keys like a virtuoso. He waited a moment as if listening, then grinned as numbered grids ran down the screen.

"One down," Derek read aloud. "The Chinese naval authorities have been advised by their own security—"

A Dragon laughed. "The Bureau of Green Dragons."

"That the meet is confirmed as two hundred miles due west of here," Derek said. "And now . . . the *pièce de résistance.*"

Again, his fingers flew over the keys. "Done," he said. "The Red communications are now jammed. Nothing goes in or out. We own the airwaves."

"For how long?" I asked.

He shrugged. "They're pretty good, so they should be back up and running in twenty-four hours. More than enough time for us to declare mission accomplished."

I could only stare, trying to understand what he meant.

"Still," he said, "we're cutting it pretty close, as it is."

As I wandered back to the dredged area, I saw that *Kitty* was under way, leaving the atoll. An American flag fluttered at her stern. I thought that Duke was probably aboard, but then I saw him nearby, watching *Kitty* leave.

A platform had been erected on the beach; atop it, a tarp shaded two people: Madame Soo and the old monk I now knew was Lucky. They watched the excavation intently. The submerged crate had been excavated from the plane and now hung within a steel net dangling from the boomed ship, sand and water dripping from its barnacled sides.

It looked awfully heavy. Tons heavy.

Javier was videoing the process. Dolores stood at his side, wearing an expression I'd never seen before. *Anxiety.*

Dripping seaweed, the box slowly crossed from its watery pit to the stern of the old freighter. The back flap remained open on the freighter's stern deck, and the crate slowly lowered through the opening, coming to rest atop a grid of steel rollers in the cargo bay. When the crate was leveled, the Filipinos lashed it in place. Ten feet from where it sat, beneath the open flap, was the faded name of the freighter:

The White Rose.

Karma. Before I'd sidled into lawyering, I'd toyed with becoming a screenwriter. I was in awe of the classic black-and-white action films of earlier times, not just war flicks but adventures like *The Treasure of the Sierra Madre*, starring Bogey and based on a book by a mysterious Norwegian living in Mexico—his pen name was B. Traven—who scribed odes to the victims of unbridled, unregulated capitalism. Traven was dead, but I'd tracked down his widow in Mexico City—Mexico being safe in those days—and tried to persuade her to sell me a film option for another Traven book, *The Death Ship.* Turned out it had already been optioned, but we struck a deal for another book, *The White Rose.* Cost me $5,000, which at the time was every penny I had. Nothing ever came of it but fixed in my memory was her parting remark. Pointing at a marble bust of her late husband—a resolute-looking dude if ever there was one—the widow had said, "You look like him."

Over the years, I'd often speculated: *What if I'd become a writer?*

Another speculation: *Kitty* having departed, *The White Rose* was going to transport us from the atoll. *Would it be my death ship after all?*

As if in response, there came a sudden roar. A Chinese fighter whooshed by low overhead, circled, then made another, lower pass.

Duke said. "They're still wondering why they weren't alerted to any presence here. Keep your asshole tight, Counselor."

"Shut up," said Dolores. "Let's move."

The White Rose's foghorn sounded, and move everyone did. Madame Soo and the old monk were helped from their platform onto *The White Rose*, whose engines coughed to life. The Filipinos were casting off when the foghorn blew again, and the engines stopped.

What now? I wondered.

I soon found out.

A Chinese patrol boat was fast approaching.

Just when you thought it was safe to go back into the water . . .

Derek and the Dragons were putting their Chinese uniforms back on. Dolores was no longer in sight. The captain lowered the gangplank. I positioned myself atop it. Dolores had been right. The time had come for me to earn my money.

The patrol boat stopped in deeper water outside the reef and lowered a boat manned by a dozen sailors. The boat navigated the rocks and stopped just short of the beach. Immediately, the sailors splashed ashore and lay prone on the sand, weapons pointed at *The White Rose.* An officer strode toward us, his holster undone, hand above it.

"My map say no authorization work here," he called out to me.

As I descended the gangplank toward the officer, Derek appeared, in his uniform and cap with red star looking every inch a Chinese trooper. He saluted the officer. "Humble sir, may I speak in English for the benefit of this gentleman, who is a friend of the People's Republic of China?"

"Go on," said the officer.

"There has been a misunderstanding," said Derek. "We were ordered here. We've been attempting to contact our superiors but for some reason their communications are out."

"Electronics out, true," said the officer. "Show me your orders."

The steamer's captain—a curly-haired Greek—produced a file of documents. I wasn't surprised that they were seemingly stamped by Chinese officialdom. The captain gave them to me.

Derek and I went down to the beach, and I handed the file to the officer, who frowned as he perused the documents. As he did so, his certainty visibly crumbled. Not trusting his own eyes, he held the papers up to the sun, as if somehow he might gain an x-ray insight into their veracity. Clearly, he was wavering, and for a moment I thought our bluff had not been called; that Dolores's forged permissions had succeeded—

But then the officer froze—

Staring at Derek's wrist.

On whose underside a green dragon was tattooed. The officer drew his sidearm and shouted a command—

An arrow skewered the officer's neck like a kabob.

A silent moment, then all hell broke loose. Leave it to the Logui, Those Who Know More, to be the first to realize what was about to happen. A few had taken their bows and climbed the mast. Others had slipped back ashore and from the ridge unloosed a volley of automatic weapons fire. Sand geysers burst around the contingent of sailors on the beach and the boat.

Christ, it's starting!

I hit the deck.

Given the loss of their officer, I thought the sailors on the beach might give up, but they'd been trained well and began returning fire, as did their shipmates aboard the patrol boat. They were armed with heavier weapons and grenade launchers, and soon their answering enfilades silenced the Logui guns.

Then it was quiet.

Seemingly, the Chinese had prevailed. I looked around and saw Dolores peering from *The White Rose*'s wheelhouse, her face a mask of horror.

The Chinese fired another volley that shredded the bush where the Logui were entrenched. Nothing in reply. A Logui lay still, chest bloody.

At the sight, a feeling rose in me, one I'd never experienced before. I'm given to losing my temper, yet normally with a degree of restraint, mindful of the consequences I might provoke. Truth be told, although I think myself tough, when it comes to displaying testicular fortitude, I make myself scarce.

But not this time.

My heart seemed to swell, and I saw things through a red filter of pure fury. I had nothing to lose. Our mission was a failure. I had no future with Dolores. I just wanted to take out as many of the bastards as I could until they dropped me.

Without thinking, I snatched the rifle of a fallen Filipino, fumbled to undo the safety, stood, and squeezed off a full mag until I was out of ammo.

I had no illusions. The fight was lost. And so was all else.

Yet I still raged with the insane passion only violence can produce. I'd felt it before when I'd killed before. The primitive response that's in all men's genes. Now it was my turn to be killed, but so what?

I'd already grabbed my share of life.

Wielding my useless rifle like a club, I charged the sailors. I saw their eyes widen at the crazy *gweilo* rushing toward certain death. I saw the black muzzle of a weapon pointed at me and braced myself, thinking:

So this is how it ends. On an unnamed beach far from anywhere, for reasons unknown but for a single, simple fact . . .

I was a fool for love.

CHAPTER 61

As I prepared to die, another tremendous roar shook the island, and from out of the sun came two silver interceptors, guns strafing the line of Chinese sailors. I mean, *stitching* the poor bastards. One second they were men, the next blood and gore reduced to bite-size pieces of fly-meat on the sand. Leaving me standing there, watching the Chinese sailors dwindle to specks on the beach.

Javier had joined me and was taping them. He said, "Little bees with big stingers, those Harriers."

Harriers? Why would Richard shoot his ally's people?

The White Rose's foghorns moaned, dirgelike.

We boarded and quickly got under way.

The atoll receded, and we became just another tramp freighter, except for the wooden crate perched on rollers only feet from the stern and its inexplicably still-lowered flap.

A Filipino woman wearing a plastic cap and medical greens exited a cabin. She glanced at Javier and shook her head.

"*Oh no!*" said Javier, making for the cabin. I followed him inside.

Dolores sat beside a bed Older Brother lay on, oxygen tubes in his nose, an intravenous line in his arm, blood soaking through his heavily bandaged midsection. It took a moment before Dolores became aware of our presence, her face ravaged with grief. Sobbing, she fell into my arms.

"He's dying," she said. "Two others are dead. It's on me. I asked them to come. But I had no choice . . ."

"I know," I said. "They knew, too."

The surviving Logui entered the cabin and gathered around Older Brother. Dolores and Younger Brother amid them, they linked hands. Javier nudged me. I understood: this was a private moment where my presence didn't belong, so Javier and I left the cabin and stood on deck and stared at the crate dully gleaming in the last light—

Then the image was gone as the sun dipped below the horizon. As the sky began to darken, a sonic boom sounded, followed by another.

Then it was eerily quiet again, but just moments later, fireworks erupted far above where missiles streaked the black sky before bursting into multicolored extravaganzas. Long seconds later, the sounds of explosions reached us across the sea. Half a mile away, a jet fighter tumbled toward the sea like a broken bird.

"No contest," said Javier. "The Chinese J-Fifteens are copies of a last-generation Russian interceptor. Plenty of speed but not much else. The Harriers have the J-Fifteens locked in before the Chinese even know they're in range."

Nice to know for our own safety's sake, but what about the safety of the rest of the world? This was not the mere braggadocio of competing militaries; this was out-and-out open warfare. For sure, the hostilities would spread across the South China Sea, and the only question was not *whether* they would spread beyond it but how soon. If *The White Rose* made it to its rendezvous, would there still be a port of call to return to afterward?

The captain addressed the wheelhouse crew in Tagalog.

Javier said, "Chinese communications are back online."

Derek joined us. "Much as I'd like to muck up their Net again, can't do it from aboard the ship. Even if I tried, they'd pinpoint our location."

"They already have," said Javier.

We followed his gaze and saw the running lights of several ships. From a distance, they appeared at least frigate-size, meaning they were armed with ship-to-ship missiles. I visualized a Chinese naval officer with his finger poised above a firing button.

Javier said, "Not to worry. They're just shadowing us."

"Where?" I asked.

Javier shrugged. "Wherever. But we're bulletproof. Considering our cargo, they won't touch us."

"Why not?"

He raised his chin toward the crate. Atop it, an object gleamed despite the dimness. It was Lucky's hat. "They've got night vision. They see we've confirmed Lucky's with us."

I leaned on the railing. The black sea was riven by *The White Rose*'s wake. Through the warm, salty air, an infinity of stars pinwheeled in the sky. The vastness was humbling. So much of planet Earth I had no knowledge of, nor would I ever. I was just one among seven billion human organisms living and dying in their own small portion of the world. How much longer did I have among the living?

My thoughts were focused on three dimensions: the past I regretted. The future that was no longer. The present that was inescapable, for out in the darkness, predators waited to strike.

Derek and his Dragons had shed their Chinese military garb and were again wearing white jumpsuits, their cargo pockets stuffed with banana clips. Good thinking.

I smelled weed. Then I saw Derek with a joint in his hand, humming an oldie but goodie about this'll be the day that he died.

I took a deep hit of the joint. "Nice day if it don't rain."

"Benn, the wisenheimer," said Derek. "Another reason I couldn't figure you. Then again, what did I know back then? I was Scar, killer and all-around bad kid. If it means anything, I truly didn't know better at the time. My father was a drunk; my mother worked double shifts in a steam laundry. I slept on the floor of a one-room flat. So when there was money to be made, I went for it, and small crimes led to bigger crimes, and . . . well, you know the rest. I never did thank you. But now I will. Thank you, Benn."

"No thanks required. Uncle paid me well."

"Asshole. How about, 'You're welcome'?"

"You're welcome. And I'm glad as hell I beat your case. You made something of yourself, kid."

"Sometimes I pinch myself to make sure I'm not dreaming. Half my old boys are dead or doing life, the rest struggling to get along, but I was fortunate enough to have a good lawyer."

I held in a hit, exhaled a cloud. "No, a *great* lawyer."

The moon slid between clouds. In the changeable light, a tear glittered in the corner of Derek's eye. He said, "I want to help my boys. One thing I learned in the can? If you can make it through with your beliefs intact, you're a better person for the experience. Funny, apart from my girl, the only people I trust are ex-cons."

"Guess that leaves me out."

Derek laughed some more. "Nah. You're an ex-con who happened to avoid doing time inside. You served your sentence outside."

I was high enough to understand what he meant. It was the truth, the whole truth, and nothing but the brutal truth. I'd been in a self-imposed cell since I'd made a certain hard-right turn. The one that threw my ex-wife, Mady, from my car while I raced off to my career as a drug lawyer.

I sensed Derek was thinking something similar, the way we'd lapsed into silence and were staring at the dark sea—

The cabin door opened.

Dolores and the Logui appeared, carrying three shrouded bodies. They gathered at the railing, slid the shrouds into the sea, stood watching as they floated a moment, then left when they sank into the depths. Alone, Dolores remained.

I went to her.

I put my arm around her, and she leaned against me. "Older Brother's not dead," I said. "He's waiting for us."

Dolores gave me a teary smile. "My man," she said. "The One Who's Beginning to Know."

CHAPTER 62

Javier said, "And the dawn comes up like thunder outer China 'crost the Bay."

Javier was an educated man. He knew his Kipling, the poetic genius of blood and guts. Pa's favorite poet. And mine.

But this sun came up a pale-red disk behind gauzy clouds that merged sky and sea to a borderless leaden gray. Derek and Javier and I were still on the bridge after a long night of smoking dope and shooting the shit. The things we'd done and the opportunities we'd missed. The sad state and sadder future of mankind. Women we'd loved and lost.

Javier's lament was of his lovers and wife he hadn't seen during the fifteen years he'd been on the run. Derek had gone on a long rant of the virtues of the only woman he'd ever loved but feared losing. He didn't mention her name, but I knew it was Stella, although I didn't understand why he feared losing her. Considering our current situation, it was Stella who should fear losing Derek. When they finished emoting, they looked at me, and I told them how I'd loved and lost my ex-wife.

"Another way we're alike," said Derek. "One-woman men."

Javier smiled. "You're really a one-woman man, Benn?"

I'd knew he'd picked up on my omitting Dolores.

I'd nodded, thinking: *I am now.*

"Typhoon," said Javier studying the dim horizon.

Oh shit. I pictured *The White Rose* struggling to crest a twenty-foot wave, then capsizing and spilling us into the sea. The thing I dreaded most was drowning. Holding my breath as I sank, daylight diminishing above, the final inevitable clogging swallow of saltwater. *Please, not that way.*

Javier laughed. "Relax, Benn, you'll get worry lines. That storm's eye is three hundred miles distant, heading away from us—"

A door slammed open somewhere behind the bridge. Stella appeared.

"Eff you, Derek," she said. "This is *my* show. When is it starting?"

"Uh-oh," said Derek, quietly. "Excuse me, guys."

Stella's hair was disheveled, her face flushed with anger. She started down from the bridge, but Derek blocked the stairway. He said, "Slow and easy, baby. When the time comes, I promise you'll be there."

He went to hug her, but she pushed him away. He grabbed her arms and gently pulled her to him. After a moment, she stopped resisting and put her arms around him. He led her back to her cabin.

"More company," said Javier.

The morning mist had lifted, and there was a virtual fleet of warships within a few miles of us, ranging from patrols to frigates to destroyers. All dwarfed by the length and superstructure of Richard's amphibious assault ship, its decks bristling with helicopters and Harriers.

I raised my binoculars and saw that, to my surprise, the flags on other ships were not the Chinese red-and-gold banner but flags of countries I didn't recognize, excepting the Australian Union Jack.

"Friendlies," said Javier. "Come to support the cause."

"Regular BFFs," I said. "Exactly what is the cause?"

He shrugged. "No one told me anything except to get as much footage as possible on that crate we dredged up."

I heard the distant sound of jet engines and looked up. High above, glinting in the sunlight, a pair of J-15s painted contrails in the sky.

"Not to worry," said Javier. "After the mauling they just took, they won't dare come down to the deck. The Harriers are our air umbrella."

"Unfortunately," said Derek, who had suddenly reappeared, "there are holes in the umbrella."

I followed his gaze above, where half a dozen drones hovered. Three were close by the crate.

"Or maybe not," said Derek. He and a Dragon were fiddling with a device that looked like an oversize hair blower. Wires dangled from it to electronics still in their cases. He pointed the device at the drones. "Maybe we can blind those babies."

He pressed a button, waited, then shook his head. "Can't."

On deck, the Logui sat cross-legged in an unbroken circle of flesh touching flesh. Lean, bronzed men, not quite hard-looking but capable. Their beatific expressions brought to mind acid freaks doing group meditations fifty years ago. A generation who'd thought they'd found something but ended up losing themselves and, to a large degree, their country.

I hoped their prayers were realized.

Yet I couldn't help but wonder: Had Dolores gone too far trusting Richard? Were we now in a no-exit situation? Was Dolores following her nature and refusing to go down without a fight?

"The Chinese won't harm us," said Dolores. I hadn't noticed her join us, or that Javier and Derek had discreetly distanced themselves, allowing us privacy. "They're pragmatists; they play the long game."

"Unlike Richard, who's on the one-yard line."

"Richard thinks he's exempted from history repeating itself. The same mistake the Japanese made. Trying to conquer a billion people scattered over half a continent. Look at what that led to. This time it will be worse. Far worse. Supposing Richard's rogue op sinks half a dozen of their frigates? They'll send their big boy in. Their carrier."

"One half-assed refurbished Chinese carrier against Richard's Harriers? The Chinese carrier will be gone in a flash. Literally."

Dolores smiled. "The Chinese carrier cost a fiftieth of an American carrier. They built it for prestige purposes only. For face. The Chinese aren't afraid of the American carriers because they have carrier-killing missiles. Takes but one to sink an American carrier. If that happens, the tipping point falls. In retaliation for the carrier, the Americans nuke the Three Gorges Dam, flooding half of China's industry. Then the Chinese take out Hoover Dam, maybe add in the Hanford nuclear complex for the hell of it."

"It won't come to that. It can't."

"*Think*, Benn. While this is happening, the American president will be hiding in a bunker, paranoid, his advisors urging him to go to the silos and nuke subs. An hour later, Shanghai's a memory. Followed by New York. Peking goes, then Washington, then a thousand more mushroom clouds. Inevitably someone lobs a bomb at Israel, and the hell spreads worldwide. France, England, India, Pakistan, and North Korea. In three days, civilization as we know it is gone."

"So we're on a one-way track to eternity?"

"Not necessarily. If they solve their Lucky problem—"

"*Solve?* You mean once they *have* him."

Dolores shrugged, and again I felt as if she were dissembling, hiding something from me. She said, "*Afterward*, things will revert to the way they were. The Chinese will build their islands while the Americans vocally oppose their claim to the South China Sea. Behind the scenes things will be negotiated. Give and take."

I raised her face to mine. "Tell me . . . why did Richard save us?"

"He didn't save *us*. He preserved us until he can take Lucky."

"What's he waiting for?"

Her reply was to look pointedly at the crate with Lucky's hat atop it sitting on rollers just a few feet from the opened stern flap. "If he approaches us prematurely, he's afraid we'll dump Lucky over the side. He needs to personally hand Lucky to the Chinese, or they won't pay him. Not that I suspect they will, anyway."

"They're gonna stiff him?"

She smiled. "He'll be a stiff, all right."

"Why would they kill Richard?"

"I didn't say *they* would."

Javier rejoined us, followed by Stella and Derek. I gave Derek a look, and he shrugged. Stella seemed preternaturally calm, but I sensed something simmering beneath her placid surface. They stood looking out to sea, where two patrol boats were bouncing over the waves, fast approaching us. One flew the Chinese flag, the other the American flag.

The White Rose's engines stopped.

The ship was dead in the water.

CHAPTER 63

The Chinese patrol boat reached us first. Dolores nodded to our captain, who gave an order, and the Filipino crewmen draped a ladder over the side of our hull. The Chinese swarmed up it like a horde of ants: armed and determined-looking. First a squad of sailors, automatic weapons unslung. Then a quartet of civilians laden with duffel bags. Then an officer—a wide man with a narrow face—who wore the shoulder boards of a full colonel. Then, very slowly, a large, extremely old man whose knotted arms bulged as he slowly lifted himself rung by rung.

"Eff me," whispered Derek. "It's General Ming Chan himself."

I recognized the same ancient man Derek had met with in Chinatown. I'd learned who and what Ming Chan was but still didn't know why he'd met with Derek.

A hoarse voice broke the silence. "Mother of all fuckers."

It was Duke. From the bridge, he glared at Ming Chan.

But Ming ignored him as another figure appeared, lightly clambering from the ladder to the deck: Missy Soo, trim in customized army pants tucked into high-fashion boots. She glanced around, then paused, glaring hatefully at the bridge.

Derek was on the bridge now. He said, "Oh *no* . . ."

Duke had his arm around Stella, as if restraining her; understandable, for she bristled with hostility directed at Missy. Duke wore the same hateful expression, clearly restraining himself as well—

All at once in my mind's eye, a big piece of the puzzle fell into place: the document written in Burma in 1942 by a British Army doctor that Duke had left in a file for me to read: "Diagnosis of Rare Double Pregnancy," describing a phenomenon known as superfecundation, which may occur when a woman has sex with two different men during her same menstrual cycle, resulting in the birth of two babies who are "half twins" because they have different fathers.

And now I understood:

Missy and Stella were both Madame Soo's granddaughters, although each bore similarities to their respective grandfather: Ming and Archie. *The whole business had been ignited by a family dispute.* I'd once been a reluctant witness in a divorce trial and never before or since had seen such utter animosity, in or out of court, until now. I decided it was best to keep my eye on both Missy and Stella, who appeared to be on the verge of violence.

They were not the only ones. Duke's face was a portrait in hatred as he wielded his blackthorn stick. Ming had untied what looked like a leather-braided whip he'd been wearing around his waist, his thick brows arched angrily, good eye fixed on Duke.

It felt like the silence before a storm.

The Chinese sailors had formed a protective circle around the colonel and Ming Chan and Missy Soo. From the deck and the bridge, the Filipino crew stared at the Chinese balefully. No love lost between these undeclared enemies. I knew beneath their shirts the crew carried automatic weapons.

The White Rose was now becalmed, the humid tropical air redolent with tension. And I wondered:

Had Dolores lured the Chinese into a killing ground?

Javier was videotaping the scene. *Why?*

Dolores approached the Chinese. The sailors parted, and she addressed the colonel in English. "It's good to see you again, Colonel Tso."

"And you, Miss Dolores," replied Colonel Tso in nearly unaccented English.

So Dolores *had* been scheming with the Chinese—

There was a *clunk*, and everyone turned.

The American patrol boat that had bobbed alongside *The White Rose* had thrown a weighted ladder on our deck.

Colonel Tso seemed unconcerned. "May we begin?"

"By all means," replied Dolores.

Colonel Tso nodded to a sailor, who spoke into a phone, listened a moment, then pointed: a quarter mile distant from our stern, a Chinese freighter turned toward us.

Colonel Tso nodded again. The civilians carried their duffels to the stern, where the barnacled crate perched on steel rollers by the lowered stern flap—

"Hello, boys," said Richard as he climbed aboard, followed by half a dozen armed American sailors. Unslinging their rifles, they leveled them at their Chinese counterparts. He air-punched a jab at me, then winked at Dolores. "What's the haps, babe?"

"Not you, Dickie," said Dolores.

He grinned. "Forgot my flyboys saved your ass?"

"Noble of you. Protecting your fee."

"So smart, the lady is. One of the reasons I was crazy for you. But then you had to go off on your own. So maybe you're not so smart after all. Choosing this rust bucket over my ship. A bright girl like you should know to stick with the man who has the biggest one."

Dolores put her arm through my elbow. "I am. Not to mention Benn's teeth are real, his hair isn't dyed, he doesn't use sunlamps, and he doesn't take Cialis."

For the first time, I saw Richard falter. Dried saliva had gathered in the corners of his mouth, and his eyes were pinpoints. The maniac must've been popping reds for days, amping up for this moment. He fixed his glare on me.

"What the hell are you doing here, Bluestone?"

"Negotiating my client's business," I said.

"The negotiation's finished. Me and the colonel here, we dotted every *i* and crossed every *t*."

Yet Colonel Tso continued to ignore Richard's presence, and I realized something: *He had expected Richard to be there but didn't care; the Chinese had their own agenda that excluded him—*

From the aft deck, a hammer echoed, a crowbar squeaked. The Chinese civilians had set Lucky's hat aside and were now opening the crate. Missy stood watching, her eyes hungry. Behind her, Ming hunched, rheumy gaze on the crate.

Ignored by all, Javier videotaped.

Richard sidled up to me, spoke quietly. "Just so you know, when this is over, I'm dropping a RICO indictment on you. The predicate acts include treason and murder. This is the last time you'll see free daylight."

"So buzz off and let me enjoy it," I said.

The Chinese freighter had turned itself around and now, stern first, was reversing toward us. Like *The White Rose*, it had its rear cargo flap lowered. Clearly, the intent was for the two vessels to meet stern to stern; then the crate would move atop the rollers from *The White Rose* onto the Chinese freighter.

Richard motioned his sailors to stand aside. When they had, he held a phone out to the colonel and said, "Colonel Tso, it's time to give the okay to transferring the twenty-five million dollars to my account."

Colonel Tso shook his head. "Not until our scientists verify all is as it should be, and both sides sign the necessary documents. I have such authority. Who has authority for you?"

"You're looking at him," said Richard.

"Wrong," I said. "*I* have the authority."

"Wrong." Richard thumbed at the gray mass of the amphibious assault ship. "Along with my US Navy command, *I* was given the authority."

Dolores said, "Colonel Tso, I suggest you ask the commanding officer of the American ship to join us. If he is made aware of the situation, this man who calls himself Richard will end up in a navy brig, and all his dealings canceled."

Richard shook his head. "Dream on, Dee. The US military is conditioned to follow orders, no questions asked. The dildo in command of that assault ship will obey my orders." He moved closer to Dolores and, sotto voce, said, "You're okay for a one-night stand. Thing is, you're just garbage I left behind. After this is finished, I have a genuinely gorgeous Chinese lady waiting to spend a cushy life with me."

Dolores laughed cruelly. "Missy Soo will chew you up and spit you out."

Richard shook his head, called to Missy. "Straighten her out, baby."

As if she hadn't heard him, Missy didn't respond.

"Your papers?" Colonel Tso asked me.

I wear a money belt when I travel. It's made of a stretchable but sturdy synthetic. Strong enough to hold a .25 belly gun—which it did now; I'd found it in Duke's cabin—and large enough to hold some other things. Like a bunch of business cards. My own, and others I'd glommed over the years; cards that had belonged to the kind of people that can do—and undo—the undoable.

"In five minutes, you and your lover boy are fish food, doll," said Richard. "Colonel, please place the call. By the time the bank's on the line, Lucky will be all yours."

I glanced at the bridge. Along with Duke, Derek, and Stella, Madame Soo and the monk called Lucky were there. It was almost as if they were *waiting*.

"Papers," repeated Colonel Tso, impatiently.

I handed several business cards to Colonel Tso. Mine was bold script embossed on heavy blue paper, very classy, if I say so myself. The others were a mix of Washington prosecutors and agents, heavyweights with impressive titles. I'd taken the liberty of stamping the backs of their cards with official-looking authorizations naming yours truly as duly authorized by the laws of the United States of America. I'd bought the stamp for $49.99. The scam had worked before, dealing with minor functionaries who'd allowed my loitering where I shouldn't. My way of going low among those in high places.

But Colonel Tso was no slouch.

"Not sufficient," he said.

"Exactly," said Richard. "I'm the only one with authority. Come on, make the call—"

Colonel Tso said, "No call. No deal. China has regained Lucky without your help."

"Shit on you, Mac," said Richard. "I'll call your boss."

Ignoring him, Colonel Tso left Richard furiously punching his phone and turned his attention to the crate. Its top had already been removed, and the Chinese civilians were prying the side planks open. Already some were looking inside the crate, studying the object within through loupes, measuring its dimensions, scraping samples into test tubes, mixing in chemicals and watching colors change.

I could barely see a corner within the crate because it was elevated atop the steel roller, but I made out a massive dark shape; and then, as another plank lifted, sunlight reflected off gold and embedded green and red and diamond-white stones.

"The writing," Colonel Tso called to the civilians. "Is it there?"

Another plank fell away, and I saw the bejeweled object was a huge, golden Laughing Buddha. I supposed it bore some sort of engraving that confirmed it as genuine. Was this the Ming Treasure?

After a moment, the answer came in rapid, positive-sounding Mandarin.

Even as the Laughing Buddha was confirmed as genuine, an eerie moaning commenced, rising and falling and rising again:

"Om Mani Padme Hmm . . . Om Mani Padme Hmm . . ."

I followed Dolores's gaze to the bridge deck, where the monk I'd made as Lucky wailed a mantra:

"Om Mani Padme Hmm . . . Om Mani Padme Hmm . . ."

"What does that mean?" I wondered aloud.

Dolores said, "Six syllables describing the path of wisdom that removes impurities so the exalted mind of a Buddha can emerge."

"Now you're a hippie? What means *exalted*?"

Dolores shrugged. "A blank page, a new life."

The chugging grew louder, the Chinese freighter now a mere fifty feet away, its aft slowly backing toward *The White Rose's* aft.

Duke had hobbled from the bridge, closer—too close, I thought—to Ming. Stella was close behind him. Duke drew his .45, but Stella snatched it from his hand.

"Om Mani Padme Hmm . . . Om Mani Padme Hmm . . ."

Another voice, reed-thin and weak, joined the mantra. It came from Madame Soo. As she sang, her face seemed strangely youthful and carefree, as if she'd somehow regained her departed beauty.

"Om Mani Padme Hmm . . . Om Mani Padme Hmm . . ."

PART SIX:
THE VERDICT

CHAPTER 64

While everyone was concentrating on the emergence of the Laughing Buddha, Ming limped toward Duke, wielding his weapon of choice: the braided leather rope he wore around his waist. Duke looked for Stella, but she had left his side and stood on the aft deck near the Laughing Buddha, Duke's gun in her hand.

Ming's whip lashed at Duke, its end snapping against Duke's cheek, drawing first blood. An inch higher, it would have taken Duke's eye, no doubt Ming's intent.

He flicked his whip again, pulping Duke's ear. Again, he flicked the whip, but Duke raised his blackthorn stick, entwining the braided leather, yanking it from Ming's grip.

The old men, wincing with effort, faced off. Ming reached beneath his tunic and withdrew a short, pointed dagger. Duke unscrewed the top of the blackthorn stick and from its hollowed interior withdrew a needlelike sword. They went at each other without hesitation, thrusting and parrying. Blood spurted from their wounds and darkened their clothing. Grunting in pain, Ming put an elbow in Duke's gut. Duke went to his knees as Ming paused for breath.

From nowhere, Dr. Keegan appeared, trying to assist Duke. But Duke brushed him away, saying only, "Give me your piece."

From his satchel, Dr. Keegan took a small-caliber handgun and handed it to him. At nearly point-blank range, Duke aimed the gun at Ming. He pulled the trigger, but nothing happened.

Duke looked to Keegan. "You didn't load it?"

"The safety's on," said Keegan.

Fingers trembling, Duke found the safety. The gun went off immediately, but the shot struck Dr. Keegan, who fell atop the rollers between the crate and the opened flap. Duke turned the gun toward Ming, but before he could shoot, Colonel Tso snatched the weapon from his hand.

"Fight honorably," he said to Duke, then turned to Ming. "Kill him, General."

Round three. Ming and Duke went at each other again, grunting like wounded bulls.

Neither the Chinese or American sailors dared interfere in this last round of a fight that had begun three-quarters of a century ago. Amid an array of the most advanced weapons on earth, two men from another era were fighting to the death by hand.

Duke slipped in his own blood. Ming's thrust narrowly missed Duke's throat, a failed move that earned Ming Chan a shoulder stab that left him gasping on hands and knees. But he rose again.

And still they fought.

CHAPTER 65

Madame Soo felt as if a great burden had been lifted. At last, her destiny had appeared. Everything was clear to her now . . . except her true name. Was she Kitty or Li-ang? But then, as if by magic, the answer came to her. *She was both.* The final pieces of the puzzle had come together, and the mosaic of her life was completed.

There were so many parts to it. The dualities.

Her two dead daughters: one pure Chinese; the other Chinese-Caucasian. Her two granddaughters. So strange she loved the *gweilo* more than the one who was her image. Or maybe not so strange, for she disapproved of Missy's aggressive behavior; it reminded her of the cruel choices she'd made in her life. Choices concerning two men she'd once loved: Ming, her loyal husband; Archie, who'd first touched her.

They didn't even know how alike they were.

She watched as the two old fools dueled for her withered wedding finger. As if she'd ever wear either man's band.

The struggle went on, now reduced to sporadic thrusts between long pauses for oxygen.

"Om Mani Padme Hmm . . . Om Mani Padme Hmm . . ."

Ming Chan and Duke were unable to continue. Mere feet apart, they gasped for air, hated adversaries in the past and present, and yet . . .

now here was something new in their expressions . . . a camaraderie born of respect, a mutual understanding of life's irony.

Duke raised his bloody sword to Madame Soo, a dying knight saluting his lady.

Ming, brows knit in a scowl, ran the side of his hand across his belly, pretending to commit hari-kari like the samurais in the Japanese movies he'd always derided Li-ang for watching.

Too little, too late, thought Madame Soo.

Yet, she cared for both, in her way.

But neither was her true love.

So sad . . . and yet . . . so funny. Her last moments before joining her ancestors, watching *Yojimbo* and John Wayne fighting for her hand.

So fitting they'd fought to a draw. At last, their spilling blood over her was done. And now, as her final act, she'd make sure their nations would also be spared. She yearned for what would then follow:

Eternal sleep deep beneath the good earth of China.

Her hand found a lever set on the deck at her side.

She drew her last breath and pulled the lever.

"Om Mani Padme Hmm . . ."

CHAPTER 66

When the lever was pulled, the low grinding of a belowdecks engine began, but none of us on board was aware of it at the time. We all watched as the Chinese freighter drifted closer, narrowing the gap between its stern and that of *The White Rose*. Twenty feet now. The crate had been disassembled and the great Buddha sat, exposed, laughing in all his glory.

Missy stared at it, enraptured.

So did I, incredulous. For beneath the Buddha's right arm, the Chinese scientists had drilled a hole that partially exposed the mummified face of a monk entombed within a coffin of gold and precious stones.

And then, at long last, I finally realized the truth—

Lucky was both a monk and *the Ming Treasure.*

Duke motioned to me. "Tell Stella I tried . . ."

Richard stepped between us, pointing his pistol at me—

From above, an arrow flew, striking the deck at Richard's feet. Logui warriors on the bridge and on the radar mast had their arrows notched in drawn bowstrings.

Richard holstered his weapon, forced a crazed grin. "Fine," he said to the Logui, gesturing at me. "He's all yours." From a pocket, he pulled what seemed a piece of dry leather on which was tattooed seven numbers. It took a moment before I realized it wasn't leather but the inside of Albert Woo's cheek—

Derek had told me Albert's face had been partially removed.

Richard let me glimpse the underside of his wrist, where another seven numbers were tattooed . . . the remaining seven numbers. A revelation dulled by realization: dead men tell no tales.

"The Chinks think they ripped me off," he said to no one in particular, eyes glittering strangely. "But I still got their seed money. Ten million greenbacks. Think about it all the long days you're gonna spend in jail, *Counselor*."

I felt a slight vibration on the deck beneath my feet, and for a moment it seemed the Laughing Buddha moved. Or maybe I just imagined it, for I also imagined I heard the golden behemoth laugh, a rich, deep-throated peal—

The deck vibrated again, more strongly this time, and now I saw that the Buddha had moved toward the opened railing, although the Chinese freighter remained ten to twenty feet away.

Stella rushed at Missy Soo, her face twisted with hatred, wielding the gun she'd taken from Duke.

"*You,*" said Missy Soo, adopting a martial-arts ready position.

I moved to intercept Stella and took the gun away. If she harmed Missy, the Chinese would retaliate, the Americans would reply, and we'd all be dead. As Stella writhed in my grip, Missy lunged at her. I tried fending Missy off, but she got around me—

Ming lumbered between us and gripped both women. Beside his massive bulk, they looked like dolls. Tears flowed down Ming's disfigured cheek as he hugged both, then kissed each of their foreheads—

The Buddha lurched again, precariously close to the opening.

"*No!*" Missy screamed, breaking free and rushing down to the aft deck and placing her weight against the Buddha, desperately trying to stop its movement.

I took Stella's gun from my belt. The time had come to end Richard's life. But Stella yanked it from me and shot Missy. I snatched the pistol back, but it was too late. Blood blossomed from Missy's breast; she staggered, yet continued trying to halt the Buddha's movement.

Richard went to help her. He lent his weight to Missy's, and the Buddha stopped.

Yet Missy Soo screamed, "Get away, *gweilo* pig."

Stoned, Richard said, "No, baby, it's *me*."

The Chinese freighter floated only fifteen feet away now. Through its lowered aft flap, crewmen were readying to extend a roller that would bridge to the one on *The White Rose*, conveying Lucky across the gap.

The Laughing Buddha was still, the moment frozen.

I became aware of Dolores at my side. She was smiling.

"Lend a hand, you slackers," Richard cried to his sailors.

But none did, intuiting that this was not part of their mission.

Dolores squeezed my arm, nodded.

The Laughing Buddha had begun moving again and now was partly through the flap, teetering above the sea. Missy Soo slipped and fell from the rollers into the water. Blood trickled from her mouth, but still she gripped the tipping Buddha, which now tilted just above her.

Richard alone held the Buddha back now. Something fell from his hand to the deck. "Help me," he said to me.

I put my gun against his heart and shot him.

He cried, "Jeannie!" and fell into the sea.

No longer restrained, the Buddha slid over the side. As the remaining cables that had secured it snapped, it sank slowly, dragging Missy Soo and Richard with it. Richard reached for my hand, and I pretended to take it but didn't. His face sank beneath the surface of the clear tropical sea, which seemed illuminated by Lucky's multicolored jeweled glow.

Again, I thought I heard the Buddha, laughing.

I tossed both pistols over the side into the sea.

"I'm not gonna miss you, Dickie," I said.

Then I picked up what he'd dropped.

Both teams of sailors seemed stunned by what had happened. Dolores kissed Stella's cheek. Stella stifled a sob, smiled, entered Derek's embrace. Ming Chan crouched opposite where Duke lay, bloody and exhausted. The two men looked at each other for a long moment before Ming spoke, his voice labored.

"Thank you for fighting for my country."

"Hey, it was a blast," gasped Duke.

CHAPTER 67

Javier lowered his camera. "Helluva place for a burial. We're directly above a trench. Nothing below us but five miles of saltwater."

"*Om Mani Padme Hmm . . . Om Mani Padme Hmm . . . Om . . .*"

The monk's refrain was no longer a chant but a moan.

"Kitty," cried Duke. "Oh, my Kitty . . ."

Madame Soo lay still on the bridge. Ming Chan and Duke managed to stagger to her side. We all followed. Next to the lever she'd pulled that sent Lucky into the sea, Madame Soo lay draped in a shawl, her face peaceful in death. Her arms were folded across her breasts, her small hands closed. Stella reached to her, stopped, unsure . . .

"Go ahead," said Derek gently. "She's your grandmother."

Tears ran down Stella's cheeks as she pried Madame Soo's fingers open. In her left hand was a Hero of the Revolution medal. In her right hand was an AVG Flying Tigers ring. Stella ignored both of these as she undid Madame Soo's shawl, as if looking for something else.

She found it.

Beneath where Madame Soo's arms had been folded was an old, yellowing photograph of Kitty and a young, bespectacled Chinese man wearing a suit and tie: the young Uncle Winston Lau.

"When Uncle brought her to New York, they fell in love, but she could not live as a criminal's wife," said Derek. "They lived far apart but were always one. Duke knew he dare not communicate with Madame Soo, so he entrusted Lucky's hat to Uncle, hoping one day Uncle might return it to her. They arranged Lucky's fate. I was their go-between. Madame Soo believed in one China and didn't care if Taiwan claimed to be independent. To her, China was China; the different names were just the result of stupid men saving face. She knew if the Reds found Lucky on a South China Sea island, they'd claim he'd been there since Ming Dynasty days, which meant their sovereignty predated all other claims. And if the Taiwanese got Lucky, they'd claim that proved the Ming Dynasty capital was in Taiwan, and they were the traditional rulers. Either way, there would be a war. So she decided the best outcome was that Lucky belonged to no one."

Colonel Tso climbed onto the bridge. Scowling, he addressed Dolores.

"I am of the impression this was your true plan all along, yes?"

"Not mine," she said, looking at Madame Soo, still clasping her photograph in death. "Hers. And Mr. Mason's. And, apparently, General Ming Chan's as well."

"But you went along with it," said Colonel Tso, unholstering his pistol. "For that, there must be consequences."

"Bad idea." I pointed at the Logui above, their bowstrings drawn.

Colonel Tso looked, then holstered his weapon. "Point taken."

"Good. Let's move on to negotiating."

"What is left to negotiate? Lucky is gone."

"But not forgotten. His discovery on an atoll flying the Chinese flag and his removal from the crate were recorded on video. Seems to me that's a lot of fuel for your propaganda machine. Putting it another way, half a loaf is better than none at all."

The colonel considered a moment, glanced at Ming Chan, and said, "I'll need to make a call. No doubt my superiors will want to discuss the matter directly with you."

"You might also mention that the videos have already been electronically conveyed for safekeeping."

"Safekeeping?" asked Colonel Tso.

I nodded. "From you and yours."

He nodded. "My compliments."

"Another thing," I said. When I told him what it was, his eyes narrowed in disbelief but then slowly widened as he understood. He nodded.

Colonel Tso walked aside and murmured into his phone. Listened. Spoke some more, listened some more. Hung up and rejoined us.

"It will take some time to arrange," he said. "A few hours."

With that, the Chinese left *The White Rose*.

Stella knelt by Duke, who lay exhausted.

"She's going to need a lot of healing," said Derek.

"You're the right man for that job," I said.

"You did pretty well yourself."

"Considering I'm The Man Who Knows Least," I said, holding my hand out to Dolores.

She took it and pressed it to her lips.

PART SEVEN: POSTTRIAL

CHAPTER 68

It was late day, and Dolores and I were alone on the bridge. Derek and Stella had retreated to her cabin. Javi was on the prow, smoking a spliff. The Chinese had returned. On the stern deck below us, a crew of technicians was gathered around a bank of electronics topped by three monitor screens. Colonel Tso looked at us, nodded.

"Time for my closing argument," I said.

In the gathering twilight, Captain Starski of the American amphibious assault vessel, Dolores, Javier, Colonel Tso, and I stood facing the three monitor screens, now glowing brightly in the dimness.

On one monitor, a woman I recognized as the US deputy secretary of state sat at a desk, the American flag behind her. On another, a Chinese man wearing a Mao jacket sat stiffly in front of the red and gold-starred flag of the People's Republic of China. On the third monitor, a man I knew was the vice president of Colombia sat beside the yellow, blue, and red striped flag of Colombia. All three were waiting for me to speak.

Let them wait.

Whatever their separate agendas, I knew they all operated outside the pale of international law. Although disparate people, they had one thing in common: they were all masters of the deniable. People died and nations crumbled, but these were the Three Wise Monkeys. No see, no hear, no speak . . . and always have a fall guy in reserve.

But that was about to change. No evasiveness and no fall guy because now they were dealing with an entity they'd never experienced.

Benn Bluestone, Mouthpiece, Esq.

I said, "Before I begin, I need for you to understand that nothing is negotiable. You either accept our terms, or suffer the consequences. Here's what you get. The United States reacknowledges its support for a one-China policy—"

"Now, see here," began the deputy secretary of state.

Sometimes I think being a loyal American is akin to loving a whore. You play, you pay. Lord only knows what whoring has cost the United States in blood and treasure over the last half century. People and fortunes that could have transformed the States, hell, the entire *planet*, to be all that it could be. But all that transpired on the home front was that the rich got richer. In my adulthood alone, we've ass-screwed Southeast Asia, the Middle East, and Latin America. Not that the Chinese or the Colombians were any better. All three peoples suffered the misery imposed by governmental greed and false ambition.

If I were king—man, would I love to be—the deputy secretary of state would be in Guantanamo getting waterboarded and the Colombian and Chinese leaders locked in underground cells in the Florence Supermax.

"Zip your lip," I told her. "We've got footage of a CIA agent who called himself Richard committing treason with Chinese intelligence. The same Richard you put in command of a US Navy warship. Not to mention a host of accompanying murders, extortions, and betrayals. Do you understand?"

The undersecretary cleared her throat, nodded.

"I didn't hear you," I said. "Speak up."

"Understood," she replied, weakly.

"First and foremost, I, Javier Barrera, Derek Lau and his colleagues, Stella Maris, Marmaduke Mason, and the woman named Dolores get full immunity from any and all prosecutions by the United States, China, and Colombia."

"That could be in play, depending," said the undersecretary.

"Good start," I said, taking my time, savoring the moment. Orgasmic. I'd just given the government my middle finger. After so many years of having to beg for favors, it felt good dictating my demands.

"What does China get?" asked the man in the Mao jacket.

"The United States and China issue a joint statement that all competing national claims in the South China Sea are subject to peaceful arbitration."

"The United States supports that position," said the undersecretary.

"The People's Republic of China agrees," said Mao jacket. "I repeat, what does China get?"

Their greediness made me want to puke. Their words were conveniences of the moment, subject to future redefinitions and redactions.

I said, "China gets the video of Lucky being raised from the sea next to an atoll flying the Chinese flag, along with the close-up video of Lucky on deck. Do with it as you wish. But should you choose not to accept the offer, the video of Lucky going overboard in your presence will be released to the media. Feeding-frenzy time. China may find it difficult to explain dumping their proof of sovereignty into the sea."

"Point taken," said Mao jacket. "Continue."

"China must guarantee in the United Nations that the Strait of Malacca is deemed international waters permanently, and that China will never seek to impose a toll for passage."

After a moment, Mao jacket nodded. "Agreed."

The phonies. As if they were really giving up anything. Closing the strait would be an act of war that would escalate from a minor misunderstanding to all-out nuclear war neither side wanted. I'd added the meaningless condition as a sop for the Chinese to save face.

The undersecretary said, "The United States doesn't make deals dictated by criminals."

"Excepting all the time," I said. "Your answer is no?"

Flustered, the undersecretary said, "I . . . the United States agrees."

I turned to the Colombian vice president. He was well known for his histrionic antidrug speeches, but I had personal knowledge that he was a thief, having once, courtesy of a cooperating client, watched a "classified"—*ha!*—video of a payoff encounter in which he'd made specific mention of this for that. Yet the US government had deemed the veep as too big to fail—he being a pillar of the antidrug forces—and ignored the clear proof of his malfeasance.

"As for you, señor," I said, "the Colombian government will inform China that the present Sierra Nevada rare-earth-element mining agreement is void. It will be replaced by a new agreement allowing China to mine rare earth elements in other, proven deposits near Riohacha."

"But the contract is already in force," he protested.

"I have the floor, señor. Meaning, you shut up. As I was saying, Colombia and China will renegotiate the REE mining, moving the leased territory from the Sierra Nevada de Santa Marta to Riohacha. In return, evidence of corrupt Colombian officials being bribed to veto the Sierra Nevada as a World Heritage Site will be destroyed."

The Colombian vice president nodded. "A pleasure."

"While you're pleasuring yourself, you will reverse your government's decision, and instead *request* the Sierra Nevada be declared a World Heritage Site. *¿Comprendes?*"

"*Sí*, señor. Gladly."

"I'm glad you're glad," I said. "I want everything in writing."

No way I trusted mere words, even if I had to wait for the bureaucrats of three nations to define the agreements on paper. But to my surprise—no, to my further endless appreciation of Dolores—the papers were quickly drawn up and transmitted by computers Derek had set up, and it dawned on me that all along Dolores had been planting seeds, cultivating this outcome. With my unwitting help, she'd pitted her resourcefulness against the great powers and won.

I pointed to Javier, who was taping the exchange. Addressing the three monitor images, I said, "There's no better proof than self-incrimination. Now, no if, ands, or buts. *Sign.*"

I watched as the three nations signed and transmitted the documents to one another. Hard copies of the signed documents were given to me. I photographed them and e-mailed them to Hotmail addresses only I knew.

"One more thing," I said. "Madame Soo is to be buried in the Soo family plot in Shanghai."

Colonel Tso nodded. "I will personally ensure that."

Both squads of sailors had already departed *The White Rose*. Now Captain Starski and the colonel left. Ming was the last to go. He took the hat with him. I said nothing. Let the old man keep his memories. As he gripped a railing for support, he stared at Duke, who met his gaze.

Ming raised a bloodied arm and saluted Duke.

"See you on the other side," said Duke.

CHAPTER 69

Duke was in extremis. He'd driven himself to live this far, but now he was running on fumes. Each time his eyes closed, I thought he had departed, but always they fluttered open again, and always he scanned the horizon expectantly.

It was dark when I understood why.

Lights ablaze, *Kitty* appeared from the night. Duke gathered himself and stood, watching *Kitty* near. A railed gangplank linked the two vessels. Duke was first to cross. Midway, he tottered, then regained himself and boarded *Kitty*. He sagged to his knees, bent, and kissed the deck, then slumped, dead.

The old man had been a singularly strange bird, a weirdly cunning bastard, yet he'd been beloved. By Stella, because he had protected and raised her. By Derek, because Duke had been his grandfather's partner and friend, as well as his lover's grandfather.

Even I felt a tinge of melancholy, thinking of Duke as happy-go-lucky Archie.

We were in the doldrums, the sea dead calm. We crossed from *The White Rose*—the death ship that wasn't—to *Kitty*, opened a bottle of Duke's best, and toasted all those who had once been and all things that never were.

CHAPTER 70

Kitty cruised eastward beneath a crescent moon. No other shipping lights were visible. Dolores and I were alone on the flying bridge. Below us, on the deck, Stella leaned into Derek's arms. We could hear her, faintly sobbing.

"Poor kid," I said.

"Like me, she's had a parent who was murdered. Sadness, anger, all of it. Maybe that's why we bonded," said Dolores. "But poor she's not. My guess is she inherits Duke's estate. There's tons of gold that's now hers."

"How do you know that?"

"Richard told me. When he got wasted, he talked too much. Master spy that he wasn't, he even gave all the players code names. His was Brutalist."

"Yeah, I can see that."

"Yours was Franklin."

"Well, I liked money."

"Missy Soo was Flower."

"Venus flytrap would be more like it."

"Mine was Sangfroid."

"I don't get that one."

She tilted her head and smiled slyly. "I'll take that as a compliment. You know, there was another code name, one I couldn't figure at first. But when I realized Madame Soo was a ruthless woman who achieved her goal at the expense of her granddaughter's life, I understood why he'd coded her as the White Tigress."

"No, my love. You see so much, but you're off here," I said. "Madame Soo wasn't ruthless. She was a kind woman who chose the greater good over her personal loss. Can't you guess who Richard was *really* referring to?"

Dolores got it in a flash.

"*Oh* . . . Stella's the White Tigress. She provoked Duke into reigniting the war by offering Lucky to the Reds. She knew it would stir up trouble, and just maybe she'd get a chance to kill Missy."

"Doesn't really matter anymore," I said. "It's all over."

"According to The Man Who Thinks He Knows All."

* * *

Despite what we'd concluded, Stella acted extremely friendly and gracious toward Dolores and me now. She insisted Dolores and I stay in Duke's master cabin. We did. After we made love, Dolores fell asleep. I couldn't. Unfinished business. I roused Javier and told him what I wanted.

"No problem," he said, reaching for his camera.

We watched the replay of Lucky's last moments. When Richard reached from the sea for me to help him, I said, "Freeze that frame."

Javier did.

"Zoom in."

Richard's arm, rising from the sea for my help, filled the screen.

"Stop," I said. "Zoom in closer."

Javier did, and there on Richard's arm, clear as bold typeface, were the last seven numbers of the account. I stared at them until they were burned into my memory via an old trick: thinking in terms of telephone numbers. These were *888 6660*. Chinese lucky numbers. The first seven numbers I'd seen on Albert Woo's cheek were *0666 888*. Two peas on opposite ends of the same pod, palindrome-style.

I knocked on Derek's cabin door softly. When he opened it, I glimpsed Stella's shape, asleep in the darkness.

"I couldn't sleep," said Derek. "Too much to process."

"Good," I said. "Because I need your help."

The $10 million Richard had stolen from the Chinese was in a numbered account on the far side of the world from us. It was daylight there. Derek hooked up a satellite connection and when the bank operator answered, her voice was as clear as if she were across the street. I told her I wanted to speak to an officer regarding a numbered account.

When the officer came on, I said, "I want to transfer funds from my numbered account to my account in another bank."

"Yes, sir. The number, please."

I enunciated the fourteen digits.

"Security question: The name?"

I hesitated. Richard had made his feelings for Missy obvious. Yet at the moment before death, he'd uttered the name of his deceased wife.

"Jeannie," I said.

"To what account do you wish the money be wired to?"

I gave him my bank Swift Code and routing number and my personal account number. I'd sworn to myself not to take dirty money, but now I had another idea.

"Consider it done, sir," the officer said.

PART EIGHT: ANAWANDA

CHAPTER 71

Carefully, I raised Dolores's arm so as not to disturb her intravenous tube and brushed my lips across the back of her hand. I said, "Happily ever after."

Dolores said, "No such thing. There's only right now."

"Whatever. But right now all is well."

This was true. There had been minimal fallout concerning the incident in the South China Sea. The Reds had issued a press release to the effect that they'd discovered—and filmed—Lucky on an atoll where he'd been buried by the Ming Dynasty, thereby proving their claim that the Ming Dynasty had long ago established Chinese sovereignty over the disputed islands. To buttress this, they'd released Javier's close-ups of Lucky. Predictably, the other nations with claims to the same area challenged the Chinese to produce Lucky.

Of course, that didn't happen, and the issue became just another talking point. All sides proclaimed their commitment to a peaceful solution, but all sides continued to strengthen their military postures.

So nothing had changed at all.

Except maybe my future.

I figured there was a fifty-fifty chance that someday a Freedom of Information freak or Snowden-type would expose the clandestine deal I'd negotiated. *Pretending to be a government employee, obstruction of justice, blah, blah, blah.* Sure, I'd received a grant of immunity, but that was worthless if those who'd bestowed it were themselves coconspirators.

Bottom line?

If the saga had been a trial, although I'd walked from the courtroom a free man, in legal speak, the case was deemed dismissed *without* prejudice. Meaning if the spores of the conspiracy to conduct illegal diplomacy still existed, and if they were ever made public—

"Will you please stop thinking?" said Dolores.

"I wasn't . . . sorry, I guess bad habits die hard."

She said, "Get some good habits. Hold her."

She passed me our baby girl, and as if by magic, love welled in me. My tiny beauty was so small, I was afraid I'd drop her. Our eyes touched and she gurgled, and I—literally—felt my heart warm. The best feeling of my life. One I'd never let be taken from me.

Even if the dirt surfaced, the feds would never find me, here in the Lost City, which was forbidden to even the hardiest nature lovers who hiked the Sierra Nevada World Heritage Site.

Here, I'd start my new life.

Later, while Dolores and our girl—we'd named her Li-ang—slept, I sat outside the stone house watching the sun set behind Anawanda, letting my cares and worries drain. From somewhere a monkey howled, and I thought I heard the monk's chant . . .

Om Mani Padme Hmm . . .

My palm began to itch.

Strange that I felt the symptom of a new case coming my way, for I was no longer money hungry. I'd burned the deed to the Phuket hotel. Of the $10 million from the numbered account, I'd put four in a trust account bearing Li-ang's name. Another four I'd given to the Logui nation. I split the last $2 million with Javi. The one mil I kept would last me ten monk-size lifetimes, the cost of living in the Sierra Nevada being approximately zero.

My priorities had done a one-eighty. Derek's as well. The Yellow Submarine had undergone a massive expansion—adding Silicon techies to Derek's Green Dragons—a combination that had given birth to a new and legal brand of drone-killing software. Last I heard, they were planning a big IPO. I wished all the luck in the world to Derek and Stella, who had announced plans to marry.

The itch really was bothering me now, like a phantom feeling in an amputated limb.

I ate a mushroom and strolled in the last light, my dog at my side. Lucky was a rare silver Lab Derek had gifted me in anticipation of his impending IPO. Along with the pooch had come an invitation to Derek's marriage to Stella. All things considered, we chose not to attend, but sent a gift:

Lucky's hat.

A courier from the new Chinese mine site had brought it to me. I'd forwarded it to Derek and Stella, along with the note tucked inside it:

Your grandmother wanted you to have it.

It was signed: *Godfather Ming.*

I told the courier to express my thanks to the sender, but his expression became downcast. "I regret to inform you General Ming Chan is dead."

Now, as Lucky and I walked the forest, the mushroom enhanced my senses. I realized how beautiful the Sierra was. Felt how good it was to be alive. How majestic was Anawanda.

Lucky trotted ahead of me and began barking. I soon saw why.

A lone hiker was on the trail ahead. A stooped old man.

The monk?

No. The old man was Caucasian. He wore worn hiking boots and a battered old cap . . . which, to my surprise, bore the logo of the original Brooklyn Dodgers, before the Boys of Summer went to LA.

"Nice evening," said the old man, pleasantly.

"Yes, it is," I said, thinking it weird an old codger was playing tourist all the way up here by his lonesome, with night coming on, no less. There was something about him that seemed vaguely familiar. Apparently, the feeling was mutual.

"You remind me of a departed friend," he said.

Lucky had a nose for good people. He sat at the old timer's side and nuzzled for a stroke. The old man obliged.

I had a question I was afraid to ask, but did:

"Your friend? What was his name?"

"Our gang called him Kid Louie."

Pa? Was the old man an illusion?

He continued walking, uphill.

"Wrong way," I called out.

But he kept on walking.

"Take the down path."

"My path leads up."

"Nothing up there."

"Oh, but there is."

Before I could ponder his words, much less respond, the old man was gone in the gloaming. My palm still itched, and for a moment I was tempted to follow him, but I didn't.

My family was awaiting me.

ACKNOWLEDGMENTS

To those readers who liked *The Extraditionist* but had reservations about Benn Bluestone: Thank you for allowing the guy to redeem himself. Once again, my thanks to the astute Gracie Doyle at Thomas & Mercer, who from the beginning knew Benn was a good guy. And to the crew at Thomas & Mercer: Sarah Shaw, Dennelle Catlett, Gabrielle Guarnero, Laura Constantino, Laura Barrett, Oisin O'Malley, Sarah Burningham, Claire McLaughlin, and Jae Song.

I am infinitely grateful to my steadfast agents, David Hale Smith and Liz Parker at Inkwell.

And last, but far from least, to the patient, brilliant Ed Stackler, editor and friend extraordinaire.

ABOUT THE AUTHOR

Todd Merer worked for thirty years as a criminal attorney, specializing in the defense of high-ranking cartel chiefs extradited to the United States. He successfully argued acquittals in more than 150 trials. His high-profile cases have been featured in the *New York Times* and *Time* magazine and on *60 Minutes*. A "proud son of Brooklyn," Merer divides his time between New York City and ports of call along the old Spanish Main.